THE LAST

VALERIO MASSIMO MANFREDI is professor of classical archaeology at the Luigi Bocconi University in Milan. He has carried out a number of expeditions to and excavations in many sites throughout the Mediterranean, and has taught in Italian and international universities. He has published numerous articles and academic books, mainly on military and trade routes and exploration in the ancient world.

He has published ten works of fiction, including the 'Alexander' trilogy, which has been translated into twenty-four languages in thirty-eight countries. He has written and hosted documentaries on the ancient world, which have been transmitted by the main television networks, and has written fiction for cinema and television as well.

He lives with his family in the countryside near Bologna.

Also by Valerio Massimo Manfredi

ALEXANDER: CHILD OF A DREAM

ALEXANDER: THE SANDS OF AMMON

ALEXANDER: THE ENDS OF THE EARTH

SPARTAN

HEROES
(*formerly* The Talisman of Troy)

TYRANT

THE ORACLE

EMPIRE OF DRAGONS

THE TOWER

Valerio Massimo Manfredi

THE LAST LEGION

Translated from the Italian by Christine Feddersen-Manfredi

PAN BOOKS

First published 2003 by Macmillan

First published in paperback 2003 by Pan Books

This edition published 2007 by Pan Books
an imprint of Pan Macmillan Ltd
Pan Macmillan, 20 New Wharf Road, London N1 9RR
Basingstoke and Oxford
Associated companies throughout the world
www.panmacmillan.com

ISBN 978-0-330-44729-4

First published in Italian 2002 as *L'Ultima Legione* by
Arnoldo Mondadori Editore S.p.A., Milano

3 5 7 9 8 6 4 2

A CIP catalogue record for this book is available from the British Library.

Typeset by SetSystems Ltd, Saffron Walden, Essex
Printed and bound in Great Britain by
Mackays of Chatham plc, Chatham, Kent

I would like to thank Carlo Carlei and Peter Rader, who helped me to develop the idea for this novel in view of a cinematic adaption: their contributions significantly enriched this story.

PROLOGUE

These are the memories of Myrdin Emreis, Druid of the sacred wood of Gleva, who the Romans called Meridius Ambrosinus. I have taken upon myself the task of writing them down so that those who shall come after me will not forget the events which I have been the last to witness.

I have long crossed the threshold of extreme age and I cannot explain why my life continues to go on, so far beyond the limits which nature usually assigns humankind. Perhaps the angel of death has forgotten about me, or perhaps he wants to leave me this last bit of time so that I may repent of my many sins, of no small consequence. Presumption, foremost. I have been guilty of great pride in the intelligence gifted me by God, and I have allowed, out of pure vanity, legends about my clairvoyance – even about supposed powers that can only be attributed to our Supreme Creator and the intercession of His saints! – to take root amongst the people. Oh, yes, I have even devoted myself to the forbidden arts, to the writings of the ancient pagan priests of these lands on the trunks of trees. Yet I believe I have done no evil. What evil can come of listening to the voices of our Ancient Mother, of Sovereign Nature, the voices of the wind amidst the leafy boughs, the song of the nightingales to the moon, the gurgling of the spring waters and the rustling of the dry leaves, when the hills and the plains are cloaked with the gleaming colours of autumn in those quiet sunsets that hint at the winter.

It is snowing. Big white flakes dance in the still air and a candid mantle covers the hills that crown this silent valley, this lonely tower. Will the land of Eternal Peace be like this? Is this the image that we shall see forever with the eyes of our souls? If it were such, death would be sweet, soft the passage to our final rest.

How much time has passed! How long since those bloody, tumultuous days of hate and war, of the convulsions of a dying world which I had believed immortal and eternal, and which I saw collapse. Now, as I prepare myself to take my last step, I feel the need to hand down the story of that failing world, and to tell how the last bloom of that parched tree was carried by fate to this remote land, where it took root and gave origin to a new era.

I don't know whether the angel of death will leave me the time, nor whether this old heart will hold up to reliving the emotions that nearly broke it asunder when I was so much younger, but I will not let the immensity of my endeavour discourage me. I feel the wave of memories rising like the tide among the cliffs of Carvetia. I have once more seen distant visions that I had thought forever vanished, like an ancient fresco faded by time.

I had thought that taking up my quill and touching it to this fresh parchment would have been sufficient to recreate the story, setting it free to flow like a river through a field when the snow melts in the spring, but I was wrong. Memories throng and press, a knot fills my throat and my hand falls impotent on the white page. I must first evoke the images, restore the strength of those colours, of the lives and the voices enfeebled by the years and the distance. I must even recreate what I have not seen with my own eyes, as the dramatist plays out scenes on his stage which he has never experienced.

It is snowing on the hills of Carvetia. All is white and silent as the last light of the day is slowly extinguished.

From nations far apart you have made a single fatherland

– Rutilius Namatianus, De Reditu suo, 63

PART ONE

1

Dertona, fieldcamp of the Nova Invicta Legion,
Anno Domini 476, 1229 years after the foundation of Rome

THE LIGHT PIERCED through the clouds covering the valley, and the cypresses straightened up suddenly like guards, alert on the ridge of the hills. A shadow bending over a bundle of twigs appeared at the edge of a stubble field and vanished at once, as if in a dream. A cock's crow rose from a distant farmhouse, announcing another grey, leaden day, only to be swallowed up instantly by the fog. Nothing penetrated the mist, save the voices of the men.

'Blasted cold.'

'It's this damp that gets into your bones.'

'It's the fog. I've never seen such thick fog in all my life.'

'Nor have I. And not a sign of our rations.'

'Perhaps there's nothing left to eat.'

'Not even a little wine to warm us up.'

'And we haven't been paid for three months.'

'I can't take it any longer, I've had it with this whole thing. A new emperor practically every year, barbarians controlling all the main posts, and now, to top it all off: a snotty-nosed kid on the throne of the Caesars! A thirteen-year-old brat who hasn't even got the strength to hold up the sceptre is supposed to be running the world – the West, at least. No, this is it for me, I'm getting out. As soon as I can I'm leaving the army and going my own way. I'll find myself a little island where I can put goats out to pasture and make cheese. I don't know about the rest of you, but my mind is made up.'

A light breeze opened a breach in the mist and revealed a group of soldiers huddled around a brazier. They were waiting to go off the last shift of guard duty. Rufius Vatrenus, a Spaniard from Saguntum and a veteran of many battles, commander of the guard corps, turned to his comrade, the only one who hadn't yet said a word or sounded a complaint: 'What do you say, Aurelius, are you with me?'

Aurelius poked the tip of his sword into the brazier, rekindling a flame that crackled into life and set a swirl of sparks dancing in the milky mist.

'I've always served Rome. What else could I do?'

A long silence fell. The men looked at each other, gripped by a feeling of dismay and restless unease.

'He'll never hang up his sword,' said Antoninus, a senior officer. 'He's always been in the army. He doesn't even remember what he used to do before he joined up. He simply doesn't remember ever being anywhere else. Isn't that true, Aurelius?'

He got no answer, but the reflection of the nearly burnt-out embers revealed Aurelius's melancholy look.

'He's thinking of what's ahead,' observed Vatrenus. 'The situation is out of control again. If the reports I've heard can be believed, Odoacer's troops have rebelled and attacked Ticinum, where the emperor's father Orestes had taken refuge. They say that he's heading for Placentia, and that he's counting on us to knock some sense into these barbarians and buttress the tottering throne of his young Romulus Augustus. You know, I'm not sure we can do it this time. If you want to know what I think, I really doubt it. There's three times as many of them as of us and—'

'Wait – did you all hear that?' asked one of the soldiers, the one closest to the palisade.

'It's coming from the field,' replied Vatrenus, his gaze searching the semi-deserted camp, its frost-covered tents. 'It's the end of the night shift; it must be the daytime picket coming on duty.'

'No!' said Aurelius. 'It's coming from outside. Sounds like—'

'Horsemen,' nodded Canidius, a legionary from Arelate.

'Barbarians,' concluded Antoninus. 'I don't like it.'

The horsemen appeared all at once out of the fog along the narrow white road that led from the hills to the camp. Imposing, on their massive Sarmatian steeds covered with metallic scales, they wore studded iron helmets, conical in shape and bristling with crests. Long swords hung at their sides, and their blond or reddish locks fluttered in the misty air. Their black cloaks were worn over trousers made of the same coarse, dark wool. The fog and the distance made them look like demons out of hell.

Aurelius leaned over the paling to observe the band drawing closer and closer. The horses plodded through the puddles that had formed on the road after the rain of the night before had melted the snow, raising muddy splashes. 'They're Heruli and Skyrians from the Imperial Army, Odoacer's men probably. Looks bad to me. What are they doing here at this hour, and why weren't we notified? I'm going to report to the commander.'

He clambered down the stairs and ran across the camp towards the praetorium. The camp commander, Manilius Claudianus, a veteran nearly sixty years old who had fought as a young man with Aetius against Attila, was already on his feet, and as Aurelius entered his tent he was hooking his scabbard to his belt.

'General, a squad of Herulian and Skyrian auxiliary troops are approaching. No one said anything about them coming, and I don't like it.'

'Neither do I,' answered the officer in a worried tone. 'Deploy the guard and open the gates. Let's hear what they want.'

Aurelius ran to the palisade and instructed Vatrenus to have the archers take position. He then went down to the guard post, drew up the available forces, had the praetorian gate opened and walked out with the commander. In the meantime, Vatrenus woke the troops with a whispered alarm, one man to the next, almost in silence and without sounding the trumpets.

The commander was completely armed and wore his helmet, a manifest sign that he considered this a war zone. His guard flanked him on both sides. One man towered head and shoulders above all the rest: Cornelius Batiatus was a gigantic Ethiopian, black as coal, who never abandoned the general's side. He carried an oval shield built to measure by an armourer to cover his huge body. A Roman sword hung from his left shoulder, while a barbarian double-edged axe hung from the right.

The band of barbarians on horseback were just paces away by now, and the man at their head raised his arm as a signal to stop. He had a thick head of red hair which fell at the sides in two long braids. His shoulders were covered by a cloak trimmed with fox fur and his helmet was decorated by a crown of tiny silver skulls. His bearing denoted his importance. He turned to Commander Claudianus without getting off his horse, speaking in a rough, guttural Latin:

'Noble Odoacer, head of the Imperial Army, orders you to deliver your charge over to me. As of today, I shall assume command of this legion.' He threw a roll of parchment tied with a leather cord at his feet, adding: 'Your certificate of discharge and retirement orders.'

Aurelius stooped to pick it up but the commander stopped him with a peremptory gesture. Claudianus was from an ancient aristocratic family proud of their direct descent from a hero of the Republican Age, and the barbarian's gesture stung him as an intolerable insult. He replied without losing his composure: 'I don't know who you are and I'm not interested in finding out. I take orders only from noble Flavius Orestes, the supreme commander of the Imperial Army.'

The barbarian turned towards his men and shouted: 'Arrest him!' They spurred on their horses and surged forwards with their swords unsheathed: it was evident that they had been ordered to kill them all. The guards retaliated in kind, as a unit of archers simultaneously appeared at the bastions of the camp, their arrows already nocked to the bowstrings. They let fly, at Vatrenus's order, with deadly precision. Nearly all of the horsemen in the front line were hit, as were many of their horses. Wounded or lamed, they pulled their riders down with them in calamitous falls.

This did not stop the others, however, who jumped to the ground so they wouldn't be so easy to hit and rushed headlong at Claudianus's guards. Batiatus hurled himself into the fray, charging like a bull and delivering blows of unstoppable power. Many of the barbarians had never seen a black man, and they backed up, terrorized at the sight of him. The Ethiopian giant sheared off their swords and smashed their shields, chopping off their heads and their arms, whirling his axe and yelling: 'Behold the Black Man! I hate you freckled pigs!' In the fury of his assault, however, he had come too far forward and Commander Claudianus's left flank was left unguarded. Aurelius had just rid himself of an adversary when he saw, out of the corner of his eye, an enemy warrior lunging at the general, but his shield arrived too late to stop the barbarian's pike from sinking into Claudianus's shoulder. Aurelius shouted: 'The commander! The commander is wounded!'

Meanwhile the gates to the camp had been thrown open and the heavy line infantry was charging forward full force, in complete battle gear. The barbarians were driven off, and the few survivors leapt on to their horses and fled with their chief.

*

Shortly thereafter, on the other side of the hills, they reported to their commander, a Skyrian named Mledo who regarded them with scorn and contempt. They looked pitiful: weapons dented, clothing ripped, filthy with blood and slime. Their chief muttered, head low: 'They . . . refused. They said no.'

Mledo spat on the ground, then called his attendant and ordered him to sound the falling-in. The deep bellow of the horns rent the cloak of fog that still covered the countryside like a shroud.

*

Commander Claudianus was eased gently on to the plank bed in the infirmary and a surgeon prepared to remove the pike still stuck in his shoulder. The shaft had been sawn off to contain the damage caused by its swaying back and forth, but the tip had penetrated just below the collar bone and there was the risk of its perforating the lung as well. An assistant brought an iron to a red heat over coals, readying it for cauterizing the wound.

Trumpet blasts and cries sounded a new alarm from the bastions. Aurelius left the infirmary and ran up the stairs until he found himself beside Vatrenus who was staring at the horizon. The entire line of the hills was black with warriors.

'Great gods,' murmured Aurelius, 'there are thousands of them.'

'Go back to the commander and tell him what's happening. I can't see that we've got much choice here, but tell him we're awaiting his orders.'

Aurelius reached the infirmary just as the surgeon was wrenching the tip of the pike from the shoulder of their wounded leader, and he saw the noble patrician's face twist in a grimace of pain. Aurelius moved closer: 'General, the barbarians are attacking. There are thousands and thousands of them, and they are completely encircling our camp. What are your orders?'

Blood spurted copiously from the wound on to the hands and face of the surgeon and his assistants who were doing their utmost to staunch it while another approached with the red hot iron. The surgeon plunged it into the hole and Commander Claudianus moaned, gritting his teeth so as not to cry out. The acrid odour of burnt flesh saturated the little room and a dense smoke arose from the scorching iron which continued to sizzle in the wound.

Aurelius said again, 'General . . .'

Claudianus stretched out his free hand towards Aurelius: 'Listen . . . Odoacer wants to exterminate us, because we represent an insurmountable obstacle for him. The Nova Invicta is a relict from the past but we still frighten them. All Romans, from Italy and the provinces; he knows we'll never obey him. That's why he wants us all dead. Go at once to Orestes, he must be told what's happening here. Tell him that we're surrounded . . . that we desperately need his help . . .'

'Send someone else,' answered Aurelius, 'I beg of you. I want to stay. All my friends are here.'

'No. You must obey my orders. Only you can succeed. We still have control over the bridge on the Olubria; it will certainly be their first objective in cutting us off from Placentia. Go, now, before the circle closes in, hie to it and never stop. Orestes is at his villa outside the city with the emperor. We'll manage to hold out here.'

Aurelius lowered his head: 'I'll be back. Fight them off for as long as you can.' He turned. Behind him, Batiatus stared mutely at his commander, wounded and deathly pale, stretched out on the planks soaked with his blood. Aurelius didn't have the courage to say a word. He ran out and reached Vatrenus on the sentry walk: 'He has ordered me to go and seek reinforcements: I'll be back as soon as I can. Hold them off; I know we can do it!' Vatrenus nodded without speaking. There was no hope in his gaze, just the determination to die like a soldier.

Aurelius couldn't bring himself to speak. He stuck two fingers in his mouth and whistled. A whinny could be heard in reply, and a bay stallion trotted towards the bastions. Aurelius sprang into the saddle, spurring him towards the rear gate. Vatrenus ordered the doors to be unbolted for just long enough to let out the galloping horse and his rider, then had them closed again immediately.

Vatrenus watched as he rode off into the distance, heading towards the bridge on the Olubria. The squad guarding the bridgehead realized immediately what was happening, as a large group of barbarian horsemen detached from the bulk of the army and raced directly towards them.

'Will he make it?' asked Canidius at his side.

'You mean will he make it back? Yes. Perhaps,' replied Vatrenus. 'Aurelius is the best we've got.' The tone of his voice and his expression told a different story.

He turned back again, observing Aurelius as he raced to cover the open ground between the camp and the bridge. He soon saw another squad of barbarian cavalry emerging suddenly on the left and joining up with the squad arriving from the right, closing in like a pair of pincers to cut short his flight, but Aurelius was as fast as the wind, and his horse devoured the flat terrain between the camp and the river. Aurelius was stretched out nearly flat on the horse's back so as to offer less resistance and less of a mark for the arrows which were bound to start raining upon him.

'Run, run,' growled Vatrenus between his teeth, 'That's the way to do it, boy . . .'

He realized almost instantly that the assailants were too numerous and that they would soon overwhelm the soldiers at the bridgehead. Aurelius needed a greater lead. 'Catapults!' he shouted. The men arming the catapults were ready, and aimed their missiles at the barbarian cavalry converging on the bridge.

'Fire!' shouted Vatrenus again, and sixteen catapults discharged their arrows towards the heads of the two squads, hitting their mark. Those in the lead keeled over while those just behind them tumbled headlong over their fallen comrades. Others were crushed by the weight of their horses, while the archers stationed at the bridge picked off a number of those on the sides. First they sent a swarm of arrows horizontally into the crowd, then flung their javelins high to swoop down in the centre. Many barbarians fell, run through, as more horses stumbled and rolled over, dragging and burying their horsemen beneath them. The remaining comrades continued their charge, fanning out, yelling in fury at this reverse.

Aurelius was close enough so that his companions drawn up on the bridge could hear his voice. He recognized Vibius Quadratus, a tent mate, and shouted: 'I'm going for help! Cover me! I'll be back!'

'I know!' shouted Quadratus and raised his arm to signal the others to open a passage for Aurelius. He shot through the line of comrades like a lightning bolt and the bridge thundered under the hooves of his powerful steed. The garrison closed up compactly behind him, shields clanging tight against shields. The front line knelt while the second stood, only the tips of their spears protruding, shafts planted firmly in the ground.

The barbarian horsemen flung themselves at that little garrison in a blind frenzy, submerging that last bulwark of Roman discipline like a tidal wave. The bridge was so narrow that some of the assailants crashed into each other and were flung to the ground. Others made their way to the centre where they furiously attacked the small contingent. The Romans were pushed back, but held their line. Many of the barbarians' horses were wounded by spears, while others reared up and threw their horsemen, who ended up on the iron spikes. The combat was fierce, man against man, sword against sword. The defenders knew that every instant gained meant ground gained for Aurelius, and this could mean the salvation of the entire legion. They knew what horrible torture awaited them if they were taken alive, so they fought with utter disregard for their fate, loudly urging each other on.

Aurelius had reached the far end of the plain and turned around before bounding into the forest of oak trees before him. The last thing he saw was his comrades being overrun by the relentless vehemence of the enemy.

'He's made it!' exulted Antoninus from the camp's sentry walk. 'He's in the forest, they'll never get him now. Now we have a chance.'

'You're right,' replied Vatrenus. 'Our comrades on the bridge let themselves be slaughtered so they could cover his retreat.'

Batiatus arrived then from the infirmary.

'How's the commander?' asked Vatrenus.

'The surgeon has cauterized the wound, but he says the pike has punctured a lung. He's coughing up blood and his fever is rising.' He clenched his cyclopean fists and tightened his jaw. 'The first one of them I see I swear I'll butcher him, I'll demolish him, I'll smash him into pieces. I'll eat his liver . . .'

His comrades looked at him in a sort of admiring shock: they knew quite well that his weren't mere words.

Vatrenus changed the subject: 'What day is it today?'

'The nones of November,' replied Canidius. 'What difference does it make?'

Vatrenus shook his head: 'Just three months ago Orestes was

presenting his son to the Senate, and now he already has to defend the boy from Odoacer's fury. If Aurelius is lucky he'll get there sometime in the middle of the night. The reinforcements could leave at dawn and be here in two days' time. If Odoacer hasn't occupied all the passes and bridges, if Orestes has loyal troops he can set to march right away, if . . .'

His words were interrupted by blasts of alarm coming from the guard towers. The sentries shouted: 'They're attacking!'

Vatrenus reacted as if lashed by a whip. He called the standard bearer: 'Raise the ensign! All men at their battle posts! Machines in firing position! Archers to the palisade! Men of the Nova Invicta Legion, this camp is the last outpost of Rome, the sacred land of our ancestors! We shall defend it at all costs! Show these beasts that the honour of Rome is not dead!'

He grabbed a javelin and ran to his place on the bastions. At that very same instant from the hills exploded the howl of barbarian fury, and thousands upon thousands of horsemen made the earth tremble with their wrathful charge. They dragged chariots and wheeled carriages loaded with sharpened poles to hurl against the fortifications of the Roman camp. The defenders thronged the palisade, drawing the strings of their bows, spasmodically clutching at the javelins in their fists, pale with tension, their foreheads drenched with cold sweat.

2

FLAVIUS ORESTES GREETED his guests personally at the door to his country villa: notables from the city, senators, high army officers, all with their families. The lamps were lit and dinner was ready to be served: the lavish celebrations for his son's thirteenth birthday were about to commence. It was three months since young Romulus Augustus had risen to the throne.

Orestes had long pondered on whether it would be wise to postpone this banquet, given the dramatic situation unfolding. This unforeseen rebellion of Odoacer, with his Herulian and Skyrian troops! But in the end he had decided there was no reason to sow panic by abruptly changing plans. After all, his most seasoned division, the Nova Invicta, trained in the manner of the ancient legions, were on their way at that very moment, proceeding at a forced march. His brother Paulus was advancing from Ravenna at the head of more select troops. The rebellion would soon be quashed.

*

Flavia Serena was exceedingly ill-humoured, worried and sullen. Orestes had tried to hide the fall of Ticinum from his wife, but he had to think that she knew much more than she let on.

Orestes' gaze fell on her melancholy figure, off on her own by the tablinum door. Her attitude stung him as a harsh rebuke. She had always been against Romulus's ascent to the throne, and these celebrations irritated her beyond measure. Orestes approached her, trying to hide his inner conflict and his disappointment. 'Why so withdrawn? You are the mistress of this house and the mother of the emperor. You should be at the centre of attention, at the centre of the festivities!'

Flavia Serena looked at her husband as if the words he had just pronounced were totally devoid of sense, and replied harshly: 'You have succeeded in fulfilling your ambitions by exposing an innocent child to mortal danger.'

'He's not a child! He's practically a young man now, and he has been educated to become a sovereign. We've discussed this so often; I was hoping that you would spare me your ill humour, at least for today. What are you worried about? Look around you. It's a lovely party, our son is happy, and his tutor is satisfied as well; Ambrosinus is a wise man, and you've always trusted his judgement.'

'How can you rave on like this? What you've built is already falling to pieces. The barbarian troops of Odoacer, who had pledged to back you, have risen up in rebellion and are sowing death and destruction everywhere.'

'I shall force Odoacer to come around, and stipulate a new agreement. It isn't the first time such things have happened. They have no interest in bringing about the fall of an empire that provides them with land and money.'

Flavia Serena sighed and lowered her eyes for a moment, then raised them directly to her husband's: 'Is it true what Odoacer is going around saying? Is it true that you had promised him a reward? A third of all Italy? And then that you went back on your word?'

'No, it's not true. He . . . misinterpreted what I'd said.'

'Well, that doesn't change the situation much, does it? If he prevails, how do you think you'll be able to protect our son?'

Orestes took her hands between his. The noise of the surrounding festivities seemed to abate, muffled by the anguish that was growing between them like a nightmare. A dog barked in the distance and Orestes felt his wife's hands trembling. 'You must not worry,' he said. 'We have nothing to fear. I want you to know you can trust me, so I'm about to tell you something I've kept hidden from you all these years. I've established a special division, in complete secrecy – a loyal, cohesive fighting unit, all Romans from Italy and the provinces, trained like the legions of old. They take orders from Manilius Claudianus, an officer from the Roman aristocracy, a man who would sooner die than go back on his word. These soldiers have proven their incredible valour on our borders and I have ordered them now to return here, at a forced march. They could be here in two or three days' time. What's more, Paulus is on his way here from Ravenna at the head of another contingent. You see, you have nothing to worry about. Now, please, come and join our guests.'

Flavia Serena let herself be convinced that his words were spoken in truth, because in her heart of hearts she wanted nothing but to believe him, but as she tried to find her smile so she could take part in the reception, the dog's barking became louder and was joined by furious howling from all the others. The guests paused in their pleasantries and in that moment of silence a cry of alarm rose from the courtyard and the horns sounded the falling-in of the guard. An officer charged into the room and ran towards Orestes: 'We're being attacked, sir! There are hundreds of them, with Wulfila at their head!'

Orestes swiftly pulled a sword from a panoply which hung on the wall and shouted: 'Quickly, take up arms! We're under attack! *Ambrosine*, take the boy and his mother and hide in the woodshed. Don't move from there for any reason until I come to get you. Quickly, quickly!'

They could already hear the deafening roar of a battering ram at the gate and the entire line of fortification of the villa shook under its blows. Just as the defenders were rushing to the sentry walk in an attempt to drive back the attack, dozens of scaling ladders were being leaned up against the parapet, and hundreds of warriors were surging in from every direction, filling the air with their wild cries. The gate gave way and a gigantic horseman burst through with an acrobatic leap of his horse. Orestes recognized Odoacer's lieutenant and lunged at him, waving his sword: 'Wulfila! You traitor! You villain!'

*

Ambrosinus had managed to reach the woodshed, dragging the shaking, terrified boy behind him, but in the general confusion he had not noticed that Flavia Serena was not following. From a crack in the door, Romulus could see the tragedy unfolding. He saw the guests fall one after another to the floor in their own blood. He saw his father, challenging that beastly giant with the courage of his despair: Orestes was wounded and fell to his knees, yet he rose again, sword still in hand, and fought bravely until his energies abandoned him and he finally dropped, run through. The convulsive flickering of the boy's eyelids broke the experience up into a thousand sharp splinters and drove them deep into his memory. He heard his mother crying: 'No! Curse you! May you all be damned!' as Ambrosinus ran out to protect her. She screamed in horror, pulling out her hair and digging her nails into her face as she knelt beside her dying husband. Romulus scurried out of hiding as well. He would rather die with his parents than remain alone in that savage world! The boy gasped as the gigantic warrior dipped his hand into his father's blood and drew a red line with it across his forehead. He rushed to where his father's sword had fallen: he would take it up himself, he would destroy the enemy!

Ambrosinus, moving lightly and somehow unnoticed through that shower of darts, amidst the combatants clutching each other in hand-to-hand contest, planted himself between the boy and the sword of a barbarian who had just run up and whose blade would have taken the boy's head off had Wulfila himself not blocked the blow: 'Idiot!' he growled at the soldier. 'Can't you see? Don't you know who he is?'

The other lowered his sword in confusion. 'Take all three of them,' Wulfila ordered. 'The woman too. We'll be taking them with us. To Ravenna.'

The battle was over. The defenders had been overpowered

and put to the sword, one after another. Some of the guests had escaped through the windows into the dark countryside and others had hidden in the servants' quarters, under beds or in storehouses or in the midst of the farm tools, but many had been mowed down without pity in the fury of the attack. Even the musicians who had been delighting the guests with their melodies were dead now and lay with their eyes wide open, still holding their instruments. The women had been raped repeatedly as their fathers and husbands were forced to look on, before their own throats were slit like lambs at the slaughter.

The statues had been toppled from their pedestals in the garden, the plants and bushes had been uprooted and the fountains were flowing with blood. Blood stained the floors and splashed the frescoed walls, and the barbarians were busy finishing up the job by sacking all the precious objects in that sumptuous residence: candelabra, furnishings, vases. Those who were not able to get their hands on anything of value contemptuously mutilated the corpses or soiled the magnificent mosaic floors. The incoherent cries of those savages drunk on the butchery were joined by the crackling of the flames that had begun to devour that unfortunate house.

The three prisoners were dragged away and thrown on to a cart pulled by a couple of mules. Wulfila shouted: 'Let's get out! Out of here, I said, we have a long way ahead of us!'

His men grudgingly abandoned the devastated villa and lined up one after another on horseback, trotting along after the small convoy. Romulus wept in silence in the dark, curled into his mother's arms. In less than an hour he had fallen from imperial triumph to the most miserable of all fates. His father had been massacred before his eyes and he was a prisoner of these beasts, completely in their power. Ambrosinus sat behind them, unspeaking and shocked. He turned to look at the great rural villa going up in flames. The spiralling smoke and sparks that rose towards the sky spread an evil glow over the horizon. He had been able to save only his satchel, the one that he had brought with him to Italy so many long years ago, and just one of the thousands of books in his library: the splendidly illustrated *Aeneid* that the senators had presented as a gift for Romulus. His hand skimmed the leather cover of the volume and he thought that fate had not been so cruel after all, if it had left him with Virgil's verses for company. Prophetic, in a way.

*

Aurelius met a number of road blocks during his nocturnal ride. Odoacer had assigned garrisons to the bridges and passes, and squads of barbarian soldiers from the Imperial Army were patrolling the consular routes, so he was often forced off the road. He found himself braving almost impassable mountain paths and fords made treacherous by the autumn rains. As he began his descent towards the valley, he realized that his horse would never make it. The generous animal would fall dead if he spurred him into another gallop; he was covered with sweat and foam, his breath was short and his eyes dilated with the strain. Destiny was with him, however, as he made out a building with a familiar look in the distance: an exchange post on the via Flaminia, miraculously intact and apparently still open. As he approached, he could hear the creaking of a sign hanging from an iron bar embedded in the outer wall. It was quite rusty, but he could still discern the figure of a sandal and a phrase in well-formed capital letters: 'MANSIO AD SANDALUM HERCULIS.' A milestone in front of the building said *m.p.XXII*: twenty-two miles to the next station. If it was still standing.

Aurelius jumped off his horse and entered, short of breath. The post master was snoozing on a chair and a few couriers or customers were laid out on their cloaks on the floor, in a deep sleep. Aurelius woke the man: 'Imperial service,' he said. 'With a matter of the maximum urgency and top priority: it may be a question of life or death for a great many people. My mount is outside, but he's exhausted. I need a fresh horse, immediately.'

The man shook himself awake, opened his eyes and realized, as soon as he had focused on the soldier before him, that what he was saying had to be true. Aurelius's features were distorted with tension and fatigue.

'Come with me,' the post master said, handing him a chunk of bread and a flask of wine as they walked across the hall and down the stairs towards the stables. He could tell the man hadn't stopped a moment, not even to eat. The stalls were mostly empty, but three or four horses were just barely visible in the dim light. The post master lifted his lantern so he could see them better: 'Take that one,' he said, indicating a sturdy-looking horse with a lustrous black coat. 'He's a magnificent animal. His name is Juba. His master was a high-ranking officer, who never came back to claim him.'

Aurelius took a last bite out of the bread and swallowed a quick gulp of wine, then jumped on the steed's back and urged him up the ramp, shouting: 'On, Juba!' He emerged into the open air like a damned soul escaping the underworld, crossed the consular road at breakneck speed, and turned down a path that shone white in the moonlit landscape. The post master came out shortly thereafter with the lantern still in his hand, shouting and waving a receipt, but Aurelius was already far away and Juba's gallop faded off into the countryside.

The man repeated in a lower voice, as if talking to himself: 'You have to sign the receipt!' He was startled by a quiet neighing and noticed Aurelius's bay, steaming with sweat. He took him by the bridle and led him into the stables: 'Come on in, boy, or you'll catch your death out here. You're all sweaty, and you must be hungry. You won't have stopped to eat at all, I'll bet, just like your master.'

*

A pale glow had just begun to light up the horizon when Aurelius came into sight of Flavius Orestes' villa. He realized he'd got there too late. A dense column of black smoke rose from the ruined building and there were signs of savage destruction everywhere. He tied the horse to a tree and approached cautiously from behind an enclosure wall until he was near the main entrance. The gate doors were unhinged and scorched and lay on the ground, and the courtyard was thick with blood-clotted corpses. Many were soldiers of the Imperial Guard, although there were barbarian warriors as well, fallen in fierce hand-to-hand combat. The horror of death was still carved on to their faces, their bodies frozen in the ultimate spasm of agony.

No sound could be heard save the crackling of the flames, joined every now and then by the dry snap of a falling beam or a roof tile as it shattered on to the floor. Aurelius walked through the desolation, dismayed and incredulous as the tragedy unfolded before his eyes in all its gruesome reality. He felt suffocated, crushed as under a millstone. The stink of death and excrement tainted the inner rooms, which had not yet been devoured by the flames. The corpses of women, stripped and raped, of young maidens with their legs obscenely split open, lay next to the corpses of their husbands and fathers. Blood was everywhere – on the intricately patterned marble floors, on the beautifully frescoed walls, in the atria, the bath chamber, the triclinium, spattered on the tables and over the remaining food. The curtains, carpets and table linens were soaked with it.

Aurelius fell to his knees and covered his face with his hands. A growl of impotent fury escaped him. He felt powerless to move, his forehead practically touching his knees, as his despair grew. He was suddenly shaken by the sound of groaning. Was it possible? Possible that someone was still alive in that slaughter-house? He sprang to his feet, hastily wiped away the tears running down his face and headed in the direction of the sound. It was coming from the courtyard, from a man prostrate in a pool of blood. Aurelius knelt beside him and turned him over gently, so he could see him in the face. The man, so close to death, recognized his uniform and insignia. 'Legionary,' he whispered.

Aurelius moved even closer: 'Who are you?' he asked.

The man moaned in pain; every breath was costing him terrible suffering.

He answered: 'I am Flavius . . . Orestes.'

Aurelius shook with emotion: 'Commander,' he said, 'oh great gods . . . Commander, I'm with the Nova Invicta Legion.' And that name – ne'er defeated! – seemed a bitter mockery.

Orestes was shivering and his teeth chattered as the chill of death invaded his body. Aurelius took off his cloak to cover him. That gesture of pity seemed to hearten the man, restoring a glimmer of energy: 'My wife, my son . . .' he said. 'They've taken the emperor! I beg of you, tell the legion. You must . . . free them.'

Aurelius lowered his head: 'The legion has been attacked by overwhelming forces. I had come to ask for reinforcements.'

An expression of profound discouragement was painted on Orestes' face, but as he stared at Aurelius with tear-filled eyes, his voice still trembled with hope: 'You save them,' he said. 'I beg of you.'

Aurelius couldn't bear to meet the distressing intensity of his gaze. He looked away, saying: 'I am . . . all alone, Commander.'

Orestes seemed to ignore his words completely. With his last bit of strength he tried to pull himself up and gripped the edge of Aurelius's cuirass: 'I implore you,' he panted. 'Legionary, save my son. Save the emperor! If he dies, Rome will die. If Rome dies, all is lost.' His hand slipped lifelessly to the ground and his eyes took on the stupefied stare of death.

Aurelius closed Orestes' eyelids. He took back his cloak and walked away as the sun rose gloriously over the horizon, illuminating the full horror of the massacre as he turned his back to it. He reached Juba, who was calmly nibbling at some grass. He untied him, got into the saddle and urged him north, on the traces of the enemy.

3

The column led by Wulfila proceeded for three days in an arduous march over the snow-covered Apennine passes, and then across the foggy plain. The prisoners were worn out by fatigue and insomnia, pushed to the limit of their powers of endurance. None of them had properly slept a single night; their troubled sleep was racked by nightmares. Flavia Serena called up all the courage instilled by her strict upbringing, so that her behaviour would be an example to her son Romulus. The boy would lay his head in her lap and close his eyes, but as soon as he began to drop off, images of the massacre invaded his shaken mind, and his mother could feel his limbs cramping up painfully. She could almost see the scenes of horror dancing under his eyelids. He would awaken suddenly with a shout, his brow beaded with cold sweat, his eyes full of anguish.

Ambrosinus lay his hand on Romulus's shoulder, trying to convey a little warmth. 'Take heart, my boy,' he said. 'Destiny has dealt you the cruellest and most difficult of fates, but I know you will withstand it.'

When he noticed the boy falling asleep, he would whisper soft words into his ear, and for a little while the child's breath would come longer and his features would relax.

'What did you say?' asked Flavia Serena.

'I spoke to him with the voice of his father,' replied Ambrosinus enigmatically. 'It was what he wanted to hear.'

Flavia said nothing and continued to stare at the long winding road that descended towards the Adriatic Sea, crested with grey foam under a leaden sky. They arrived near Ravenna on the evening of the fifth day, as it was getting dark, crossing over on one of the many embankments which led through the lagoon to the group of islands where the city had been founded, now joined by a long coastal dune. The rising fog crept over the surface of the still water and seeped over the dry land, where it lapped at skeletal trees and at the isolated huts of fishermen and farmers. The cries of the night animals were muffled, distant, as was the barking of a solitary dog. The cold and damp penetrated their bones, and their fatigue and discomfort felt unbearable.

The towers of Ravenna rose suddenly before them like giants in the mist. Wulfila shouted something in his guttural tongue and the gate swung open. Dozens of galloping horses rumbled across the access bridge, then they slowed to a trot and entered the deserted, foggy city. The inhabitants seemed to have all disappeared: the doors were barred and all the windows were closed. A boat made its way down the canal like a ghost, oars slicing silently through the waters. They stopped at the entrance to the imperial palace, made of red bricks and grey Istrian stone columns. Wulfila ordered that the mother be separated from her child, and that the boy be taken to his quarters.

'Allow me to go with him,' Ambrosinus swiftly proposed. 'He's terrified and exhausted; he needs someone with him. I am his tutor and I can help him. I implore you, powerful lord, let me accompany him.'

Wulfila, flattered by that designation, to which he was hardly accustomed and which had certainly never been directed to him before, acquiesced with a grunt. Ambrosinus caught up with his disciple as they dragged him away. Romulus twisted around, crying out for his mother. Flavia Serena cast a sorrowful yet dignified look at her son, silently exhorting him not to give up hope. She walked off down the hall between two guards with a firm step, shoulders squared and arms crossed over her breasts, to conceal what her torn gown left unveiled.

Odoacer had been notified of their arrival and he awaited her, seated on the ivory throne of the last Caesars. At his peremptory gesture, Wulfila and the guards left him alone with the woman.

A chair had been prepared at the foot of the throne and Odoacer invited her to sit down, but Flavia Serena remained standing, her back straight and her eyes staring into the distance. Even though her clothing was in shreds and her hair clotted, even though her tunic was bloodstained, her forehead blackened with soot and her cheeks gouged, she radiated proud, untamed femininity. Her beauty had been insulted but was still intact, superb and delicate at one and the same time. Her neck was pure white, her shoulders curved softly and her hands crossed over her breasts could not wholly conceal their perfection. She felt the barbarian's eyes upon her even though she would not look at him, and she felt ablaze with disdain and impotent rage, but the pallor of her fatigue, hunger and lack of sleep cloaked her true emotions.

'I know you despise me,' said Odoacer. 'Barbarians, you call us, as if you were somehow better. Yours is a race prostrated by its own vices, by power and corruption! I had your husband killed because he deserved it. He had betrayed me by going back on his word. I had to make an example of him, so that everyone would understand that you cannot deceive Odoacer with such impunity! The example had to be such a good one that everyone, everywhere, would understand, and be terrified by it! And don't imagine that you can count on your brother-in-law Paulus: my troops have surrounded his army and destroyed it. But I've had enough of all this blood! I do not intend to make this country suffer. I want it to be reborn; the arts must be revived, work in the fields and the shops must flourish again. This land deserves better than Flavius Orestes and his child emperor. It deserves a true sovereign who will guide and protect it like a husband guides and protects his wife. I will be that sovereign, and you shall be my queen.'

Flavia had remained still and silent until that moment. She finally reacted, and her voice was as cutting as a blade: 'You don't know what you're saying. I descend from those who have fought you off for centuries, and chased you back into the woods where you can live like the beasts that you are. I am nauseated by your stench, your ignorance, your savagery. I hate the sound of your voice and your language, which seems like the barking of a dog, not the tongue of a human being. I am disgusted by your skin, which can't bear the light of the sun, by your hair of straw, by your moustaches, always filthy with the remains of your food. Is this the marriage bond that you desire? The exchange of feelings you dream of? Kill me, now, my life doesn't matter to me. I will never marry you!'

Odoacer clenched his jaw. Her lashing words had wounded and humiliated him. He knew that nothing could win over such scorn, and yet the feeling of boundless admiration that had struck him as a young man when he had first entered the Imperial Army was still keen and unchanged – admiration for those ancient cities, their forums and basilicas, their columns and monuments, their streets and ports and aqueducts and arches, their solemn inscriptions in bronze, their baths and their houses. Their villas were so beautiful they seemed the residence of the gods, not of mere men. The empire was the only place in the world where life was worth living.

He looked at Flavia and found her more desirable than ever, even more so than the first time he had seen her, when she was just twenty and was betrothed to Flavius Orestes. She had seemed so distant to him then – as lovely and unattainable as the star that he would watch as a child, stretched out in his parents' nomadic cart under the night sky, in the midst of an endless plain. Now she was at his mercy and he could have her whenever he wanted, even in that very moment, but that was not what he wanted, not yet.

'You'll do as I say,' he told her, 'if you want to save your son. If you don't want to see him killed before your eyes. Get out of here now.'

The guards entered and escorted her to the western wing of the palace.

*

Ambrosinus was looking through the keyhole as he heard the men's low voices. He called Romulus to his side: 'Look,' he said, 'it's your mother.' He brought his index finger to his mouth in warning as he stepped aside so the boy could see.

The small cortège soon passed beyond his restricted line of vision, but Ambrosinus put his ear to the door and counted their steps until he heard the click of a door opening and closing.

'Twenty-four. Your mother's room is twenty-four paces from ours, and may be on the other side of the corridor. We're probably in the women's quarters. I lived here for a while a couple of years ago, and your mother also knows the place well. This could be an advantage for us.'

Romulus nodded, accustomed as he was to following his tutor's elaborate reasoning even when he could make neither head nor tail of it, but was not particularly convinced. The door to their room was bolted from the outside and guarded by a warrior armed with an axe and sword. What chance was there that he'd ever see his mother again?

He lay on the bed, exhausted by too many emotions and by enormous fatigue. Nature took its course and Romulus soon fell into a deep sleep. Ambrosinus covered him with a blanket, patted the boy's head softly and then lay down himself, hoping for some rest. He refrained from extinguishing the lantern because he was sure that the darkness would have aroused images from which he might not be able to defend himself. He wanted to stay vigilant on such a night, teeming with vengeful shadows.

He couldn't say how much time had passed when a sound struck his ear, followed by a dull thud. Romulus was deeply asleep and apparently hadn't heard anything: he was still in exactly the same position as when he had first lain down. Ambrosinus got up and heard another noise, a sharp metallic click this time, directly outside the door. He shook the boy: 'Wake up, quickly. There's someone at the door.'

Romulus opened his eyes without realizing at first where he was. He became painfully aware of his surroundings as he looked around at the walls of his prison. The door had opened, creaking, and a cloaked, hooded shape appeared in the doorway. Ambrosinus's glance fell to the tip of the sword in the figure's hand and he instinctively moved to shield the boy, but the man uncovered his face.

'Quickly,' he said, 'I'm a Roman soldier. Nova Invicta Legion. I've come to save the emperor. Now! We've no time to lose.'

'But how can I—' began Ambrosinus.

'It doesn't matter. I promised to save him, not you.'

'I've never seen you, I don't know who you are . . .'

'My name is Aurelius and I've just killed the guard.' He turned around and dragged in the body.

'I won't come without my mother,' said Romulus at once.

'Then move, in the name of the gods,' replied Aurelius. 'Where is she?'

'Down that way,' offered Ambrosinus. Then, grappling for some proof that he was indispensable to the escape effort: 'What's more, I know how to get out of here. There's a passage that leads to the women's gallery in the imperial basilica.'

They headed to the door of the room where Flavia Serena was being held prisoner. Aurelius inserted his sword between the door and the jamb, prised the bolt and managed to draw it out. At just that moment a guard appeared on his rounds: shouting in alarm, he ran towards them with his sword drawn. Aurelius faced the barbarian, knocked him off balance with a feint and ran the man through from side to side. The guard collapsed without a moan and the legionary entered Flavia's room: 'Quickly, my lady, I've come to free you. There's not a moment to lose.'

Flavia saw her boy and Ambrosinus and her heart skipped a beat: destiny had unexpectedly come to her aid.

'This way,' said Ambrosinus. 'There's a direct passage to the women's gallery. Perhaps the barbarians don't know about it.' They hurried down the corridor, but the shouting of the guard that Aurelius had killed had drawn the attention of the others, who were appearing at the end of the hall. Aurelius managed to close an iron grating behind them, just in time, then ran on with his fleeing companions. Shouts sounded from every direction, torches lit up the courtyard and the windows, clanging weapons and excited cries seemed to surround them. Just as Ambrosinus was about to open the hidden door that led to the women's gallery, some soldiers sprang out of a side staircase. A giant of a man – Wulfila! – flanked by two others.

Ambrosinus had gone on ahead of his companions and found himself cut off from them. Consumed by anguish, he crouched behind the arch that concealed the door to the gallery, and helplessly watched the attack. The three warriors hurled themselves at Aurelius, who stood shielding Flavia and Romulus. Ambrosinus closed his eyes and grasped the pendant hanging from his neck with his left hand. It was a twig of mistletoe set in silver. He concentrated all the powers of his spirit in Aurelius's arm, which struck lightning-swift and chopped off the head of one of the barbarians. It rolled between the man's legs and for a moment the last contractions of his still-beating heart twitched through his body, spurting blood copiously through his neck before he fell backwards.

Aurelius halted Wulfila's blow with the dagger he held in his other hand, then abruptly leapt aside, tripping the third man who was about to attack. He spun back around with fierce energy and his dagger cleaved the air, landing between the shoulder blades of his fallen aggressor, and nailed him gasping to the ground. Aurelius turned then to face his most formidable adversary. Their swords clashed with deafening force as both delivered a sequence of deadly blows, sparks spraying all around them. Both swords were crafted of fine, hardened steel, and the frightful strength of the barbarian threatened to best the skill and agility of the Roman.

The shouts of the other barbarians were drawing closer, and Aurelius realized that he would have to rid himself of his adversary or face a horrible death at their hands. Swords locked tight between the chests of the two warriors, each tried to cut the other's throat, hands clutching each other's wrists. At that moment, so close that they were staring each other down, Wulfila's eyes widened in sudden surprise: 'Who are you?' he cried. 'I've seen you before, Roman!'

All he had to do was immobilize Aurelius for a few more

moments and his comrades would be upon them, ending their fight and answering that question, but Aurelius managed to free himself by butting him hard in the face. He drew back to lunge at the barbarian, but slipped on the slick blood of his fallen enemies and fell to the ground.

Wulfila was about to finish him off, but Romulus, who until that moment had been holding on tightly to his mother, frozen by fear, recognized his father's murderer. He twisted free, grabbed the sword of one of the dead men and hurled himself at Wulfila. The giant could see him coming out of the corner of his eye and threw his dagger, but Flavia had moved forward to protect her child and took the blow full in the chest. Romulus began screaming, horrified, and Aurelius took advantage of his adversary's momentary distraction to strike. Wulfila jerked back his head, but his face was slashed from his left eye to his right cheek. He howled in rage and pain, continuing to wave his sword.

Aurelius pulled the boy off his mother's body and dragged him down the staircase that his aggressors had emerged from. Ambrosinus shook off his fright and made to follow them, just as a squad of guards appeared. The old man backed into the shadow of the arch and then slipped behind the door that led to the gallery.

*

Ambrosinus found himself on the inside of the long marble balcony that faced the basilica's nave. The apse was dominated by a large mosaic of Christ the Almighty, its golden reflections shining with pale light. He walked swiftly to the balustrade and crossed the presbytery and the sacristies, where he found the narrow corridor built into the church's external wall that led outside. He tried to imagine where Aurelius might come out and how they might try to escape. He trembled at the thought of the boy exposed to such deadly peril.

*

Only one escape route remained for Aurelius, and it led directly through the palace baths. He emerged into a large room covered by a barrel-vaulted ceiling, dimly lit by a couple of oil lamps. The huge pool built into the floor was filled with water, once crystal clear, that the negligence of the palace's new owners had allowed to become filthy and algae-coated. Aurelius tried the door that led to the street but it was locked from the outside. He turned to the boy: 'Can you swim?' he asked. Romulus nodded as his eyes focused with disgust on that smelly cesspool.

'Then you get in after me. We have to swim down the drainage pipe that connects the pool with the canal outside. My horse is not far from there. The water is going to be very dark, and cold, but you can do it, and I'll be helping you. Hold your breath and let's go.'

He lowered himself into the pool and then helped Romulus in. They ducked under and Aurelius began to make his way up the water drainage pipe. He put his hands forward to feel for the bulkhead that separated the pool from the canal. It was closed. His heart sank, but he was determined to find a way. He could feel the boy's panic through the black water and realized how close he was to drowning. Aurelius succeeded in slipping his hands under the base of the bulkhead and slowly pushed it up with all his strength until he could feel it yield, little by little. Blindly he grabbed the boy and shoved him past the obstacle, then made it through himself and let the bulkhead drop shut behind him. His lungs nearly bursting, he surfaced along with Romulus. The child seemed about to faint; he was livid with the cold and his teeth were chattering helplessly. He couldn't leave the boy in the water while he went for his horse. He pushed him up on to the bank, soaked and shivering, then hoisted himself up, dragging Romulus quickly to shelter behind the southern corner of the palace.

'The fog is rising,' he said. 'Lucky for us. Don't lose hope, we can make it now, but you stay here and promise me you won't move.'

The boy did not reply at first; he seemed to have lost every contact with reality. Then, with a barely perceptible voice, he said: 'We have to wait for Ambrosinus.'

'He's old enough to take care of himself,' responded Aurelius. 'We'll need all the luck we have to get out of here ourselves. The barbarians are already searching the grounds.' They could hear the uproar as men on horseback rushed from the stables at the northern wing of the palace, heading out to patrol the roads. Aurelius ran off to retrieve Juba from the old rundown fish warehouse where he'd hidden him.

He took the horse by its halter and retraced his steps, careful not to make the slightest sound. When he was not far from where he had left the boy, he heard a voice cry out in Herulian: 'Here he is! I've found him! Stop!' Romulus scurried away from his hiding place, running along the eastern side of the palace. They had flushed him out!

Aurelius jumped on to his horse and burst into the vast open space in front of the facade of the imperial palace which was illuminated by a great number of lit torches. He saw Romulus racing at breakneck speed, chased by a group of Herulian warriors. Aurelius spurred on his horse and stormed into their midst, running through a couple of the barbarians from behind, one to his left and the other to his right, before they understood what was happening. He overtook the others and reached Romulus. Grabbing the boy under his arm, Aurelius urged on his horse: 'Go, Juba. Go, boy!' Just as he was about to hoist Romulus up on to the saddle, one of their pursuers sent an arrow flying. It hit Aurelius full in the shoulder. He tried to resist, but, as a painful spasm racked the muscles in his arm, he had to let the boy go.

Romulus tumbled to the ground but Aurelius refused to give up. He tightened his legs against the horse's flanks and swiftly twisted Juba around so he could yank up the boy with his good arm, but just at that moment Ambrosinus burst forth from a side door and threw himself on the emperor, flattening him to the ground as he shielded him with his own body.

*

Aurelius realized that he didn't have a chance. He swerved down a narrow side street, jumping his horse over the canal that crossed it and proceeded at a mad pace towards the city walls where an old breach which had never been repaired allowed him to career up the side as if going up a ramp. He came down on the other side without great difficulty.

A group of barbarian warriors on horseback erupted from one of the doors, brandishing torches and intent on stopping his escape. Aurelius raced to the embankment that crossed the lagoon and tried to put as much distance as possible between himself and his pursuers. The fog would do the rest. But the unbearable pain in his shoulder interfered with his control of the horse, who was losing speed. Through the darkness he could see a thick grove of trees and bushes growing alongside the swamp. He pulled up on the reins, and slipped to the ground. He tried to hide in the water, sliding down the bank, in the hope that his pursuers would ride on, but they immediately realized his intent and drew up short. There were at least half a dozen of them; they would soon see him and he would have no chance against them.

He unsheathed his sword and prepared to die like a soldier, but at that very instant a whistle pierced the air. One of the barbarians crumbled to the ground, struck by an arrow. A second was hit in the neck and fell backwards, vomiting blood. The remainder realized that with their torches lit they were clear targets in the darkness and they were about to toss them away when a third arrow pierced the stomach of another horseman, who howled in pain. The others fled, terrified, from that invisible enemy hidden by the fog of the swamp.

Aurelius tried to climb up the bank, pulling his horse after him, but he slipped backwards, completely drained of strength. The pain was insufferable, his vision clouded over and he seemed to be sinking into the fog in an endless fall. In a brief flash of consciousness he thought he saw a hooded figure bending over him, and there was the slow gurgling of water sliced by an oar. Then nothing.

4

AMBROSINUS GOT UP FROM the ground and helped Romulus up as well. Completely soaked, his clothes soiled with algae and mud, his hair plastered to his forehead, the boy was shivering and his lips were blue. Ambrosinus took off his cloak and wrapped it around the child's shoulders, saying: 'Come on, now. We'll go back inside.' They were completely surrounded by Wulfila's guards who threatened them with their unsheathed swords.

Ambrosinus passed through their ranks with his head held high, helping the boy along and whispering words of encouragement as they walked down the halls and up the stairs, back towards their detention chamber. Romulus said nothing, shuffling along with an uncertain step, tripping over his shredded clothes and over the cloak itself, much too long for him. His limbs were stiff and aching, and his soul was tormented by the image of his mother falling under the dagger of his father's assassin. He hated the man who had deceived him with the hope of saving them. He had just caused worse trouble, and made his future look even more frightening. He raised his eyes to his tutor's and asked: 'My mother . . . she's dead, isn't she?'

Ambrosinus lowered his head without answering.

'Is she dead?' insisted the boy.

'I'm . . . I'm afraid so,' replied Ambrosinus, putting his arm around the boy's shoulders and drawing him close, but Romulus twisted away, shouting: 'Let me be! Leave me alone! I want my mother! I want to see her. Where have you put her? I want to see her!' He rushed at the barbarian guards, furiously beating his fists against their shields. They snickered and started teasing him, pushing him off one against the other. Ambrosinus tried to get hold of him and calm him down, but he wouldn't be caught. He seemed out of his mind. In truth, the boy was devastated. There was no glimmer of hope in his life, no escape from the horror. He was so inconsolable that his tutor feared he might try to take his own life.

'Let him see his mother,' Ambrosinus implored the guards. 'Perhaps he'll give vent to his feelings and then be able to settle down. I beg of you, if you know where they've put her, let him see her. He's only a frightened boy, have pity on him.'

The barbarians stopped laughing as Ambrosinus stared into their eyes, one by one. His look was so intense, such disquieting power radiated from those blue eyes, that the guards dropped their gazes, as if subdued by some mysterious energy. Then, the one who seemed the squad leader said: 'Not now. You have to go back to your room; these are our orders. I will refer your requests to my commander.'

Romulus had finally quietened down, worn out and exhausted, and they were taken back. Ambrosinus said nothing, because anything he could say would only worsen the situation. Romulus slumped down at the far side of the room, his head leaning against the wall and his eyes staring. Every now and then he would sigh and shudder. His tutor would then get up and draw nearer to examine his expression and try to understand what part of his spirit was vigilant and what was lost to delirium. In this disturbed state of intermittent sleep they passed the rest of the night.

When a little milky light had seeped into the room through a couple of loopholes high up on the wall, they heard a noise at the door. It swung open and two maidservants appeared. They carried a tub of water, fresh clothing, a jar of unguent and a tray with some food. They put everything down on a table and approached Romulus, bowing and kissing his hand deferentially. Romulus let himself be washed and dressed, but refused to eat despite Ambrosinus's persistence. One of the maids, a girl of about eighteen, was very gentle and pretty. She poured some hot milk and honey in a cup and said: 'Please, my lord, drink this at least. It will give you a little strength.'

'Please!' insisted the other girl, just a little older than the first. The thoughtfulness in her gaze was intense and sincere. Romulus took the cup and drank in long gulps. Then he set it back down on the tray and thanked them.

Under normal conditions the boy would never have thanked a servant, Ambrosinus thought. Perhaps that situation of extreme pain and solitude made him appreciate any gesture of human warmth, no matter where it came from. When the girls got up to leave, the old man asked them whether they had noticed any particular comings and goings that morning in the palace. They shook their heads.

'We need your help,' said Ambrosinus. 'Any information that you can give us could be precious. Crucial, even. The emperor's life may be at stake.'

'We'll do what we can,' answered the older girl, 'but we don't understand their language and often don't know what they're saying.'

'Could you take out a message?'

'They search us,' replied the girl, blushing, 'but we can repeat a message, if you want. Unless they have us followed. There's great hostility and suspicion in the palace against anyone who is Latin.'

'I understand. What I need to know is whether a Roman soldier was captured last night, a man of about forty-five, powerfully built, with dark hair, greying a little at the temples, and black eyes. His left shoulder was wounded.'

The girls exchanged a glance and said that they hadn't seen anyone who fitted that description.

'If you should see him, dead or alive, please let me know as soon as possible. One last thing: who sent you?'

'The master of the palace,' answered the older girl. 'Noble Antemius.' Ambrosinus nodded: he was a senior functionary and had always been faithful to the emperor, whoever the emperor happened to be, without asking questions. Evidently it seemed only right to him that he should serve Romulus, until a successor had been named.

The girls walked out, and their light steps faded into the heavier stride of the guards who were escorting them. Romulus curled into a corner of the room in obstinate silence, refusing to accept any invitation to converse on the part of his tutor. He simply didn't have the strength to climb out of the abyss that he'd fallen into. To judge from the fixed, uncaring expression of his eyes, lost in the void, he was continuing to slip down deeper, but then his eyes would glitter with untold emotion and the tears would begin to run down his cheeks, wetting his clothing.

More time passed: it must have been nearly noon when the door opened again and the guard Ambrosinus had spoken to the night before appeared on the threshold and said: 'You can see her now, if you like.' Romulus immediately shook himself out of his torpor and followed him out without even awaiting his tutor, who joined the two of them. Ambrosinus had not spoken because he knew that there were no words that could light up that chasm, and because he believed that nature protected her little ones, and only she could heal such painful wounds.

They walked towards the southern wing of the palace, to the now-deserted quarters of the palatine guards. They went down a flight of stairs and Ambrosinus realized that they were headed for the imperial basilica, which he had entered from the women's gallery such a short time ago. They crossed the nave and went down into a crypt, partially invaded by the brackish water of the lagoon. The central altar and the small presbytery rose out of the water like a little island, linked to the church floor by a walk-way of bricks. They crossed the crystalline water which sparkled over an ancient mosaic that depicted the dance of the seasons. Flavia Serena's body was lying on the marble altar table. White as wax, covered by a white wool blanket that fell on both sides, her hair had been combed and her face cleaned and lightly made up. One of the palace maidservants must have composed her body with great care.

Romulus stared at his mother at length, as if her lifeless body might miraculously awaken under the warmth of his gaze. His eyes then filled with tears and he wept his heart out, his forehead pressed against the cold marble. Ambrosinus, who had drawn close without daring to touch the boy, let him give vent to his feelings. Romulus finally dried his eyes and whispered something that Ambrosinus could not quite make out. The boy turned to the guards standing by, barbarian soldiers in Wulfila's charge, and his tutor was struck by the firmness with which he said: 'You'll pay for this. All of you. May God damn you to hell, you pack of rabid dogs.'

Not one of them understood the boy's words, pronounced in archaic Latin, like the curse he had uttered. His tutor was relieved, but above them, standing on a small gallery near the apse, Odoacer had observed the scene. He turned to one of his servants and asked: 'What did he say?'

'He swore revenge,' replied the servant summarily. Odoacer sneered indulgently, but Wulfila, half hidden in the shadows behind him, seemed the physical manifestation of that curse. The wide slash inflicted by Aurelius's sword disfigured his face, and the stitches that the palace surgeon had applied made his swollen cheeks look even more repugnant. His lips contracted into a grotesque grimace.

Odoacer turned to the guard standing next to him: 'Take the boy back to his room and bring me the old man: he must know a thing or two about last night's raid.' He cast a final look at Flavia Serena's body, and in the darkness no one could see the expression of profound regret that passed through his gaze for an instant. He turned away and walked off, followed by Wulfila, headed towards the imperial apartments. One of the guards went down into the crypt and murmured something to the commander. Romulus was immediately separated from his tutor who was taken away by the newcomer. The boy called after him: '*Magister*!' Ambrosinus turned around. 'Do not abandon me!'

'Do not fear. We shall see each other soon. Keep up your courage, and do not let anyone see you cry. Never, for any reason. You have lost both of your parents, and there is no sorrow in life greater than this. Now you can only rise from the depths of your grief. And I will be there to help you.' He walked away after the guards.

*

Odoacer was waiting for him in the imperial apartments, in the room which had been the study of Julius Nepos and Flavius Orestes himself.

'Who was the man who attempted to free the prisoners last night?' Odoacer asked, mincing no words. Ambrosinus was staring at the long shelves, full of scrolls and books; how many of them he had consulted, when he had had occasion to visit this sumptuous residence in the past! Odoacer was greatly irritated by his attitude and shouted: 'Look at me when I talk to you! And answer my questions!'

'I don't know who he was,' was the old man's calm reply. 'I had never seen him before.'

'Don't lie to me! No one would have attempted such an undertaking without a prior agreement. You knew about him, and perhaps you know where he is now. You had better tell me: I have ways to make you talk.'

'I don't doubt that,' replied Ambrosinus, 'but even you can't force me to say what I don't know. Just ask the men in the escort: from the moment in which we left the villa, we were in contact with no one but your barbarians. There were no Romans in the group you sent in for the massacre, and none of Orestes' men survived, as you know well. What's more, I myself prevented that man from carrying out his plan to take away the boy . . .'

'Only because you didn't want to put the child at risk.'

'Of course. I would never have agreed to such a plan! Hopeless from the start, and the price was horrendous. It may have been the last thing he intended, but his rash gesture resulted in disaster. My lady, the empress, would still be alive if it weren't for him. I could never have approved of such folly, for a very simple reason.'

'And what would that be?'

'I detest failure. He was certainly a very courageous man, and that dog of your guard will remember him for some time: he sliced his face from side to side. I know you want revenge, but I cannot help you. Even if you cut me to pieces, you will learn nothing more than what I have already told you.'

He spoke with such calm and self-assurance that Odoacer was impressed: a man like that could be very useful to him, a man with the wit and wisdom to guide him through the maze of politics and court intrigue that he was about to be drawn into. However, the tone he'd used in saying the words 'my lady, the empress' left no doubts concerning his convictions and his loyalty.

'What will you do with the boy?' Ambrosinus asked him.

'It's no affair of yours,' replied Odoacer.

'Spare him. He cannot harm you in any way. I don't know why that man attempted to liberate him, but he's no worry for you in any case. He acted alone: if this had been a plot, the choice of the time and place would have been different, wouldn't you say? A greater number of men, accomplices along the way, an escape route: do you know that I had to suggest a way to escape myself?'

Odoacer was surprised by the old man's spontaneous admission, and struck by the logic of his words. 'How did he manage to find your apartments, then?'

'I don't know, but I can imagine.'

'Well?'

'That man knows your language.'

'How can you be certain?'

'Because I heard him speaking with your soldiers,' replied Ambrosinus.

'And how did they get out?' insisted Odoacer. Neither he nor his men had managed to explain how Romulus and Aurelius had been found outside the palace when all the escape routes were closed off.

'This I do not know because we were separated by your men's raid, but the child was wet and smelled terrible. One of the sewers, I'd say. But what difference does it make? You can't be afraid of a boy of not even thirteen. What I'm telling you is that that man acted alone. And he was badly wounded. He may even be dead by now. Spare the boy, I beg of you. He's little more than a child: what harm could come of it?'

Odoacer stared into his eyes and felt suddenly dizzy, pervaded by an inexplicable feeling of uncertainty. He lowered his gaze in the pretence of weighing his words, then said: 'Go now. You will not wait long for my decision. Do not entertain any hope that last night's episode will be repeated.'

'How could it possibly?' replied Ambrosinus. 'Our every move is being watched by dozens of warriors . . . an old man and a boy! But if you'll accept my advice . . .'

Odoacer did not want to humiliate himself by asking, but he was curious to hear what this man, who was capable of unsettling him with a mere glance, would say next. Ambrosinus understood and continued speaking: 'If . . . if you eliminate the child, it would be seen as a serious abuse of your power – by the Emperor of the East, for instance, who has many supporters here in Italy, many spies, and a great number of soldiers. He would never recognize your authority under such circumstances. You see, a Roman can take the life of another Roman, but . . .' he hesitated an instant before pronouncing the word: 'a barbarian cannot. Even the great Ricimerus, your predecessor, in order to govern was forced to hide behind insubstantial imperial figures. If you spare the boy, you will be seen as magnanimous and generous. You will gain the sympathy of the Christian clergy, which is very powerful, and the Emperor of the East will have to act as though nothing has happened. He doesn't really care who is in command in the West, because it changes nothing for him, but he is very concerned with . . . the way things look. Remember what I'm saying: if you keep up appearances, you will be able to stay in control of this country for as long as you live.'

'Keep up appearances?' repeated Odoacer.

'Listen. Twenty-five years ago Attila imposed a tax on

Emperor Valentinian the third, who had no choice but to pay. But do you know how he worked it? He named Attila General of the Empire and paid the tax as if it were his salary. In reality, the emperor of Rome was a tributary of a barbarian chief, but the appearances were saved and with them, his honour. Killing Romulus would be an act of useless cruelty and a terrible error politically. You are a man of power now, and it's time that you learn how to wield that power.' He nodded respectfully and turned away before Odoacer could think of making him stay.

As soon as the door closed behind him, a side door opened and Wulfila stepped in: 'You must kill him, immediately,' he hissed, 'or there will be no end to episodes like last night's.'

Odoacer regarded him coolly; this man, who in the past had carried out every sort of foul deed upon his orders, seemed suddenly distant and completely foreign to him, a barbarian with whom he no longer had anything in common.

'You know nothing but blood and killing, but I want to govern, understand? I want my subjects to dedicate themselves to their occupations and interests, not to plots and conspiracies. I will make my own decision regarding this matter.'

'You've gone soft with the whimpering of that kid and the chattering of that charlatan. If you don't feel up to the task, I'll take care of it.'

Odoacer raised his hand as if to strike him, but stopped at a palm's breadth from Wulfila's butchered face. 'Don't you dare challenge me!' he said sharply. 'You will obey me, without any discussion. Go now, I have to reflect on this. When I've decided I'll see that you're called.'

Wulfila walked back out, slamming the door behind him. Odoacer remained alone in the study, pacing back and forth, pondering what Ambrosinus had said. He called a servant and ordered him to call Antemius, the master of the palace. The old man appeared promptly and Odoacer had him sit down.

'I've made my decision,' he began, 'regarding the destiny of the young man called Romulus Augustus.'

Antemius lifted his watery and apparently inexpressive eyes. He had a tablet on his knee and a quill in his right hand, ready to take notes.

Odoacer continued: 'I feel pity for that poor child who has no blame for the treason of his father and I have decided to spare his life.' Antemius could not help but draw a sigh of relief. 'In any case, last night's episode clearly demonstrates that his life is in danger and that someone could use him to sow war and disorder in this country which is so badly in need of peace. I will send him to a safe place, where he will be watched over by trustworthy guardians and assigned an allowance consonant to his rank. The imperial emblems will be sent to Emperor Basiliscus in Constantinople, in exchange for his nominating me *magister militum* of the West. One emperor is more than enough for the world.'

'A wise decision,' nodded Antemius. 'The most important thing is—'

'Keeping up appearances,' concluded Odoacer. Antemius looked up in surprise: that rude soldier was learning the rules of politics quickly.

'Will his tutor accompany him?' asked the old man.

'I have nothing against that. The boy can dedicate himself to his studies.'

'When will they leave?'

'As soon as possible. I want no more trouble.'

'May I know the destination?'

'No. Only the escort commander will be informed of that.'

'Must I prepare for a long journey or a short one?'

Odoacer hesitated a moment: 'A rather long journey.'

Antemius nodded and withdrew with a respectful bow, returning to his quarters.

*

Odoacer immediately convened the officers of his personal council, the men he most trusted. Among them was Wulfila, still irritated after his recent confrontation with his commander.

Lunch was served. When they were all sitting down and each had taken his portion of meat, Odoacer raised the question of where the boy should be sent for his internment. One of the men proposed Istria, another Sardinia. Someone spoke up: 'These destinations are too distant and difficult to control. There is an island in the Tyrrhenian sea, bare and inhospitable, poor in every sense, close enough to the coast, yet sufficiently far away. There's an old imperial villa still standing there, set on a completely inaccessible cliff. It is partially in ruins but still habitable.' He got up and went to the wall on which a map of the empire was painted, pointing at a spot in the Gulf of Naples: 'Capri.'

Odoacer did not reply immediately, evidently considering the various proposals. After a short while, he said: 'This does seem the best destination. Isolated enough, but easy to reach if neccessary. The boy will be escorted by a hundred warriors, the best we have. I don't want surprises. Make all the necessary preparations; I will let you know when the moment to leave has arrived.'

The destination decided upon, conversation roamed to other matters. Everyone was in a fine mood. There they were, in the bosom of supreme power, with reasonable expectations for a grand life ahead of them: property, servants, women, herds, villas and palaces. They were euphoric and inclined to drink beyond measure. When Odoacer turned them out, most were drunk and needed their servants' assistance to find their quarters and take a little afternoon rest – a Latin custom which they had eagerly adopted.

Wulfila was still quite sober, thanks to his endless capacity to guzzle wine. Odoacer held him back.

'Listen,' Odoacer began. 'I've decided to put you in charge of the boy because you're the only man I can trust for this mission. You've already told me how you feel about the situation; now let me tell you how I feel. If anything happens to him, anything at all, you will be held responsible and your head would be worth less than the scraps I just fed to the dogs. Is that clear?'

'Completely,' responded Wulfila. 'I think you'll come to regret your decision about the boy. But you are in command here,' he added, with a tone that clearly meant 'for now'. Odoacer took in his words, but preferred to remain silent.

*

On the morning of their departure, Romulus's door was opened and two maidservants entered to wake him and prepare him for the journey.

'Where are they taking us?' asked the boy.

The two girls exchanged a look, then said in a low voice to Ambrosinus, who had got up as well: 'We don't know for sure, but Antemius is certain that you'll be headed south. From the quantity of provisions he's been asked to prepare, he thinks about a week's journey, maybe more. Gaeta, or Naples, perhaps, or maybe even Brindisi, but he thinks that's less likely.'

'And then?' asked Ambrosinus.

'That's all,' replied the maid. 'Whatever your destination is, it will be forever.'

Ambrosinus lowered his head in an attempt to hide his emotions. The girls kissed Romulus's hands, murmuring: 'Farewell, Caesar, may God protect you.'

Shortly after, Romulus and Ambrosinus were escorted outside by Wulfila's men, from the door facing the basilica. The basilica's door was open and they could see a coffin covered with a pall at the end of the nave, surrounded by lit lamps. The solemn funeral rites of Flavia Serena were about to begin. Antemius, watched closely by one of Odoacer's men, approached Romulus and greeted him with great deference, kissing his hand. He said: 'Unfortunately, you will not be allowed to participate in your mother's funeral, but perhaps it's better this way. Have a safe journey, my lord, and may God assist you.'

'Thank you, Antemius,' said Ambrosinus with a nod of his head. He got into the carriage and held the door open for Romulus, but the boy took a few steps towards the basilica threshold.

'Farewell, mother,' he whispered.

5

The image began slowly to take shape. At first a confused glimmer, a greenish reflection. Then the edges became more defined in the pale morning sun: a huge pool full of green water, with a mask in the form of an open-mouthed satyr which spilled in a trickle of water. Wide cracks in the damp, curving vault overhead let in a little light, which danced over the surface of the water and the walls. Clusters of maidenhair ferns hung from the ceiling and the mutilated remains of statues stood on pedestals all around. An old nymphaeum, abandoned.

Aurelius tried to sit up, but his sudden gesture made him moan in pain. Several frightened frogs dived into the stagnant water.

'Stay calm, now,' sounded a voice behind him. 'You have a nice big hole in that shoulder and it could open up again.'

Scenes of his flight through the lagoon flooded Aurelius's memory: that terrified child, that beautiful woman, so pale in death; the sharp stab of grief was much worse than the aching of his body. He turned; the person who had spoken was a man of about sixty, leathery skin parched by the salty sea air. He was wearing a knee-length tunic of coarse wool and his bald head was covered by a wool cap.

'Who are you?' Aurelius asked.

'I'm the one who put you back on your feet. My name is Justinus and I was once a respected medical doctor. I stitched you up as best I could with fishing line, and I washed out the wound with vinegar, but you were in sorry shape. Your clothes were soaked with blood, and you lost even more on the boat as I took you across the lagoon.'

'How can I thank you—' began Aurelius, but he stopped as he heard the sound of footsteps at the other end of the vast building. He turned and saw a woman, dressed like a man: goatskin trousers and cloak, hair so short he could see the nape of her neck. She wore a bow over her shoulder and was carrying a quiver by its sling. Her hands were rough and strong looking, while her lips were well shaped and her nose fine and straight, aristocratic even.

'She's the one you have to thank,' said the man, pointing. 'She saved your skin.' He gathered his satchel and the tin bucket he had used to wash out the wound, and left, nodding goodbye.

Aurelius looked at his shoulder: it was red and swollen, as was his arm, all the way down to his elbow. He had a terrible headache and his temples were pounding. He fell back on the straw pallet he had been lying on, as the girl came close and sat down on the ground next to him.

'Who are you?' asked Aurelius. 'How much time has passed?'

'A couple of days.'

'I slept for two days and two nights?'

'Let's say you were unconscious for two days and two nights. Justinus said that your fever was high and that you were delirious. You said the strangest things . . .'

'You saved my life. Thank you.'

'It was five against one. I thought I should balance up the odds.'

'Incredible aim you have, at night, with the fog . . .'

'A bow is the ideal weapon in such unstable surroundings.'

'My horse?'

'They'll have caught him for sure. Eaten him, maybe. Tough times, my friend.'

Aurelius sought out her gaze but she escaped him.

'Do you have any water? I'm dying of thirst.'

The girl poured him some from an earthenware jug.

'Do you live in this place?' he asked.

'It's one of my . . . shelters, shall we say. It's lovely, isn't it? Big, spacious, hidden from curious eyes. But I have others.'

'What I mean is, do you live in the lagoon?'

'I have since I was a child.'

'What's your name?'

'Livia. Livia Prisca. And you?'

'Aurelianus Ambrosius Ventidius, but my friends call me Aurelius.'

'Do you have a family?'

'No, no one. I don't remember ever having had a family.'

'That's impossible. You have a name, and isn't that a family ring you are wearing?'

'I don't know. Maybe it was given to me, or maybe I stole it. Who can say? My only family has been the army. My comrades. I can't remember any further back.'

The girl couldn't quite make sense of what he was saying. Perhaps the fever had shaken his mind. Or perhaps he didn't want to remember. She asked him: 'Where are your comrades now?'

Aurelius sighed. 'I don't know. Dead, probably. They were extraordinary fighters, the best: the legionaries of the Nova Invicta Legion.'

'The Nova Invicta, you said? I never thought it really existed. The legions belong to the past, with battles on the open field, infantry against infantry, cavalry against cavalry. You say all your comrades are dead, and yet you managed to survive. Strange. In the city they're saying that a deserter tried to kidnap the emperor. There's a sizeable price on his head.'

'And you're interested in collecting that reward, aren't you?'

'If I were, I would already have done something about it, don't you think? You would have woken up in prison or swinging from the gallows, or you would have died as they were taking you in. We would never have met.'

Her tone was light and ironic. She had begun to fuss with her fishing net and avoided looking her guest in the eye. He couldn't understand whether these were the harsh manners of one used to living in the wild, or whether she was timid. Aurelius fell silent, as if listening to the cries of the swamp birds getting ready to migrate or to the monotonous dripping of water into the great green pool. His comrades thronged into his mind. He had been unable to save them or help them. Submerged in a sea of enemies. He imagined their bodies left unburied, riddled with wounds, prey to stray dogs and wild animals. Vatrenus, Batiatus, Antoninus, their commander Claudianus. It broke his heart, and tears rose to his eyes.

'Don't think about it,' said the girl as if she were looking him in the face. 'The survivors of a massacre always feel guilty. Sometimes for the rest of their lives. Guilty of being alive.'

Aurelius didn't answer and when he spoke again he tried to change the subject: 'How can you live in a place like this? A woman, alone, in a swamp?'

'We are forced to live like barbarians to continue living as Romans,' answered Livia in a low voice, as if talking to herself.

'You know the writings of Salvianus!'

'So do you, I see.'

'Yes . . . scraps of knowledge that somehow come to mind from my past. Words . . . images, at times.'

Livia got to her feet and came closer. Aurelius raised his eyes to observe her: a ray of light filtered from a crack in the wall, light that had pierced the morning fog, and it spread over her slender figure like a diaphanous aura. She was fascinating . . . beautiful, even. His gaze fell to her breast; the medal hanging at her neck bore the image of a wide-winged eagle. She noticed his look and her expression changed instantly. She considered him with an inquisitive, almost searching glance. In his mind's eye, Aurelius suddenly saw a city in flames – a dilated, distorted image – and over that sea of flames he could see the necklace with the eagle floating down lightly like a leaf twirling in the air. Livia shook him out of his reverie: 'Does it remind you of something?'

Aurelius looked away: 'What?'

'This,' replied the girl. She took the medal in her hand and knelt down next to him, raising it to the level of his eyes: a bronze circle a little bigger than a five-solidus coin, decorated with a small silver eagle.

'No,' answered Aurelius sharply.

'Are you sure?'

'Why should it?'

'It looked as though you recognized it.'

Aurelius turned on his pallet and lay down on his side. 'I'm tired,' he said. 'I'm exhausted.'

Livia didn't say another word. She turned away and disappeared under an arch. He could hear bleating; there must be animals somewhere close by.

She reappeared with a bucket of milk and poured some in a cup. 'Drink,' she said. 'It's fresh, and you haven't eaten for days.'

Aurelius drank and the warmth of the milk filled his body and mind with an unbearable weariness. He lay back on the straw and drowsed off. Livia sat next to him and stayed to watch him for a while. She was looking for something in his features but she couldn't say what, exactly. The situation was making her feel very uneasy; an uneasiness born of hope but mixed with the feeling that such hope was absurd. Impossible.

Livia shook her head, as if to chase away a worrisome thought, and got up. She reached her boat, pushed it into the water and took off across the lagoon until she came to a cane thicket, where she stopped and lay back on the bottom of the boat, waiting. Stretched out on the fishing net, she watched the sky as it slowly darkened. Flocks of ducks and wild geese flew high overhead in long lines, over huge puffy clouds reddened by the setting sun. She could even hear their calls as they prepared for migration. A blue heron took flight, slow and solemn, low over the water's surface. The fields and canals sounded with the dreary croaking of frogs.

The autumn and the flight of the migrating birds always made her feel melancholic, even though she had lived through many a season on the swamp. She would have liked to fly far away herself, towards another world, beyond the sea, to forget about that dank swamp, the familiar but disquieting walls of Ravenna, shrouded in fog for so many months a year. The damp, the gloomy rain and the cold wind from the east that chilled your bones. But when spring returned and the swallows came back to their nests among the ruins, when the sun sparkled again on myriad tiny silver fish, she felt hope rise up again within her, hope that the world could have a new start, be born again, somehow.

She had always lived like a man. She had learned how to survive in a harsh and often hostile environment, to defend herself and to attack when necessary, no holds barred. Her body and her soul had been hardened, but she'd never forgotten her roots, the few years that she had lived serenely with her family in her home town. She remembered the traffic, the markets, the ships at port, the fairs and festivals, the ceremonies of many different religions. She remembered the white-robed magistrates who administered justice, seated in their high-backed chairs in the forum. She remembered the Christian priests who celebrated the mass in a church glittering with mosaics. She remembered the plays at the theatre and the lessons of her teachers at school. She remembered what civilization was.

Then, she remembered, one day the barbarians came. A horde of them from the east, small and ferocious, their eyes long and their hair pulled back to look like the tails of their bristly little horses. She thought she remembered the prolonged lament of the horns, echoing from the walls to sound the alarm, the soldiers, running on the rampart walkways, taking position, preparing for a long, stubborn resistance. The commander was away on a mission. The officer who took command was very young. Little more than a boy. Much more than a hero.

The sound of an oar shook her from her thoughts. She sat up and listened: a boat was approaching the shore. A couple of men got out; the first was elderly, but well dressed and very dignified looking, while the other was slender, not too tall and quite finely featured, a man of about fifty. Livia had seen him before; he was the older man's personal guard, if she wasn't mistaken. She left the cane thicket and approached them: 'Antemius,' she greeted the elder of the two. 'I thought you'd never get here.'

'It wasn't easy for me to leave the city. I'm under their surveillance and I don't want to rouse suspicion. I had to wait for a valid pretext. I have important news, but if I'm not mistaken, you have something to tell me as well.'

Livia took him by the arm and accompanied him towards an abandoned farmhouse that had sunk into the swamp down to the window-level. She didn't want their conversation to be overheard.

'The man that I saved the other night is the one who tried to abduct the emperor from the imperial palace.'

'Are you sure?'

'As sure as I can be. He was being chased by Odoacer's troops, and when I told him that in the city they were looking for a deserter who had attempted to carry off the emperor, he didn't even try to deny that it was him.'

'Who is he?' asked Antemius.

'He's a legionary from the Nova Invicta. An officer, perhaps . . . I'm not sure.'

'The unit that Orestes was secretly training to be the pillar of the new empire. Annihilated.'

Livia thought of the anguish in Aurelius's eyes as he remembered the sacrifice of his comrades: 'Is it true that no one was saved?' she asked.

'I don't know. Some may have been taken as slaves. Tomorrow the army commanded by Mledo that Odoacer sent to wipe out the legion should be returning. If there were any survivors we should hear about it. That soldier's raid on the palace was a disaster. He did kill off a dozen barbarians, which pleases me no end, but he involuntarily brought about the death of the empress, Flavia Serena. The whole palace is up in arms now. The barbarians suspect everyone of everything. I was afraid that the life of the emperor himself was in peril, but fortunately Odoacer has decided to spare him.'

'Very generous on his part, but I can't say I'm convinced. Odoacer never does anything for nothing, and that boy represents a lot of problems for him.'

'You're wrong,' said Antemius. 'Odoacer is beginning to understand how politics work. If he killed the emperor he would have to deal with the hate and scorn of the Roman population. The Christian clergy would certainly compare him to Herod, and the eastern crown would assume that he was aspiring to take the empire himself. If the boy is spared, he will be considered magnanimous and forgiving, and will not give rise to dangerous mistrust in Constantinople.'

'Do you really think that anyone cares about Romulus Augustus in Constantinople? Emperor Zeno backed Julius Nepos, the last Emperor of the West, after Flavius Orestes had deposed him, and he offered him his own properties in Dalmatia during his forced exile. As far as I know, they make fun of the boy in the East. They call him Momylus instead of Romulus, imitating the pronunciation of a little child.'

'But Zeno himself has been dethroned. Basiliscus reigns in his place, and Basiliscus is now in Pyrgos, in the Peloponnese, at only three days' navigation from here. I have sent a small delegation, disguised as fishermen. They should already have met with him, and his answer may reach us at any moment.'

'What have you asked?'

'To provide refuge for the emperor.'

'And you believe he will consent?'

'I've made him an interesting offer. I think so.'

The sun was setting on the vast, silent lagoon, and a long train of warriors on horseback stood out against the red disc as it sunk into the dark, flat countryside.

'Mledo's advance guard,' observed Antemius. 'Tomorrow we will know for certain whether any of your soldier's companions survived.'

'Why are you doing this?' asked Livia.

'What?'

'Trying to save the boy. There's no advantage in it for you, either.'

'Not in particular, but I've always been faithful to the family of Flavia Serena. Fidelity is a virtue of old men; we're too tired to change our attitude or our ideals.' He sighed: 'I served her father for years and I would have done anything I could to help her, had I had the time, had that soldier not got mixed up in this.'

'Perhaps he had a good reason.'

'I would like to hope so. It would be a pleasure to meet him, if you can arrange it.'

'If Basiliscus agrees to give asylum to that boy, what will you do?'

'I will free him.'

Livia, who had been walking in front of him, spun around: 'You'll do what?'

'What I said. I'll free him.'

Livia shook her head and looked at him with a derisive grin: 'Aren't you a little old for such adventures? Where would you find men who will agree to carry this out? You've already said that Odoacer is willing to spare his life. Isn't that enough for you? It's best to leave things as they are.'

'I know you will help me,' Antemius continued as if she had not spoken.

'Me? I wouldn't dream of it. I've already risked my life saving that poor soul. I don't intend to challenge destiny in a hopeless match.'

Antemius took her by the arm: 'You have a dream yourself, Livia Prisca, and I can help you to attain it. You'll be given a huge sum of money: enough to pay off whoever you choose to involve in this endeavour, and enough left over to accomplish your own plans. But this is all premature: we need to have Basiliscus's response first. Let us go back now; my prolonged absence might be noticed.'

They walked towards Antemius's boat. His escort was sitting on the shore.

'Stephanus is my secretary and body guard. My shadow, you could say. He is aware of everything that is going on. He could be our contact in the future.'

Stephanus could not quite hide his admiration as he stared at her, as if appealing for her consent.

'As you wish,' shrugged Livia, 'but I believe you are too optimistic, and too trusting. Basiliscus couldn't care less about Romulus's life.'

'We'll see,' was the old man's reply. He got into the boat and Stephanus set himself at the oars, but not before he had taken a last look at the girl. Livia stood still on the bank, watching them as they slipped off into the darkness.

6

THE COLUMN JOURNEYED ALONG the embankment that crossed the lagoon from north to south, down the ridge of an ancient chain of coastal dunes, until it reached the mainland. A dirt road that began at that point joined up a few miles later with the paved road known as via Romea, because it was the preferred route of pilgrims from all over Europe travelling towards Rome to pray at the tombs of the apostles Peter and Paul. Wulfila advanced at the head of the column on his battle horse, armed with his axe and sword. A coat of mail covered his torso, reinforced with metal plates on the shoulders and chest. He rode in silence, apparently absorbed in his thoughts, but in reality nothing in the fields or along the road escaped his predatory gaze. A couple of guards flanked him on the right and left, scrutinizing every corner of the vast territory opening up before them.

Two squads of a dozen warriors each scoured the countryside on both sides of the road at a distance of about half a mile from the main column, to head off any possible raids. Behind Wulfila were about thirty horsemen, followed by the carriage with the prisoners. The rear guard of twenty men closed the column at a suitable distance.

Inside the carriage, Ambrosinus sat opposite Romulus. He would point out details of their journey to the boy from time to time: villages or farmhouses, ancient monuments fallen to ruin. He tried to encourage conversation, with very little success. The boy answered in monosyllables or withdrew into himself. His tutor would then pull out the *Aeneid* from his satchel and read, raising his eyes every now and then to check their surroundings, or he would take out a tablet and a travelling inkwell. He would dip in his quill and write, for hours at a time. When the carriage crossed an inhabited area, one of the guards ordered the curtains to be closed: no one could see who was travelling inside.

The journey had obviously been planned with great diligence. When the convoy stopped the first night, at the twenty-fifth milestone on the road, the old dilapidated exchange post seemed to have been partially renovated. A light was on inside and someone was fixing dinner for the guests. The guards camped a short distance off and made their own meal: a porridge of millet seasoned with lard and salted meat. Ambrosinus sat opposite Romulus as the host served some pork with stewed lentils, stale bread and a jug of well water.

'It's not much of a meal,' he admitted, 'but you must eat. Our journey will be long and you are very weak. You must regain your strength.'

'Why?' asked the boy, eyeing the steaming food without any appetite.

'Because life is a gift from God and we cannot throw it away.'

'It's a gift I didn't ask for,' replied Romulus, 'and all I have before me is imprisonment without end. Isn't that right?'

'No one can speak of endless conditions in this world. Change is constant. Turbulence, upheaval. He who sits on the throne today may be biting the dust tomorrow. He who weeps may find hope with the new dawn. We must hope, Caesar, we must not surrender to misfortune. Eat something, please, my boy. Do it for me, you know how much I care about you.'

The boy took a sip of water, then said flatly: 'Do not call me Caesar. I am nothing, and perhaps I never have been.'

'You are wrong! You are the last of a great race of the lords of the world. I was present when you were acclaimed by the senate of Rome. Have you forgotten already?'

'How long ago was that?' interrupted the boy. 'A week? A year? I can't remember, actually. It's as if it never happened.'

Ambrosinus decided not to insist. 'There's something that I've never told you. Something very important.'

'What?' asked Romulus distractedly.

'How I first met you. You were only five, and your life was in danger. It was in the middle of an Apennine forest, not far from here, if my memory serves me. It was a dark winter's night.' The boy lifted his face, curious about the story despite himself. His tutor was a wonderful narrator. With just a few words he could create an atmosphere, give substance to shadows, life to ghosts from the past. Romulus took a piece of bread and dipped it in the stewed lentils, under the satisfied gaze of Ambrosinus, who had begun to eat too.

'Well, what happened then?' asked Romulus.

'You had been poisoned. You'd eaten poisonous mushrooms. Someone, by mistake or intentionally, had put them in your food . . . eat a little meat.'

'Mightn't this meal be poisoned as well?'

'I don't think so. If they had wanted to kill you, they would have already done so. Do not fear, my boy. Well, you see, I found myself there by chance. I was tired and hungry, worn out by a long journey and numb with cold, when I saw a light in that tent in the middle of the forest and I felt something inside me. A strange emotion, like a sudden revelation. I entered without being stopped, as if I were a ghost. Perhaps God himself assisted me: he covered the guards' eyes with fog and I found myself inside your tent. You were lying in your bed. So small you were! And so pale, your lips were blue. Your parents were out of their minds. I gave you an emetic and you vomited away all that poison. I became a member of your family then and I've never left you.'

Romulus's eyes filled with tears at the mention of his parents, but he forced himself not to cry. He said: 'You should have let me die.' Ambrosinus put a little meat into the boy's mouth, and Romulus swallowed it whole. 'What were you doing in that place?' he asked.

'What was I doing there? Well, it's a long story, and if you like I'll tell it to you along the way, but finish eating now so we can go to rest. Tomorrow we'll have to get up at dawn and travel all day.'

'*Ambrosine . . .*'

'Yes, my son.'

'Why do they want to keep me prisoner my whole life? Because my father had me named emperor? Is that why?'

'I think so.'

'Listen,' he said, his face suddenly lighting up, 'I have a solution. I'm willing to give it all up, my title, my possessions, my crown. I just want to be a boy like all the others. You and I can go away somewhere. We'll find work, we can become street singers, telling stories in the squares. You're so good at that, *Ambrosine*! We'll earn a living somehow and we won't bother anybody. We'll see lots of new places, we'll travel beyond the sea to the land of the pygmies, to the mountains of the moon. Won't that be grand? Won't it? You go tell him, please. Tell him that I want to give up everything, even . . .' he lowered his head so as not to show the shame on his face, 'even avenging my father. Tell him I want to forget everything. Everything! And that he'll never hear anyone mention my name ever again. As long as he lets us go. Please? Will you go and tell him?'

Ambrosinus looked at the boy with great tenderness: 'It's not so simple, Caesar.'

'You're a hypocrite! You call me Caesar yet you won't obey my orders!'

'I would if it were possible, but it's not. These men have no power to grant you anything. Odoacer could, of course, but he is in Ravenna, and he has given orders that no one would dare to argue with. And you must never call me a hypocrite again. I'm your teacher and you owe me respect. Now, if you don't mind, finish your dinner and go straight to bed. No arguing.'

Romulus obeyed meekly and Ambrosinus watched him chewing a last bite of bread before disappearing into the next room for the night. He pulled his tablet out of the satchel and continued to write by the flickering light of the lantern. From outside came the boisterous exclamations of the barbarians who were beginning to recover from the fatigue of the journey as the beer they drank in abundance warmed their spirits. Ambrosinus listened in: it was a good thing that the boy was sleeping and that he couldn't understand their language. Many of them had taken part in the raid on Orestes' villa, and were boasting about the sacking, the rapes, the violence and the defilement of every sort that they had inflicted on their victims. Others were part of Mledo's army which had annihilated the Nova Invicta Legion. They told stories of atrocities, torture, mutilation of live prisoners – a succession of horrors, of cruelty beyond any imagining. Ambrosinus realized with anguish that these were the new rulers of the world.

As these dark thoughts obsessed him, Wulfila abruptly appeared, his gigantic figure towering over the bivouac. His wide drooping moustache, long side burns, bristly head of hair and the long braids which fell to his chest made him look like one of the Nordic gods venerated by the Suebians, the Chatti and the Scanians. Ambrosinus swiftly blew out the lantern, so it would seem that everyone inside the exchange post were sleeping. He put his ear to the wall, still peering out of the half open window.

Wulfila shouted something, a curse of some sort, and they all fell silent. He continued: 'I told you idiots to shut your traps! We don't want to attract attention. The less we're noticed, the better it is.'

'Come on, Wulfila!' protested one of his men. 'Who are you afraid of? Even if someone does hear us, what could happen? I'm not afraid of anything! What about the rest of you?'

'Shut up!' ordered Wulfila harshly. 'And the rest of you as well, that's enough! Post the guards on two lines at a distance of one hundred paces from each other. If anyone abandons his assigned position for any reason, he'll be executed immediately. You others get to sleep. Tomorrow we'll be marching until after dark. We'll set up camp at the base of the Apennines.'

The men obeyed and mounted the guard while the others spread their blankets on the ground and lay down for the night. Ambrosinus went to the door and sat outside on a stool, immediately catching the eye of one of the sentries. He did not acknowledge the man, and looked up instead towards the sky to observe the constellations: Cassiopeia was low on the horizon and Orion shone high overhead, nearly in the centre of the sky. He searched for the North Star. The star of the little dipper; it made him think of his childhood, when his teacher, a Druid of venerable age, taught him to find his bearings by the stars and orient himself in the dark, in the open countryside or amidst the waves of the sea. He could predict the eclipses of the moon and read the passing seasons on the earth by means of the eternal motion of the stars.

He thought of the boy and his heart swelled up with pity. He had persuaded him to eat something, and had dissolved a powder in his water to make him sleep. How could he persuade him to return to his life? And if he succeeded, what kind of future could he possibly offer him? How many days, months and years would they spend in the prison that awaited them? Endless imprisonment? How many paces would it take to measure the narrow space? How long would they be able to bear their hateful persecutors?

The verses of a poem drifted into his mind from long ago and far away:

Veniet adulescens a mari infero cum spatha
pax et prosperitas cum illo
aquila et draco iterum volabunt
Britanniae in terra lata

A sign reaching out to him from a remote past in that moment of infinite sadness. What kind of a sign? Who had sent it?

He recited the words to himself again, slowly and softly, in a singsong. For a little while, his heart felt as light as a bird rising to take flight. He walked back into the rundown hovel that had once been a *cursus publicus* station, busy and teeming with customers. Cold and deserted now. He lit his lantern from the fireplace embers and entered the bedroom to lie down next to Romulus. He raised his lamp to light up the boy's face. He was sleeping and his breathing was slow and even. His boyhood flowed sweetly under his golden skin. He was a beautiful child; his proud, delicate features recalled his mother's. Flavia Serena. Ambrosinus remembered her body stretched out on the cold marble under the vault of the imperial basilica. He swore in his heart that he would build a future for that boy. At any cost, even at the cost of his own life. He would have gladly given his life in love for the woman who had appeared to him long ago at the bedside of her dying child, on a cold winter's night in an Apennine forest. He lightly touched the boy's cheek, extinguished the lamp and lay down on the bed with a long sigh. His heart sank into a strange and unknowing serenity, like the surface of a lake on a windless night.

*

Aurelius turned over on the straw mat, still deeply drowsy; he couldn't say whether the sound he'd heard was coming from a dream or from reality. Certainly, he was dreaming and his eyes were not yet open when he voicelessly murmured 'Juba'. The neighing became louder and clearer and was accompanied by the splashing of hooves in water. He shouted then, 'Juba!' and the whinny he heard in reply was real and expressed all the joy of reuniting with a friend one had feared lost forever.

'Juba, good boy, my good boy, come on, come on boy,' he called. His mud-covered horse, grey and spectral in the morning fog, was walking towards him through the knee-deep water. Aurelius reached out and embraced him, overwhelmed by emotion. 'How did you find me? How did you do it? Look at you! All dirty, full of scabs . . . you must be hungry, you poor thing, so hungry . . . wait, here.' He went over to the niche that Livia used for storage and came back with a bucket full of spelt that the horse eagerly dipped his head into. Aurelius took a rag, soaked it in some water and began to stroke his coat until it was shiny again. 'I don't have a curry comb, my friend, we'll have to make do. Better than nothing, wouldn't you say?'

When he had finished he stepped back to take a look at Juba. He was magnificent: fine, long legs, slender ankles, muscular chest, proud head, quivering nostrils, arched neck adorned with a splendid blue-black mane. He cleaned the saddle as well and adjusted the stirrups, and when he saw that Juba had had his full of food and water, he diligently saddled and bridled him, believing that he was a sign sent by his unknown ancestors from the other world. He took his sword belt and slung it over his shoulder, put on his hobnailed boots, took the horse by his bridle and headed to where the water was lowest.

'Aren't you forgetting anything?' asked a voice behind him, and the echo reflected by the huge vault repeated 'anything?'

Aurelius turned around with surprise and then embarrassment. Livia stood in front of him with a harpoon in her hand, wearing a sort of loin-cloth of tanned leather, with two bands of the same leather crossed over her breasts. She had just come out of the water which still dripped off her muscular body. She threw the fishing net she'd been holding in the other hand on to the ground in front of her. It was full of big mullet, still wriggling, and an enormous eel which twisted like a snake around the handle of the harpoon.

Aurelius said: 'My horse came back.'

'I can see that,' replied Livia. 'I also see that you were about to leave. You could have waited until I came back, to say "thank you".'

'I was leaving you my armour,' he said, pointing to the cuirass, shield and helmet abandoned in the corner of the large room. 'You can do a lot with it.'

Livia spat on the ground. 'I can find all the scrap iron I need whenever I like.'

'I would have come back, sooner or later, to thank you. I would have left you a message if I'd had something to write on. I can't stand saying goodbye, going away. I wouldn't have known what to say and . . .'

'There's nothing to say. Just go. Get out of here with your stuff and don't ever come back. Nothing could be easier.'

'It's not like that. These last few days I've . . .' He looked up slowly from the ground along her body as if afraid to meet her gaze. 'I've never had anyone take care of me like this, a girl like you, so young and courageous. You're like no one else I've ever met in my whole life. I thought that if I waited, each day would become more difficult for me . . . I was afraid . . . that I wouldn't be able to leave.' Livia did not answer.

His eyes moved up now to meet hers, but stopped again for a barely perceptible instant on the pendant she wore at her neck, the little silver eagle. Livia noticed, and when he finally looked into her eyes, they were not as bitter as he had expected. She was looking at him with a mix of curiosity and rough affection. 'You don't need to talk such nonsense. If you want, you can go. You don't owe me anything.'

Aurelius could not say a word.

'Where were you going?' prompted Livia.

Aurelius lowered his head again. 'I don't know. Away. Far from these places, from the stink of these barbarians and from our own corruption. Far from this relentless decadence, from my own memories, far away from it all. And you? Will you stay in this swamp for ever?'

Livia drew closer: 'It's not the way you think it is,' she said. 'There's hope being born in this swamp. And it's not a swamp, it's a lagoon. It's full of life, and the breath of the sea.'

Juba snorted humbly and pawed at the ground as if he didn't understand the delay. Livia grasped the medal that hung from her neck and held it tightly. Aurelius shook his head: 'There's no hope anywhere. Only destruction, pillaging, oppression.'

'Then why did you try to abduct that boy?'

'I didn't want to abduct him. I wanted to free him.'

'That's hard to believe.'

'It's true, whether you believe it or not. It was his father who asked me to save him, as he lay dying. I got to the villa in Placentia after the massacre. I was coming from the field where my legion was already surrounded by a throng of enemies; I left them to seek help. When I found him he was still breathing. He begged me with the last life he had in him to save his son. What else could I do?'

'You're crazy. You're lucky it didn't go well. What would you have done with him if it had?'

'I don't know. Taken him somewhere with me. I would have taught him to work the land, raise bees, plant olive trees and milk goats. Like a true Roman.'

'And you wouldn't like to try again?' rang out a voice behind them.

'Stephanus! What are you doing here?' demanded Livia. 'Our pact was never by day and never here.'

'You're right, but there's an urgent reason. They've left.'

'For where?'

'No one knows. They've taken via Romea, headed for Fanum. I believe they'll go south on via Flaminia at some point. We're trying to learn more.'

'What are you talking about?' asked Aurelius.

'About freeing a boy,' replied Stephanus, 'and we need your help.'

Aurelius looked at him and shook his head incredulously: 'A boy . . . Him?'

Stephanus nodded: 'Him. Romulus Augustus Caesar, Emperor of the Romans.'

7

Aurelius shot an amazed look at the man, then turned towards his horse and started adjusting the saddle straps as if he were about to leave: 'I wouldn't dream of it,' he said.

'Why?' insisted Stephanus. 'You already tried once, and you were alone; it was hopeless from the start. Now we're offering you our support and help, for the same identical mission, multiplying the chances for success. Why should you refuse?'

'It was different before. I did it because it seemed right and because I thought I had a hope of succeeding by taking them completely by surprise. And I did nearly succeed. I don't know what your motives are and I don't know you. After my raid, surveillance will have been intensified. No one will manage to get close to the boy any more, that I'm sure of. Odoacer will have set his whole army around him.'

Stephanus drew closer: 'I represent a group of senators who maintain direct contact with the Eastern Roman Empire. We're convinced that this is the only way to prevent Italy and the West from sinking into complete barbarism. Our envoy met with Emperor Basiliscus in the Peloponnese and has returned with an important message. The emperor is willing to offer Romulus hospitality and protection at Constantinople, and to provide him with an annuity worthy of his rank.'

'And that doesn't seem suspicious to you?' asked Aurelius Basiliscus, as far as I know, is nothing more than a usurper. How can you trust him? How do you know he won't treat the child even worse than this barbarian?'

'This barbarian had the child's parents massacred,' observed

Stephanus. Aurelius turned towards him and met his firm and apparently impassable gaze. His Oriental accent reminded him of the way certain comrades from Epirus spoke.

'What's more,' Stephanus continued, 'he is destined for imprisonment without end in an isolated, inaccessible place, condemned to live with his nightmares and terror for the rest of his days, awaiting the moment in which any change in his warders' mood decrees his death. Can you imagine the abominations a child could be subjected to at the mercy of those brutes?'

Aurelius remembered Romulus's eyes at the moment in which he had been forced to let go, his shoulder pierced by an arrow: desperation, impotent rage, infinite bitterness. Stephanus must have noticed that his arguments were hitting their mark, and continued: 'We have friends at Constantinople, very influential friends. They will be able to protect him.'

'What about Julius Nepos?' insisted Aurelius. 'He has always been the East's candidate for the Western throne. Why should Basiliscus change his mind now?'

Livia tried to intervene but Stephanus stopped her with a look: 'Nepos has fallen completely out of favour; he'll be left to grow old in his villa in Dalmatia, isolated from the rest of the world. We have a very ambitious plan in mind for this child, but in order to succeed we must shield him from all danger. He must receive an adequate education and training and grow up in the imperial house in a tranquil, serene position. He must not be touched by doubt or suspicion, until the moment comes when he is ready to reclaim his legacy.'

Livia decided to speak up. 'Leave Aurelius alone,' she said, turning towards Stephanus. 'Fear is fear. He tried once, risked dying and has no intention of trying again.'

'That's right,' confirmed Aurelius without batting an eye.

'Exactly,' shot back Livia. 'We'll do fine on our own. I'm the one that saved him, not the other way around. What direction did you say the convoy took?'

'South,' replied Stephanus. 'They're on the road for Fanum.'

'They must mean to cross the Apennines.'

'Most probably, but we're not sure. We'll soon find out.'

Aurelius continued to adjust the straps on his horse as if the conversation no longer involved him. Livia pretended not to notice and continued talking with Stephanus: 'Is it true that Mledo has returned?'

'Last night.'

'Were there any prisoners?'

Aurelius spun around and his eyes glared with tension: fear, hope, trepidation. Those few words had managed to disintegrate his apparent equilibrium.

'About fifty, I'd say, but I could be wrong; it was nearly dark.'

Aurelius came closer: 'Did you recognize . . . anyone?'

'How could I?' replied Stephanus. 'The only one that stood out was a gigantic black man, an Ethiopian, I'd say. At least six feet tall, loaded down with chains.'

'Batiatus!' exclaimed Aurelius, his face lighting up. 'It has to be him!' He grabbed Stephanus's cloak: 'He's a friend; I fought alongside him for many years. I beg you, tell me where they've taken him. Other comrades may be with him.'

Stephanus looked at him with a touch of irony: 'You're ready to try another dramatic break-out?'

'Will you help me or won't you?'

'Strange question for someone who has just refused his own help.'

Aurelius bowed his head: 'I'll do anything, but just tell me where they've been taken, if you can.'

'To Classis, but that doesn't mean much. That's the port of Ravenna; from Classis you can go anywhere in the world.'

Aurelius showed signs of crumbling: his joy at learning that his friend was alive was crushed by the awareness that there was nothing he could do for him. Livia saw the grief and discouragement in his expression and felt pity for him: 'They may be taking them to Misenus, near Naples. The other base of the imperial fleet is there; it's almost completely out of commission, but they sometimes need rowers. It's also the most important slave market on the peninsula. You can try to reach the base and get information. With a little time and patience you may be able to find him. If your friend is as big as Stephanus says, he certainly won't pass unobserved.

'Listen,' continued the girl with a calmer, more conciliating tone, 'I'll be heading south to follow the convoy that's accompanying the emperor. We can start off together, if you like. Then you'll go your way, and I'll go mine.'

'You're going to try and liberate the boy . . . alone?'

'That's my affair, isn't it?'

'Maybe not.'

'And what could make you change your mind?'

'If I found my comrades, would you help me to free them?'

Stephanus intervened: 'There's a large reward, ten thousand silver solidi, for whoever brings the boy to the old port of Fanum on the Adriatic sea. A ship will be waiting there to take him to the East every first day of the new moon, at dawn, for two months, beginning with the moon of December. The ship will be easy to recognize: a standard with a monogram of Constantine will be hoisted astern. With all that reward money you'll be able to buy your friends back, if you find out where they are.'

'But if I found them first, they could prove vital on this mission. They are the best combatants on earth, but above all they are Roman soldiers, loyal to the emperor,' said Aurelius.

Stephanus nodded, seemingly satisfied: 'What must I tell Antemius?'

'Tell him we'll be leaving today, and that I will keep him informed as best I can,' said Livia.

'I will,' replied Stephanus. 'Well then, good luck.'

'We'll need it,' replied Livia. 'I'll let you out. I want to be sure no one has seen you.'

They reached Stephanus's small, flat-bottomed wooden boat, designed for navigating the lagoon. A servant was sitting at the oars. Livia climbed with amazing agility on to a large willow whose branches stretched over the water. She scanned the area: not a soul to be seen. She signalled to Stephanus, who got into the boat. Livia stopped him: 'What did Antemius offer Basiliscus to convince him to accept his proposal?'

'This I do not know. Antemius doesn't tell me everything, but in Constantinople everyone knows that nothing happens in the West without Antemius knowing about it. His prestige and power are enormous.' Livia nodded. 'That soldier . . . do you really think we can trust him?'

'He's like a small army on his own,' admitted Livia. 'I know a fighter when I see him. I can recognize the gaze of a lion, even if he's wounded. But there's something else in his eyes that reminds me of . . .'

'Of what?'

Livia's lips crinkled in a bitter smile: 'If I knew, I'd be able to give a name and a face to the only person who left a mark in my life and in my soul. Apart from my father and mother, who died such a long time ago.'

Stephanus was about to say something, but Livia had already turned her back to him and was walking away, with that slow, silent, predatory pace of hers. The servant bent his back and dipped the oars into the water, and the little boat slowly drifted away from the shore.

*

The column escorting Romulus's carriage crossed the countryside along a narrow, arduous trail that skirted Fanum to avoid the great number of curious onlookers who would have lined the way and perhaps interfered with their progress. The orders for silence and secrecy must have been very strict, and Ambrosinus did not fail to note the digressive manoeuvre: 'I believe our itinerary is leading us to a pass on the Apennines. We'll be back on via Flaminia soon, and we'll be crossing the highest peak through a tunnel excavated in the mountain. It is called *forulus*, an extraordinary work of engineering designed at the time of Emperor Augustus and completed by Emperor Vespasianus. This zone is rough and mountainous, my boy, and crawling with brigands. It is dangerous to cross the pass on one's own. The authorities have tried time and time again to rid the countryside of this nuisance, even by establishing special guard corps, without success. It is poverty that produces brigands: they are mostly farmers impoverished by exorbitant taxes and famine, who have had no choice but to take to the bush.'

Romulus seemed to be looking at the thick groves of oak and ash which flanked the road and at the herdsmen who here and there were watching some poor thin cows grazing. He was listening, however, and responded thoughtfully: 'Laying taxes that ruin people is not only unjust; it is stupid. A man brought to ruin pays no taxes, and if he becomes a bandit he obliges the state to spend much more, just to make the roads safe.'

'Your observation is perfect,' Ambrosinus complimented him, 'but perhaps too simple to be put into practice. Governors are greedy and government officials often stupid, and these two problems give rise to frightful consequences.'

'But there must be an explanation behind all this. Why do governors have to be necessarily greedy, and officials necessarily stupid? You have often taught me that Augustus, Tiberius, Hadrian and Marcus Aurelius were wise and honest princes who punished corrupt governors – but perhaps not even this is true: perhaps men have always been stupid, greedy and evil.'

At that moment Wulfila passed alongside them, galloping up to a hill which would allow him to scrutinize the surrounding countryside and watch his men's movements. The ugly wound that disfigured him was beginning to scar over, but his face was still quite red and swollen and a purulent liquid seeped from the stitches. Perhaps that was why he was always in such a bad mood. He would fly into a rage for any reason, and Ambrosinus avoided arousing his suspicion or misgiving in any way. However, he was contemplating a plan to win over the brute's trust and perhaps even his gratitude.

'It's understandable that you have such a negative vision of the world just now,' he answered Romulus. 'I would be surprised if you didn't. In reality, human destiny – and even the destiny of a people or an empire – is often conditioned by causes and events which are beyond man's control. The empire defended itself for centuries against the barbarian attacks. Many emperors were elected to the dignity of their rank by their soldiers at the front, and died at the front, sword in hand, without ever having seen Rome or discussed any matter whatsoever with the Senate.

'The attack was often multilateral, coming in waves from various directions, and waged by many populations at once. This is why the great wall was built, at such expense, extending from the mountains of Britannia to the deserts of Syria. Over three thousand miles long! Hundreds of thousands of soldiers were recruited. As many as thirty-five legions were called up at once, with nearly half a million men! No expense, no sacrifice seemed too great to the Caesars in order to save the empire, and civilization with it, but in doing so they did not realize that costs had become intolerable, and that the taxes they levied to cover them impoverished the farmers, the breeders, the craftsmen, destroying trade and even reducing the number of births! Why put children into the world to have them live in misery and deprivation?

'Eventually, it became impossible to stave off the invasions, and so our leaders imagined that they could settle the barbarians peaceably within our own borders and recruit them into our army so they could fight off other barbarians . . . It was a fatal error, but perhaps they had no choice: poverty and oppression had killed off patriotism in the citizens, and it became necessary to use mercenaries – who have now turned into our masters.'

Ambrosinus fell silent, aware that this was not just a history lesson for his pupil. He had called up very real and very recent events for the boy, events that had wounded him to the quick. That sad boy sitting opposite him was the last Emperor of the Western Empire, after all – an actor in the immense tragedy, despite himself, not a mere spectator.

'Will you write all these things in your history?' asked Romulus.

'I do not aspire to writing history: others can do that much better than me, using more elegant language. I only want to leave a memory of my personal affairs and the events I've witnessed directly.'

'You'll have time to do that. Years and years of imprisonment. Why did you want to come with me? You could have stayed in Ravenna or gone back to your homeland, in Britannia. Is it true that the nights have no end there?'

'You already know the answer to your first question. I care for you deeply and I am firmly devoted to your family. As far as the second, it's not quite—' began Ambrosinus, but Romulus interrupted him.

'That's what I'd like for myself. A night without end. A sleep without dreams.' The boy's eyes were empty, and Ambrosinus did not know how to answer.

*

They travelled all day, and the tutor tried to be sensitive to every change of mood of his pupil, without losing sight of what was happening outside. They didn't stop until dusk. The days had become very short, and marching hours were limited. The barbarian soldiers lit a fire, and a few of them disappeared on a horseback raid through the countryside, returning with some chickens tied in bunches and slaughtered sheep hanging from their saddles. They must have sacked some isolated farms. Their easy prey was soon skinned and feathered and roasting on the embers.

Wulfila sat on a rock apart from the others and awaited his portion. His face was dark and his features were exaggerated dramatically by the reflection of the flames. Ambrosinus, whose eye was always on his enemy, walked up to him slowly and in full light so he wouldn't become riled or suspicious. When he was close enough to make himself heard, he said: 'I am a doctor and an expert in medicines. I can do something for that wound: it must hurt terribly.'

Wulfila sneered and made a gesture as if to squash an irritating insect, but Ambrosinus did not move and carried on regardless: 'I know what you're thinking: you've been wounded many a time before, and sooner or later the lesion has healed and the pain has passed. It's very different in this case. One's face is the most difficult part of the body to cure, because your soul emerges more in your face than anywhere else. It is much more sensitive and much more vulnerable as well. That wound is infected, and if the infection spreads it will devastate your appearance beyond all recognition.'

He turned back towards the carriage, but Wulfila's voice stopped him: 'Wait.'

Ambrosinus took his satchel and had the soldiers bring him some wine which he used to wash the wound, squeezing out the pus until the skin bled clean. He removed the stitches, applying a paste of malva and wheat bran and then bandages.

'Don't think even for an instant that I'm grateful to you,' grumbled Wulfila when Ambrosinus had finished.

'I certainly would not expect that.'

'Why did you do it then?'

'You are a beast. Your pain can only make you more ferocious. I did it in my own interest, Wulfila, and in the boy's.'

He returned to the carriage to put away his satchel. A soldier arrived with some roast meat on a spit which the old man and the boy ate. The air was cold; they were in the mountains at the end of autumn and the hour was late. Ambrosinus preferred to ask for another blanket rather than lie down next to the fire, as the others were doing. The heat made their stink unbearable. Romulus ate the meat and even drank some wine, at his tutor's insistence, which gave him a little energy and desire to live.

They stretched out next to each other under the starry sky.

'Do you understand why I did that?' asked Ambrosinus.

'Cleaned that butcher's face? Yes, I can imagine why you did it; you mustn't stroke a ferocious dog the wrong way.'

'Yes, that's it, more or less.'

They fell into silence, listening to the crackle of the fire as the soldiers kept adding dry branches, and watching the sparks that whirled up into the sky.

'Do you pray, before sleeping?' asked Ambrosinus.

'Yes,' replied Romulus. 'I pray to the spirits of my parents.'

8

Livia spurred on her horse along a narrow trail that climbed towards the mountain ridge, then stopped to wait for Aurelius who had taken another route through the woods. From the crest they could easily spy the opening to the Flaminia tunnel which crossed the mountain from side to side. They took up position behind some beech shrubs, and didn't have to wait long before a group of Heruli on horseback emerged. Their commander appeared at the head of about thirty armed soldiers and then came the carriage, followed by the rear guard.

Aurelius started as he recognized Wulfila, and instinctively looked at the bow Livia had strapped across her back.

'Don't think about it,' said the girl, catching on. 'Even if you managed to hit him, the others would overpower us, and they'd probably take out their anger on the boy.'

Aurelius bit his lip.

'The time will come,' insisted Livia. 'We must have patience now.'

Aurelius watched the rickety carriage until it disappeared round a bend in the road. Livia put a hand on his shoulder: 'There's unresolved business between the two of you, isn't there?'

'I killed some of his best men, tried to carry off the prisoner in his custody and sliced his face in two when he tried to stop me. I've turned him into a monster for the rest of his days: is that enough for you?'

'So it's simply revenge, is it? I would have said a question of life or death.'

Aurelius didn't answer. He was chewing on a blade of dry grass and looking down towards the valley.

'Don't tell me that was the first time you'd met.'

'It's possible that I'd seen him before, but I don't remember. I've met more barbarians than I can count through all these years of war.' But in that moment he saw himself face to face with Wulfila in the corridor of the imperial palace, sword against sword, and the hoarse voice of his adversary saying: 'I know you, Roman! I've seen you before.'

Livia stood in front of him and looked searchingly into his eyes. Aurelius looked away.

'You're afraid to look into yourself, and you don't want anyone else to do it either. Why?' demanded Livia.

'Would you strip nude here in front of me?' he replied, eyes inflamed.

She stared back without batting an eye: 'Yes,' she said. 'If I loved you.'

'But you don't love me. And I don't love you. Right?'

'That's right,' replied Livia with a voice just as firm as his.

Aurelius took Juba by the bridle and waited until the girl untied her bay. 'We have a mission to carry out that will keep us side-by-side for some time. We will have to work together very closely and we have to be able to count on one another blindly. Each of us must avoid making the other uncomfortable or troubled. Do you understand what I'm trying to say?'

'Perfectly,' responded Livia.

Aurelius began to descend the mountain side, leading Juba by the reins. 'If we want to attempt to rescue the emperor,' he said, changing the subject, 'it has to be along the way. Once the convoy has reached its destination, it will be impossible.'

'Two against seventy? Doesn't sound like a good idea to me – and your wound hasn't completely healed. We can't risk failing again.'

'Well, what do you propose then? You must have a plan. Or are we just going to continue on without rhyme or reason?'

'First we have to find out where they're headed, then we'll

come up with a plan for breaking in and carrying off the boy. There's no other way: we didn't have time to enrol any men of our own in Ravenna, and even if we had, Odoacer's spies are so numerous that the plot would have been uncovered immediately. Even though this may seem strange to you, our main advantage lies in the fact that no one knows we exist. No one would ever suspect that two wayfarers could attempt such a feat. You nearly succeeded the first time just because no one could have expected such a sortie. If we do involve others, it must be far away from Ravenna, where no one knows anything about us.'

'And what money are we to use in . . . involving others?'

'We will have money available for us in a number of places throughout Italy. Antemius has deposits in many banks and I have a letter of credit from him. Do you know what that means?'

'No. But what's important is that you can find the money. I haven't lost hope of finding my comrades.'

'Neither have I. I know how important it is for you.' Her tone revealed a depth of feeling stronger than the spirit of camaraderie that had united them over the last days.

They kept up with the convoy, advancing about twenty miles a day, but staying at a considerable distance from it. The surveillance of the barbarians surrounding the carriage had become more lax. The strength of their numbers, the powerful presence of Wulfila and the absolute lack of any threat as far as their eyes could see all contributed to easing the tension, as well as the discipline.

They crossed the Apennines and descended the Tiber valley.

'If we should find my comrades,' said Aurelius all at once, 'would you help me to rescue them?'

'I imagine so. Granted that we find them. It depends on how many of them there are, but please don't raise your hopes too high. Misenus is a possibility, but just one among many others.'

'It's strange, I badly want to find them, and yet I'm afraid . . . afraid to find out what happened to the others.'

'You did what you could,' said Livia. 'Don't torment yourself. What happened happened and we can't change it . . .'

'That's easy for you to say. The legion was my whole life. Everything I had.'

'You never had a family?'

Aurelius shook his head.

'A wife? A lover?'

Aurelius looked away: 'I've had the odd encounter. Nothing lasting. It's difficult to join your life with someone when you have no roots.'

They advanced slowly for a while without speaking, then Livia broke the silence again. 'A legion!' she said. 'It seems incredible. The original legions were done away with ages ago when Emperor Gallienus judged them too heavy and slow to stand up against the hordes of invading barbarians on their fast horses. No military unit has been called a legion for at least forty years. Why set one up now?'

'The plan was extraordinary. First of all, the territory in Italy rarely allows for deployment of a vast contingent of cavalry, and the impact of our infantry forces on the march would have been formidable: Orestes wanted his people to see a silver eagle shining in the sun. He wanted the Romans to regain their pride, to see foot soldiers advancing with the ancient suits of armour and the great shields, making the earth tremble beneath their feet. He wanted discipline to triumph over barbarity, order over chaos. We were all so proud to be part of it. Our commander was a man of virtue and incredible valour, austere and just, jealous of his honour and ours.'

Livia looked at him: his eyes sparkled and his voice vibrated with intense feeling as he spoke. She would have liked to delve into these emotions, but she saw that the convoy seemed to be slowing down in the distance and she signalled to Aurelius to stop.

'No, it's nothing,' she reassured him after a moment. 'Just a herd of sheep crossing the road.'

They proceeded at the edge of a wood that flanked the road at a distance of three or hour hundred feet.

'Please, continue with what you were saying,' coaxed Livia.

'The men were chosen one by one from other units: officers and soldiers, auxiliaries and engineers, mostly Romans from Italy and from the provinces. Several barbarians were enlisted as well, but only men of proven loyalty whose families had served the state for generations. They were concentrated at a secret base in Noricum, and trained for nearly a year there. When the legion ventured into battle for the first time in an open field, the effect was devastating: we penetrated the enemy ranks with the power of a war machine, causing enormous casualties. We had maintained the best of ancient techniques and joined them with the most modern.'

'What about you? Where were you recruited?'

Aurelius rode on for a little while as if absorbed in his thoughts, staring straight ahead. He kept to the hillside between the trees, so they would not be surprised by Wulfila's scouts who incessantly scoured the sides of the valley to head off any surprise attacks. They were probably more worried about brigands than any unlikely attempt to rescue the boy.

'I told you,' replied Aurelius suddenly. 'I've always been part of the legion. I don't remember anything else.' The tone of his voice left no room for argument. They continued on in silence; Livia would break off every now and then, wandering up hill or down, unable to take her companion's mute obstinacy. When their paths crossed they exchanged a few words about the itinerary or the terrain and then moved on. Aurelius was clearly reliving the drama of his comrades' massacre and his failure to save them. Ghosts certainly rode at his side, the bleeding shadows of youths cut down in their prime, of men cruelly tortured to their last breath. The place echoed with their screams, their appeals from the depths of the underworld.

They proceeded at that pace for several hours until the sky began to darken and the convoy drew up for the night. Livia noticed a hut on the hillside about a mile from Wulfila's camp. She pointed it out to her companion: 'Maybe we can stop there for the night, and find shelter for our horses as well.' Aurelius nodded and urged his Juba towards the wood on the hill.

He entered cautiously to make sure no one was inside. It looked like a refuge for herdsmen bringing their cows to pasture. There was straw in the corner, and behind the building were several bales of hay, stored under a makeshift shed. Nearby, a little stream of water poured into a trough carved from a sandstone boulder. It trickled over the top and flowed down between the moss-covered stones to form a natural basin. The little crystalline lake that had collected there reflected the sky and the trees all around. The forest glowed at dusk with the colours of autumn. Wild vines twisted around the oak trunks with their big vermilion leaves and little clusters of purple grapes.

Aurelius tended to the horses and tied them under the shed, giving them a little hay. Livia ran to the lake, stripped and plunged in. She shivered at the contact with the icy water, but her desire to wash herself was stronger than the chill. Aurelius was coming down the slope when he saw her nude body splashing in the clear water. He watched her for a few moments, awestruck by her beauty. Then he turned away, confused and upset. He wanted to draw her close and tell her how much he wanted her, but the thought that she might reject him was unbearable. He walked over to the trough and washed himself as well, first his chest and arms and then the lower part of his body. When Livia returned she was wrapped in her travelling blanket and was carrying two big trout strung on the harpoon she held in her right hand.

'They were the only ones left,' she said, 'and they were probably ready to die. Go down and get my clothes; they're hanging on a branch near the lake. I'll get the fire going.'

'You're crazy. They'll see the smoke and send someone up here.'

'They can't check every trace of smoke in the countryside,' she replied, 'and besides, we'll see them coming from up here. If anyone tries it, I'll string him up like these trout and drag him into the forest. Give him an hour or two, and only his bare bones will be left. Even wild animals are going hungry these days.'

Livia cooked the fish as best she could, feeding the flames

with little pine twigs, which raised a bright crackling fire, but no smoke. When they were ready, Aurelius took the smaller trout for himself, but Livia switched it with the bigger one. 'You have to eat,' she insisted, 'you're still weak, and when it's time for a fist fight I want a lion at my side, not a sheep. You go to sleep now. I'll take the first guard shift.'

Aurelius didn't answer, and walked towards the edge of the clearing where he leaned against a huge old oak tree. Livia watched him as he stood motionless, eyes wide and staring, facing the night as it descended from the mountain with its shadows and its ghosts. She would have gone close, if only he'd asked her.

*

Wulfila ordered camp to be set up near a bridge that crossed a tributary of the Tiber and his men began to roast the sheep and rams confiscated from the shepherd who had so incautiously crossed their path a few hours before. Ambrosinus was worried: 'The emperor detests mutton,' he said.

The barbarian burst out laughing: 'The emperor detests mutton! Oh what a pity, how terrible! Unfortunately, the imperial cook has refused to move from Ravenna and the bill of fare here is limited. Either he eats mutton or he goes to bed on an empty stomach.'

Ambrosinus drew closer: 'I've seen chestnuts in the forest. If I may, I could gather a few and make a very tasty and nutritious sweet for him.'

Wulfila shook his head: 'You're not moving from here.'

'What are you afraid of? You know that I'd never abandon the boy for any reason in the world. Allow me to go: it won't take me long, and you'll have your share as well. I can assure you that you will never have eaten anything so delicious.'

Wulfila grudgingly agreed, so Ambrosinus took a lantern and started off into the wood. The ground under the knotty trunks was covered with spiny chestnut husks; many of them had split, revealing their lovely fruit, red-brown as tanned leather. He gathered up quite a few, thinking that this place must surely be uninhabited if such precious fruits were left to the bears and boars. He walked back to the camp with his lantern put out, furtively approaching the spot where Wulfila seemed to be holding a meeting with his officers.

'When do I leave?' asked one of them.

'Tomorrow, as soon as we get to the plain. You'll take a half a dozen men with you and go directly to Naples. There you will contact a man named Andrea da Nola who you'll find in the quarter of the palatine guards. You'll have him arrange for our transport to Capri. The entire escort will come along, as well as the boy, his tutor, and servants for them and for us. Tell him that everything should be made ready for us: living quarters, food, wine, clothing and blankets. Everything. We may need slaves: make sure they don't get them from Misenus. Some of the ones that Mledo captured at Dertona are there and I don't want them in our way. Understand? If anything goes wrong I'll hold him personally responsible. Let him know that I'm not forgiving with bunglers.'

Ambrosinus thought he had heard enough and made his way light-footed to the opposite side of the camp, where the men were turning the spits of mutton over the campfire. He found a corner where he could roast his chestnuts, then crumbled them in a mortar and mixed them with boiled must from the convoy supplies. He formed several flat little cakes and crisped them again on the open flame. He served them proudly to his lord. Romulus was amazed: 'My favourite sweet! How did you do it?'

'Wulfila is starting to give me a little freedom; he knows that he can't treat me too badly if he wants his face to heal. I just went into the forest and gathered some chestnuts, that's all.'

'Thank you!' exclaimed Romulus. 'They remind me of feast days at home, when the cooks prepared them on slate slabs in the garden. I can still smell the must bubbling away! No fragrance is sweeter or more intense.'

'Eat!' said Ambrosinus. 'Don't let it get cold.'

Romulus bit into the cake and his tutor continued: 'I have

news. I know where they are taking us. I heard Wulfila talking to his men as I was leaving the wood. Our destination is Capri.'

'Capri? That's an island.'

'Yes, it is an island, but it's not far from the coast. It can actually be quite pleasant, especially in the summer when the climate is good. Emperor Tiberius built luxurious villas there, and he lived in the most beautiful one of all during the last years of his reign: villa Jovis. After his death—'

'It's still a prison,' interrupted Romulus. 'I'll have to live the rest of my days in the company of my most hateful enemies. I won't be able to travel, to meet other people, to have a family . . .'

'Let us take what life gives us, my son, one day after another. The future is in the hands and the mind of God. Never give up! Do not lose heart, don't resign yourself to anything. Remember the great examples of the past; keep in mind the teachings of wise men like Socrates, Cato and Seneca. Knowledge is nothing if it doesn't gives us the means for dealing with life. You know, the other day, I had a premonition: an old prophecy of my native land came to me, almost miraculously, I would say. It has changed my outlook. I realize that we are not alone, and other signs will soon come. Believe me, I can feel it.'

Romulus smiled, seemingly more in pity than in relief: 'You're raving mad, *Ambrosine*,' he said, 'but you do make good chestnut cakes.' He began eating again, and Ambrosinus watched him with such satisfaction that he nearly forgot that he hadn't touched a bit of food himself. He brought what was left to Wulfila, as promised, hoping to gain a little more of his goodwill.

The next day they awoke at dawn and watched the departure of the advance squad as it headed south. Then the convoy started up again, stopping only for a light meal at midday. The climate was becoming milder as they proceeded. Big white clouds sailed across the sky, pushed by the western wind; at times they would condense into towering black masses and flood the earth with sudden, violent downpours. Then the sun would return to illuminate the humid, glossy fields. The oaks and ashes gave way to pines and myrtles; the apple trees were replaced by olive trees and grape vines.

'Rome is behind us now,' said Ambrosinus. 'We're approaching our destination.'

'Rome!' murmured Romulus, thinking of when he had entered the senate-house in his imperial robes, accompanied by his parents. It seemed like a century had passed, rather than just a few weeks. His youth and his adolescence, the most beautiful age of man, were opening up for him while his heart was oppressed by grief and by dark imaginings.

9

WHEN WULFILA NOTICED THE water vendor, she was still some distance away. She stood on the right side of the road, a wineskin strapped over her shoulder and a wooden bowl in her hand. She looked much like a number of other beggars and wretches they had met along the way, but the sun had become hotter, and the noonday hour and absence of springs alongside the road had whetted the thirst of both the men and their horses.

'Hey, over here,' he said in his own language when they were close enough. 'I'm thirsty.'

The girl understood from his gestures and attitude that he wanted a drink, and she passed him a full bowl. Although she was awkwardly bundled up in a worn cape, her beauty shone through, inciting the salacious comments of the barbarians.

'Hey, let's get a better look at you!' one of the warriors yelled, yanking the cape from her shoulders, but she dodged him with a swift twist of her torso. She gave a little smile anyway and held out her hand to have a few coins in exchange for the cool water she poured into the bowl.

'Since when do we have to pay for water?' shouted another man. 'If I pay a woman I want a lot more!' He managed to grab her around the middle and pull her close. He could feel her slender waist and shapely hips, muscles taut under her skin. 'What firm flesh! You're not as starving as you look,' he exclaimed in surprise, but at that moment another voice piped up: 'I'm thirsty.'

The girl realized it was coming from the carriage, just a few steps away. She wriggled free and went closer, moving aside the curtain covering the window. What she saw was a boy of twelve or thirteen with light brown hair and big dark eyes, dressed in a white tunic, sleeves embroidered with silver thread. With him was a grey-bearded man of about sixty, balding at the top of his head. He was wearing a simple grey wool gown, with a little silver pendant hanging at his neck.

'Get out of here!' Wulfila immediately pulled the curtain closed and dragged the girl away forcefully, but the man sitting inside moved aside the curtain again and said loudly: 'The boy is thirsty.' At that moment, his eyes met the girl's and he realized that she was not what she seemed. She was trying to tell him something or prepare him for something, and he gripped Romulus's arm as if to alert him for an unexpected event. The water vendor leaned in and, momentarily hidden from Wulfila, passed a metal cup to the man, and the wooden bowl full of water to the boy. As he drank, she whispered in Greek: *'Chaire, Kaisar.'* Hail Caesar! The boy managed to control his surprise while his companion responded in the same language: *'Tis, eis?'* Who are you?

'A friend,' she replied. 'My name is Livia. Where are they taking you?'

Right at that instant, Wulfila intervened, pulling her back again and putting an end to their conversation.

Inside the carriage, Romulus turned to his tutor wide-eyed, unable to interpret the strange encounter: 'Who could she have been, *Ambrosine*? How did she know who I was?' But the man's attention was drawn to the cup he was still holding in his hand. He turned it over and discovered a seal in the shape of an eagle impressed on the bottom with the letters: LEG NOVA INV.

'Legio Nova Invicta,' he said in a low voice. 'Do you know what this means, Caesar? That the soldier is about to try again, and he's not alone this time. I don't know whether to be pleased or worried, but my heart tells me that this is a favourable sign of an auspicious event. We have not been abandoned to our destiny. I know that the premonition I had several days ago is true . . .'

Wulfila had pushed Livia to the side of the road, but she looked at him with a pleading expression: 'My bowl, good lord! I need it.'

'All right,' agreed Wulfila. 'But get moving!' He accompanied her back to the carriage but after she had retrieved her bowl, he pushed her to the edge of the road, not leaving her side for an instant. She had just enough time to exchange a look with the two prisoners, without saying a word. She watched the carriage at length until it disappeared over a little hill, not moving until the sound of the horses' hooves and carriage wheels had completely faded away. At that point she turned towards the mountain and saw a lone horseman, observing her from the top of a hill: Aurelius. She entered the forest then, following a winding path that led to the base of the hill. Aurelius was there, holding the second horse by its bridle. Livia jumped into the saddle.

'Well?' he asked. 'You had me worried.'

'I failed. He was about to say something when Wulfila pulled me back. If I had raised my voice he would have become suspicious and held me there, but at least they've realized that we're following them, I think. The man who is with the emperor is impressive; his gaze is quite penetrating. He's surely a man of great intelligence.'

'He's a damned troublemaker,' replied Aurelius, 'but he's the boy's tutor and we'll have to include him in whatever plan we decide to act on. What about the boy: did you manage to see him?'

'The emperor? Yes, of course.'

'How is he?' asked Aurelius, without hiding his anxiety.

'I'd say he's well, but there's a great melancholy in his eyes. The loss of his parents must have been a terrible blow for him.'

Aurelius meditated in silence for a few moments, then said: 'Let's see if we can establish some kind of contact with him again. The guards don't seem so cautious any more; perhaps they're convinced that no one is interested in their prisoners.'

'The others, perhaps. Not Wulfila. He's distrustful, suspicious.

He has the eyes of a wolf, that one; you'll never catch him off guard. He has the situation completely under his control and nothing escapes him. I'm sure of it.'

'Did you see his face?'

'As clearly as I'm seeing you now. You've left him a nice souvenir, no doubt about it. If he's seen himself in a mirror, even just once, I wouldn't want to be in your shoes when he catches up with you.'

'That will never happen,' replied Aurelius. 'He'll never catch up with me . . . alive.'

They rode the whole afternoon until dusk, when they saw Wulfila's column changing route near Minturnus. The old via Appia was no longer usable. The swamps which had once been cleared, at least partially, by the drainage canals built by Emperor Claudius, had again flooded vast areas of the roads and fields, due to a complete lack of maintenance. The stagnant water briefly mirrored the flaming sun, but then took on the leaden tone of the reflected sky. Far off, over the sea, storm clouds were gathering, and there was a distant rumble of thunder from the west: perhaps it would rain.

The atmosphere, charged with humidity and swamp vapours, was suffocating. Both Aurelius and Livia were drenched with sweat but they continued on so as not to lose contact with the imperial caravan which was again proceeding at a fast pace in an attempt to gain ground before nightfall. Aurelius stopped to drink from his flask, and Livia handed him her bowl, having used up all her own water reserves for Wulfila's men. She brought it to her lips and drank in long gulps. As the bottom of the bowl was left uncovered, Livia's face lit up.

'Capri!' she said. 'They're going to Capri.'

'What?' asked Aurelius, bewildered.

'They're going to Capri. Look, I told you that man was intelligent.' She showed Aurelius the bottom of the bowl where a word was scratched in, using the tip of a stylus: CAPREAE.

'Capri!' repeated Aurelius. 'It's an island in the gulf of Naples, bare and rocky and completely wild, inhabited only by goats.'

'Have you been there?'

'No, but I've heard it described by several of my friends who come from near there.'

'I can't believe it's as bad as you say,' objected Livia. 'There must be some reason why Emperor Tiberius chose it as his residence. I'm sure that the climate is good, and mild, and I can imagine the scent of the sea mixing with the fragrance of the pines and broom.'

'Even if you are right,' replied Aurelius. 'It's still a prison. Come on, let's look for some shelter for the night up towards the hills. The mosquitoes will eat us alive down here.'

They found a little hut of reeds and straw, perhaps once used by farmers to safeguard their harvest, now obviously abandoned. Livia toasted some spelt flour in the bottom of a metal bowl, and mixed it with a little water and crumbled cheese for their dinner. Sitting near a small fire made with dry branches, they ate without speaking, listening to the continuous croaking of frogs which rose from the swamp.

'I'll stand guard first,' said Livia, hanging her bow over her shoulder.

'Are you sure?'

'Yes. I'm not tired, and I prefer to sleep when night has set in completely. Try to get some rest.'

Aurelius nodded, tied Juba to the trunk of a sorb, and entered the hut where he stretched out on his cloak. He watched for a while as his horse ate the ripe red fruit, then lay down on his side and tried to fall asleep, but thoughts of his companion-in-arms intruded, making him feel restless and aroused. He would have liked to let instinct take over, but the fear of inevitable separation once the mission was over held him back.

*

Livia had screened off the fire and sat in the dark, watching the lights in the enemy camp down on the plain. Some time had passed, she couldn't say how long, when she suddenly noticed the shadows of several barbarians on horseback riding alongside the swamp with their torches lit. A simple reconnaissance, no doubt, but that scene sparked off a memory that had long lain buried: a troop of barbarian horsemen galloping towards the shore of the lagoon, against a background of the sea in flames, rushing towards a lone man, who stood waiting for them. She shivered as if struck by a cold wind, and turned towards the hut. Aurelius slept deeply, worn out by their long journey and debilitated from lack of food. Livia was suddenly prompted to take a firebrand and creep closer. She crouched down next to him and reached out her hand to uncover his chest. Aurelius sprang up with his sword in fist and pointed it at her throat.

'Stop! It's me,' said Livia, pulling back.

'What in the name of the gods were you doing? I might have killed you!'

'I didn't think you would wake up, I just wanted to . . .'

'What?'

'I wanted to cover you up. Your blanket had slipped off.'

'You know full well that that's not true. Tell me the truth or I'll leave straight away.'

Livia got to her feet and went to stand next to the fire. 'I . . . I think I know who you are.'

Aurelius came close to the fire and seemed to be observing the little blue flames that licked at the embers. He looked straight into Livia's eyes. There was a cold shadow in his gaze, as if his soul had sunken into a muddy tide of memories, as if an old wound had started to bleed again. He turned his back to her abruptly: 'I don't want to hear it,' he said with a flat voice.

'The night is still young,' responded Livia. 'We have plenty of time for a long story. You just said that you wanted the truth from me. Remember?'

Aurelius turned back towards her slowly, lowering his head in silence, and Livia continued: 'One night, long ago, many years ago, my city – the city where I lived and grew up, where my house and my parents were – was suddenly attacked after a long, long siege. The barbarians gave themselves over to the sack and massacre. Our men were all run through on their swords, our women raped and taken into captivity, our houses plundered and set ablaze. My father died trying to defend us. He was chopped to pieces before our eyes, on the very threshold of our home. My mother escaped, holding me by the hand. We ran through the dark, on an old sentry road behind the aqueduct. We were completely overcome by panic. The streets were lit up by the fires. Shouting and moaning and cries of madness echoed from all around, raining from the sky like flaming hail. The city was full of dead bodies, and blood flowed everywhere. I was exhausted and frantic, and my mother had to pull me along. We reached the shore of the lagoon where a boat was about to put out to sea. It was filled to the brim with people trying to escape, and it was the last: other boats were already far out, and they were disappearing, swallowed up by the darkness, beyond the furthest reflection of the fires.' She stopped for an instant, looking deep into Aurelius's soul, her eyes brimming with tears. Nothing. Compassion, yes, pity, but no sign of recognition. Of remembrance.

'Go on,' he said.

Livia covered her eyes with her hands as if trying to protect them from those nightmarish images branded into her heart, memories that had remained confined for so long in the abyss of her mind. She forced herself to continue: 'The boat was already pulling away and my mother started to cry, screaming for them to wait, the water was at her knees . . .'

A flash of anguish crossed Aurelius's gaze and Livia moved even closer, until he could smell the salty fragrance which emanated siren-like from her body. A rush of heat enveloped him like a whirlwind of flames and he felt panic crushing his heart like a boulder.

Livia went on, implacable: 'There was a man. Standing at the stern, a young Roman officer. His armour was bloodied. When he saw us, he got out, into the water, helped my mother up and took me into his arms as she settled into the last remaining place. He held me by the waist and pushed me up towards my mother's outstretched arms, but I saw dark water beneath me and I clutched onto his neck. And that's when I tore this off,' she said, touching the medal with the silver eagle hanging at her neck. 'My mother managed to grab me and she held me tight while the boat slowly pulled away. That's the last image I have of him: standing there, dark against an inferno of flames, with a troop of barbarian soldiers galloping up behind him, like demons, waving torches. That soldier was you. I'm sure of it.'

She stroked the little silver eagle between her fingers. 'I've always worn this since that night, and I've never lost hope of finding the hero who saved our lives, sacrificing his own.'

She fell still and stood in front of her companion, waiting for his response, for a sign that she had reawakened his awareness of the past, but Aurelius said nothing. He closed his eyes tight to press back the tears, to prevail somehow over the emptiness that yawned before him.

'That's why you are drawn to this medal. You know it belongs to you. It's the badge of your division, the Eighth *Vexillatio Pannonica*, the heroic defenders of Aquileia!'

Aurelius shuddered at her words, but regained control. He opened his eyes and looked at the girl tenderly, taking her by the shoulders. 'That young soldier is dead, Livia. He's dead, understand?'

Livia shook her head while tears ran down her cheeks.

'He's dead. Like all the rest. There were no survivors in that garrison. Everyone knows that. It's just a dream you had when you were a little girl. Think about it: given the situation you've described, is there any chance that that young man might have lived, and that you'd meet up with him again after all these years?' But as he spoke he saw Wulfila's face twisted in fury, heard his voice shouting: 'I know you, Roman! I've seen you before!'

'These things only happen in fables. Give it up.'

'Really? Well then, tell me something. Where were you the night Aquileia fell?'

'I don't know, believe me. It happened too long ago, beyond the confines of my memory.'

'Maybe I can prove it to you. Listen to me. While you were sleeping just now, I wanted to see if . . .'

'What?'

'If you have a scar on your chest. I . . . I think I remember that that soldier was bleeding from a wound on his chest.'

'Lots of soldiers have scars on their chests. Brave ones, anyway.'

'And why are you always attracted to this medal?'

'I'm not looking at the medal. I'm looking at . . . your breasts.'

'Get away from me!' screamed Livia in a fit of anger and disappointment. 'Leave me alone! Leave me alone I said!'

'Livia, I . . .'

'Leave me alone,' she whimpered softly.

Aurelius walked away as she crouched over the last embers, cradling herself and covering her face. She wept in silence.

She couldn't move, until she realized that she was chilled to the bone. She lifted her head and saw Aurelius leaning against an oak tree, a shadow among the shadows, alone with his ghosts.

10

Aurelius walked to the stream, took off his corselet and tunic and began to wash his chest with the clean, cold water, lingering over the scar that creased his skin right at the junction of his collar bone. The freezing water made him shiver at first, but then gave him a sensation of strength and energy after a troubled, mostly sleepless night. A sudden cramp made him shut his eyes and wince, but it wasn't the scar that caused the pain. It came from a hard bump at the base of his skull, the result of some fall or other, who knows when and who knows where. As the years passed, that acute pain, prolonged and throbbing, was coming more frequently and seemed more intense.

'They're moving!' cried Livia. 'We have to go!'

Aurelius dried off without turning, slipped on his tunic and corselet, slung his sword over his shoulder and climbed up the short slope to where Juba was calmly grazing on the dewy grass. He jumped into the saddle and galloped off, followed by Livia. When they slowed to a walk, Aurelius observed: 'The weather is changing. My pains always let me know.'

Livia smiled: 'My grandfather used to say the same thing. He was quite a character: thin, bony and practically toothless! I remember him as if it were yesterday. He was a veteran, you see, and had fought with Emperor Valentinian the Third at Adrianopolis against the Goths. He would get these stabs of pain when the weather was about to change, although he couldn't even tell you where they came from, he was so full of scars and mended breaks! He was never wrong; six or seven hours might go by, but it would always start to rain. Or worse.'

Below them the long procession of Heruli and Skyrian warriors escorting the carriage of the young emperor and his tutor wound through the last stretches of the swamp. Wet, glossy-coated buffalo would emerge from the bog as they passed, moving a few steps away. Others sprawled on the road to dry themselves in the morning sun; they would get up lazily, the huge, muddy beasts, and move away from the horses towards the meadow strewn with purple thistles and golden dandelions. Italy's most fertile plain began to open before them, fields yellow with stubble or brown with overturned earth where ploughs had passed. A little ruined sanctuary marked the territory of some ancient Oscan tribe. A shrine placed at the meeting of three crossroads, once dedicated to Hecate, had been replaced by a Christian image: Mary with the holy child in her arms.

*

They continued until evening, when the convoy stopped not far from the banks of a stream. The men started to set up tents for the officers and prepare their own spots for the night. Farmers coming home from the fields, tools in hand, and children cavorting in the day's last light paused to watch them with curiosity but soon headed off for their villages and homes, from which spirals of smoke were starting to rise. After darkness fell, Livia pointed to some distant lights in the plain: 'That's Minturnus,' she said, 'once famous for its wine.'

Aurelius nodded and absent-mindedly quoted a couple of hexameters: '*Vina bibes interum Tauro diffusa palustres inter Minturnas . . .*' Livia was shocked: she'd never heard a soldier quote Horace in verse and with a classic pronunciation! His past continued to escape her.

'We have to make contact,' said Aurelius. 'Tomorrow they'll have to head south towards Naples or southeast towards Capua, but in either case, without the cover of these hills we won't be able to continue following them. We'll be seen if we go down to the plain, with all these villages and farmhouses. Strangers never pass unobserved.'

'What's that?' Livia interrupted him, pointing to a winking light near a grove of willow trees close to the stream. Aurelius watched attentively and after a while that intermittent flashing brought something to mind: it seemed to be the communication system used by the reserved imperial postal service!

He watched more carefully, and the signals soon began to take on meaning. Disconcerting. *'Huc descende, miles gloriose.'* Come down here, swaggering soldier. He shook his head as if he couldn't believe his eyes, then turned to Livia and said: 'Cover me and keep the horses ready in case we need to get out fast. I'm going down.'

'Wait . . .' protested Livia, but she didn't have time to finish; Aurelius had already disappeared into the thick vegetation. She could hear the leaves rustling for a while as he passed, then nothing.

Aurelius was trying not to lose sight of the light sending out those curious signals. He soon realized that it was a lantern, held high by an old man to illuminate his path. The light gleamed on his bald head: Romulus's tutor! Followed by a barbarian warrior. A few steps further and he could hear their voices. 'Stay back, give me a little room! I'm used to doing certain things in private; where do you think I'll run to, you animal? It's dark, and you know I'd never abandon the emperor!'

The barbarian muttered something, then leaned back against the trunk of a willow. The tutor walked a little forward, hung the lantern on a branch and arranged his cloak on a bush so that it looked like a person crouching. He walked a few steps further and vanished, swallowed up by the forest. Aurelius, who had come very close, was perplexed. What to do now? He couldn't call out or signal his position; the barbarian would hear him immediately. He moved towards the point where he'd seen the old man disappear and found himself near the bank of the river, where the foliage was even thicker and darker. A quiet voice abruptly sounded behind him, less than a step away.

'Crowded here, isn't it?'

Aurelius spun around and Ambrosinus found his sword at his throat, but he did not flinch.

'Good boy now,' he said, 'Everything's all right.'

'How—'

'Quiet. We only have the time for a crap.'

'By Hercules—'

'I'm Ambrosinus, the tutor of the emperor.'

'That much I know.'

'Don't interrupt me, just listen. Surveillance is heightened because we're approaching our destination. They won't even leave me alone to take a shit any more! You must also know, I imagine, that they're taking us to Capri. How many of you are there?'

'Two. Me and . . . a woman, but—'

'Yes, the water vendor. Well, for heaven's sake, don't try it again on your own, it would be suicide. If they catch you, they'll flay you alive. You need someone who can give you a hand.'

'We have money. We plan on recruiting—'

'Be careful! A mercenary is always ready to change his master; be sure to find someone you can trust. The other night I heard a couple of Wulfila's officers talking about Roman prisoners sent to Misenus to serve on the fleet. It might be worth your while to try there.'

'I certainly will,' replied Aurelius. 'Can you find out more?'

'I'll try. In any case, stay close behind us. I'll leave traces whenever I can. I see that you can read the light code. Can you use it as well?'

'Of course, but how did you know that I would see you?'

'The cup: I realized it was a signal, so I answered by scratching our destination into the bottom of the bowl. Then I thought that if you weren't stupid you'd be following us from the hills and your vantage point would allow you to see my light – just as I've seen your fires. Now I must go. Even if I were constipated, I've taken too long!'

Ambrosinus moved off, recovering his lantern, his cloak and his companion, who was still waiting to escort him back to camp.

*

He found Romulus leaning against a tree, looking off into nothingness.

'You must react, my boy!' admonished Ambrosinus. 'You can't go on like this! You're just at the start of your existence and you must begin living again.'

Romulus didn't even turn. 'Living? What for?' and he slipped back into his silence.

Ambrosinus sighed, 'And yet, there is hope for us . . .'

'Hope scribbled on the bottom of a cup, right? Once hope was kept in a box, if I remember correctly. Pandora's box.'

'Your sarcasm is out of place. That soldier has already tried to save you and he is more determined than ever to free you.'

Romulus nodded without enthusiasm.

'That man has risked his life for you, and he's willing to do it again. He considers you his emperor, and this is so important for him that he won't give up such a desperate endeavour. He deserves much more than just a nod from you.'

Romulus didn't answer at first, but from his look Ambrosinus realized that he'd struck a chord.

'I don't want him to risk his life again, that's all. What's his name?'

'Aurelius, if I remember well.'

'That's a common name.'

'You're right, but he is not a common man. He behaves as though he is commanding an entire army at your orders, and yet he's all alone. Your life and your liberty are the most precious things in the world for him. His faith in you is so blind that he's ready to face any danger, although the wound he suffered in his last attempt to save you hasn't even healed yet. Think about this when you no longer have the courage to take your life into your own hands, when you behave as if your life were not worth living. Think about it, little Caesar.'

He turned and walked towards the tent to prepare some dinner for his pupil, but before entering he turned his gaze to the shadowy forested hills and muttered between his teeth:

'Hold fast, *miles gloriose*! By all the devils and all the gods, hold fast.'

*

'He called me *miles gloriosus*, can you believe it?' panted Aurelius at the top of the hill. 'Like I was some character from a play. I was about to cut his throat.'

'The old man's, I suppose. Was it him?'

'Yes, of course.'

'He's read Plautus, that's all. And so have you, I see. You're quite an educated man. Rare for a soldier, especially these days. Haven't you ever asked yourself why?'

'I have other things to think about,' Aurelius cut her short.

'Can you tell me what's happening or is that too much to ask?'

'He confirmed that they're going to Capri, but there's something else. He has heard that some Roman prisoners have been sent to Misenus, near Naples, to serve on the fleet's galleys. If only I could find them!'

'That shouldn't be so difficult. A little money gets a lot of information. What's our next move?'

'I was thinking about that on my way up. He was sure of their destination, and there's no sense in us risking exposure by going down to the plain. We should get there before them and prepare our raid as well as possible.'

'But first you want to find your comrades.'

'It's in everyone's interest. I need men that I can rely on completely, and there was not one man in my entire division who I could not trust. We'll put together an assault unit and plan our attack.'

'What if they change destination as we're headed for Naples?'

'I don't think they will, but it's a risk we have to run. The longer we remain within sight of them, the greater our chance of making an unfortunate encounter, especially on open ground. I think we should break away from them tomorrow. We can set off after we see which road they're taking and precede them. We're much faster than they are.'

'As you wish. Perhaps you're right. It's only that . . . oh, I don't know, as long as we were nearby I felt that he was safe.'

'Under our protection. That's true. I've felt the same way, and I'm sorry to go, but I must say we're leaving him in good hands. That crazy old man surely cares for the boy very much, and he's smarter than all those barbarians put together. Let's rest now. We've been riding all day and we've only eaten biscuits and a piece of cheese.'

'I can promise you we'll eat well in Naples. Do you like fish?'

'I'd rather a side of beef.'

'You're a meat eater, so you must come from the plains. A farm in the countryside.'

Aurelius didn't answer. He detested Livia's digging into his past. He took off Juba's saddle and bit, leaving on his halter, so that he could graze freely. Then he laid out his blanket.

'I'd eat nothing but fish,' said Livia.

'I was forgetting that you are an aquatic creature yourself,' replied Aurelius, stretching out. Livia lay down beside him as they silently watched the stars glittering in the immense vault of the night sky.

'Do you ever dream at night?' asked Livia.

'The best night is passed without dreams.'

'You always answer with someone else's words. Plato this time.'

'Whoever he is, I agree with him.'

'I can't believe that you never dream!'

'Never dreams. Only nightmares.'

'What do you see?'

'Horror . . . blood, screaming . . . and fire, fire everywhere, an inferno of flames. Or a sensation like freezing, as if my heart were turning into a piece of ice. And you? You have a dream, I remember you telling me about it. A city in the middle of the sea.'

'It exists.'

'So this little Atlantis really exists?'

'Oh, it's only a village, with lots of huts. We fish and sell salt, but that's enough for us. We're free and no one dares to hazard into our waters: sandbanks and quagmires, shoals made treacherous by the tides. The coast mutates from day to day, from hour to hour actually.'

'Go on.'

'It was founded by my companions in misfortune, the refugees of Aquileia. Others came afterwards: from Gradus, Altinum, Concordia. We arrived the very night of the onslaught. We were frantic, hopeless, exhausted. The fishermen knew about a little group of islands in the middle of the lagoon separated by a wide canal, like a bit of a river which was lost in the sea. The ruins of an ancient villa stood on the biggest island, and that's where we took refuge. The men gathered dry grass for us to lie down on. The younger women stretched out to nurse their babies and someone managed to light a fire amidst those tumbledown walls. The next day the carpenters began to cut down trees and build houses, the fishermen went out to fish. Our new homeland was born. We were all Veneti, apart from a Sicilian and two Umbrians from the imperial administration: we called our town Venetia.'

'That's a nice name,' said Aurelius. 'Sweet. Sounds like the name of a woman. How many of you are there?'

'Nearly five hundred – and the first generation born in the city is already growing up, the first Venetians. So much time has passed that even our accent sounds different from the way they speak on the mainland. Isn't that marvellous?'

'And no one has ever bothered you?'

'Several times, but we've defended ourselves. Our realm is the lagoon. From Altinum to Ravenna, our men know every corner of it, every shoal, every beach, every little island. It's indefinable, ambiguous: neither land nor sea, nor sky; when the low clouds merge with the foaming waves, it's all three things together – invisible, often, foggy in the winter and misty in the summer, flat like the surface of the water. Each one of those islands is covered by thick woods. Our children sleep cradled by the song of the nightingale and the cries of the gull.'

'Do you have a child?' asked Aurelius suddenly.

'No, but the children of each one of us belong to everyone. We share everything we have and we help one another. Everyone's vote is counted when we elect our leaders. We have revived the old republican constitution of our ancestors, of Brutus and Scaevola, Cato and Claudius.'

'You talk about it as if it were a real nation.'

'It is,' replied Livia, 'and like Rome at its start, it attracts fugitives and refugees, the unfortunate and the persecuted. We build flat-bottomed boats that can go anywhere, like the one that carried you that night you were fleeing Ravenna. We've begun to build ships that can face the open sea. New houses spring up nearly every day, and the time will come in which Venetia will be the pride of the earth and the lady of the sea. This is my dream. That's why I've never had a man, nor a child. I've been alone, ever since I lost my mother to a sudden disease.'

'I can't believe that a girl so . . . beautiful, has never had . . .'

'A man? Why not? Maybe I've never met the one I have in mind. Maybe because everyone feels honour-bound, or empowered, to protect a girl left all alone. I had to prove that I could be self-sufficient, and that kind of attitude doesn't attract men. Quite the opposite. You know, every one of us in my city has to be ready to fight. I learned to handle a bow and a sword before I ever learned to cook or sew. We women take up arms when the need arises. We learn to distinguish the sound of a wave driven by the wind from a wave pushed by an oar. And we urinate standing up, like men, when we stand guard.'

Aurelius smiled at this, but Livia continued. 'In any case, we need men like you to build our future. When we've finished this mission, would you come to settle with us?'

Aurelius did not answer, confused by her unexpected proposal. After a moment of silence, he replied: 'I would like to tell you how I feel, but it's as if I were trying to walk in the dark over unknown territory. I have to take one step at a time. Let's try to free that boy, that will be something in itself.'

He brushed her lips with a kiss. 'Please get some rest,' he said. 'I'll stand guard first tonight.'

11

Aurelius and Livia arrived near Pozzuoli two days later as evening approached. The days had become very short and dusk came early, in a halo of reddish mist. This, the most beautiful region of Italy, showed few signs of the devastation of the north or the desolation and poverty of the central regions. The extraordinary fertility of the fields allowed two harvests a year and provided food for all, with enough left over to sell at a high price in less fortunate places. There were still vegetables and flowers in the gardens, and the barbarian presence was not nearly as strongly felt as in the north. People were kind and solicitous, the children noisy and a bit exasperating, and the strong Greek accent of the Neapolitans could be heard everywhere. They bought food at the Pozzuoli market which was held on alternating days of the week inside the amphitheatre. The arena, once soaked with the blood of gladiators, now played host to stands selling turnips and chickpeas, pumpkins and leeks, onions and beans, cabbage, greens and seasonal fruit like figs, red, green and yellow apples and bright red pomegranates, split in two on display, the pips inside gleaming like rubies. A true feast for the eyes.

'It's like coming back to life again!' exclaimed Aurelius. 'Everything is so different here!'

'You've never been?' asked Livia. 'I have. A couple of years ago, I helped Antemius's men to escort the bishop of Nicaea to Rome.'

'I've never been further south than Palestrina. Our division was always stationed in the north; in Noricum or Moesia or

Pannonia. The climate is so mild here, the earth so generous, the people so gracious. It's like another world!'

'Now can you see why people who come to this land never want to leave?'

'Absolutely,' said Aurelius, 'and to be honest, I'd much rather settle down here than in your swamp.'

'Lagoon,' Livia corrected him.

'Lagoon, swamp, what's the difference? Where do you think they'll sail from?' he asked, abruptly changing the subject.

'The port of Naples. Without a doubt. It's the shortest route to Capri. They'll be able to stock up on everything they need for their stay at the warehouses as well.'

'Let's get moving then. We want to get there as soon as possible and this land is too tempting. Even Hannibal and his army went soft with the pleasures to be had here.'

'The indolence of Capua . . .' nodded Livia. 'You've read Titus and Cornelius Nepos. An education typical of a good family from middle if not high society. And if the name you bear is your own—'

'It's mine,' Aurelius cut her short.

*

They reached the port of Naples late the next morning and blended into the crowd thronging around the market and the wharves to listen in on the local gossip. They ate bread and roast fish at a peddler's stand and admired the beauty of the gulf and the impressive mass of Mount Vesuvius with the plume of smoke that the wind carried eastward. Towards evening, they saw the imperial convoy arrive: the armour, shields and helmets of the barbarian soldiers seemed like monstrous contraptions in the peaceful, festive and multicoloured atmosphere of the port. Children scampered between the horses' legs, trying to get close enough to the warriors to sell them sweets, toasted seeds and raisins. When Romulus descended from his carriage, they swarmed around him, fascinated by his embroidered robes, his aristocratic features and his despondent expression. Neither

Aurelius nor Livia could resist catching a glimpse of him. They covered their faces, he with a wide-brimmed straw hat and she with a shawl, as they walked along the wharf, sheltered under the shade of the portico that flanked its entire length. The boy emperor was quite close, surrounded by his young subjects.

'Won't you come and play with us?' demanded one.

'Yes, come, we have a ball!' exclaimed another.

A child handed him a piece of fruit: 'Want an apple? It's good, you know.'

Romulus smiled at them all, a bit awkwardly, not knowing how to respond. Wulfila got off his horse and chased them all away with his booming voice and terrifying appearance. A group of porters finished unloading the goods destined for Capri, the last prison of the last Emperor of the Western Roman Empire. A couple of large ships drew up alongside the pier and began to board the men and the goods. The last to embark was the boy accompanied by his tutor.

Ambrosinus lifted the hem of his robe as he stepped aboard, revealing his bony knees. He was looking around as if he expected to recognize someone or something. For the briefest instant his eyes met Aurelius's, in the shadow of the portico, under the brim of his hat, and the expression of his face and the fleeting nod of his head acknowledged that he had seen him.

The ship cast off the moorings as the sailors called out orders for departure: as some weighed anchor and pulled in the lines, others set the sails to the wind. Livia and Aurelius came out of the shadows and walked to the end of the pier, keeping their eyes on the tiny figure of Romulus standing at the stern, which got smaller and smaller as the distance increased. The wind tousled his hair and puffed up his robes and perhaps even dried his tears on that melancholy, misty evening.

'Poor little boy,' said Livia.

Aurelius continued to stare at the boat, quite far away now, and he thought he could see Romulus raising his hand as if saying goodbye.

'Maybe he saw us,' he said.

'Perhaps,' echoed Livia. 'Let's go back now. We don't want to be noticed.'

They stopped in front of an inn called the Parthenope, as announced by a weather-eaten sign displaying what must have once been the figure of a siren.

'There was only one room,' said Aurelius as they climbed the stairs. 'We'll have to share it.'

'We've slept under worse conditions and I've never complained,' she said as if daring him to disagree. 'And we have a pact, don't we? So we run no risk sleeping in the same room. Isn't that right?'

'Of course,' replied Aurelius, but the look in his eyes and the catch in his voice said otherwise.

Livia took the lantern and went in. The room was small and unadorned, but decent enough. The furnishings consisted of two cots and a chest. There was a jar full of water in the corner and a basin. A bucket stuck in a niche in the wall was covered by a metal lid. A tray with a piece of bread, a small whole cheese and two apples had been placed on the chest. They washed their hands and ate in silence.

As they were preparing for sleep, there was a knock at the door.

'Who is it?' asked Aurelius, flattening himself against the wall next to the door with his hand on his sword.

No answer. Aurelius gestured to Livia that she should open it, while he waited with his weapon in fist. Livia, holding her own dagger in her left hand, slowly lifted the bolt with her right, and then swiftly flung open the door. The corridor was deserted, dimly lit by a lamp hanging from the wall.

'Look,' said Aurelius, pointing to the floor. 'They've left a message.'

There was a little folded piece of parchment paper on the ground. Livia picked it up and opened it: two handwritten lines and a small *sphraghis*, an oriental-type seal with three intertwining fret designs.

'Antemius's signature,' said Livia, beaming. 'I was sure he wouldn't have left us on our own.'

'What does it say?' asked Aurelius.

'Stephanus has deposited some money with a banker in Pozzuoli. We'll be able to recruit the men we need, and I'll be able to get a message back to Antemius through the courier carrying the letter of credit. It's a system we've used in the past, and it's always worked very well.'

'I want my comrades. Even if a single one of them has survived, I want to find him.'

'Calm down. We'll do everything we can, but it's not said that we'll succeed.'

'Ambrosinus said that Roman prisoners were taken to Misenus.'

'And that's where we'll go to look for them, but nothing will be certain or easy. If we find them there, they'll be slaves, understand? Slaves. Chained, probably. Certainly under close surveillance. Trying to free them might expose us to enormous risks and jeopardize our main mission.'

'There is no mission more important to me. Do you understand that?'

'You gave me your word.'

'So did you.'

Livia bit her lip: there was no way out but his. He would never change his mind.

*

They started out the next morning just before dawn. A cold north wind had swept away the mist, and a crescent moon shone low over the surface of the sea. Capri lay clearly at the horizon, rocky and dry, topped by thick brush. To the south, a thin stream of smoke rose from Mount Vesuvius, black as a mourner's veil against the lightening sky.

At sunrise they met Antemius's banker, a man called Eustatius, in a little isolated church outside the walls, at a chapel dedicated to the Christian martyr Sebastian. The image of the saint, tied to a pole and pierced with arrows, struck Aurelius like the lash of a whip. His mutilated memory tried frenetically to make a lost contact, awakening the deep sense of anguish prowling in his soul. It took an immense effort to control himself, to hide his emotions.

'We need some information,' said Livia, pretending not to notice Aurelius's reaction.

'You can count on me,' replied Eustatius, 'for whatever I can do.'

'We've heard that several Roman soldiers who were taken prisoner have been brought to Misenus to serve on the galleys.'

'I doubt it. Most of the military port is in disuse,' replied Eustatius. 'This season's ships have been pulled aground for repairs. The rowers are used for other jobs.'

'Such as?' asked Aurelius anxiously.

'Manning the sulphur mines or salt works. Others are used as gladiators in illicit games. The activity's illegal, but the betting goes sky high. Believe me, as a banker I know. If it's soldiers you're looking for, my guess is you'll find them there.'

'Where?'

'Inside the *piscina mirabilis*.'

'What's that?'

'It's an old cistern that was used to store drinking water for the fleet's ships. Imagine a huge underground basilica; it's absolutely amazing. Since the aqueduct is no longer in use, it's become the perfect hiding place for these shameful orgies. I can assure you that there are many Christians among the spectators, betting enormous sums on the most highly ranked champions. You'll need a pass to get in,' he added, and handed them a small smooth bone tablet inscribed with a trident, the three-pronged spear used in gladiator combat.

Livia took the money and the pass, signed a receipt and wrote a few lines for Antemius in code. They were about to leave, when the banker stopped them.

'Wait, there's something else. If you can, find yourself a room at the *Gallus Esculapi*; it's a tavern near the old dockyard. It's the favoured haunt of the bookmakers and gamblers. If you're asked: 'What do you say to a little swim?' answer 'Couldn't ask for better.' It's the password used by frequenters. What else? Oh yes, you realize of course that organizing or even participating in gladiatorial games is punished by death.'

'Of course,' said Aurelius. 'It's an old law of Constantine's but that doesn't mean it's respected.'

'That's true, but be careful anyway. When convenient, laws are applied to the letter, and if you should be the unfortunate one to find yourself under the edge of the axe . . . Good luck!' said Eustatius.

They rode all day without stopping, going past Lake Lucrinus and Lake Avernus and reaching Misenus after sunset. It wasn't difficult to find the *Gallus Esculapi* tavern at the old *Portus Iulius* dockyard. The great hexagonal basin was partially silted up, and the port entrance was only big enough to let one ship through at a time. It held only five warships in all, many of which showed signs of years of negligence. They were under the charge of a *magister classis*, whose worn standard dangled inertly from one of the yards. What had once been the base of the imperial fleet, a basin designed to contain two hundred warships, had become a dried up millpond full of decaying wrecks.

Livia and Aurelius entered the tavern after sundown and ordered chicken soup and vegetables. The air rang with the cries of gulls and the calls of women rounding up their children for dinner. The place was already quite crowded: a bald, red-faced host was serving white wine to the regulars sitting at their tables rolling dice or playing knuckle bones or morra. It was evidently the domain of games and gambling, but where were the bookmakers? Livia looked around and noticed a few tables grouped around the only window, where several disreputable looking characters were sitting. Their faces were scarred and their arms tattooed like the barbarians. Gallows-birds. She nudged Aurelius.

'I've seen them,' he said. He called over the host and said: 'I'm new to these parts but, you know, I like this place and I'd like to make the acquaintance of some of these fine people. Bring a carafe of your best to those men over there.' The host did so and the wine was accepted with an ovation.

'Hey, stranger! Come over and have a drink with us, and bring the little chickie with you. You do believe in sharing with your friends, don't you?'

'Give me some money,' whispered Aurelius to Livia. He approached their table with a half smile and said: 'You don't want that one around. She's no chick. She's a wolf, and she bites.'

'Oh, come on!' protested a second man as he got up from the table, an ugly scoundrel with a mouth full of rotten teeth. 'Come over to the party, sweetheart!' He approached Livia, who was still sitting at her table and laid a hand on her shoulder, fingers moving down towards her breast. Lightning fast, she grabbed his testicles with her left hand and squeezed, as she swiftly pulled out her dagger with her right. Without letting go, she sprang to her feet and jabbed it at his neck. The wretch yelled with all the breath he had in him, but he couldn't move with that blade at his throat and he couldn't get free of her steel fingers. Livia continued to squeeze until the man fainted in pain and collapsed to the ground. The girl slipped the dagger back into her belt and continued eating her soup as if nothing had happened.

'I told you she bites,' said Aurelius, impassive. 'Can I sit down?'

The others moved over wordlessly. Aurelius poured himself some wine and ostentatiously placed a couple of silver coins on the table. 'I've heard that you can make a lot of money here, if you're tipped off to the right man.'

'You like to get straight to the point, from what I see,' said the man who seemed to be their leader.

'If it's worth it to me.'

'Well, you're in the right place all right, but you need a patron saint, if you get my gist.'

Aurelius took the tablet with the trident and flashed it for an instant before putting it back in his pocket: 'Like this one?'

'I see you know the ropes. Do you like to go to bed early?'

'Me? I'm a regular night owl.'

'What do you say to a swim at midnight?'

'Couldn't ask for better.'

'How much do you want to bet?'

'Depends. Is there anyone worthwhile?'

The man got up, grabbed him by the arm and took him aside as if to confide a great secret: 'Listen, there's this Ethiopian. A giant. Tall as a tower and all muscle. Looks like Hercules himself. He's massacred every one of his opponents.' Aurelius's heart skipped a beat: Batiatus! he would have liked to yell, but he suffocated the excitement that he felt at knowing his friend was alive.

'Everyone's been betting big money on him, but seeing that the gold's not a problem for you, I'd like to make you my partner. Let's bet everything you have on the black man losing. I guarantee he'll lose, and we'll split the winnings, but I need at least five gold solids, or it's not worth it to me.'

Aurelius pulled out his money bag and weighed it in his hand. 'Money's not a problem, but I'm not stupid. Why should the big guy lose at all?'

'Two reasons. The first is that he has to fight three against one tonight. The second is a surprise. You'll see for yourself. I don't know you, handsome, I can't risk telling you any more than that. I've already said too much. So how much are you betting?'

'I told you, I'm not stupid. You'll see your money tonight, just before the show begins.'

'Agreed,' said the man. 'At midnight, when you hear the admiralty's bell ringing.'

'I'll be there. Oh, let me tell you something. Remember her?' he said, pointing at Livia. 'She is nothing but a wet chick compared to me. No tricks, all right? Or I'll rip off your balls and force you to eat them. Now go and collect that animal before he wakes up and she changes her mind and smashes his head like a pumpkin.' The man grunted in assent and went to take care of his battered crony. Aurelius and Livia disappeared into the alley.

'Batiatus is alive!' exclaimed Aurelius, beside himself with joy. 'Can you believe it? He's alive!'

'All right, I heard you. And who is Batiatus?'

'One of the men in my division. He was my commander's personal body guard. He's a huge Ethiopian, more than six feet tall and strong as a bull. He's worth ten men, I'm telling you. If we manage to free him, I know we can liberate the emperor. And if he's alive, maybe so are some of the others. Oh gods, if only it were true . . .'

'Don't get your hopes up. In the first place, how do you plan to set him free?'

Aurelius put his hand on the shaft of his sword: 'With this. What else?'

'I imagine you'll need a hand.'

'It would help.'

'You have a strange way of asking for things.'

'I'm not asking for anything. I'm trying to help you bring your mission to completion.'

'True. Let's get started, then, we'll have to prepare everything we need. What did that other pig tell you?'

'That everyone will be betting on the black man, since he always wins, but he asked me for a large sum to bet on him losing, and says that he'll arrange it.'

'Do you think they mean to poison him?'

'I doubt it. He's worth too much.'

'Drug him?'

'Maybe.'

'I don't like it. We'll have to be on our guard.'

They returned to the tavern and made careful plans. 'We'll need horses,' observed Aurelius. 'Three or even four, you never know. I can take care of that. I noticed an exchange post at the entrance to the city; my military insignia should get us what we want, but I'll need more money.'

Livia dipped into their reserves and Aurelius left, not returning until after dark.

'It's all taken care of,' he said. 'The post master was a good man, an old-fashioned functionary who knows when not to ask too many questions. He'll have the horses waiting for us at the mill located at the third milestone near the coast. I said that I was expecting friends and that we'd be leaving tomorrow before dawn.'

'What about our weapons?' asked Livia.

'They'll presumably be searching people at the entrance. Do you think you can hide them under your cloak? You'll have to look like a woman, do you know what I mean?'

'Perfectly,' replied Livia, not flustered in the least. 'Please leave now. Knock when you come back.'

When Aurelius entered, he was astonished at Livia's metamorphosis. Her eyes sparkled, accented by a thin line of bistre, and he wanted to tell her how beautiful she was, but the toll of a bell sounded from the port.

'The admiralty's bell,' said Aurelius. 'Let's go.'

12

People started arriving a few at a time, in silence and complete darkness, mostly men, but women as well and even a few children. They were searched at the entrance, and any weapons found had to be left with the guard. The only light was a small lantern used to check the passes similar to the one which Aurelius had received from Eustatius.

Aurelius and Livia stood in line awaiting their turn. Livia had arranged her hair and was wearing a veil that she had bought at the market which accentuated her feminine grace. The crowd began to buzz as the sound of heavy footsteps and dragging chains was heard, and parted to make way for the combatants who were to fight that night. Among them was a black man a full head taller than the rest: Batiatus! Aurelius pushed closer even as Livia tried to hold him back. When he was near the lamp, he bared his head and said: 'Hey, sack of coal. I bet a mountain of money on you tonight, try not to disappoint me!'

Batiatus turned towards the voice and found his old comrade in arms standing before him. His eyes glittered in the semi-darkness, and emotion was close to betraying both of them, but Aurelius gave a quick wink and immediately covered his head, turning away. The lanista, the gladiators' trainer, yanked on the chain and Batiatus stumbled down the stairs that led to the heart of the immense cistern.

Suddenly Aurelius saw Vatrenus pass by as well, and could not hold back his tears. A chunk of his past life suddenly re-emerged in that dark, sinister place; companions he had thought lost were alive and at hand, raising immense hope in him and terrible fear: fear that everything would sink back into the void, fear that he would not be up to the task, that he would fail as he had failed to liberate Romulus at Ravenna. Livia understood what was going through his mind; she held his arm tight and whispered: 'We can do it. I know we can do it! Bear up now, we're going in.'

The guard was about to put his hands on Livia, but Aurelius growled: 'Hey, keep those paws off her! She's my fiancée, not that whore of your mother.'

The man muttered something in irritation, but he must have been used to such insults. 'You get over here and let me search you, then – and show me your pass, or I'll make you sorry you ever opened your mouth,' he said, putting his hand on a sort of cudgel he had hanging from his belt.

Aurelius showed him the tablet and raised his arms, grumbling, as the guard searched him. 'You can go,' he said, finding everything in good order, and he turned away to check some newcomers.

Aurelius and Livia began to descend the long flight of stairs that led to the base of the cistern, and found an incredible spectacle before them: the grandiose *piscina mirabilis*, lit up by dozens of torches, a reservoir capable of holding enough water for an entire city. It was divided into five aisles, each supported by tall arches. The walls and floor were smoothly polished, and the pavement sloped on both sides towards the centre to form a lime pit, a little channel closed by a gate which had to be opened occasionally to expel the limey silt which would deposit on the bottom over time. Looking up, towards the ceiling on the eastern wall, they could see the original water inlet from the aqueduct; once used to fill up the cistern, it was now closed by a gate. A long rusty smear and a slight dripping sound made it clear that there was still water in the aqueduct supply line, but it was probably shunted off towards secondary collectors. Directly across from the inlet, on the west wall, was the old outlet pipe, which had once supplied the fleet tanks with water from the top surface, the cleanest and most pure. Now the entire system, that had quenched the thirst of sailors and soldiers in the world's most powerful fleet, was nothing but an empty abyss, a reservoir of blind, bloody violence, of man's most shameful instincts.

Aurelius noticed the buckets of water with butchers' brooms near some of the pillars that must have been used to sweep away the blood. A wooden shed leaned up against the back wall, probably a changing room for the gladiators.

Livia passed the sword and dagger to Aurelius and kept the other weapons for herself. 'Where should I take position?' she asked.

Aurelius looked all around: 'The best thing for you to do is to go back towards the entrance. You'll be able to keep an eye on the entire situation from up there and cover our escape. Remember, don't ever lose sight of me. As soon as you see me attack, shoot down anyone who gets in my way. I'm counting on you.'

'I'll be your guardian angel.'

'What's a guardian angel?'

'A kind of winged genius that we Christians believe in. They say that each one of us has one protecting us.'

'Whatever you can do to cover my back will be fine. There's my bookmaker. You go and take position.'

Livia walked lightly up the stairs and flattened into the shadows behind the half-closed entry door. She took her bow out from under her cloak and placed the quiver full of sharp arrows on the ground. Aurelius was approaching the swindler.

'Ah, our mysterious friend with the money. Willing to bet that the black man will lose, then?'

'I've just seen him. He's frightening! You were right, a real Hercules. How are you going to tame him?'

'That's a secret. I can't say.'

'You tell me the secret, and I'll hand over the money,' he said, shaking the bag he held in his hand.

The man looked at it greedily. 'If I say it's a sure thing, you can trust me. Look, this is my share,' he said, indicating a pile of gold solids.

Other bookmakers near him were shouting: 'Come forward!

On with the bets, folks, the show is about to begin! Who's betting on the black titan?' As the buzz and the confusion grew, a group of servants began to set up a kind of iron barrier that marked off the field of combat, while a group of armed men at the end of the room took position. Aurelius looked up towards Livia and nodded towards the security guards, whom she had already spotted.

The first pair of combatants entered the marked off space and the duel began, amidst the increasingly excited goading of the crowd, thronging close. These preliminary fights were just a warm up for the most eagerly awaited event: the ordeal of the black Hercules!

Very little time remained. What had the bookmaker meant about a secret? Aurelius thought he should make him spit it out at any cost, even with a dagger to his ribs; in the confusion, no one would notice. He saw that a huge amount of money was accumulating on the table and was gripped by panic. How could he be so certain that the black man was going to lose? Their eyes met for an instant and the man gestured as if to say: 'Are you in?'

The guards seemed distracted by the fight, which was getting more furious by the moment as it drew towards its rapid conclusion. Struck in the shoulder, one of the combatants vacillated and his adversary ran him through. The delirious screaming of the crowd exploded into thousands of echoes which shattered against the arches and pillars.

Just then, Aurelius's ears, which were used to picking up the slightest sound even at the height of a battle, made out some turmoil on his left, coming from the changing room. He slipped along the wall and got close enough to see. Four men had tied up Vatrenus and they were gagging him, while his armour and salleted helmet were being donned by another gladiator of the same build and height.

So that was their strategy! They had realized that Batiatus never dealt a death blow to the man wearing that armour and they were getting ready to punish him for it: Batiatus would be taken by surprise and finished off by an enemy disguised as a friend, and the gamblers would win an enormous sum of money. In his heart, Aurelius thanked the gods who were giving him this magnificent gift, and he crouched into a corner to brood on his fury and channel all of his power into revenge.

They were letting Batiatus out. Wearing only a loin-cloth, his muscular body gleaming with sweat, he carried a small round shield and a short, curved Saracen sword. The crowd roared while the servants dragged away the fallen gladiator by hooking him through the heel. The man disguised as Vatrenus followed close behind. Aurelius saw his moment. He rushed into the changing room, surprising the two guards. He beheaded the first with a swipe of his sword and stuck his dagger hilt-deep into the other's chest. Both men fell over without uttering a cry.

'Vatrenus, it's me!' he said, untying his friend and removing the gag.

'By Hercules! How did you get here? Hurry! Batiatus is in danger.'

'I know. Let's go.'

As they ran out, Livia, anxious at losing sight of Aurelius, spotted them. She nocked the arrow and pulled the bowstring, ready to strike.

Vatrenus and Aurelius made their way through the noisy crowd, trying to get to the front. Batiatus was faced with three adversaries, but he was clearly striking out much more violently at the two at his sides, and not the man directly in front of him, who he must have thought his friend.

They arrived just as the stand-in for Vatrenus – after a series of spectacular but off-the-mark blows, typical of a sham skirmish – suddenly went directly for the base of the giant's throat with a well-aimed lunge. At the same instant, the real Vatrenus yelled at the top of his lungs: 'Batiatus! Beware!' Batiatus had a flash of recognition and dodged to avoid the death blow, but the blade cut through the skin on his left shoulder.

Aurelius had already knocked over the barrier and run through one of the surviving gladiators, while Vatrenus took care of the other. Batiatus recognized his friend fighting bare-faced alongside him and, having recovered his balance, charged at Vatrenus's double and felled him with a single slash of his sword. Before the throng could comprehend what was happening, the three of them burst forward with their weapons outstretched, cutting through the crowd and running to the stairs.

'This way!' shouted Aurelius. 'Hurry!' Pure pandemonium broke loose, with the terrified onlookers scattering in every direction.

The guards gave chase, but Livia was waiting for them. The first two were struck with deadly precision, one in the chest and the other in the middle of his forehead. A third was nailed to the ground just a few steps from the stairs. The others, about twenty in all, managed to reach the base of the stairway and set off in pursuit, shouting out in alarm. The custodian leaned over the gallery to see what was going on, but Livia gave him a push that sent him tumbling over. His scream was only interrupted by a brutal meeting with the floor one hundred feet below.

Aurelius and his comrades had almost reached the exit when the door snapped shut from outside, with the sound of a bolt being drawn. The guards were close behind them on the stairs and the four fugitives had no choice but to turn around and face them. Batiatus grabbed the first within reach and dashed him into the others like a rag doll, sending them all rolling down the stairs. Then he turned and shouted 'Get back!' His friends moved aside as he lunged at the door like a battering ram. Shoved off its hinges, it crashed to the ground and the four of them ran outside. One of the guards had been crushed by the falling door, while the other took off at the mere sight of that black demon emerging from a cloud of plaster dust.

'This way! Follow me!' shouted Livia, but Aurelius headed towards the flood gate of the water supply circuit.

'They wanted a swim and they'll have one, by Hercules!'

'There's no time!' pleaded Livia. 'We have to go! Now!'

But Aurelius was already at the winch with Batiatus at his side. The gears were rusty and jammed, but the giant's force released the mechanism. The gate lifted and the water rushed inside with the din of a waterfall. The desperate cries of the crowd issued from the narrow door opening like a choir of damned souls from the depths of hell. The two friends were already running after Livia and Vatrenus down the slope to where Aurelius had tied their horses.

A shout reached them: 'Wait for us! We're coming with you!'

'Who are they?' demanded Aurelius, looking back.

'Companions in misfortune!' replied Batiatus, panting. 'Move it! There's not a moment to lose!'

Aurelius and Livia leaped on their horses and guided the others to the mill at the edge of an olive grove where three more steeds were waiting.

'I didn't think there'd be so many of you! The lightest pair up,' ordered Aurelius. 'Batiatus, that one's yours!' he added, pointing at a massive Pannonian steed, black as coal.

'I'll bet he is!' shouted Batiatus, springing into the saddle. At that moment, a trumpet sounded sharp blasts of alarm.

'Let's go!' cried Livia. 'They'll be on us any moment!'

They galloped through the olive wood until they reached a cave dug into the tufa, a shelter for the sheep that grazed at night among the stubble. Completely concealed from view, they watched as the fields filled with shadowy figures on horseback, their burning torches slicing through the darkness like plunging meteors. Shouts, angry orders and calls echoed in every crag and cranny, but the old comrades in arms saw nothing and heard nothing. Out of their minds with joy and still unbelieving, they embraced each other with fervour. They recognized each other in the dark without the need for sight, by their smells, by the sounds of their voices broken by emotion, by the rock hardness of their bodies, like old mastiffs returning from a midnight round up: Aurelianus Ambrosius Ventidius, Rufius Aelius Vatrenus and Cornelius Batiatus, soldiers of Rome, Romans by Roman oath.

PART TWO

13

THEY SET OFF AGAIN immediately at a gallop towards Cuma, where a little fishermen's village rose on the sea near the ruins of the once-glorious Greek city. Livia seemed to know the territory quite well and she moved in the semi-darkness with great speed and confidence. The escape of four slaves, the killing of half a dozen guards and the flooding of the *piscina mirabilis* had caused such an uproar that it was in their best interest to find a safe and out-of-the-way haven. Batiatus was so enormous that he would attract people's attention no matter where he was, so they had to find a way to get by unobserved. They decided to avoid lodging houses, taverns and public places. Livia had them take haven in a part of the dead city which was said to be the ancient lair of the Sybil of Cuma, a dark cave supposedly frequented by demons. She figured that one more black demon would only serve to stoke the popular imagination.

They stopped inside the tumbledown city walls and Livia took her companions inside the cave, actually a kind of artificial trapezium-shaped tunnel dug into the stone. They managed to light a feeble fire, and then Livia stitched up Batiatus's wound, bandaging it as well as possible. She gave him her blanket to cover himself, as the others tried to settle in that uncomfortable shelter. Aurelius gathered up a quantity of dried leaves; some he threw on the fire, obtaining more smoke than flames, while the others he spread out on the ground so they would have something to stretch out on. Livia took all the food she had out of her satchel, too little for all of them: some cheese and olives and a loaf of bread. She offered it to those exhausted men.

'It's not much, just enough to fool our stomachs for tonight. Tomorrow we'll see what we can find. We all need our rest now; it's almost dawn.'

'Rest?' said Batiatus. 'You must be joking, girl! There are too many things we have to tell each other. Do you know who we are? How much we've gone through together? Gods in heaven, I just can't believe it. This fellow says: "Hey, sack of coal, don't disappoint me with all the money I've bet on you." I turn around to spit in the son of a bitch's face, and who do I see? Aurelianus Ambrosius Ventidius in flesh and blood, right in front of me! By Hercules, I thought I was going to drop dead right then and there, and I said to myself, "What can a no-good like him be up to here? Want to bet that the bastard came all the way here just to free his good old friend?"' His voice trembled as he spoke and his eyes twinkled like a child's. '"Want to bet that he tracked me down in this disgusting hole?" But then, I think, "How did he ever find me in this shit hole, who told him I was here . . ." Gods in heaven, I still can't believe it. Punch me, I want to know if I'm dreaming.'

Vatrenus dealt him a heavy blow on the head: 'See? You're awake! Everything's all right now, black man. We made it, we made it out! We fucked them all! Can you imagine, once the public authorities got there, how many respectable people, how many devoted matrons, they found floundering in the water? Caught red handed at a clandestine gladiators' fight? If only I'd been a frog, to see their faces! Can you imagine how many people will be sneezing and coughing tomorrow in the city?'

Aurelius burst out laughing, and all the others with him, laughter that left them gasping for air, laughter as liberating as the cry of a babe who has been in fear's grip too long.

Livia watched them silently. Their male camaraderie was fascinating, a concentration of all men's best virtues: friendship, solidarity, sacrifice, enthusiasm. Not even their rough barracks talk, which she certainly wasn't used to, bothered her in the midst of their glee.

Then, suddenly, silence fell: the silence of remembrance and regret; the silence of the common memories of men who had faced the same dangers and suffered the same pain and the same toil for years, with only their friendship to comfort them, only the esteem and faith they had in each other; the silence of deep feeling and incredulous delight at finding each other again, against all possible odds, against the most adverse destiny. She could almost see the thoughts that passed through their moist eyes, under their furrowed brows; she could see their past in their callused hands, their scarred limbs, their shoulders that seemed to sag under the weight of their arms. They were thinking of the comrades who were no longer with them, those they had lost forever, of their commander, Claudianus, wounded and then slain by the fury of his enemies, deprived of the patrician honour of sleeping in the mausoleum of his ancestors.

It was Aurelius who broke that emotion-laden silence as he intercepted the curious glances of his comrades towards Livia. They must have been asking themselves who she was and how she had ended up in such a place with them.

'This is Livia Prisca,' he said. 'She comes from a village of huts on the lagoon between Ravenna and Altinum, and she's the chief here, whether you like it or not.'

'You're kidding. You're the chief here, although I could pull rank on you,' shot back Vatrenus.

'No. She saved my life and she gave me something worth fighting for. She's a woman who's a lot like a man . . . but better, in many ways. And she's the one . . . that is, she'll pay you to join us in a mission, a mission that I'll be leading. Is that clear?'

Batiatus shook his head, perplexed, but Livia interrupted, nodding towards the two men who had joined them in their escape: 'What about them? Who are they? Can we trust them?'

'We're grateful that you've let us come with you,' said one of them. 'You've saved our lives. My name is Demetrius, I'm a Greek from Heracleia and I'm a prisoner of war. I was captured by the Goths at Sirmium while I was patrolling the Danube in my boat, and then sold to Odoacer's Heruli. I was sent here to serve in the fleet because I was a sailor. I'm an excellent swordsman, that I can assure you, and no one can best me in the art of knife-throwing. This is my friend and comrade in arms Orosius. He's taken part in military campaigns all over the world, and his skin is as tough as leather.'

'They are worthy men,' added Vatrenus. 'They've always acted fairly, in all the time we've been together. They detest the barbarians as we do, and their only dream is to become free men again.'

'Do you have families?' asked Aurelius.

'I had a family,' answered Demetrius. 'A wife and two boys of fourteen and sixteen, but I've heard nothing of them for five long years. They lived in the village near our winter camp. While I was away on a reconnaissance mission down the river, the Alans set up a bridge of boats during the night. They took our people by surprise and massacred them. When I returned, I found only ash and coal and black mud, under torrential rain. And corpses. Everywhere. Were I to live a hundred years, I will never forget that scene. I turned them over one by one, so much anguish in my heart, expecting at any moment to see a beloved face . . .' His voice broke and he fell still.

'I had a wife and a daughter,' began his companion. 'My wife's name was Asteria and she was as lovely as the sun. One day, when I returned on leave from a long campaign in Mesia, I found that my city had been sacked by the Rugians. Both my wife and my daughter had been carried off. I'd heard that the tribe was still in the area, and my commander sent out native guides with a ransom request, but those savages demanded an exorbitant sum. I knew I would never be able pay them off. Then they vanished back into their immense grasslands, just as they had appeared. Since then, I've dreamt of nothing but setting out after them. But where? How? At night, before I fall asleep, I try to imagine where my wife and daughter have ended up, under what sky, and I wonder what my little girl looks like now.' He bowed his head without saying another word.

They were stories like many others he had heard, but Aurelius was moved none the less. He had never truly resigned himself to this catastrophe. He had never shared the dream of the city of God as proclaimed by Augustine of Hippona. He had never imagined cities in the sky amidst the clouds. The only city for him was Rome of the seven hills, protected by Aurelian's wall, founded on the divine Tiber. Rome, violated yet immortal, the mother of all lands and of all lands daughter, repository of the most sacred memories. He asked them: 'And now that you are free, where would you like to go?'

'We have no place to go,' replied Orosius.

'We have nothing. No one,' echoed Demetrius. 'Take us with you on this mission of yours.'

Aurelius looked at Livia, unsure. She nodded: 'They seem the right sort, and we certainly need men.'

'They may not want to stay on when they've heard what we plan to do.'

The men looked each other grimly in the face at these words.

'If you don't tell us, how will we ever know?' prompted Batiatus.

'What's all this mystery about? Out with it!' said Vatrenus.

'You can trust us. Our friends know this. We've always tried to protect each other in the fights,' insisted Demetrius and Orosius.

Aurelius exchanged a rapid glance with Livia, who nodded again.

'We want to liberate Emperor Romulus Augustus from Capri, where he is being held prisoner.'

'What did you say?' asked Vatrenus incredulously.

'What you heard.'

'By Hercules,' swore Batiatus. 'That's a big job.'

'A big job! It's pure foolishness! He'll be watched over day and night by a multitude of guards,' exclaimed Vatrenus.

'Freckle-faced pigs,' Batiatus commented again. 'I hate them.'

'Seventy in all. We've counted them,' said Livia.

'And there are five of us,' said Vatrenus, looking hard at the others.

'Six,' said Livia.

Vatrenus shrugged.

'Don't underestimate her,' warned Aurelius. 'She nearly tore the balls off a fellow bigger than you down at the port. If I hadn't stopped her, she'd have slit his throat like a goat's.'

'Not bad,' observed Orosius, giving Livia the once-over.

'Well?' asked Aurelius. 'Remember you're free men now. You can walk off and we'll still be friends. You'll buy a drink for me one day, when we meet in some brothel.'

'You'd never manage it on your own,' said Batiatus.

Vatrenus sighed: 'I get it. We've fallen from the frying pan into the fire, but at least it seems like we might have some fun getting the job done. There's not any money in it, is there? I'm stony broke and . . .'

'One thousand gold solids a head,' said Livia, 'when the mission is completed.'

'By the gods!' exclaimed Vatrenus. 'For a thousand solids I'll bring you Cerberus up from the underworld.'

'What are we waiting for?' asked Batiatus. 'Looks like we all agree, right?'

Aurelius raised his hand to ask for a bit of silence: 'My friends, the task that awaits us may prove more difficult than anything any of us has ever done. We have to find a way on to the island, free the emperor and then take him across Italy to a point on the Adriatic coast where a ship will be waiting to take him to safety. This is where we'll be paid by Livia and by those who have assigned her this mission.'

'What then?' asked Vatrenus.

'That's asking too much!' replied Aurelius. 'It was quite a feat just getting you out of that inferno! Who knows? Maybe each of us will go his own way, or the emperor will want to take us with him, or perhaps . . . Who can say? I'm dead tired and we all need to get some sleep. With the light of day we'll be able to think straight. The first thing we'll have to do is find a boat so we can get close enough to the island to study the situation, and then we'll see. We'll have to come up with a foolproof plan before we act. Who'll stand the first guard tonight?'

'The first and only, since it's almost dawn. I will,' offered Batiatus. 'I'm not tired, and besides, I'm practically invisible in the dark.'

They were weary and weak, conscious that their punishment would be atrocious were they ever tracked down, but they had taken fate back into their own hands and would never let it go again, for any reason in the world. They would rather face death.

*

The first days of their stay in Capri were almost pleasant. The colours of the island were extraordinary: the deep green of the pine forests and of the myrtle and lentiscus bushes, the bright yellow broom and the silvery grey wild olives under a turquoise sky made Romulus feel as if he had fallen into some sort of Elysium. The moon's tremulous light danced on the waves of the sea at night as they foamed white over the pebbles on the shore and around the great rocky pinnacles that towered hugely over the water. The wind brought the salty odour of the sea all the way up to the steps of the great villa, along with all the myriad fragrances of that enchanted land. This is how Romulus as a boy had imagined the island of Calypso, where Ulysses had forgotten his native Ithaca, bare and stony, for seven long years.

The breeze carried the smell of figs, of rosemary and mint, along with far-off island sounds: bleating, shepherds' calls, shrieking birds wheeling in the crimson sky at dusk. The sailboats returned to port like lambs to the fold, smoke rose in lazy spirals from the houses set low on the tranquil bay.

Ambrosinus began immediately to gather herbs and minerals, sometimes in Romulus's company, although their jailers never lost sight of them. He taught the boy the virtues of certain berries and roots, and explained the movements of the constellations in the sky. He pointed out the big and the little dippers, and the north star: 'That is the star of my land,' he recounted, 'Britannia, an island as big as all of Italy, green with forests and fields, inhabited by immense flocks of sheep and by herds of red bulls with great black horns. At its outermost reaches,' he said, 'the nights of winter last six months and the sun in summer never sets. Its light continues to illuminate the sky until midnight.'

'An island as big as Italy!' repeated Romulus. 'How is that possible?'

'It's absolutely true,' Ambrosinus assured him, reminding him of how Admiral Agricola had completely circumnavigated the island at the time of Emperor Trajan.

'But beyond . . . beyond those endless nights, what comes then, *Ambrosine*?'

'Beyond lies the outermost land above sea level. Ultima Thule, surrounded by a wall of ice two hundred cubits high, beaten day and night by freezing winds, guarded by sea serpents and monsters with fangs like daggers. No one who reached those lands has ever returned alive, except for a Greek captain from Marseilles called Pytheas. He described a huge whirlpool that swallows up the waters of the Ocean for hours and hours, then vomits them up with a frightening clamour, fraught with skeletons of boats and of sailors, spitting them so far that miles and miles of beaches are inundated.' Romulus's eyes filled with wonder, and for a moment he forgot his troubles.

During the day, they wandered around the vast courtyards and walkways overhanging the sea. When they found a place to sit in the shade of a tree, Ambrosinus would give lessons to his pupil, who listened intently. As the days passed, however, space seemed to narrow and the sky became distant and indifferent. Everything seemed frightfully unchanged and unchanging: the flight of the seagulls, the armed guards patrolling the bastions, the lizards basking under the last sun of autumn and skittering into the cracks in the walls when the sound of a step drew close.

The boy was gripped then by sudden anguish and piercing melancholy, and he would stare at the sea for hours without moving. At other times he was overcome by rage and desperation and would throw stones hard at the wall, dozens, hundreds of stones, under the bemused eyes of the barbarian guards, until he fell over, out of breath and drenched with sweat. His tutor watched him then with tenderness, but did not let himself be moved to pity. He would reprimand the boy instead, reminding him of the dignity of his forebears, the austerity of Cato, the wisdom of Seneca, the heroism of Marius, the incomparable greatness of Caesar.

One day, as he saw him breathless and exhausted over that foolish, pointless game, humiliated by the jeers of his jailers, he approached Romulus and laid a hand on his shoulder: 'No Caesar, no. Save your strength for when you shall grasp the sword of justice.'

Romulus shook his head: 'Why are you trying to fool me? That day will never come. Don't you see those men up there on the walkway? They're prisoners of this place just as we are. They will grow old in boredom and weariness until they send in others to replace them, but I'll still be here. They'll come and go, but it will always be me here, like the trees and the walls. I'll grow old without ever being young.'

A bird's feather drifted slowly from on high. Romulus grabbed it and crumpled it tight. He opened his fist, looking his tutor straight in the eyes: 'Or will you build me wings of feathers and wax, like Daedalus did for Icarus? Shall I take off from here?'

Ambrosinus lowered his head: 'If only I could, my boy. If only I could! But there is something, maybe, that I can do for you. Something I can teach you: do not allow your soul to be imprisoned in your body.' He raised his eyes to the sky: 'See that gull up there? Do you see him? Let your spirit fly with him . . . up there, on high. Take a long breath . . . again . . . another,' he placed his hands on the boy's temples, closing his eyes. 'Fly, my son, close your eyes and fly. Fly past this misery, beyond the walls of this crumbling house, over the cliffs and the forests. Fly towards the disc of the sun and bathe in its infinite light.' He lowered his voice as tears trickled slowly from the boy's closed eyes. 'Fly,' he said softly. 'No one can imprison a man's soul.' Romulus's breathing, rapid at first like that of a frightened puppy, slowed to the calm rhythm of an easy sleep.

Other times, when none of this helped, when there were no words that had meaning any more, Ambrosinus would go and sit in a corner of the courtyard and dedicate himself to writing his memories. Romulus would go off on his own, drawing lines in the sand with a stick, but then little by little he would draw nearer, observing him out of the corner of his eye, trying to imagine what his tutor was setting down in his neat, regular hand.

One day he showed up and asked: 'What are you writing?'

'My memories. You too should be thinking about writing, or reading at least. Reading helps us to forget our troubles; it liberates our spirits from the anxiety and boredom of everyday life, and puts us in contact with another world. I've asked to have books for your library, and they'll be arriving today from Naples: not only philosophy and geometry and agricultural manuals, but also beautiful stories: Heliodorus's Ethiopian tales, the pastoral love of Daphnis and Chloe, the adventures of Hercules and Teseus and the voyages of Ulysses. You'll see! Now I have some things to take care of, and then I'll prepare your dinner, so don't go off too far. I don't want to have to shout myself hoarse.'

Ambrosinus placed his book on the bench he had been sitting on, closed the inkwell and put away the quill. He walked to the ancient imperial library, once the repository of thousands and thousands of volumes from every part of the empire, in Latin and Greek, Hebrew and Syrian, Egyptian and Phoenician. Now the niches that had contained the shelves were empty as blind eye sockets, staring at nothing. Only a bust of Homer, blind as well, remained, white as a ghost in that big dark room.

Romulus wandered aimlessly around the huge courtyard, but every time he passed near Ambrosinus's book he gave it a distracted look. Abruptly he stopped and stared at it longingly. Perhaps he shouldn't read what he'd written but after all, if his tutor had left it there unguarded and without forbidding him to touch it, maybe he wouldn't mind if he had a look. He sat down and opened it. On the title page was a cross with the letters alpha and omega at the ends of the arms. A sprig of mistletoe was drawn beneath, looking like the silver pendant that Ambrosinus wore round his neck.

The evening was warm and the last swallows gathered at the centre of the sky, calling each other, as if reluctant to leave their empty nests to migrate towards warmer climes.

Romulus smiled and said softly: 'Off with you, now! You who can, fly away. You'll find me here next year in this very place. I'll stay and guard your empty nests.'

Then he turned the page and began to read.

14

I was not even born yet when the last eagles of the Roman legions left Britannia, never to return. The emperor was recalling all of his troops, and thus my land was abandoned to its destiny. Nothing happened at first. The authorities continued to govern the cities by the laws of their fathers and the magistrature of the empire, maintaining contact with the distant court of Ravenna, hoping that sooner or later the eagles would return. But one day the barbarians of the north who live beyond the Great Wall invaded our lands, sowing death, destruction and hunger with their unending raids and plundering. We asked the emperor for help, in the hope that he had not forgotten us, but there was certainly nothing he could do. A flood of barbarians was threatening the eastern confines of the empire. Ferocious, untiring horsemen with olive skin and slanted eyes had arrived from the boundless Sarmatian plain. Like spectres from the deep of night, they destroyed everything in their path. They never rested nor slept, only laying their heads on the necks of the shaggy horses. They macerated the meat that they ate by storing it under their saddles.

The high commander of the Imperial Army, a hero named Aetius, drove back the slant-eyed barbarians with the aid of other barbarians in a tremendous battle that lasted from dawn to dusk, but he could not restore our legions to us. Our envoys implored him, reminding him of the ties of blood, laws and religion that had bound us together for centuries. In the end he was deeply moved, and promised to do something. He sent us a man named Germanus who was said to be gifted with magic powers, entrusting him with the standard of the legions of Britannia: a dragon of silver with a purple tail that seemed to come to life as the wind blew. He could do no more than this, and yet the sight of that ensign was enough to stir our demoralized spirits and arouse our sleeping pride. Germanus was a valorous and charismatic leader. His flashing, feverish eyes, his cries as shrill as a hawk's, his hooked hands gripping the standard and his unwavering faith in law and civilization worked a miracle. He led his men into battle crying 'Hallelujah!' And the barbarians were repulsed. Many citizens took up arms and stood vigil over the Great Wall, restored the parts in ruin and guarded the abandoned castles. This day of sweet victory has been known ever since as the Hallelujah battle.

As the years passed, people returned to their own occupations, and only a few poorly equipped groups of badly trained troops were left to guard the High Lands from the towers of the Wall. So when the barbarians launched a surprise attack, they massacred the defenders. They picked our men off the Wall with their hooked pikes, stringing them up like fish. The attackers spread then towards the south, taking the undefended cities by storm, burning, destroying. What terror they inspired! Their faces were painted black and blue and they spared no one, not women nor children nor elders.

Another embassy was sent to Aetius, the high commander of the Imperial Army, to plead for help once again. But once again, the most he could do was to send Germanus, who had succeeded before in instilling vigour and determination in the hearts of Britannia. Germanus had long abandoned the practice of arms. He had become the bishop of a city in Gaul and was famed as a saint, but he would not shirk his duty, and he returned to our island for the second time. He reunited forces, and convinced the inhabitants of the cities to forge swords and spears and to march against the enemy. Unfortunately, the outcome of this battle was not conclusive, and Germanus himself was seriously wounded.

He was brought to the forest of Gleva and laid on the grass at the foot of an age-old oak tree, but before dying he made the army chiefs swear that they would never surrender, that they would continue to defend themselves by building a permanent, disciplined corps, modelled on the Roman legions, to protect the Great Wall. Their banner would be the dragon which had already led them to victory.

I witnessed these events directly. I was still quite young, but I had been instructed in the Druidic arts of medicine, prophecy and the study of the heavenly bodies. I had travelled in many countries and learned many important things. They called me to cure the dying hero. There was nothing I could do for him but relieve the pain of his wound, but I still remember his noble words, the flash in his eye that not even death could extinguish. When Germanus died, his body was taken to Gaul and buried at Lutetia Parisiorum where he still rests today. His tomb is venerated as a saint's and visited by many pilgrims from both Gaul and Britannia.

That corps of selected warriors was established in accordance with his wishes, commanded by the best men of Britannia, descendants of the highest Roman and Celtic nobility. It was stationed in a fort of the Great Wall near Mons Badonicus, or Mount Badon, as we call it in our Carvetian dialect.

Several years passed, and it seemed that Germanus's sacrifice had procured peace in our lands, but this was not to be. A series of very cold winters and arid summers decimated the herds of the northern barbarians, causing a great famine. Attracted by the mirage of the rich cities on the plain, they attacked a number of places along the Great Wall, putting the defenders' resistance to a severe test. I myself was at the fort of Mount Badon as their doctor and veterinarian. The commander, a man of great dignity and valour named Cornelius Paullinus, had me called. By his side was his deputy commander, Constantine, called Kustennin in the language of Carvetia, a man who held the office of consul.

Paullinus spoke with an expression of grave worry and discouragement. 'Our forces can no longer hold out against enemy attacks unless someone comes to our aid. You'll leave immediately for Ravenna to speak with the emperor, along with the dignitaries I have chosen for this mission. Make him see that we need reinforcement troops, remind him of the faith of our cities and of our people in the name of Rome. If he cannot send an army our houses will be burned, our woman raped, our children carried off in slavery. You'll hold vigil at the door of the imperial palace, day and night if necessary, refusing food and drink until he has seen you. You are the only man I know who has travelled across the seas to Gaul and Iberia. You know many languages besides

Latin and you are an expert in medicine and alchemy. I'm sure you will win over his esteem and consideration.'

I listened without ever interrupting him. I could not help but be aware of the extreme gravity of the situation and of his great trust in me, but in my heart of hearts I knew that such an expedition would be exceedingly risky and have little hope for success. Most of the provinces of the empire were in the hands of turbulent populations, the roads were fraught with danger and it would be nearly impossible to find food for myself and my companions along the way. Sizeable obstacles all, but nothing compared to the final challenge: being received by the emperor and obtaining his help.

I replied: 'Noble Paullinus, I am ready to do what you ask. I shall gladly risk my own life for the salvation of my homeland if necessary, but are you certain this is the best solution? Would it not be better to come to an agreement with noble Wortigern? He is a valorous combatant of great strength and courage and his warriors are numerous and well trained. This would not be the first time they will fight at our side against the barbarians of the north, if I remember correctly. His father was Celtic and his mother Roman, and that strengthens his ties with all the people of this land. Your deputy, Kustennin, knows him very well.'

Paullinus sighed, as if he had been expecting just this objection. 'It's what I have tried to do, but Wortigern demands too high a price: power over all of Britannia: dissolution of the citizens' assemblies, abolition of the ancient magistratures and closure of the senate's chambers wherever they may be. I fear that the remedy would be worse than the disease. The cities which have already submitted to his power suffer violent tyranny and harsh oppression. I will come to a similar decision only if I am forced to do so, only if all the other alternatives have been exhausted. What's more . . .'

He broke off as if he dared say no more, but I believed I could express his unspoken thoughts. I said: 'You are a Roman from your feet to the roots of your hair, son and grandson of Romans, perhaps the last of this race. I can understand you, even though I believe that it is impossible to stop time, to turn back the wheel of history.'

'You are wrong,' replied Paullinus. 'That's not what I was thinking,

although in my heart I have continued to dream that the eagles would return. I was thinking of the day that we brought Germanus to you, mortally wounded, from the battlefield. There in the forest of Gleva, so that you might cure his wounds . . .'

'I remember that day well,' I admitted. 'There was little I could do.'

'You did enough,' said Paullinus. 'You gave him the time to receive his last rites and absolution from a priest, and to pronounce his last words.'

'That you alone heard. He murmured them into your ear before taking his last breath.'

'And now I shall reveal them to you,' continued Paullinus. He brought a hand to his forehead as if trying to concentrate all the force of his memory and power of his spirit there. Then he said:

"Veniet adulescens a mari infero cum spatha,
pax et prosperitas cum illo.
Aquila et draco iterum volabunt
Britanniae in terra lata."'

'They seem the words of some old popular song,' I replied after having reflected on them. 'A young warrior who comes from the sea bringing peace and prosperity. That's a very common theme. Similar songs always spring up in times of war and famine.'

However, it was evident that for Cornelius Paullinus they had another meaning. He said: 'But these were the last words of a hero at the moment of his death. There must be another meaning, deeper and more important, essential to the salvation of this land and all of us. The eagle – 'aquila' – represents Rome and the dragon – 'draco' – is our ensign, the standard of the legion of Britannia. I know that everything will become clear when you have reached Ravenna and the emperor. Go, I implore you, and carry out this mission.'

So intense and inspired were his words that I accepted what he asked of me, even if those strange verses aroused no particular vision in me. Before the senate of Carvetia, meeting in a plenary session presided over by Kustennin, I swore that I would return with an army to liberate our land once and for all from the barbarian threat. I left the next day. Before going to the port with my travel companions I cast a last look at the Great Wall, at the purple-tailed dragon fluttering from the tallest tower. A figure wearing a cloak of the same colour stood on the rampart walkway: Cornelius Paullinus and his hopes vanished slowly behind me in the light mist of an autumn dawn.

We set sail with a favourable wind, headed for Gaul, where we set ashore at the end of October. The journey we embarked upon then was long and tiring, as I had predicted. One of my companions fell ill and died after falling into the icy waters of a river in Gaul, and another was lost in a blizzard as we crossed the Alps. The last two died in an ambush laid by brigands in a forest of Padusa. I was the only survivor and when I reached Ravenna I tried without success to be received by the emperor: a faint-hearted fool already in the hands of other barbarians. Of no avail were my pleas or the fasting that Paullinus had demanded of me. In the end, weary of my presence, the servants chased me away from the palace atrium with sticks.

Exhausted by the long wait and my hunger, I fell prey to desperation and left that city and its arrogant men. I wandered from village to village, asking for hospitality from the farmers and paying for their dry bread or cup of milk with my skills as a doctor and veterinarian. I practised both professions equally well, and there was no doubt that I was keener sometimes to help innocent beasts of burden than obtuse and brutal human beings.

What had happened to their noble Latin blood! The countryside was infested by bands of brigands, the farms inhabited by miserable peasants oppressed by intolerable taxes. What had once been proud cities encircled by turreted bastions along the glorious old consular roads, were now nothing more than ghosts of crumbling walls invaded by dark ivy. Emaciated beggars at the thresholds of the villas fought the dogs for food scraps, coming to blows over the stinking guts of butchered animals. There were no grape vines on the hills, nor the silvery olive trees that I had dreamt of as a boy, reading the poems of Horace and Virgil at school in Carvetia. No white oxen with crescent horns turned up the earth with their ploughs. Nor were there farmers sowing seed: only coarse, half-wild shepherds urging flocks of sheep and goats over arid pastures, and packs of pigs rooting under oak trees for acorns. Famished all, beasts and men.

We had placed our hopes in this land! Order, if one could call it that, was maintained by troops of barbarians who made up most of the imperial army, more loyal to their own chiefs than to the few remaining Roman officers. They tormented the people much more than they defended them. The empire was nothing more than a larva, an empty husk like its emperor. Those who had been the lords of the earth were now under the heel of rude, arrogant oppressors. How often would I peer into those brutalized faces, those filthy brows dripping with servile sweat, to search for the noble features of Caesar and Marius, the majestic lineaments of Cato and Gracchus! And yet, like a beam of sun may suddenly penetrate dense clouds in the midst of a tempest, sometimes, without any apparent reason, the proud valour of their ancestors would flash from their eyes, and this made me hope that all was not lost.

In the cities and villages, the religion of Christ had taken root everywhere, and the crucified God looked down upon his faithful from altars sculpted in stone and marble, but in the countryside, temples dedicated to the ancient divinities still stood, concealed and somehow protected by dense thickets. Unknown hands laid offerings before their broken, mutilated images. Sometimes flutes and drums sounded from the heart of the wood or the peaks of the mountains to call believers to conjure up the dryads from the forests, the nymphs from the streams and lakes. Then, from the fragrant musk in the deepest caves, Pan himself would appear, feral with his cloven hooves, with his enormous phallus distending from his obscene groin, witness to orgies never finished nor forgotten.

The priests of Christ announced the saviour's imminent return and His final judgement, and exhorted the people to abandon the thought of earthly cities and raise their eyes and their hopes to the City of God. And so, day by day, the love of the Roman people for their homeland was dying. The cult of their forebears vanished and their most sacred memories were left to the purely academic studies of the rhetors.

I lived this way for years, survival my only care, unmindful of the reason that had pushed me so far from my native land, certain that there as well, at the foot of the Great Wall, all had fallen into ruin, all was lost, dead my friends and companions, extinguished their hopes for liberty and dignity and civil living. How could I possibly attempt to return, with what money and what supplies, if what I was able to earn barely sufficed to ease the pangs of my hunger?

Only one desire remained, one dream: to see Rome! Despite the ferocious plundering she had suffered more than half a century before at the hands of Alaric's barbarians, Rome still stood, one of the most beautiful cities of this earth, protected more by the aegis of the Supreme Pontiff than by the violated walls of Aurelian. The Senate still met there in the ancient curia, to perpetuate a revered tradition rather then to make decisions which no longer involved their authority. So one day I set off, dressed as a Christian priest, perhaps the only figure that still instilled a bit of reverential fear in the brigands and thieves, and it was during this journey across the Apennines that my fate abruptly changed, as if Destiny had suddenly remembered me, recalling that I was still alive and perhaps could still accomplish something in that desolate land.

It was an October evening. Dusk was falling and I sought some shelter for the night, gathering up dried leaves to serve as my bed under an overhanging rock, when I thought I heard a moan coming from the forest. It seemed the cry of a nocturnal animal or the hoot of the scops owl, which sounds so much like a human voice, but I soon realized that it was the wailing of a woman. I got up and followed that sound, slipping amidst the shadows of the wood, light and invisible, as I had learned to move in the sacred wood of Gleva when I was a boy. All at once I saw, at the centre of a clearing, a camp guarded by both Roman and barbarian soldiers, all of them fitted out in the Roman manner. A fire was burning at the centre of the camp and one of the tents was illuminated. The moaning was coming from there.

I drew closer and no one stopped me, because at that moment my ancient Druidic art allowed me to make my body so insubstantial that it seemed nothing more than one of the many shadows of the night. When I spoke I was already inside the tent and they all turned towards me, astonished, as if I had materialized out of nowhere. The man before me had a powerful build and his face was framed by a dark beard which gave him the look of an ancient patrician. His pronounced jaw was tightly clenched, and his deep, dark eyes revealed the anguish that weighed on his heart. Next to him, a beautiful woman was weeping disconsolately, alongside a bed where a little boy of perhaps four or five lay, apparently lifeless.

'Who gave the order to call a priest?' asked the man, perplexed. There must have been something in my humble appearance, in my dirty, wrinkled clothing, that made me look more like a beggar than a minister of God.

'I am not a priest . . . not yet,' I replied, 'but I am an expert in the art of medicine and perhaps I can do something for that child.'

The man stared at me with fire and tears in his eyes, and said: 'This child is dead. He was our only son.'

'I don't believe that,' I answered. 'I still sense the breath of his life in this tent. Let me examine him.' The man nodded with the resignation of despair, and the woman looked up at me with a gaze full of wonder and hope.

'Leave me alone with him, and before dawn I will give him back to you,' I said, surprising myself with my own words. I couldn't understand how, in that solitary place, I could feel the ancient science of Roman knowledge and the heredity of my Druidic powers unite at the bottom of my soul in a potent concentration of raw energy and serene comprehension. Although I had lived for all those years forgetful of myself and my dignity, all at once I knew that I could put colour back into the wan cheeks of that creature, and light into the eyes that seemed dimmed under his closed lids. The signs of his poisoning were evident, but I could not see how far the process of intoxication had gone. The man hesitated, but the woman convinced him. She pulled him away by his arm, whispering into his ear. She must have thought that I couldn't hurt the child any more than the disease she believed him to be suffering from.

I opened my satchel and took stock of what remained, realizing that at least, throughout all those years, I had never let my supply of medicines run out. I had continued to collect herbs and roots when the seasons were right and to treat them in keeping with the rules of my art. I put some water to warm on the brazier and prepared a potent infusion that would force his organism to react. I heated up stones and wrapped them in clean cloths, arranging them all around his cold body. I poured the hot, nearly boiling water into a wineskin and placed it on his chest. I had to reawaken a whisper of life in that little body before

I applied the remedy. When I saw little drops of sweat forming on his cyanotic skin, I instilled the infusion in his mouth and nose and noticed a slight reaction, a nearly imperceptible contraction of his nostrils.

The world outside was immersed in silence. I could no longer hear the weeping of his mother. Perhaps that lovely, proud woman was resigned to such a terrible loss? I instilled a few more drops and saw a stronger reaction, and then a visible contraction of his stomach. I pressed down hard and the little one vomited a greenish, foul-smelling fluid that left me no doubts. I instilled more of the emetic potion; more contractions followed and then a stronger retching and still more convulsions. Then the little boy lay back as if exhausted. I undressed him and washed him and covered him with a clean blanket. He was drenched with sweat but he was breathing now and his heartbeat was picking up: a faltering rhythm that to me seemed louder and more triumphant than the roll of a drum. I examined his stomach contents and my doubts were fully confirmed. I left the tent and found his parents in front of me. They were sitting on a couple of stools in front of the campfire, and there was a powerful excitement in their eyes. They had heard their son retching; an unmistakable sign of life. Yet they had held strong to their promise and left me alone with the boy.

'He will live,' I said with studied, subdued emphasis, and I added immediately: 'He had been poisoned.'

They ran into the tent and I could hear the mother sobbing for joy as she embraced her child. I walked away from the camp, towards the guards' campfire so as not to disturb a moment of such intense emotion, but a strong voice stopped me. It was him, the father.

'Who are you?' he asked. I turned around and faced him as he stared at me as if seeing me for the first time. 'How did you get into my tent, surrounded by armed guards? How did you bring my son back to life? Are you . . . a saint or an angel from heaven? Or are you a spirit of the wood? Tell me, I beg you.'

'I am only a man, with some knowledge of medicine and natural sciences.'

'We owe you for the life of our only son, and there is no sufficient recompense for this on this earth. Ask whatever you like, and if it is in my power it will be granted.'

'A warm meal and a piece of bread for tomorrow's journey will be enough,' I answered. 'My greatest reward was seeing that child breathe again.'

'Where are you headed?' he asked me.

'Rome. To see the City and its marvels has always been the dream of my life.'

'We are going to Rome as well. Please, remain with us. You will be safer and your journey will be free of troubles. Both I and my wife ardently hope that you will wish to remain with us forever and care for our son. He will need a teacher, and who could teach him better than you, a man with so much knowledge and such miraculous skills?'

His were words that I had hoped to hear, but I told him that I would consider his offer and give him my answer in Rome. In the meantime, I would help the child to recover fully, but he, the father, would have to find the assassin, a man who hated him to the point of poisoning an innocent child.

The man seemed to be struck by a sudden awareness, and replied: 'This is my affair. The culprit will not escape me. Please accept my hospitality and my food, and rest for what remains of the night. A rest well deserved.'

He told me that his name was Orestes and that he was an officer of the Imperial Army. As we were speaking, his wife, Flavia Serena, joined us. She was so moved that she took my hand to kiss it. I withdrew it quickly and bowed to render her homage. She was the most beautiful and most noble person I had ever seen in my life. Not even the terror of losing her son had affected the harmony of her aristocratic features nor dimmed the light in her amber-coloured eyes, which had only become more intense in her trepidation and suffering. Her bearing was dignified but her gaze was as soft as a springtime dawn. Her high forehead was crowned by a braid of dark hair with violet reflections, her fingers were long and tapered, her skin diaphanous. A velvet belt accented the soft curves of her hips under her dress of light wool. At her neck she wore a silver chain from which a single black pearl hung, nesting between her immaculate breasts. I had never in all my life seen a creature of such enchanting beauty, and from the first moment I laid eyes on her I knew

I would serve her devotedly for the rest of my days, no matter what destiny had in store for us.

I bowed deeply and asked permission to retire. I was very tired, having spent all my energy in that victorious duel against death. I was accompanied to a tent and I fell exhausted on to a little cot, but I spent the hours which separated us from dawn in a sort of lethargic stupor, broken by the screams of a man being tortured. It must have been the man whom Orestes suspected of having administered the poison. The next day I did not ask nor did I care to find out who it was, as I already knew enough: the father of that boy was surely a man of great power if he had enemies so fierce that they would plot against his son's life. When we moved on, we left the tormented corpse tied to a tree trunk behind us. Before evening, the forest animals would have left nothing but the bare bones.

So I became the boy's tutor and a member of that family, spending many years in an enviable position, living in sumptuous houses, meeting important people, dedicating myself to my favourite studies and experiments in the field of the natural sciences, and nearly forgetting the mission for which I had been sent to Italy so many years before. Orestes was often away on risky military expeditions and when he returned he was usually accompanied by the barbarian chiefs who commanded the army units. Every year there were fewer Roman officers. The high aristocracy preferred to join the Christian clergy and become shepherds of souls rather than leaders of armies. This was true for Ambrose, who at the time of Emperor Theodosius had abandoned a brilliant military career to become the bishop of Milan, and for our own Germanus, of course, our leader in Britannia who had cast away his sword to take up the staff.

Orestes was of a different temperament. I learned through time that as a young man he served under Attila the Hun, distinguishing himself on the basis of his wisdom and intelligence. There was no doubt that his final objective was power.

He esteemed me greatly and he often asked my opinions, but my main task remained that of educating his son Romulus. He delegated me with his paternal duties, since he was so often completely absorbed in his climb to top military rank, until one day he obtained the title of

Patrician of the Roman people and was given command of the Imperial Army. At that point he made a decision that would profoundly influence all of our lives and somehow give birth to a new era.

Julius Nepos was the reigning emperor. He was a cowardly and incapable man but a friend of the Emperor of the East, Zeno. Orestes decided to depose him and seize the imperial purple. He told me about his decision and even asked me what I thought. I replied that his plan was pure folly: how could he imagine that his destiny would be any different from that of any of the other emperors who had succeeded one another on the throne of the Caesars? What tremendous danger would he be exposing his family to?

'This time it will be different,' he replied and refused to say more.

'But how can you be certain of the loyalty of these barbarians? All they want is money and land. As long as you can provide these, they will follow you, but when you can no longer make them rich, they'll find someone else who can, someone more powerful and more open to their demands and their boundless avidity.'

'Have you ever heard of the Nova Invicta Legion?' he asked me.

'No. The legions were abolished long ago. You know well, my lord, that military technique has undergone considerable evolution in the last hundred years.' I thought of the legion that Germanus had founded before dying at the foot of the Great Wall, a legion to guard the fort at Mount Badon. Perhaps it no longer existed.

'You're wrong,' retorted Orestes. 'The Nova Invicta is a select unit made up of Romans from Italy and the provinces. I've reorganized the legion in complete secrecy and it's been ready for action for years, at the command of an absolutely upright man of great civil and military virtue. They are advancing this way at a forced march, and they will soon make camp not far from our residence in Aemilia. But that's not the only surprise. I won't be the emperor.'

I looked at him, stunned, while a terrible thought began to worm itself into my brain: 'No?' I asked. 'Who will the emperor be then?'

'My son,' he answered. 'My son Romulus, who will also assume the title of Augustus. He will bear the names of the first king and the first emperor of Rome, and I will shield him by maintaining the high command of the Imperial Army. No one and nothing will be able to hurt him.'

I said nothing because I knew that anything I said would be useless. He had already decided and nothing would dissuade him from his plans. He didn't even seem to be aware that he was exposing his own son, my pupil, my boy, to such extreme danger.

That night I went to bed late and sat up at length with my eyes wide open, unable to sleep. Too many thoughts assailed me, not least of all the vision of those men advancing at a forced march to shield the boy emperor: legionaries of the last legion, sworn to supreme sacrifice for the destiny of the last emperor . . .

⋆

Here the story finished and Romulus raised his head, closing the book. He found Ambrosinus standing in front of him: 'Interesting reading, I suppose. I've been calling you for ages and you haven't even bothered to answer. Dinner is ready.'

'I'm sorry, *Ambrosine*! I didn't hear you. I saw that you had left this here and I thought . . .'

'There's nothing in that book that you can't read. Come now, let's go.'

Romulus put the book under his arm and followed him towards the refectory: '*Ambrosine* . . .' he said suddenly.

'Yes?'

'What does that prophecy mean?'

'That prophecy? It certainly isn't a complicated text to understand.'

'No, it's not, but . . .'

'It means:

A youth shall come from the southern sea with a sword,
bringing peace and prosperity.
The eagle and the dragon will fly again
over the great land of Britannia.

'It's a prophecy, Caesar, and like all prophecies, difficult to interpret. It speaks to the hearts of the men that God has chosen for his mysterious designs.'

'*Ambrosine* . . .' started up Romulus again.

'Yes.'

'Did you . . . love my mother?'

The old man bowed his head and nodded gravely. 'Yes, I loved her – a humble, devoted love, that I would never have dared confess even to myself, but for which I would have been ready to give my life at any instant.'

He turned to the boy and his eyes gleamed like embers in the dark when he said: 'The man who made her die will pay for it with the most atrocious death. I swear it.'

15

Ambrosinus had disappeared. For some time he'd been devoting himself to exploring the less apparent corners of the villa, especially the old quarters which were no longer in use, where his insatiable curiosity was fed by a number of disparate objects which he found exceptionally interesting: frescoes, statues, archival documents, laboratory materials and carpentry tools. He spent his time repairing old implements that had fallen into disuse ages ago, like the mill and the forge, the oven and the latrine with running water.

The barbarians considered him some kind of eccentric lunatic and snickered as he passed, making fun of him. All but one: Wulfila. He was all too aware of the old man's intelligence. He let him roam freely in the villa, but not outside the external circle of walls, unless he was subject to strict surveillance.

Romulus imagined that Ambrosinus had forgotten about the Greek lesson they were supposed to have that day; he must have found some new engrossing activity. The boy wandered down to the lower part of the villa which descended along the slope. There were very few guards down there because the wall was high and had no access from below, ending in a steep, rocky precipice. It was a cool day in late November, so clear that from the highest vantage points he could see the ruins of the Athenaion of Surrentum and farther off the cone of Mount Vesuvius, iron red against the intense blue of the sky. The only sounds to be heard were his own footsteps on the pavement and the whisper of the wind through the leafy fronds of the pines and age-old holm-oaks. A robin redbreast took flight with a slight fluttering of wings, an emerald green lizard scuttled to hide in a crack in the wall. That little universe acknowledged his passing with barely perceptible murmurs.

There had been a terrible racket coming from the soldiers' quarters all night after the arrival of a shipload of prostitutes, but Romulus did not feel tired from lack of sleep. How could he be tired when there was no activity, no plans, no prospects, no future? At that moment he did not feel particularly unhappy, nor especially happy, since there was no reason for either emotion. His soul reached out absurdly and uselessly to the world around him like a spider's web in the wind. The clean air and the tranquil breath of nature were reassuring. He hummed a little children's song that for some reason had just come into his mind.

He thought that perhaps he'd get used to his cage, after all. One can get used to anything and his fate was certainly not worse than that of many others. On the mainland there were massacres and wars and invasions and famine. He need only succeed in wiping the image of Wulfila from his mind. The thought of him was the only thing that could shake the apathy that he had fallen into and set off wild convulsions in his spirit, unleashing an anger that he could not allow himself nor sustain, a fear that was no longer justified, an oppressive sense of shame that was as troublesome as it was inevitable.

All at once he felt the strange sensation of a gust of air against his face: intense, concentrated, smelling of moss and the trickle of hidden water. He looked around but saw nothing. He was about to move when he felt the same sensation again, clear and strong, accompanied by a barely discernible hiss of the wind. He realized suddenly that it was coming from below him, from the holes of a clay grate for draining off rainwater. He glanced around surreptitiously: there was no one to be seen. He took the stylus from his pocket, knelt down and began scraping at the grate which was emitting that curious sigh. When he'd cleaned all around, he prised up one side with a stick and lifted out the grate, placing it alongside on the pavement. He took another quick look around, then stuck his head into the hole. The vision before him was astonishing, even more impressive upside down: a vast cryptoporticus adorned with frescoes and grotesques, opening up into the heart of the mountain.

One of the side walls had crumbled, forming a sort of slide that he could use to drop down on to the floor below. He entered and pulled the grate back over his head, slipping down without much difficulty. A dreamlike sight unfolded before his eyes: beams of light filtered from the drainage grate above him, revealing a long paved passageway flanked to the right and left with statues of the Roman emperors, each on a marble pedestal, their storied cuirasses and faces illuminated by the changeable light that poured in from above. The boy walked on, overcome by wonder: each pedestal reported that man's endeavours, his honorary titles, his triumphs over his enemies.

With every step he felt increasingly overwhelmed by the sheer mass of history. What a heritage he had weighing on his fragile shoulders! He strolled slowly, reading the inscriptions, repeating those names and titles under his breath: 'Flavius Constans Julianus, Restorer of Rome, Defender of the Empire. Lucius Settimius Severus, Particus Maximus, Germanicus, Particus Adiabenicus, High Pontiff. Marcus Aurelius Antoninus, Pius Felix, semper Augustus, High Pontiff, six times Tribune of the People. Titus Flavius Vespasianus, Augustus. Claudius Tiberius Drusus Caesar, Britannicus. Tiberius Nero Claudius, Germanicus, Father of the Country, High Pontiff. Augustus Caesar, son of the divine Julius, High Pontiff, seven times Consul . . .'

A light layer of dust had settled on those impressive effigies, on their thick eyebrows, on the deep wrinkles that furrowed their brows, on the draping, the weapons and the decorations, but none of them showed signs of disfigurement or mutilation. The place must be some sort of sacrarium, created in secret. By whom? Julianus, perhaps, the first of the figures, whom the Christians had condemned to infamy with the name of Apostate, inaugurating the line-up of the lords of the earth with his own frowning, melancholy image.

Now Romulus, trembling with emotion and astonishment,

found himself in front of the northern wall of the cryptoporticus. Before him was a vertical slab of green marble, decorated at the centre with a laurel crown in relief made of gilded bronze. Inside this, in capital letters, were the words: CAIVS IVLIVS CAESAR. Caius Julius Caesar! Beneath, in cursive letters, was an enigmatic expression: *quindecim caesus*, that Romulus repeated softly: 'Stricken fifteen times.' What could it mean? Caesar had been struck by thirty-eight dagger blows as everyone knew from their history books, not fifteen, and why would such a sad reminder of the Ides of March appear in a grandiose epigraph of precious marble, bronze and gold? It made no sense: an inscription that commemorated the slaughter of the greatest of all Romans.

What could that number mean? He thought of all the acrostic and enigmatic puzzles that his tutor proposed so often to sharpen his mind and keep boredom at bay. He read the letters forwards and backwards; there must be a trick of some sort, a key to interpreting that strange expression.

No sound came from outside except the monotonous chirping of the sparrows. In that empty, suspended atmosphere, the boy's mind frenetically explored any and every combination to find a solution. He realized that someone would be noticing his absence soon and that all hell would break loose in the villa. Ambrosinus himself would be in danger. His mounting anxiety honed all the powers of his intellect and his thoughts alighted like a butterfly on those words, breaking them down into a series of numbers that added up to a total of fifteen. The sum of V, V and V: the Vs of gilded bronze that appeared in the words CAIVS IVLIVS. The inscription which followed – *quindecim caesus* – had deliberately been written in cursive letters instead, where the 'u' was not equivalent to 'v' as it could be in a capital letter. That must be the key to the solution! He pressed his trembling hand in succession on the three Vs: they receded into the slab but nothing happened. He sighed resignedly and was turning to go when he suddenly had another idea: the phrase said '*quindecim*' which meant three times five, not three fives in a row. He turned back and pressed all three Vs in the words CAIVS IVLIVS at once. The three letters receded and he heard a sharp metallic click, the sound of a counterweight, the creaking of a winch and then a puff of air emanated from the sides of the slab as the huge stone revolved upon itself and opened.

Romulus grabbed the edge, pulled hard so that it turned a little on its hinges and put a stone in place so it couldn't close behind him. He took a deep breath and went in.

A sense of marvel rushed over him as soon as his eyes became used to the dusky light: before him was a magnificent statue, sculpted using different coloured marbles that imitated natural tones. It carried real metallic weapons, finely embossed.

Romulus slowly ran his eyes over the statue, exploring every detail, from the knotted footwear rising up his muscled calves to the storied cuirass with images of gorgons and sea monsters with scaly tails. His face was austere, his nose aquiline, his eyes flashing with the fierce pride of the *dictator perpetuus*. Julius Caesar himself! A strange light seemed to flutter over the surface, like the reflection of invisible waves, and he realized that a shifting blue light was illuminating the statue from below, from a carved marble well-head that he had taken for an altar at first. Romulus leaned over the edge; all he could see at the bottom was a light blue glimmer. He dropped a stone and listened for long seconds before he heard the splash of the stone being swallowed up into water. The drop must be tremendous!

He backed away and walked around the statue, examining it with greater attention. He had never seen such realism in any statue of bronze or marble. The belt bearing the sheathed sword seemed real. He climbed up on to one of the capitals and reached out a shaky hand until he could grasp the hilt, trying to avoid the withering stare of the dictator. He pulled. The sword docilely followed his hand and began to emerge from the sheath that contained it. He'd never seen such a blade before! Sharp as a razor, shiny as glass and dark as night. There were letters carved into it, but he couldn't quite make them out. He held it tight with both hands at a palm's width from his face and he quivered at the sight like a leaf in the wind. This was the sword that had subjugated Gauls and Germans, Egyptians and Syrians, Numidians and Iberians. The sword of Julius Caesar!

His heart beat wildly and he thought again of Ambrosinus, who must be terribly worried at not finding him anywhere. Wulfila would be enraged. He considered putting the sword back in its place but a force greater than his will stopped him. He would not, and could not, separate himself from it.

He took off his cloak and wrapped it around the sword then retraced his steps and moved the slab back into place. He shot a last glance at the stern dictator before he disappeared from sight and whispered: 'I'll only keep it a little while. Don't worry, I'll bring it back . . .'

It took some doing to get back up out of the hole, but he managed, looking all around and waiting for the moment in which no one could see him. He slipped behind a row of bushes and scurried between a double line of clothing hung out to dry until he succeeded in reaching his room. He hid the bundle under his bed. Outside, the entire villa resounded with cries and shouts and spreading uproar as the guards could not seem to find him. He went down to the ground floor and walked through the stables, plastering some of the chaff on to himself before he came out into the open. One of the barbarians noticed him immediately and shouted: 'He's here! I've found him!' He grabbed the boy brutally by one arm and dragged him towards the guards' house. Romulus recognized the moaning coming from within and his heart leaped in his chest: Ambrosinus was paying dearly for the temporary disappearance of his pupil.

'Let him go!' he shouted, wriggling away from his warder and hurrying inside. 'Let him go immediately, you bastards!' Ambrosinus was immobilized on a stool with his hands tied behind his back. He was bleeding profusely from his nose and mouth and his left cheek was swollen. Romulus ran towards him and hugged him tightly: 'Forgive me, forgive me, *Ambrosine*!' he cried. 'I didn't want . . .'

'It's nothing, my boy, nothing at all,' he replied. 'The important thing is that you're back. I was worried about you.'

Wulfila grabbed him by the shoulder and yanked him backwards, sending him sprawling: 'Where were you?' he screamed.

'I was in the stables. I fell asleep on the straw,' replied Romulus, leaping back on his feet and confronting him bravely.

'You're lying!' shouted Wulfila, dealing him a backhanded blow that hurled him violently against the wall. 'We looked everywhere!'

Romulus wiped away the blood dripping from his nose and approached him again with a courage that Ambrosinus could barely believe. 'You didn't look well enough,' he retorted. 'Can't you see I still have chaff on my clothes?' Wulfila raised his hand to slap him again but Romulus stared at him unperturbed, saying: 'If you dare touch my tutor again, I'll slit your throat like a pig. I swear I will.'

Wulfila burst into noisy laughter. 'With what?' he sneered. 'Get out of my sight now and thank your God that I'm in a good mood today. Get out of here now, you and that old cockroach!'

Romulus untied Ambrosinus's bonds and helped him to get up. The tutor saw something in the eyes of his disciple, a fierceness and pride, that he had never seen before, and was greatly struck by this unexpected miracle. Romulus held him up lovingly, leading him towards his quarters amidst the laughter and jeers of the barbarians, but their euphoric and almost frenetic rejoicing revealed just how terrified they had been a few moments before. A boy of just thirteen had eluded the surveillance of seventy of the best warriors of the Imperial Army for more than an hour, throwing them all into utter panic.

*

'Where were you?' asked Ambrosinus as soon as they were alone in their apartments.

Romulus took a damp cloth and began to clean his face. 'Somewhere secret.'

'What? There are no secret places in this villa.'

'There's a cryptoporticus under the pavement of the lower courtyard and I . . . fell in,' he fibbed.

'You aren't any good at telling lies. Tell me the truth.'

'Well, I went in on my own, by moving away a drainage grate. I could feel a puff of air coming up so I prised it out and dropped myself down.'

'And just what did you find down there? I hope it was worth all the knocks I suffered for your sake.'

'Before I answer I have to ask you a question.'

'Let's hear.'

'What do you know about the sword of Julius Caesar?'

'Strange question, my boy. Let me think . . . ah, yes, when Caesar died, there was a long period of civil wars, with Octavianus and Mark Antony on one side, and Brutus and Cassius on the other. You'll remember that they were the ones who had conspired against Caesar on the Ides of March and had had him murdered. As you know well, the final battle was in Philippi, in Greece, where Brutus and Cassius were defeated and killed. That left Octavianus and Mark Antony, who shared power over imperial Rome for several years – Octavianus in the West and Mark Antony in the East – but their relationship soon deteriorated, because Antony had repudiated Octavianus' sister to marry Cleopatra, the fascinating queen of Egypt. Antony and Cleopatra were defeated in a great naval battle at Actium, and fled to Egypt where they committed suicide, first one and then the other. Octavianus remained the sole lord of the earth and accepted the title of Augustus from the Senate. At that point, he had the Temple of Mars the Avenger built in the Roman forum and there he placed the sword of Julius Caesar. In later centuries, however, when the barbarians began to threaten Rome at close range, the sword was taken from the temple and hidden. I think it was Valerianus or Gallienus, or perhaps some other emperor. I even heard that Constantine had taken it away to Constantinople, his new capital. They say that at some point the sword was replaced with a copy, but no one knows where the original ended up.'

Romulus gave him an enigmatic yet triumphant look and said: 'You'll know now.' He went to the window and door to make sure that no one was around, then, under the curious gaze of his tutor, bent under the bed and pulled out the bundle he had hidden there.

'Look!' he said, and bared the gleaming sword. Ambrosinus was speechless in amazement. Romulus held out the blade on his open hands and the polished steel shone in the semi-darkness. The golden hilt was exquisitely carved in the shape of an eagle's head with topaz eyes.

'It's the sword of Julius Caesar,' said Romulus. 'Look at this inscription: *"Caii Iulii Caesaris ensis ca . . ."'* he said, starting to read out the letters that formed it.

'Oh Great God,' Ambrosinus interrupted him, stretching his trembling fingers towards the sword. 'Oh, Great God. The Calibian sword of Julius Caesar! I had always thought it had been lost for centuries. How did you find it?'

'It was on his statue, inside its sheath, in a hidden place. One day, when their surveillance becomes more lax again, I'll take you there and you can see it for yourself. You won't believe your eyes. But what was that word you said before? What's a Calibian sword?'

'It means "forged by the Calibians," a people of Anatolia who were famous for their ability to produce invincible steel. They say that when Caesar won the Pontic war at Zela . . .'

'When he said "Veni, vidi, vici"?'

'Exactly. Well, they say that a forge master whose life he had saved built a sword for him using a block of siderite, iron fallen from the sky. This meteor, found on a glacier on Mount Ararat, was tempered by fire, hammered incessantly for three days and three nights, and hardened in the blood of a lion.'

'Is that possible?'

'More than possible,' replied Ambrosinus. 'Certain. We'll know right away if you've found the strongest sword in the world. Come on, take it in fist!'

Romulus obeyed.

'Now strike that candelabrum, with all your might.'

Romulus delivered the blow: the sword whirled through the air with a sharp whistle but missed its target by a hair's breadth. The boy shrugged and prepared to try again, but Ambrosinus's hand held him back.

'I'll get it this time, you'll see,' said Romulus. 'Watch . . .' but he was stopped by his tutor's rapt gaze.

'What is it, *Ambrosine*? Why are you looking at me like that?'

The swing that had missed the candelabrum had slashed a cobweb hanging in the corner of the room neatly in two, leaving only the top half for the spider that had woven it. The cut was so clean and so perfect that they were awestruck.

Ambrosinus walked towards it and whispered incredulously: 'Look, my son, look! No sword in the world is capable of this.'

He watched spellbound as the spider abandoned his halved trap, dangled for an instant in the golden dust of a ray of sun penetrating from a crack in the shutter, then disappeared into the darkness. He turned to look at Romulus. The boy's eyes glittered with the same light of fierce pride as when he had dared to face up Wulfila in the guardhouse: a light he'd never seen before, the same sharp, metallic reflection that gleamed on the edge of that blade, in the golden eyes of the eagle. And the ancient verses poured from his lips like a prayer: '*Veniet adulescens a mari infero cum spatha* . . .'

'What did you say, *Ambrosine*?' Romulus asked, wrapping the sword back up in the blanket.

'Nothing, nothing,' replied his tutor. 'Only that I'm happy. Happy, my boy.'

'Why? Because I've found this sword?'

'Because the time has come for us to leave this place, and no one will be able to stop us.'

Romulus said nothing. He put away the bundle and left, closing the door behind him. Ambrosinus fell on to his knees on the floor and gripped the twig of mistletoe which hung from his neck. He prayed, from the depths of his heart, that the words he had just pronounced might come true.

16

Romulus was sitting on a wooden bench, poking at an ant hill with a little stick. The minuscule community, already settled in for the winter, were panic stricken, the ants running every which way to try to save the queen's eggs. Ambrosinus was walking by at that moment and he stopped: 'How is my little Caesar?'

'Not well. And don't call me that. I'm nothing.'

'And you're letting your frustration out on those poor innocent creatures? In proportion you've caused a tragedy no less awesome than the fall of Troy or the great fire of Rome in Nero's time.'

Romulus tossed away his stick in a temper: 'I want my father, I want my mother. I don't want to be alone, and a prisoner. Why does fate have to be so cruel?'

'Do you believe in God?'

'I don't know.'

'You should. No one is closer to God than the emperor. You are his representative on earth.'

'I don't remember an emperor who lived more than a year after taking the throne. Perhaps God should choose more long-lasting representatives on this earth, wouldn't you say?'

'He shall, and his power will mark his chosen one in an unequivocal way. Now stop wasting your time with the ants and go back to the library to study. You'll have to tell me about the first two books of the *Aeneid* today.'

Romulus shrugged: 'Stupid old stories.'

'That's not true. Virgil tells us the tale of the hero Aeneas and his son Julus, a boy just like you who became the founder of the greatest nation of all times. They were refugees, in desperate conditions, and yet they found the courage and the will to build a new destiny for themselves and their people.'

'Anything's possible in mythology, but the past is the past and it certainly doesn't touch me now.'

'Really? Then why are you keeping that sword under your bed? Isn't that a relic from a stupid old age?' He glanced at the sundial at the centre of the courtyard and seemed suddenly to remember something. He turned his back to the boy without another word and disappeared into the shadows of the portico. A few moments later Romulus saw him going up a stair that led to the parapet of the wall facing the sea. He stood there, straight and still, while the wind ruffled his long grey hair.

Romulus got up, but before directing himself towards the library he shot a last glance at Ambrosinus, who now seemed intent on one of his experiments. He was looking out over the sea and writing with his stylus on his inseparable tablet. Perhaps he was studying the movement of the waves, or the migration of the birds, or the smoke that rose increasingly from the mouth of Vesuvius, accompanied by a threatening rumble.

He shook his head and walked towards the library door, but just then Ambrosinus turned and waved him over. Romulus obeyed and ran towards his tutor, who was wordlessly pointing at a spot in the middle of the sea. Directly in front of them, still small because of the distance, was a fishermen's boat, a nutshell on the blue expanse.

'Now I'll show you an interesting game,' said Ambrosinus. He took a shiny bronze mirror from the folds of his robe and directed it at the sun, projecting a small flittering light alongside the boat, and then on the bow and then on the sail, with amazing precision.

Then Ambrosinus started to move his wrist with a series of quick, studied movements, making the little dot of light appear and disappear intermittently on the boat's deck.

'What are you doing?' asked Romulus in surprise. 'Can I try?'

'Not just yet. I'm speaking with those men on the boat using light signals. It's a system called *notae tironianae*. It was invented by one of Cicero's servants named Tiro, five centuries ago. At first, it was just a system for taking down dictation quickly, but it later became a code of communication for the army.'

He hadn't even finished his explanation when a similar signal was returned by the boat.

'What are they saying?'

Ambrosinus answered him with eyes full of emotion: 'They're saying: "We're coming to get you. The Nones of December." Which means . . . in exactly three days. I told you we wouldn't be abandoned!'

'You're not teasing me?' asked Romulus incredulously.

Ambrosinus hugged him: 'It's true!' he replied with a tremulous voice. 'It's true, at last.'

Romulus was trying hard to control his emotions. He did not want to let his hopes be crushed again. He asked only: 'How long have you been doing this?'

'A couple of weeks. We had many things to discuss.'

'Who started first?'

'They did. They got a message to me through one of the servants who goes down to the port to do the shopping in the morning, so I was ready with my mirror well polished. It was nice to speak to someone from the outside world for a change.'

'And you never told me anything . . .'

Shocked, Romulus looked first at his tutor, who winked at him with a smile, and then back at that little boat so far away. Their conversation was soon struck up again, breaking off when the sound of footsteps indicated that the guards were making their rounds. Ambrosinus took him by the hand as they descended the stairs and headed towards the library.

'I didn't want to raise your hopes until I was sure, but now I'm convinced that they can succeed. There's just a handful of them, but they have a very powerful weapon . . .'

'What weapon?'

'Faith, my boy. The faith that moves mountains. Not faith in God, they're not used to counting on him. They have faith in man, despite the darkness of our age, despite the collapse of all our ideals and our certainties. Let's go and study now. I can teach you the *notae tironianae* if you like.'

Romulus looked up at him admiringly: 'Is there anything you don't know, *Ambrosine*?'

His tutor's face became suddenly thoughtful: 'Many things,' he answered, 'many of the most important things in life. I've never had a child, for example, a home, a family . . . the love of a woman.' He glanced affectionately at his young charge and the shadow of regret passed through his eyes.

*

The boat continued on its route, rounding the northern tip of the island.

'Are you sure you got that straight?' asked Batiatus.

'Of course. It's not the first time we've exchanged messages,' replied Aurelius.

'There's the eastern promontory, and that's the north cliff,' observed Vatrenus. 'By Hercules, it's as straight as a wall – and you say we're going to scale the face of it, take away the boy against the wishes of seventy ferocious guards, drop back down to the sea, hop in the boat and take off *insalutato hospite*?'

'More or less,' replied Aurelius.

Livia slackened the sheet, easing off the sail, and the boat came to a stop, drifting lightly on the waves. The barren rock jutted out directly above them, topped by the wall of the villa.

'This is the only point of access for us,' continued Aurelius. 'Precisely because no one would consider it possible to get up from this side. We've seen that it's only patrolled twice: once during the first guard shift and again during the third, just before dawn. So we have nearly three hours to complete our mission.' He overturned an hourglass filled with water and pointed at the various levels marked on the glass: 'An hour to climb up, half an hour to rescue the boy, half an hour to climb back down and the last hour or so to return to the coast, where the horses will be waiting for us. Batiatus will remain at the base to guard the boat and man the ropes while the rest of us go up. Livia will be waiting for us on the upper walkway of the villa's north wall.'

'How's she going to do that?' asked Vatrenus.

Aurelius exchanged a look with Livia: 'Using the oldest trick in the world. The Trojan horse.'

Batiatus examined the rock face with his eyes, foot by foot, up to the top wall, and sighed: 'What a lucky man I am to stay put on the ground! I wouldn't want to be in your shoes.'

'It's not all that terrible,' protested Livia. 'It's already been done by one man alone who made it to the top climbing bare-handed.'

'I can't believe that,' retorted Batiatus.

'Well, it's true. At the time of Tiberius, a fisherman had caught an enormous lobster that he wanted to give to the emperor as a gift. Since they wouldn't let him in the front gate, he climbed straight up from the sea.'

'Great Hercules!' exclaimed Vatrenus. 'And how did it turn out?'

Livia cracked a half smile: 'I'll tell you when our mission has been accomplished. I say we go back now, before the wind changes.' She shortened the sheet as Demetrius manned the boom, setting the sail to take advantage of the wind. The boat turned in a wide curve, pointing its bow towards the mainland. Aurelius looked up at the bastions of the villa, where he distinctly saw a spectral figure appear: a gigantic warrior wrapped in a black cloak swelling in the breeze. Wulfila.

*

Three days later towards nightfall, a large cargo ship entered the little port of Capri and the captain called out to the dockers, throwing them out a line. The helmsman tossed another rope from the stern and the boat drew up. The dockers lowered a gangplank and the stevedores began to unload the smaller packages: bags of wheat and flour, beans and chickpeas, jars of wine, vinegar and concentrated must. Then they towed a lift up alongside for the heavier loads: six huge earthenware doliums weighing two thousand cotili each, three full of olive oil and three of drinking water for the villa garrison.

Livia, crouching at the stern amidst the bags, made sure that no one was watching and approached one of the doliums. She took off her cloak and lifted the lid of the first which was full of water. She threw in a coil of rope and then lowered herself in, pulling the lid back over her head. A little water splashed out, but the crew were all busy with unloading and no one noticed. One after another the enormous containers were lifted and placed on a cart drawn by two pairs of oxen. When the cart was fully loaded, the driver snapped his whip and shouted at the beasts, and the cart started up along the steep, narrow road that led towards the villa.

By the time it arrived, the lower part of the island was already in shadow, while the last reflections of the setting sun still reddened the cirrus clouds in the sky and the rooftops of the old villa. The gate was thrown open and the cart entered the lower courtyard with a great clattering of its steel wheels on the cobblestones. Geese and chickens began to squawk and scatter and the dogs set to barking until a group of servants and porters came out to unload its cargo.

The head of the servants, an old Neapolitan with a wizened face, called out to his men who had already prepared the hoist on the upper loggia. They used a winch to lower the platform until it was level with the floor of the cart. The first of the doliums was turned on its side, rolled over to the platform and secured with ropes and wedges. The head servant cupped his hands around the side of his mouth and yelled: 'Heave ho!'

The servants began to pull the winch handles and the platform pulled free, squeaking and groaning. It swung back and forth precariously, slowly making its way up towards the upper loggia.

*

On the other side of the island, Batiatus jumped to the ground at the base of the cliff and pulled the boat into the shelter of a little beach circled by sharp rocks. The weather was changing: gusts of cold wind rippled the waves on the sea, raising puffs of foam. A front of black clouds advanced from the west, pierced by the intermittent flash of lightning. The rumble of thunder mixed with the deep roar of Mount Vesuvius off in the distance.

'All we needed was a storm,' complained Vatrenus, unloading two coils of rope from the boat.

'All the better for us,' observed Aurelius. 'The guards will stay holed up inside and we'll be freer to move. Let's get started, men.'

Batiatus secured the stern line to a boulder and signalled to Demetrius to pay out the anchor from the bow. Then they all leapt ashore. They wore corselets of reinforced leather or metallic mail over their tunics, close-fitting trousers, a sword and dagger at their belts and iron helmets. Aurelius walked to the base of the cliff and took a deep breath as he always did when he was about to face the enemy. From below, the first part of the rock face seemed to have a bit of an incline that might not make it too arduous to climb.

'Two of us have to go up to that ridge, there where the colour of the rock gets lighter,' he said. 'I'll carry the rope that I've threaded with pegs; we'll be able to use it as a ladder. You, Vatrenus will carry the sack with the stakes and the hammer. Livia will be throwing us down the rope that will help us up the second gradient, the steeper of the two. If she's not there, we'll free climb. If that fisherman could do it, so can we.' He turned to Batiatus. 'You'll have to hold the bottom end of the rope taut when you see us ready to come down, so that it won't swing in the wind. We don't want the boy to become frightened or to be thrown off-balance and fall, especially if it starts to rain and the ropes become slippery. Let's move while there's still a bit of light.'

Vatrenus grabbed his arm: 'Are you sure your shoulder will hold out? Maybe Demetrius should go first; he's lighter than you are.'

'No, I'm going first. My shoulder is fine, don't worry about me.'

'You're a stubborn bastard and if we were still at camp, I'd show you who's in command, but here you decide. All right, men, let's go.'

Aurelius put the roll of rope over his shoulder and started to climb. Vatrenus made his way up directly behind him, carrying the heavy leather sack that held the hammer and tent stakes that they would use to secure Aurelius's rope as soon as they reached the ledge.

*

In the villa's lower courtyard, they were hoisting the fifth of the big doliums when a sudden gust of wind made the platform sway. A second gust augmented the swing so that the enormous jar, already halfway between the courtyard pavement and the upper loggia, tore the fragile straps that were holding it and crashed to the ground. It shattered at impact with the pavement, spraying shards of clay over a huge area, and depositing a large pool of oil. Several of the men were injured and others, completely drenched in oil from head to toe, staggered around unsteadily. The head servant swore and kicked them as he yelled: 'It had to be the oil jar, didn't it, you damned idiots! I'll make you pay for this, you can be sure I'll make you pay!'

Livia peeked from under the lid of her jar and ducked down quickly as she realized that the platform had been lowered again and they were securing the lid and tilting her dolium to load it up. She held her breath until the water level inside stabilized, then put a reed in her mouth to breathe. As the platform was being raised, the squeaking of the entire structure increased as it swung back and forth in the intensifying wind. From inside the jar, the whistle of the wind sounded like a muffled moaning. Livia could feel her heart beating faster and faster in the dark of that confined liquid prison, that stone womb. She was knocked around with every swing of the jar, confusing her orientation and balance.

Beyond her powers of endurance, Livia was about to drive her sword through the wall of the jar, despite the terrible risk, when she sensed that the loading platform had settled on to a firm surface. She forced herself to hold her breath as the servants rolled the dolium across the floor and her air supply was cut off entirely. They finally set the big jar upright, presumably next to the others. She lifted her head above the surface of the water and took a deep breath, blowing liquid out of her nose. She waited until she could no longer hear any footsteps, then extracted her dagger and stuck it into the slit between the neck of the jar and the lid, running it along the edge until she found the securing rope and cut through it. She was exhausted and her limbs were stiff and nearly paralysed by the cold.

*

A short distance away, Ambrosinus and Romulus were in the imperial apartments, preparing for escape. They wore comfortable clothing and felt shoes to allow them to move rapidly in complete silence. The old man gathered up everything that would fit in his satchel: all his powders, herbs and amulets. Then he added the *Aeneid*.

'That's useless weight!' protested Romulus.

'On the contrary. It is the most precious thing I have in here, my son,' replied Ambrosinus. 'When we flee and leave everything behind us, the only treasure that we can take with us is our memory. The memory of our origins, of our roots, the stories of our ancestors. Only memory can allow us to be reborn. It doesn't matter where, it doesn't matter when. If we conserve the memory of our past greatness and the reasons we've lost it, we will rise again.'

'But you come from Britannia, *Ambrosine*. You are a Celt.'

'That's true, but at a time so terrible when everything is collapsing and dissolving, in which the only civilization of this world has been struck to the quick, we cannot say that we are not Romans. Even those of us who come from the most remote periphery of the empire, those of us who were abandoned, long ago, to our destiny. But you, Caesar, are you bringing nothing with you?'

Romulus took the sword out from under the bed. He had wrapped and tied it carefully with some string, adding a strap so he could carry it over his shoulder.

'I'm taking this,' he said.

*

Aurelius found himself at about thirty feet from the craggy ridge that cut the rock face in two, when all of a sudden lightning lit up the cliff bright as day, followed by the crack of thunder. A drenching rain began, the footholds became slippery, and they could barely see for the water dripping down their faces. With every passing instant the coil of rope that Aurelius wore over his shoulder became heavier, soaked through and through. Vatrenus could see him struggling under his load and tried to get as close as possible. He found a foothold and nailed a stake into the rock as high up as he could reach. Aurelius managed to draw closer and set his foot down on the stake, hoisting himself up until he could clutch at a rock spike emerging from the mountain on his right. From that point on, the slope was more accentuated and allowed them to advance with greater confidence up to the ledge underlying the sheer rock wall. It was a kind of calcareous embankment covered by debris which had fallen from above over the millennia. Aurelius dropped the rope and leaned back to help his companion up as well.

Vatrenus took the mallet from his sack and nailed two stakes into the rock. He tied the length of rope to them and let it roll down to their landing spot. Batiatus grabbed it and energetically yanked on it to make sure it was secure.

'It's holding,' commented Vatrenus, satisfied.

Pulled tight, with the thirty or so pegs that Aurelius had threaded through the rope about three feet apart all the way down, the rope nearly looked like a ladder.

'The boy will make it down for sure,' said Aurelius.

'What about the old man?' asked Vatrenus.

'Him, too. He's swifter than you'd think.' He looked up, trying the shield his eyes from the downpour: 'I don't see Livia yet, damn it. What shall we do? I'm not waiting much longer; I'll go up alone.'

'You're crazy. You'll never make it. Not in these conditions.'

'You're wrong. I'll use the stakes. Pass me the bag.'

Vatrenus looked at him unbelievingly, but just then a handful of little stones hit them from above. Aurelius looked up again and saw a small figure standing on the villa walls, waving.

'Livia!' he exclaimed. 'Finally.'

The girl threw the rope but the bottom end swung free about ten feet above Aurelius's head.

'No! It's too short!' cursed Vatrenus.

'It doesn't matter. I'll climb up on your shoulders and try to grab it. Once I'm up, you nail in the stakes one by one, up to the point where the rope ends, so we can get them down without too much trouble. All right, let's try it.'

Vatrenus bent over, fuming. Aurelius stood on his shoulders and his friend pushed him up as high as he could. Then he climbed, skinning his hands, his arms, his knees, leaving bits of flesh on the sharp outcroppings, until he managed to grasp the bottom end of the rope. Pulling himself up required enormous effort. The wind kept getting stronger and stronger, swinging the rope to the left and right, smashing him up against the bare rock, as his cries of pain became lost in the roar of the storm. In the distance, sinister blood-red reflections flashed from the mouth of Vesuvius. The cord was soaking wet and very slippery, and he was often dragged down by his own weight, so that he lost in an instant ground that had taken him great efforts to gain, but he started back up again each time, stubbornly, gritting his teeth, ignoring the fatigue and pain that tormented every muscle and every joint. The sharp pangs of his old head wound stabbed into his brain.

Livia followed his every movement with spasmodic tension. When Aurelius was finally close enough, she leaned her whole upper body over the parapet and grabbed his arms, pulling with all her might. With a final shot of energy, Aurelius clambered over the parapet and held her tight in a joyous embrace under the drenching rain. She broke away: 'Hurry! We have to help Vatrenus and the others.'

Below, Demetrius and Orosius had reached the ledge by climbing up along the rope ladder. Using the stakes that Vatrenus had driven into the rock as footholds, they arrived at the lower end of the rope that Livia had thrown down. One by one, they tied it to their waists and scrambled up rapidly, pulled by their comrades from above. Vatrenus went up last.

'I told you we'd make it!' exclaimed Livia triumphantly. 'Now we've got to find the boy before the guards make their rounds.'

17

The rampart walkway was deserted and the pavement, with its large slabs of schist, shone like a mirror in the sudden flashes of lightning. The doliums that had been hoisted up earlier were against the wall and Livia grimaced, remembering her recent experience in one of their bellies.

'There's a platform behind those jars with a goods elevator,' she said. 'We could have Orosius and Demetrius lower us with a winch to the courtyard and reach the library from there. That's where they're waiting for us, right?'

'You're right, but we would make an easy target if they saw us swaying on the lift,' objected Aurelius. 'Better to go from the inside. It can't be too difficult to get to the courtyard, and there will be a light on in the library to guide us to them.' He turned to Orosius: 'You remain here on guard, to keep our escape route open. Count slowly to one hundred ten times after we've gone: if we're not back by then, go to where Batiatus is waiting and put out to sea. If we can we'll join you on the mainland within two days' time. Otherwise, it will mean that our mission ended badly, and you and Batiatus will be free to go wherever you like.'

'I'm sure you'll return safe and sound,' replied Orosius. 'Good luck.'

Aurelius gave him a half smile, then waved his companions over. They started down the stone stair that led to the lower level, Aurelius first with his sword in hand, then Livia, Vatrenus and Demetrius last.

The stairwell was completely dark, although occasional lightning streamed through the narrow loopholes on high. As they made their way down, they began to notice a slight luminescence radiating on to the walls and tufa steps. Aurelius gestured to the others to proceed with caution as they advanced towards the light. The steps ended in a corridor lit by a few oil lamps hanging from the wall at the door to each room.

Aurelius beckoned them on, whispering: 'There's a hall here, lined with doors that I would guess are bedrooms. When I give you the signal, cross the hall as quickly as you can. We should be able to reach the second flight of stairs that will lead us downstairs, to the ground level. Come on now, there's not a soul to be seen.'

'Go on, we'll be behind you,' said Vatrenus, but as soon as Aurelius moved, a door opened on his left and a barbarian warrior came out with a half-naked woman. Aurelius leapt at him with his sword and ran him through from side to side before he realized what was happening. The girl started to scream, but Livia was already behind her, covering her mouth with her hand. 'Quiet!' she hissed. 'We don't want to hurt you, but if you make a sound I'll cut your throat. Understand?' The girl nodded convulsively. Demetrius and Vatrenus swiftly bound her wrists and ankles and gagged her, dragging her into a dark corner.

*

Downstairs, in the old triclinium, Wulfila was just finishing his dinner. 'Did you hear something?' he asked his lieutenant, one of the Skyrians who had fought under Mledo.

'What?'

'Shouting.'

'The men are upstairs having a good time with the latest shipload of whores from Naples. Nothing to worry about.'

'No, that was no cry of pleasure,' he insisted, getting to his feet and taking up his sword.

'So what? You know that some of the men like to get their thrills that way. What I'm worried about is that these trollops are going to wear out our brave young warriors. All they think about is fucking lately.'

The words were not out of his mouth when they heard another cry, of rage and pain this time, suffocated in a death rattle.

'Damnation!' swore Wulfila, reaching the window that let on to the courtyard. There was only one light to be seen, inside the library, but he could make out a confused scuffling of shadows, a glittering of blades in the dark and then more screams and cries of agony.

'We're being attacked. Sound the alarm, fast!'

The officer called a guard who blew into the war horn, again and again, until another horn answered and yet another, and the entire villa resounded with that tremendous noise. A flash of lightning lit up the great courtyard and Wulfila recognized Aurelius, who was tussling with one of his men who had tried to bar his passage. There seemed to be three more men with him, shielding the old man and the boy.

'No!' he howled. 'Him again!'

He raced into the corridor with his sword in hand shouting like a mad man: 'I want him alive! Bring him to me alive!'

Aurelius realized they would be upon them in a matter of moments. He led his comrades towards the flight of stairs, as other warriors burst forth, brandishing lit torches. They reached the upstairs corridor but found it blocked by a number of armed guards. Livia attacked from the left and Vatrenus and Demetrius from the right, trying to draw them away from the stairs so that Aurelius could clear a passage to the walkway above.

Ambrosinus was flat against the wall, holding Romulus tight as the boy tried to wriggle away so he could jump into the fray. The old man was consumed by utter distress: their escape was already doomed, before it had even got underway. Aurelius delivered a great downward blow but his adversary eluded him and the Roman's sword shattered into pieces against the pillar of the stair. Romulus did not hesitate an instant. As Aurelius drew back, defending himself as best he could with his dagger, the boy shouted: 'Try this one!' and tossed him his sword.

The fabulous weapon sailed towards Aurelius, flashing like a lightning bolt in the night, and his fist rose to seize it. He wielded it solidly in hand now, with all its inexorable force.

Nothing could resist that blade. Cascades of sparks sprayed out on impact with shields and axes. It cut through helmets and penetrated skulls as if slicing through air. When it hit the pillar again, myriad incandescent splinters shot through the air accompanied by an acute, deafening clangour. The horrified survivors were mowed down one by one as Livia pulled Romulus and Ambrosinus up the stairs, now free from any obstacles. Aurelius stayed behind for a moment to cover their retreat; as he stood in the middle of a mass of lifeless bodies, the splendid, bloodied weapon in his fist, he saw Wulfila. There was no more than a swift exchange of glances between the two warriors and then Aurelius vanished behind his comrades.

Before their pursuers could catch up with them, they closed and bolted the walkway door behind them. Wulfila, an instant too late, lunged at the massive ironclad door, raining punches and howling in impotent rage. He shouted: 'Quickly, to the east ramp! There's no way out from there!' He ran down the stairs, meeting up with another group led by his lieutenant.

'You go down the outside stairs to the storehouses, quickly. We'll smoke them out between two fires!' he ordered. They raced off, disappearing at the end of the corridor.

On the upper walkway, Aurelius and his men were running towards the parapet where Orosius was anxiously awaiting them, guarding the only escape route.

'The boy first!' ordered Aurelius. Orosius leaned over, shouting at the top of his lungs to make himself heard over the din of the storm. Batiatus heard him and prepared to receive the fugitives. Demetrius, Vatrenus and the others formed a semicircle around Romulus as he readied himself for the climb. The boy's heart sank as he looked down: the cliff face glittered like steel and the sea below was boiling with foam amidst razor-sharp rocks. The boat, tossed here and there on the waves, looked as fragile as a nutshell at that distance. He took a deep breath as Orosius tried to secure him to the rope with a makeshift harness, but at that moment Livia, who had climbed up to the top of the parapet, saw Wulfila's men in the distance, closing in on them from both left and right, and she sounded the alarm.

'The jars!' she shouted, leaping to the ground. 'We can use the jars against them! The first and the third are full of oil!' Her comrades ran over and even Orosius abandoned the rope to give them a hand. They tipped over the two huge jars and rolled them in opposite directions. The containers slid uncontrollably to the right and left, crashing first against the parapet and then against the inner wall, picking up speed until they smashed violently against the wall. They broke to pieces and liberated a shiny wave that reached the two groups as they ran at full speed. The first warriors slipped and fell, and the torches they held in their hands set fire to the oil, raising whirling flames at both ends of the walkway. Some of the men, transformed into living torches, dived into the sea and disappeared beneath the waves. Others crashed down the cliffs, bouncing from one rock to another like disjointed puppets.

As more ran up to take their places, Aurelius knew that they had no choice but to fight to the last. He gritted his teeth and gripped the sword that his emperor had given him. He would throw it into the sea with his last spark of energy before he died, so that it would never fall into the hands of the enemy. As the five warriors squared off for their last fight, however, Romulus suddenly called out: 'Follow me! I know a way out!' And he ran towards a little ironclad gate, drawing the bolt.

Aurelius grasped the boy's intent and leaned over the parapet, shouting and waving at Batiatus to cast off the moorings and set out to sea. He threw the rope down, since he no longer had any hopes that they would be able to escape that way. He ran to the gate and followed his comrades down the stairs. The storm was abating, although the reverberations of the volcano, nursing its rage in the darkness, were becoming louder and louder in the distance. They negotiated the courtyard by creeping along the shadows of the north wall, until Romulus reached the tree-lined lane that would keep the fugitives out of sight until they could get to the drainage grate that would give them access to the cryptoporticus. Romulus yanked it open and the others followed him in.

'What luck that Batiatus is not with us,' said Vatrenus. 'He'd never fit through here.'

They dropped down one after another, but in the meantime one of the servants, awakened by all that uproar, saw them and started yelling. The furious barking of dogs echoed his cries and a group of guards ran over with torches and lanterns, searching the grounds.

'Where are the intruders?' demanded a guard.

The servant didn't know what to say: 'I swear, it was right here that I saw them. I'm sure of it!'

They were immobile under the drainage grate; their pursuers were standing right above them, and they could see their faces lit by the lanterns they held in their hands.

The guard insisted, but the man could only shrug, as the dogs roamed back and forth, whimpering. The barbarian gave him a hard push backwards, swearing, and led his men to another spot to continue their search. Romulus lifted the grate a bit to make sure that they had really all gone, and then started to let himself down to the floor of the cryptoporticus, and the others followed suit. The underground chamber was pitch black. Ambrosinus took out his flint and after a few tries managed to light a wick that he kept coiled up in a jar full of a black substance that seemed like tallow. The tiny smoking flame soon grew into a little globe of white light that guided them through the impressive display of imperial monuments. They finally reached the great green marble slab. Aurelius and the others could not hide their amazement, both at Ambrosinus's miraculous flame and at that incredible parade of Caesars represented in the splendour of their draped robes and armour.

'Great gods,' murmured Vatrenus. 'I've never seen a place like this in all my life.'

'Jesus!' echoed Orosius, widening his eyes at all those marvels.

'Romulus discovered them,' Ambrosinus said proudly, pointing at his disciple, who was approaching the marble slab. Romulus turned to Aurelius and said: 'You haven't seen anything yet. This is where the sword you're holding comes from. Look!'

He placed his fingers on the three Vs and pushed. They could hear the noise of the counterweights and mechanisms going into action. Under their increasingly astonished gazes, the huge slab began to revolve until they saw before them, erect on his pedestal, the statue of Julius Caesar, his silver armour gleaming, polychrome marble simulating the purple of his tunic and robes, his face pale and frowning, carved by a great artist in the most precious Luni marble.

The silent stupor of the little group was suddenly interrupted by Demetrius's alarm: 'They've found us!' he shouted. 'They've seen the light!'

Glimmering torches could in fact be seen at the end of the cryptoporticus, accompanied by shouting: Wulfila himself was leading his guards down the landslide and along the hall of statues.

'Inside, fast!' urged Romulus. 'There's a way out, through this cell!' The great slab closed behind them. The din of the weapons beating against the marble and the enraged voice of Wulfila echoed through the underground chamber, and although the thickness of the monolithic slab formed an indomitable defence, their striking weapons and wild fury poured into that tiny space and filled the group with anguish. The still air was thick with impending threat. They looked at each other in dismay, but Romulus showed them the well-head from which the mysterious flashing blue light came, as if it were in contact with the world beyond.

'This well leads into the sea,' piped up Romulus, 'and it's our only way out. Let's go. We can't do anything here.' Beneath the eyes of all his companions, before they had time to say a word, he dived into the well-head. Aurelius didn't hesitate an instant and dived in after him. Livia went next, and then Demetrius, Orosius and Vatrenus. Ambrosinus was last, and his fall through that narrow opening seemed never ending. Contact with the water gave him a sense of panic and suffocation but then, immediately after, of peace. He felt as if he were floating in a gurgling liquid, surrounded by a pulsating celestial light. The lamp he'd been holding in his hand fell and slowly sank until it hit the bottom, and that luminous globe lit the waters up with a brilliant, intense sapphire blue. He pushed upwards with all his might and reached the surface, emerging among his companions who were already swimming to the shore. They were inside a grotto that communicated with the outside world through a small opening, so low on the surface that it was practically invisible. Aurelius and the others were astounded at the flame that continued to burn beneath the water, but Ambrosinus was looking around himself with no less wonder. Vatrenus drew closer, indicating that light that seemed to spring from the very bottom of the sea: 'What is this miracle? Are you a sorcerer?'

'Greek fire,' replied Ambrosinus with studied nonchalance. 'An old recipe of Hermogenes of Lampsacus. It even burns under water.' His gaze continued to wander around him, contemplating the magnificent images of the gods of Olympus that emerged from the waters of that sea cave: Neptune, on a carriage drawn by horses with fishes' tails; Amphitrite, his wife, with her retinue of ocean nymphs; scaly-chested tritons puffing up their cheeks as they blew into sea shells. The unreal light, reflected and diffused by the lapping of the waves, seemed to breathe life into them, animating their faces and staring marble eyes. An ancient nymphaeum! Secret and abandoned.

Romulus was raptly observing the figures himself. 'Who are they?' he asked.

'Images of forgotten gods,' replied Ambrosinus.

'But . . . did they ever exist?'

'Of course not!' gasped Orosius. 'Only one true God exists.'

Ambrosinus's gaze was enigmatic. 'Perhaps,' he replied, 'as long as someone believed in them.'

A long silence followed. The magic of the place had overwhelmed them all. The blue light shimmering over that great rocky vault, those images, the distant rumble of thunder and the powerful ebb and flow of the sea after the storm inspired a sense of almost supernatural wonder in all of them. Chilled to the bone, exhausted from their efforts, they felt their souls invaded none the less by an inexpressible happiness, intense and profound.

Romulus was the first to break the silence: 'Are we free?' he asked.

'For now,' answered Aurelius, 'although we're still on the island. But if it weren't for you, we'd all be dead. You acted as a true leader.'

'What do we do now?' asked Vatrenus.

'Batiatus must have realized that we couldn't follow our original plan, and he will have cast off. He may still be cruising somewhere nearby. We have to try to reach him or have him reach us.'

'I'll go and see,' said Livia. 'You stay here with the boy.' Before Aurelius could protest, she dived into the water, crossed the grotto with a few strokes and swam out into the open sea. She continued along the coast until she found a point she could climb on to. She clambered up as high as she could to be able to see a wide expanse of sea and waited, trembling miserably from the cold. The clouds began to clear and the moon cast a pale glow on the waves. On the mainland, Vesuvius hurled red flashes at the rain clouds that galloped through the sky, pushed by the western wind.

She suddenly started. From behind a promontory a boat had appeared with a small light at its bow. An unmistakable figure stood at the stern, manning the rudder.

'Batiatus! Batiatus!' she shouted.

The boat altered course and neared the shore.

'Where are you?' asked the helmsman.

'Over here! This way!'

'At last!' said Batiatus as soon as he was close enough. 'I was beginning to lose all hope. Have all of you made it?'

'Yes, thank God. The others are hidden not far from here, in a cave. I'll have them come out.'

Batiatus slackened the sail while Livia dived back into the

sea and swam to the grotto, where she excitedly informed the others.

One by one, the fugitives swam out towards the open sea in the direction of the boat as Batiatus urged them on: 'Hurry, hurry! I've just seen a ship leaving the port; hurry or they'll find us!'

Livia swam out alongside Romulus and helped him into the boat before getting in herself. It was Ambrosinus's turn next. Vatrenus, Orosius and Demetrius followed. Aurelius had climbed on to one of the rocks outside the cave to get a better look around when he saw a red glow spreading over the waves to his left: a warship, oars out. Wulfila was at the bow, and the ship was headed towards Batiatus's boat. Aurelius did not hesitate an instant. He shouted, with all the breath he had in him: 'Wulfila, I'm waiting for you. Come and get me barbarian, if you have the courage! Come and get me, scar face!'

Wulfila turned towards the coast and in the light of the torches he saw his enemy standing on a rock, the invincible sword in his hand. He shouted: 'Put about! Put to shore, I said! I want that man, and I want that sword, at any cost!'

Batiatus understood, and trimmed his sail to the wind, setting off towards the mainland as Romulus cried: 'No! No! We have to help him! We can't abandon him. Turn back. Turn back, I say! It's an order!'

Livia came close: 'Do you want to make his sacrifice futile? He's done it for you. He attracted their attention so we could get away.' She turned towards the island and the image of Aurelius standing on the shore in the light of the torches dissolved into another image, far off in time: a Roman soldier standing immobile on another shore, stormed by a troop of barbarians against the background of a city in flames; herself a little girl, slipping away on a boat full of refugees, over the black waters of the lagoon. Like now.

She wept.

18

THE CREW RAISED THE fore lantern at Wulfila's orders, illuminating the rocky shore where Aurelius stood motionless, sword in hand.

Several of the men drew their arrows and aimed, imagining that their commander meant to give them a clear shot at an already easy mark, but Wulfila restrained them. 'Put those bows down! I want his sword, I said! If it falls into the sea we'll never find it. Draw up to shore!' he shouted at the helmsman. 'I want him alive!'

From a distance, Vatrenus was trying to make out what was happening, and suddenly understood.

'Strike the sail,' he ordered Batiatus. Livia was startled at his words and dried her eyes, reading hope into that abrupt command.

Batiatus obeyed without understanding and the boat slowed down.

'Why are we stopping?' he asked.

'Because Aurelius is luring them on to the rocks,' replied Vatrenus. 'Look at him!'

'Ship to starboard!' rang out Demetrius's voice from the bow. Another smaller vessel, loaded with warriors, was approaching, lanterns and torches blazing from the parapets and yards. It was still a couple of leagues away, but moving steadily closer.

'What shall we do?' asked Demetrius. 'They'll spot us soon and then they'll be on us.'

'Wait!' exclaimed Romulus. 'Let's wait as long as we can, *please*!'

Just then the din of the wooden hull disintegrating against the rocks reached their ears, immediately drowned out by the much louder roar of the volcano as it belched smoke and sparks into the sky. In his fury to get at his enemy, Wulfila had jammed the bow between the rocks, and the waves were lifting the stern, sending everyone on the deck rolling. They scrambled and grasped for a hand hold at the railing, cursing. Wulfila sought to right himself, still intent on his adversary, but Aurelius dived into the water and disappeared.

Ash began to rain on the deck of Livia's boat in the deepening darkness, followed by a hail of fiery lapilli.

'We must leave now,' said Ambrosinus, 'or it will be too late. The paroxysmal stage of the eruption is beginning. If the barbarians don't get us, these lapilli will set the boat aflame and take us all to the bottom with her.'

'No!' pleaded Romulus. 'We must wait.' He anxiously scanned the black surface of the sea as the second enemy ship approached, shielding their view of Wulfila's ship being tossed mercilessly now by the breakers. The volcanic rocks rained down faster, igniting small fires on the deck near Livia and on the coiled ropes. The enemy ship had not yet advanced far enough to see the wreck of Wulfila's ship, but they would soon spot Livia's.

'How many of them are there?' asked a worried Orosius, scrutinizing the enemy crew as they crowded now at the bow, shrieking and waving their weapons.

'Enough,' replied Vatrenus. He turned to Livia. 'If you want to save the boy, we have no choice.' Livia nodded unwillingly.

'Set sail!' ordered Vatrenus. 'Fast, let's get out of here!'

Batiatus manned the sheet, assisted by Demetrius at the helm, and they slowly picked up speed, but just then a sword burst from the seething foam, gleaming in the torchlight, followed by a muscular arm, a head and a powerful chest.

'Aurelius!' cried out Romulus, beside himself with emotion.

'It's him!' shouted his comrades, rushing to the railing. Vatrenus tossed out a line and hoisted him on board. He was exhausted and only the embrace of his friends prevented him from collapsing on to the deck. Livia held him close, as he swayed, only half conscious, and Romulus couldn't stop staring at him, not daring to believe that he was alive and well, and not just the figment of a cruel dream destined to fade with the breaking day.

The dense cloud of soot spewed by the volcano spread over the sea, coating the waves which lapped at the shores of the island, and Livia's boat disappeared from sight. The crew of the second ship could now hear the cries of their comrades, floundering among the floating planks. Wulfila had managed to climb on to a rock and was bellowing orders. The ship drew up, keeping at a safe distance so as not to meet the same fate as the other, and the shipwrecked warriors swam towards it and clambered aboard, one after another. When Wulfila finally reached the ship himself, he gave immediate orders to set off after the fugitives, but the helmsman, an old sailor from Capri who knew those waters well, dissuaded him. 'If we put out to sea, none of us will come out of this alive. I can't see past my nose, and it's raining fire, look!'

Wulfila grudgingly turned towards the mainland. The black sky was scored by a myriad flaming meteors and he could feel the terror creeping through his men, people of the north who had never seen the likes of this. He bit his lip at the thought that he'd let a thirteen-year-old boy and an old man escape from a fort manned by seventy of his best warriors, but what pained him far worse was the loss of that fabulous sword. He'd thought of nothing but possessing it himself, since the very first moment he'd seen it gleaming so awesomely in his enemy's fist.

'Back to port,' he barked, and the ship put about; its sailors were all men from the islands, well aware of the danger they were in, and they rowed vigorously but calmly under the orders of the helmsman. The barbarians, on the contrary, shook with fear at every tremor and watched panic stricken as the fire from hell descended from the sky. The soot spread everywhere, the stench of sulphur filled the air and the horizon throbbed with bloody light.

*

Livia's boat advanced slowly through the utter dark. Orosius was at the very tip of the foremast from which the lantern hung and he peered out in the attempt to spot sudden obstacles or danger, although it was clear that chance alone would decide their common fate in those frightful conditions. The tension on board was thick; no one spoke for fear of distracting his comrades intent on their manoeuvres as they navigated blindly. Demetrius, perched on the forward yard with his legs hanging overboard, tried to guide their route as best he could, trusting more in his instinct than anything else. Ambrosinus approached Vatrenus. 'Which way are we bearing?' he asked.

'Who knows? North, I hope. It's the only chance we have.'

'Perhaps I could help . . . if only . . .'

Vatrenus shook his head sceptically. 'Forget it, we're confused enough as it is. I've never seen anything like this.'

'And yet, it's not the first time. It happened before, four hundred years ago. The volcano buried three cities with all their inhabitants. Not a trace remained of them, but Pliny describes the eruptive stages of the volcano precisely. That's why I proposed tonight; I thought that the general confusion would make our escape easier. I was wrong. The paroxysmal phase started hours later than what I'd predicted.'

Vatrenus stared at him in surprise.

Aurelius, who had regained full consciousness, approached them. 'What did you want to help us with?' he asked.

Ambrosinus was about to answer when Demetrius's voice sounded from the bow: 'Look!'

The cloud of soot had begun to clear and the nearly imperceptible glimmer of the waves in front of them announced the first light of day. They were rounding Cape Misenum, which was raising its head above the blanket of smoke and ash that covered the sea, and the dawning sun was illuminating its top. They all gazed at that sudden vision as the soot dissipated and the boat was struck by the rays of the sun rising behind the peaks of the Lattari mountains.

The night was behind them: the terror, the anguish, the exhaustion of their troubled escape and the relentless pursuit of the barbarians, their unspoken fear that hope would vanish like a dream with the light of day. The sun shone on them like a benevolent God, the rumble of the volcano died off in the distance like the last thunder of a storm. The breeze carried intense fragrances from the land, and the blue of the sea and of the sky mingled in a triumph of light.

Romulus drew close to his tutor: 'Are we free, now?'

Ambrosinus wanted to explain that not all danger had been vanquished, that the journey awaiting them would be rife with hardship and peril, but he didn't have the heart to dim the joy he saw shining in the boy's eyes after so long. Trying hard to control the emotion he felt, he answered: 'Yes, my son. We are free.'

Romulus nodded repeatedly as if trying to convince himself of the truth of those words, then approached Aurelius and Livia, who had been watching him. With a tiny voice, he said: 'Thank you.'

*

The boat set ashore at a deserted spot on the coast near the ruins of a maritime villa about thirty miles north of Cuma. Livia jumped into the water and made sure she was the first to touch land, to make it clear that the command of the mission was still firmly in her hands.

'Sink the boat,' she shouted at Aurelius. 'Then follow me, all of you, quickly. This way!' She pointed at a rundown shack, barely visible behind a thicket of trees, a little less than a mile away. Aurelius helped the boy get out into the shallow water as Batiatus and Demetrius started to hack away at the keel with axes, to Ambrosinus's distress.

'Why? Why sink the boat? There's no safer way of getting around! Stop, I beg of you, listen to me!' he pleaded.

Livia had turned back, frustrated at their stalling. 'I told you to follow me! There's not a moment to lose. They'll be out looking for us by now. Don't you realize that this boy is the most wanted person in the whole empire?'

'Yes, of course,' replied Ambrosinus, 'but given the circumstances, the boat is really the safest . . .'

'That's enough! I want no arguing. Just follow me, and be quick about it!' ordered Livia harshly. Ambrosinus obeyed reluctantly, turning back to watch the boat as it slowly sank. Orosius was already in the water and Demetrius after him; Aurelius, Vatrenus and Batiatus leapt out and on to the shore as well, promptly catching up with the group that Livia was guiding through the thick vegetation along the coast.

'I still can't believe it,' panted Vatrenus. 'Just six of us, and we managed to break into a fort and screw seventy armed guards.'

'Just like the old days!' exulted Batiatus. 'With one very agreeable difference,' he added, winking at Livia who shot him back a smile.

'I can't wait to count up all those pretty little gold coins,' continued Vatrenus. 'A thousand solids, you said, isn't that right?'

'One thousand,' confirmed Aurelius, 'but don't forget that we haven't earned them yet. We still have to cross Italy from one side to the other, and reach the spot we've agreed upon.'

'Just where is this place?' asked Vatrenus.

'It's a port on the Adriatic Sea where we'll find a ship waiting for us. The boy will be out of harm's way and we'll have all our money.'

Livia stopped in front of the shack and cautiously inspected the ruins, holding her bow and arrow at the ready. She heard a low snorting and immediately came upon six horses and a mule tied by their reins to a rope stretched between a pair of iron poles. Juba was among them, and began to paw the ground as soon as he got wind of his master.

'Juba!' shouted Aurelius, running to untie him. He embraced the horse like an old friend.

'See?' said Livia. 'Eustatius did a good job, didn't he? Stephanus has excellent connections around here. Everything's going just as we planned.'

'I am glad to see Juba again,' replied Aurelius. 'There's no better horse in the whole world.'

Ambrosinus walked up to Livia, who was loosening her horse's ties and preparing to climb into the saddle. 'I'm responsible for the emperor's safety,' he said firmly, looking her straight in the eye, 'and I think I have the right to know where you are taking him.'

'I'm the one who's responsible for the boy's safety now, seeing I've freed you both from your prison. I do understand your concern, but I have not been acting on my own initiative, understand? I'm just carrying out the instructions I've received. We'll take the boy to the Adriatic coast, and he'll leave from there for a place where the barbarians will never catch up with him and where his imperial dignity will have its due . . .'

Ambrosinus darkened: 'Constantinople! I suspected as much. You want to take him to Constantinople. A nest of vipers! The struggle for power spares no one, neither brothers nor sisters, parents nor children . . .' He hadn't noticed that Romulus had sidled towards him and had probably not missed a single word of his passionate outburst, but it was too late now, and the boy had to be made aware of the situation. He laid a hand on his shoulder and pulled him close, as if to defend him from this new threat, no less perilous than the others he'd had to face. 'The emperor would have no one to protect him there,' he went on. 'He would be at the mercy of that capricious, arbitrary bunch. I beg of you, leave him with me.'

Livia lowered her gaze uneasily. 'He's not just any ordinary boy and you know that well. You can't simply take him wherever you like. Besides, you wouldn't get very far without us. You'll be allowed to accompany him, if you want, but please, take a mount now, and let's get moving; we're in danger here. We're still much too close to the coast.' She urged her horse down the trail that led into a thicket.

'It's just a question of money, isn't it? All you care about is the money!' Ambrosinus shouted after her.

Aurelius pressed the mule's reins into his hand. 'Don't be foolish. Do you have any idea of what they would have done to her if she'd been captured as she was trying to free you? No one risks his life for money alone, and we've all put our lives on the line for you, more than once. Now get moving, understand?'

'Can I ride with you?' asked Romulus.

Aurelius shook his head. 'You'd better ride with your tutor. We have to be free to move quickly if there's an attack.' And off he flew.

Disappointed, Romulus climbed behind Ambrosinus who rode his mule down the trail without a word. Vatrenus, Orosius, Demetrius and Batiatus brought up the rear in pairs, proceeding at a quick gait. They soon reached the top of a hill, from which they turned to observe the coastline. The sea glittered under the rays of the sun high over the crests of the mountains. The shape of their boat could still be discerned as it went down in the swirling waters. In the opposite direction, the snow-white peaks of the Apennines topped the dark green firs of their wooded slopes.

The climb became steeper and the horsemen were forced to slow their pace. Vatrenus pushed on to flank Livia and Aurelius at the head of the group, which was more at risk.

'There's something I'm still wondering about,' he said all at once, turning to Livia.

'What's that?'

'What happened to the fisherman who climbed up the north wall to take a lobster to Tiberius Caesar?'

'The emperor wasn't too happy about it. He was so annoyed that an intruder had managed to enter his villa – which he had imagined inaccessible – that he had his guards take the lobster and rub it against the poor man's face before kicking him out.'

Vatrenus scratched his head. 'The devil! It went much better for us, all things considered.'

'So far,' said Aurelius.

'Yes, right. So far,' admitted Vatrenus.

*

About one hundred feet behind them were Ambrosinus and the boy on muleback.

'Do you really think they'll take me to Constantinople?' asked Romulus.

'I'm afraid so,' replied Ambrosinus. 'Actually, I'm certain of it. Livia didn't deny it when I asked her; I suppose we can take that as a confirmation.'

'Is that really so awful?'

Ambrosinus didn't know how to answer.

'Tell me,' insisted Romulus. 'I have a right to know what's awaiting me.'

'The fact is that I don't know myself; all I can do is make assumptions. One thing is clear: someone sent Livia to free you from Capri. Aurelius's presence led me astray at first, since I knew he had already tried to liberate you in Ravenna. It seemed reasonable that he might try again. The fact that he had a woman with him didn't strike me as odd. She could have been his girlfriend; many soldiers have a lover who they marry when they're finished with the military. But I was wrong: evidently, she's the one in command and she has the money to pay the others off when the job is done.'

'Then it's true what you said . . . they only did it for the money.'

'Even if that were true, we must still be grateful towards them. Aurelius is right: no one risks his life for money alone, but money certainly helps. There's nothing wrong with a man trying to improve his conditions, and these are men cut adrift, without an army to serve or even a homeland.'

'Then why did you say those things? What can happen to me if I'm taken to Constantinople?'

'Nothing, most likely. You'll live in the very lap of luxury.

However, you are still the Emperor of the West, and this in itself puts you at risk. Someone may want to use you against someone else, like a pawn in a table game, and pawns are readily sacrificed if the player has a better move in mind. You'd be the one to suffer, in any case. Constantinople is a corrupt capital.'

'So they're no better than the barbarians.'

'Everything has its price in this world, my son. If a people attain a high level of civilization, a certain level of corruption is bound to develop as well. I'm not saying that it's in a barbarian's nature to be corrupt, but before long they develop a taste for fine clothing, refined foods, perfumes, beautiful women, luxurious dwellings. All of this costs money, lots of money, the kind of money that only corruption can produce. Remember that just as there is no civilization without a certain share of barbarity, there is no barbarity without the germ of civilization. Can you understand that?'

'Yes, I think so. What world is this that we live in, *Ambrosine*?'

'The best possible world. Or the worst possible, depending on how you look at it. In any case, I greatly prefer civilization over barbarity.'

'Well what is civilization then?'

'Civilization means laws, political institutions, guaranteed rights. It means professions and trades, streets and communications, rites and solemnities; science, but art as well. Great art; literature and poetry like that of Virgil, whom we've read so many times together. Art is the exercise of the spirit that makes men similar to God. An uncivilized person, on the other hand, is much more similar to an animal. Does that make sense to you? Being part of a civilization gives you a particular pride, the pride of participating in a single collective endeavour, the greatest that man has ever attempted to achieve.'

'But ours – I mean, our civilization – is dying, isn't it?'

'Yes,' replied Ambrosinus, and he fell into a long silence.

19

'BEAUTIFUL, ISN'T IT?'

Aurelius jumped. Romulus had surprised him by coming out of the dark behind him as he was whirling the sword in the light of the fire, hypnotized by the bluish reflections of the blade, as iridescent as the eyes on a peacock's tail.

'I'm sorry,' he replied, handing Romulus the sword. 'I forgot to give it back to you. This is yours.'

'You keep it for now. You'll certainly get better use out of it.'

Aurelius gazed at the weapon: 'It's absolutely incredible. With all the blows it suffered – and dealt! – there's not a single nick, not a scratch. It's like the sword of a god!'

'It is, in a way. This sword belonged to Julius Caesar. Have you looked at the inscription?'

Aurelius nodded and ran his finger over the sequence of letters engraved in a barely perceptible groove at the centre of the blade. 'I have, and I couldn't believe my eyes. Yet there's some mysterious force that emanates from this weapon – it penetrates under your skin, into your fingers, your arm, all the way to your heart . . .'

'Ambrosinus says it was forged by the Calibians in Anatolia from a block of iron fallen from the sky. It was tempered in the blood of a lion.'

'And this hilt! No combat sword has ever had such a precious hilt, only ceremonial swords. The neck of the eagle meets your grip like none other that I've ever held in the palm of my hand; it turns the sword into an extension of your arm . . .'

'It's a fearsome instrument of death,' said Romulus, 'crafted for a great conqueror. You are a warrior; it's only natural that you're fascinated by it.' He looked over to where Ambrosinus was busily arranging his things near the fire. 'See Ambrosinus? He's a man of science, and he's worried about saving the instruments of his art. They got soaked when we dived into the grotto. His powders, his herbs . . . and my copy of the *Aeneid*. It was given me on the day of my acclamation.'

'What about that booklet?'

'It's his personal journal. With his story . . . and ours.'

'Do you think he's written about me as well?'

'You can be sure of that!'

'What a pity that no one will ever read it.'

'Why do you say that?'

'It was immersed in water. Not much could have been saved.'

'No, not a word was lost. Indelible ink. Another one of his formulae. He knows how to make invisible ink as well.'

'You're making that up.'

'No I'm not! As he's writing you see nothing, as if he'd dipped his quill into plain water, but then all at once, when he . . .'

Aurelius interrupted him: 'You care very much for him, don't you?'

'I have no one else in the world,' replied Romulus shyly, as if seeking a denial, but Aurelius said nothing, and Romulus watched him sheath the sword with smooth, harmonious grace, like the gesture of a priest. They stood staring at the campfire until Romulus broke the silence: 'Why wouldn't you let me ride with you today?'

'I told you. If I'm to protect you, I have to be free to do so.'

'That's not why. You just want to be free of everyone, don't you?' Before Aurelius could respond, the boy walked over to where Ambrosinus was laying a blanket over his dried leaves.

*

Demetrius stood guard at the edge of the camp and Orosius was off at a distance, at the top of a little hill, posted to spot anyone arriving from the west. The others – Batiatus, Livia, Aurelius and Vatrenus – were preparing for the night.

'It's strange,' said Vatrenus. 'I should be dead tired and yet I don't feel like sleeping.'

'We've done too much over the last day,' said Aurelius. 'Our bodies don't want to believe it's time to take a rest.'

'Makes sense,' agreed Batiatus. 'I've done practically nothing, and I'm ready to drop.'

'I don't know . . . I'd like to sing,' said Vatrenus. 'Like we used to do, around the campfire. Do you remember? By the gods, do you remember what a voice Antoninus had?'

'How could I forget,' nodded Aurelius. 'And Canidius then? And Paullinus?'

'Even Commander Claudianus had a good voice,' added Batiatus. 'Remember? Some times he'd show up, after doing his inspection rounds, and he'd sit by the fire with us. If we were singing he'd start to sing to himself, softly, and then he'd have them bring some wine and we'd all have a glass. He'd say: "Drink up, boys, it'll warm you up a little." Poor commander . . . I can still see his last look as the enemy swarmed around him . . .' The black giant's eyes shone in the dark as he recalled the cruel scene.

Aurelius raised his head and the two of them exchanged a long look in silence. For an instant an enquiring expression passed through Aurelius's eyes, a hint of suspicion that Batiatus didn't miss. 'I know what you're thinking,' he said. 'You're wondering how we managed to get out of Dertona alive, aren't you? You want to know how we saved our skins . . .'

'You're wrong, I—'

'Don't lie; I know you too well. Have we ever asked you why you never came back? Why you didn't come back to die with your comrades?'

'I came back to free you, wasn't that enough?'

'Shut up!' ordered Vatrenus. He said it softly, with a calm, still voice. 'I'll tell you how it went, Aurelius, then we'll forget about it, once and for all, and we'll never bring it up again, all right? I didn't want to, but I see that I have to. Well, after you left, Aurelius, we started fighting. We were being attacked on all sides, and we fought for hours. And hours. And hours. First from the palisades, then from the rampart. Then outside, in square formation, all on foot, like in Hannibal's time. And while there were always less of us and we were fighting with tooth and nail, they continued to send fresh troops, waves of them: one, another, and yet another. They heaped arrows on us, storms of them. Then, when they saw that we were debilitated, bloodied, exhausted – it was nearly dusk by then – they sent in the armoured horses, their riders swinging axes, for the kill. They butchered us one by one. We saw tens of our comrades fall, hundreds of them, incapable even of holding up their weapons at the end. Some fell on to their own swords, putting an end to their suffering, while others were hacked to pieces while still alive . . . left lying on the ground without legs, without arms, left screaming to bleed to death in the mud . . .'

'I don't want to hear this!' shouted Aurelius, but Vatrenus took no heed. 'It was then that their chief came in: Mledo, one of Odoacer's lieutenants. There were maybe only about one hundred of us left, I'd say, disfigured and depleted, filthy with blood and dirt, and completely shattered. You should have seen us, Aurelius . . . you should . . . have seen us!' His voice shook: Rufius Aelius Vatrenus, the hardened soldier, the veteran of a hundred battles, had covered his face and was sobbing like a child. Batiatus's hand was on his shoulder, giving him little pats to calm him down.

It was Batiatus who continued: 'Mledo yelled something in his language and the slaughter ceased. A herald ordered us to throw down our arms and our lives would be saved. We threw them down; what else could we do? They chained us together and dragged us, kicking and spitting at us, to their camp. Many of them wanted us tortured to death – we had downed at least four thousand of their comrades, and wounded countless others – but Mledo must have had orders to spare a certain number of men to be used as slaves. We were taken to Classis and sent off in different directions. Some of us to Istria, I think, to the stone quarries, others to Noricum to chop trees. We were sent to Misenus where you found us. That's all there is to say, Aurelius. Now I'm going to sleep if I'm not needed here.'

Aurelius nodded deeply. 'Go,' he said. 'Go to sleep, black man. Sleep, if you can, and you too, Vatrenus, my friend. I never . . . doubted you. All I ever hoped was to find you alive, I swear. There was nothing I would not have given to find you alive. Life is all that remains to us.' He walked off and went to sit against the trunk of an oak tree, near Juba. Livia was not far off and must have heard the whole thing, but she said nothing and neither did he. Aurelius would have cried, but he couldn't. Inside him, his heart had turned to stone and the thoughts in his brain writhed like serpents twisting in their nest.

*

On the other side of the camp, Romulus was lying on his blanket but could not sleep. He felt that something terrible was happening among his travel companions, but couldn't understand what it was about and feared that he was the cause of their arguing. He tossed and turned but found no peace.

'You're not sleeping?' asked Ambrosinus.

'I can't.'

'I'm sorry, it's my fault. I shouldn't have told you those things about Constantinople and all the rest. I wasn't thinking. Forgive me.'

'Don't be troubled on my account. I could have imagined as much; why else would they have organized such a risky endeavour, unless politics were involved? Or money, like you said when you were shouting at Livia.'

'I was beside myself; you mustn't attach importance to what I said.'

'But you were right. They are nothing but mercenaries: Livia and Aurelius and all the others who've joined up with them.'

'You're unfair. Aurelius tried to free you at Ravenna without the promise of any reward whatsoever. His only reason was that your father had asked him to do so as he was dying. Don't forget this: Aurelius was the man who heard your father's last words. There's something of your father in him, and that's very important.'

'That's not true.'

'Have it your way, but it is true.'

Romulus tried to calm down and stretch out his cramping limbs. The hoot of a scops owl sounded in the distance like a cry of desolation and he shivered under his blanket.

'*Ambrosine* . . .'

'Yes.'

'You don't want them to take me to Constantinople, right?'

'I don't.'

'What can we do to prevent it?'

'Very little. Nothing, actually.'

'You'll come with me, won't you?'

'How can you doubt that?'

'I don't doubt it; but if it were up to you, what would you do?'

'I'd take you away with me.'

'Where?'

'To Britannia. My homeland. It's lovely, you know? The greenest of islands, with beautiful cities and fertile fields, with majestic forests of gigantic oaks, of beech and maple trees that lift their leafless boughs to the sky in this season like giants beseeching the stars; vast meadows where flocks and herds graze; and here and there are grandiose monuments of circular stone whose meaning is a mystery, known only to the priests of our ancient religion: the Druids.'

'I know who they are. I read about them in Julius Caesar's *De Bello Gallico*. Is that why you wear that sprig of mistletoe at your neck, *Ambrosine*? Because you are a Druid?'

'I have received instruction in their ancient wisdom, yes.'

'And yet you believe in our God?'

'There is but one God, Caesar. Only the roads that men take to find him are different.'

'But in your journal, you described Britannia as a turbulent land. The barbarians are just as ferocious there, aren't they?'

'It's true. The Great Wall no longer holds them back.'

'Is there no peace in this world? Is there nowhere we can live in peace?'

'Peace must be conquered, because it's the most precious thing man can possess. Rest now, my son. God will inspire us when the moment comes. I am certain of it.'

Romulus didn't answer. He curled up under his blanket, listening to the monotonous hoot of the owl echoing through the mountains, until he was overcome by such weariness that he closed his eyes.

The stars slowly crossed the sky as the cold north wind turned the air to crystal. The flames of the campfire flared up, giving off an intense, brilliant light, and then were rapidly extinguished. Only the pale glow of the embers remained on the vast dark mountain.

*

Halfway through the night, Aurelius relieved Demetrius, and Vatrenus took over for Orosius. Years of army life had made them so used to the routine that they would awaken at just the right time, as if their minds could somehow measure the movement of the stars as they slept. They began their journey again at dawn, after a frugal meal. Eustatius had packed the horses' bags with provisions: bread, olives, cheese and a couple of wineskins. Ambrosinus gathered the things he had left to dry near the embers and placed them in his satchel. Romulus rolled and tied his blanket with the expertise of a soldier.

Livia passed by just then, holding her horse's bridle. 'You're very good at that,' she said. 'Where did you learn?'

'I had a military instructor for two years, an officer from my father's guard. He died that night of the assault on our villa in Placentia. They cut off his head.'

'Would you like to ride with me today?' asked Livia, fitting the horse's bit.

'No, it doesn't matter,' said Romulus. 'I don't want to be a bother to anyone.'

'I'd like it if you did,' insisted Livia.

Romulus hesitated a moment before answering: 'All right, as long as we don't talk about Constantinople and all that stuff.'

'Fine,' nodded Livia. 'No Constantinople.'

'But first I have to tell Ambrosinus. I wouldn't want him to feel offended.'

'I'll wait.'

Romulus returned a few moments later. 'Ambrosinus says all right, but don't go too fast.'

Livia smiled. 'Come on, hop up,' she said, and then adjusted him in front of her.

The column began its journey towards the pass that appeared in the distance like a saddle between two snowy peaks.

'It will be cold up there,' said Romulus, 'and that's where we'll be tonight.'

'You're right, but then we'll begin our descent towards the Adriatic, my sea. We'll find the last flocks of shepherds heading towards the low pastures for the winter. There may be some newborn lambs. Would you like that?'

'I'm also an expert in agriculture and animal breeding. I've read Columella, Varro, Cato and Pliny. I've practised beekeeping and I know the techniques for pruning and grafting, the right season for mounting and how to make wine from must . . .'

'Just like a Roman of old.'

'I've learned all this for nothing. I don't think I'll ever be able to practise these arts. My future doesn't depend on me.'

Livia didn't answer his words, which sounded almost like a rebuke. It was Romulus who broke the silence. 'Are you Aurelius's girlfriend?'

'No, I'm not.'

'Would you like to be?'

'I don't think it concerns you. Did you know that I was the one who saved him that night he tried to free you at Ravenna? He had an awful wound in his shoulder.'

'I know. I was with him when he was hit. But that doesn't make you his girlfriend.'

'No, it doesn't. We've joined together for this mission.'

'What about afterwards?'

'Each of us will go our own way, I suppose.'

'Oh.'

'Disappointed?'

'I guess it's none of my concern, is it?'

'I guess not.'

They travelled another couple of miles in silence. Romulus whiled away the time observing the nearly deserted countryside. It was enchanting. They passed a lake that reflected the limpid blue sky. A pack of boars rooting at the edge of the forest ran off to hide. A huge male deer raised his head for a moment, standing still and majestic against the dawning sun before escaping with a single bound.

'Is it true that you did it for the money?' Romulus asked abruptly.

'We'll have a reward, just like any soldier who serves his country, but that doesn't mean that's why we did it.'

'Why then?'

'Because we are Romans and you are our emperor.'

Romulus said nothing. The wind picked up, a cold northeasterly wind that had brushed the snow-covered Apennines. Livia felt the boy shiver and she covered him with her cloak, drawing him softly close and wrapping her arms around him. He stiffened at first, but then abandoned himself to the warmth of her body. He closed his eyes and thought that he could perhaps be happy again.

20

THEIR JOURNEY LASTED THREE more days across mostly uninhabited lands, through forests and up steep, secluded paths where they would be unlikely to make unwanted encounters. When they stopped to set up camp, Aurelius would reconnoitre the area with one of his men or with Livia to ensure there were no hidden risks, but they never found anything that alarmed them; their enemies had probably never managed to discover which way they were directed. This was not so far-fetched; there was no reason to believe that their traces had ever been evident. The darkness of the night and the volcanic ash had masked their route, their boat had been sunk and the horses had been waiting for them inland.

Everything seemed to be proceeding well. Their march had been planned so that the day of their arrival on the coast would coincide with their appointment with the Byzantine ship. The atmosphere among them had become more relaxed. Their easy banter and joking pleased Romulus, who continued to ride with Livia. Aurelius smiled at him, and often rode at their side. He would sometimes even chat as they set up camp in the evenings, but he was still keeping his distance. Romulus imagined that their imminent separation was on his mind.

'You can talk to me,' he said to Aurelius one evening, as he sat off to the side eating his dinner. 'It won't oblige you in any way.'

'It's a pleasure to talk with you, Caesar, and an honour,' replied Aurelius with a smile, taking in his provocation without reacting, 'and I'd be inclined to talk with you often, but soon we'll be separated, unfortunately, and friendship would just make our parting more difficult.'

'I didn't say I wanted to be your friend,' shot back Romulus, swallowing his disappointment. 'I just said we could exchange a few words sometimes, that's all.'

'I'd like that,' said Aurelius. 'What shall we talk about?'

'About you, for example. What will the rest of you do when you've turned me over to my new keepers?'

'Turning you over doesn't seem the right expression.'

'Maybe, but that's the essence of it.'

'Would you have preferred to remain in Capri?'

'Not as things stand now, no, but then I don't know what's in store for me. My choice – if I'd ever had a choice – would be between two different types of imprisonment, if I understand correctly, but since I know nothing about what awaits me, how can I express a preference? A free man can choose, whereas I'm shuffled against my will from one authority to another; the second may well make me regret the first.'

Aurelius admired his reasoning and could find no way to refute it. He said only: 'I hope not. With all my heart.'

'I believe you. Well, what will you do . . . afterwards?'

'I don't know. We've hardly spoken about it during this journey. None of us has precise ideas. Perhaps we're a little afraid of the future. One day, that same day of the barbarian attack, Vatrenus said that he'd had enough of this life; that he'd decided to go and live on an island where he could put goats to pasture and work the land. By the gods, it seems a century ago and yet only weeks have passed since then! I can't say I took him seriously at the time, but now, given such an uncertain, bleak future, that seems like a good option to me, a good life . . .'

'Tending goats on an island. Why not? I'd like that kind of life myself. If I could decide about my future, that is. But I can't.'

'That's nobody's fault.'

'Yes it is. Whoever does not prevent an injustice is its accomplice.'

'Seneca.'

'Don't change the subject, soldier.'

'Six or seven of us cannot fight off the whole world, and I don't want the lives of my comrades to be endangered again. They've done all they could do: they deserve the reward that's been promised them and the freedom to choose how to live their lives. Maybe we'll go to Sicily; Vatrenus has some land there. Or perhaps each one of us will go his own way. Who knows, maybe someday we'll go east as well, and we'll come to visit you in your sumptuous palace. What do you think? Would you invite us to dinner at least?'

'Oh, that would be fantastic! I'd be happy, and proud . . .' he broke off abruptly, realizing that there was no room for feelings here. 'I think I'd better go to sleep,' he said, getting up. 'Thanks for your company.'

'Thank you, Caesar,' replied Aurelius, nodding his head. His gaze followed the boy as he made his way through their camp.

They travelled all the next day on rough terrain, covering long stretches on foot so as not to risk laming their horses. They followed the course of a little stream: an arduous road to reach the sea, but one that permitted them to avoid inhabited areas where their passage would be noticed. Every now and then the small valley would open into a clearing and they'd see shepherds tending their flocks or farmers collecting branches in the woods to burn in their hearths that winter. They all had a gruff, unruly look, with long beards and unkempt hair; they wore goatskin shoes and worn, patched clothing, ill-designed to defend them from the cold northern wind. As the column passed they would stop, no matter what they were doing, and mutely watch as the group made its way through the forest. Armed men on horseback were not an everyday sight; prepared to defend themselves, or to strike out for that matter, they were fearsome in these people's eyes. Once Romulus noticed several boys his age, with some younger girls. They were struggling, bent double under the weight of baskets full of wood. Their bare legs were livid with the cold, their noses dripped and their lips were cracked and dehydrated. One of them plucked up his courage, laid his oversized load by the wayside and drew near, holding out his hand.

Romulus, who was riding with Livia, said: 'Can we give him something?'

'No,' replied Livia. 'If we did, we'd find a swarm of them downhill and we wouldn't be able to get rid of them. They would draw attention to us, and we just cannot afford that.'

Romulus looked at the boy, at his empty, stretched-out hand and at the expression of disappointment in his eyes as they rode away. He turned to look back again, trying to let his gaze express his desire to help. It wasn't up to him; nothing was. When they were about to enter the wood again, he raised his hand to wave goodbye. The emaciated boy replied with a sad smile, moving his hand as well, before taking up his load again and trailing off into the brush.

'I'm sorry, but that was necessary,' said Livia, intuiting Romulus's thoughts. 'We are often forced to do things in life that revolt us, but we have no choice. The world we live in is harsh and unmerciful, governed by chance.'

Romulus did not answer and yet the sight of such poverty made him realize that those poor children would have considered his existence in Capri a blessing from heaven, perhaps even a luxury. There was no condition in this world so miserable that a worse one could not be found.

As time passed and their journey continued, the stream became a torrent, rushing between smooth boulders, forming eddies and cascades. At the end it flowed into another watercourse that Ambrosinus identified as the Metaurus. The temperature became milder, a sure sign that they were nearing the sea and the end of their adventure, although none of them could yet predict how it would wind up. The forests thinned out and gave way to pastures and cultivated land as they approached the coast. They found it increasingly difficult to steer clear of the many little villages in their path as they crossed stretches of via Flaminia. On the last day of their journey, they ran across an old abandoned *mansio*, marked by a milestone. The sign that hung outside was rusty, but a fountain still flowed to fill the troughs, large basins carved in sandstone from the Apennines. They had been built for the horses once housed in the exchange post, but were now frequented by transient flocks, as evidenced by myriad cloven hoof marks and by the abundant dung all around.

Livia went in first, on foot, to ensure the place was safe, leaving her horse's reins to Romulus. She pretended to draw water from the fount, and as soon as she saw that no one was around, whistled to the others to join her. Romulus tied the horse and scampered over, entering and looking about. The plaster walls still bore the graffiti left by thousands of wayfarers over centuries of use, many of which were obscene. High up on one wall was a fresco painting of a map in which he recognized Italy. There were the islands, Sicily and Sardinia, the coast of Africa below and the coast of Illyria above, with all the seas, mountains, rivers and lakes coloured in. A red line traced the *cursus publicus*, the network of roads which had once been the pride and glory of the empire, with all of its rest stations and the distances recorded in miles. Above it he could still make out the map's title, TABULA IMPERII ROMANI, half deleted by water seepage. His attention was caught by the wording CIVITAS RAVENNA, illustrated by a miniature of the city with its towers and walls, and he was suddenly gripped by fear. He turned away quickly and met Aurelius's eye; each of them saw in the other's gaze the distressing memories that image had brought to mind: the imprisonment, their failed escape, the death of Flavia Serena. Ambrosinus began rummaging around in search of materials; when he'd found a couple of rolls of partially-used parchment at the bottom of a broken cupboard he began busily recopying one of the routes marked out on the wall map.

The others entered as well and began to lay out their blankets. Demetrius had noticed a field of stubble downhill of the *mansio*, with heaps of straw here and there, so he went to collect some to make up their beds for the night. The surface layers were grey and mouldy, but the straw underneath was still blond, and dry for so late in the season; it would certainly keep them warm. A hedge of maple and brambles lined the side of the field, beyond which the low brush extended almost all the way to the sandy coast. To his left he could see the mouth of the Metaurus, the river they'd been following over the last few days. Behind them was the forest, stretching out on the north and west. Vatrenus inspected it on horseback to rule out any hidden danger, and noticed large piles of oak and pine logs, secured with twine to stakes driven into the ground, at a short distance from the boundary with the cultivated field. There must be loggers in the area, who traded timber with the coastal populations. In the distance was the sea, rippled by Boreas's breath, but not rough, and the weather conditions were mild enough so that the ship would be able to draw ashore without major problems.

Ambrosinus wanted to show his gratitude towards the men who had risked their lives for them, so when the time came, he prepared a special dinner for all, flavouring it with the herbs and roots he'd found along the way. He'd even managed to scrape together some fruit: the last few wild apples hanging from a tree in what must once have been the exchange post's orchard. He lit a fire in the old fireplace and although huge splits in the ceiling let them see the stars, the crackling of the flames and the light of the hearth spread a sense of cheer and intimacy that allayed their sadness over their imminent separation.

No one mentioned the fact that Romulus would be gone the next day – that they would perhaps never see him again, that the little emperor would fulfil an unknown destiny on the other side of the world, in an immense metropolis, amidst the intrigues of a corrupt, murderous court – but it was clear that they were thinking of nothing else, from the sidelong glances they cast towards the boy, from the half-hearted phrases that every so often escaped them, from the rough, seemingly thoughtless caresses they gave him as they passed.

Aurelius chose to take the first guard shift, and went to sit near the troughs, staring out at the sea which had become leaden. Livia approached him from behind.

'Poor boy,' she said. 'All this time he's been trying to form a bond with us, especially with you and me, and we've never let him.'

'It would just have been worse,' said Aurelius without turning.

A flock of cranes migrating in the night shrieking like banished souls.

'They'll reach the Bosporus before he will,' said Livia.

'You're right.'

'The ship should be here before dawn. They'll take the boy and give us our reward. It's a lot of money: you and your men will be able to start a new life, buy land, servants, livestock . . . you deserve it.'

Aurelius didn't answer.

'What are you thinking of?' asked Livia.

'The ship might not arrive on time. It might even be a few days late.'

'Is that worry or hope in your voice?'

Aurelius seemed to be listening to the syncopated call of the cranes which was fading into the distance. He sighed. 'It's the first time in my life that I've had something like a family, and tomorrow it will be all over. Romulus will go towards his destiny and you . . .'

'And so will I,' Livia said resolutely. 'These are hard times. We're forced to watch this world of ours die, and we're powerless to do anything to stop it. Each one of us needs a purpose, a goal, a reason good enough to want to survive all this ruin.'

'Do you really want to return to that lagoon? Wouldn't you like . . .'

'What?'

'To come with us . . . with me.'

'But where? I told you, a new hope is being born in that lagoon. Venetia is my homeland, strange as that may seem to you. It may look like just a group of shacks built by refugees fleeing the destruction of their cities, but it's much, much more than that.'

Aurelius flinched imperceptibly at those words and Livia continued: 'I'm certain that it will soon become a true city. That's why I need the money I'll be given tomorrow: to reinforce our defences, to fit out our first ships, to build new houses for new immigrants. You should unite with us, you and your comrades. We need men like you. Our cities have been razed to the ground, but their spirit lives on in Venetia; cities like Altinum, Concordia, Aquileia! Your city, Aurelius! Aquileia.'

'Why do you continue to torment me so?' snapped Aurelius. 'Can't you just leave me in peace?'

Livia knelt before him, her eyes glistening. 'Because maybe I can give you back that past that has been wiped from your mind. I knew it the first time I saw you. I knew it from the way you looked at this, even if you continue to deny it.' She raised the medal that hung at her neck and placed it squarely in front of him, like some sacred relic that would heal him from a mysterious disease. Her eyes were bright with passion and with tears. Aurelius felt suddenly engulfed by powerful emotion, by the desire he had futilely suffocated for so long. He felt her lips drawing closer, her breath mixing with his in an ardent, unexpected kiss, long dreamed of yet never hoped for. He embraced her and kissed her as he never had any woman in his whole life, with infinite sweetness, with all the energy that welled up from his heart. She wrapped her arms around his neck without moving her lips from his, every part of her trembling body pressing against him, her full breasts, her smooth stomach, her long nervous legs. He lay her on the ground on his cape, and took her, like that, on the dry grass, the odour of the earth mixing with the scent of her hair. And he remained inside her afterwards, to prolong the intimacy that filled his heart and that he wished would never end. He wrapped her up in his cloak and held her tight, delighting in the warmth of her body and the fragrance of her skin.

Then Livia left him with a kiss. 'Aurelius,' she said, 'I wish there could be a future between us, but I'm sure that the ship will be here soon. When the sun rises everything will seem different: difficult, problematical, the way it's always been. You'll follow your comrades, fleeing from the ghosts of your lost memories, and I'll return to my lagoon. We'll always have the memory of these days, of the love we've stolen on our last night together, the memory of this incredible adventure, of this kind and unfortunate boy that we've loved without ever having the courage to tell him. Perhaps one day you'll decide to come looking for me, and I'll welcome you, if it's not too late. Or perhaps I'll never see you again because the vicissitudes of life will have kept us apart. Farewell, Aurelius, may your gods protect you.'

Livia walked away towards the old tumbledown *mansio*. Aurelius was left alone under the black sky, listening to the voice of the wind, and to the cranes fending their way through the darkness.

21

THE HOOTING OF AN OWL echoed repeatedly from the willow grove near the river, then a light moved back and forth over the bridge which crossed the torrent. Livia, inside the *mansio*, seemed asleep, reclining near a breach in the wall. The noise startled her into consciousness; she got to her feet and slipped silently through the crevice. Aurelius, who had finished his stint on guard duty, was sleeping wrapped in his blanket on the opposite side of the room. Demetrius was outside now, sitting on the ground against his shield, and Livia reasoned that he'd be watching the coastline in the hopes of sighting the ship. She circled the southern corner of the building and reached the pen at the back where the horses were tied. She kept her hand over her horse's muzzle as she sneaked off with him, so he wouldn't give her away. Juba didn't even seem to notice her, or perhaps her odour was so familiar that he wasn't distracted from his rest.

Livia proceeded west down the slope on foot. When she reached the river valley where she could no longer be spotted from above, she mounted her horse and turned right, through the willow woods, towards the bridge and the sea.

Ambrosinus, still inside the *mansio*, hadn't closed an eye all night and had not failed to notice her movements. His decision had been made; he approached Romulus and nudged him gently until he awakened.

'Shhhh!' he whispered in his ear, to prevent any noisy reaction.

'What's wrong?' asked Romulus softly.

'We're leaving. Now. Livia has gone out; the ship may be arriving.'

Romulus hugged him tightly and his embrace expressed all the boy's gratitude for that unexpected deliverance; Ambrosinus could feel his longing to be free, to leave that hurtful, bitter world behind. He whispered: 'Careful not to rustle the straw as you get up. We must move like shadows.' He led the boy to the door that opened on to the little garden behind the house. Romulus looked around, waited until Batiatus's thunderous snoring reached its peak, then followed his tutor on tiptoe out of the door. The horses to their left pawed the ground nervously. Juba shook his proud head and snorted loudly. Ambrosinus signalled for the boy to stop and flatten himself against the wall.

'Let's give him a moment to calm down,' he said, 'and then we'll head towards the forest. We'll find a safe place to hide and wait there until this has all blown over. Then we'll begin our journey, you and I alone.'

'But if I run away, Aurelius and his friends won't have their reward! They'll have worked so hard and risked their lives for nothing.'

'Shhh!' insisted Ambrosinus. 'This is no time to start having qualms! They'll cope.'

The horse's excitement was growing instead of abating, and Juba finally reared up and struck the wall with his front hooves, letting out a high whinny.

'Let's get out of here immediately,' said Ambrosinus, taking the boy by his arm. 'That animal is waking everyone!' He was about to set off when a steel hand sank into his shoulder, paralysing him.

'Stop!'

'Aurelius,' said Ambrosinus, recognizing him in the darkness, 'let us go, I beg of you. Restore this boy's freedom, if you care for him at all. He has suffered so much . . . let him go free.' But Aurelius, without loosening his grip, was looking in another direction.

'You don't know what you're saying,' he replied. 'Look, over there, near those trees.'

Ambrosinus peered in the direction Aurelius was indicating:

he saw a confused rush of threatening shadows and he felt his heart sink in his chest.

'Oh most merciful God . . .' he murmured.

*

Livia, in the meantime, had reached the bridge and could make out a figure behind a tamarisk bush, holding a lantern in the early dawn. She spurred on her mount until she was close enough to recognize him: 'Stephanus!'

'Livia,' came the other's response.

'We chose a difficult route through the woods, but we managed to arrive in time regardless. Everything went well. The boy and his tutor are safe, and our men did a magnificent job. But where is the ship? It's nearly sunrise, and it should have been here last night. Embarking him in full daylight will be risky – and anyone could have seen you signalling like that!'

Stephanus interrupted her abruptly. 'The ship isn't coming any more.'

'What did you say?'

'You heard me well, unfortunately. The ship won't be coming.'

'Was it attacked? Sunk?'

'No, no shipwreck. It's simply that . . . things have changed.'

'Listen, I don't like this. I've risked my life for this mission, and so have my men . . .'

'Calm down, please. It's not our fault. In Constantinople, Zeno has reconquered the throne usurped by Basiliscus, but he needs peace to consolidate his power. He can't antagonize Odoacer, and as you know well, Julius Nepos has always been his candidate for the Western throne.'

Livia suddenly realized the alarming implications of what he was saying, for all of them. 'Has Antemius been informed of all of this?' she asked.

'Antemius had no choice.'

'Damnation! But this will mean the boy's death!'

'No it won't. That's why I'm here. I have a boat a little further up north, near the mouth of the river. We can go to my villa in Rimini, you'll all be safe there, but we must be quick; we're too exposed here.'

Livia jumped into the saddle: 'I'm going to tell them what's happened.'

'No, wait,' shouted Stephanus. 'Look, up there!'

Livia looked towards the hillside and saw a group of barbarian horsemen encircling the *mansio* from the south, while others emerged from the brush to join them. Stephanus tried to hold her back. 'Wait, they'll kill you!' He tripped and his lantern fell to the ground, shattering and spilling its oil which burst into flames. Livia took one look at the field of stubble and the heaps of straw and didn't hesitate an instant. She pulled her bow from its saddle strap, set the tip of one of her arrows on fire and shot it up in a high arch into the straw, followed by a second and a third, until the huge piles slowly began to give off dense clouds of smoke.

'You're mad!' shouted Stephanus, getting up. 'You'll never succeed.'

'That remains to be seen,' shot back Livia.

'I can't stay here any longer, I have to get back,' said Stephanus, visibly frightened by the turn events were taking. 'I'll be waiting for you in Rimini. Save yourself, for the love of God!' Livia barely nodded her head and raced off on her horse towards the hillside.

*

The barbarians were so intent on surrounding the old *mansio* that they noticed nothing at first. They had left their horses and were advancing on foot with their swords drawn, awaiting a signal from their commander: Wulfila.

The atmosphere was immersed in that unreal silence that falls upon nature when the voices of the nocturnal animals cease and the diurnal creatures do not yet dare to welcome the sun, the silence which separates the darkness of night from the first light of day. Only the sign hanging from the post creaked painfully as the first sea breeze touched it. Wulfila gave the signal, abruptly lowering his left hand which had been raised above his head. They stormed into the building, brandishing their weapons and plunging them into the unsuspecting bodies still buried in sleep. Just moments later, their furious swearing made it clear that they'd discovered the trick. There was only straw under the blankets: the *mansio*'s guests were gone.

'Find them!' screamed Wulfila. 'They have to be around here somewhere. Look for their traces, they have horses with them!' His men rushed outside, only to find fire consuming the field, the flames licked high by the gathering wind. It seemed a miraculous event, since Livia was still hidden from sight at the bottom of the river valley.

'What the devil is happening?' snarled Wulfila, who could not provide an explanation for that sudden change in scene. 'It must have been them, damnation! Find them! They're still close by!'

The men obeyed, scattering all around, scouring the terrain until one of them found tracks of horses and men heading towards the forest. 'This way!' he shouted. 'They went this way!'

They all set off on the chase, but Livia realized what was happening and came out into the open to attract the enemy's attention. Another one of her fire arrows hit its mark, spreading the flames, whilst a second flew through the air and struck one of the barbarians. Livia yelled: 'This way, you bastards! Come and get me!' She began prancing back and forth halfway up the hill, vanishing behind a thick curtain of smoke only to emerge farther down to strike again with her deadly darts.

On Wulfila's signal, three of his men separated from the group and raced at her, while the flames, fed by the wind, had transformed the entire field into a roaring brush fire. Livia's pursuers were upon her, but she ran one of them through, dodged another and hurled herself at the third with her sword in hand. He charged her, screaming like a madman, but she managed to throw him off balance with a feint. She crashed into the side of his horse and sent him sprawling into the blaze. The shrieks of the barbarian, transformed into a human torch, were soon drowned out by the din of the flames. Livia galloped off through the hellish fields until she reached the edge of the forest and appeared all at once to her comrades with her sword in fist and her hair spread on the wind, like an ancient goddess of war.

'We have to get out of here!' she shouted. 'We've been betrayed! Follow me, fast! They'll be upon us any moment!'

'Not before we've left them something to remember us by!' replied Aurelius, and he gestured to his men posted behind the piled-up logs that Vatrenus had seen the night before. At his signal, they used their axes and swords to chop through the twine and Batiatus gave them a push and sent them rolling. The huge trunks quickly picked up speed as they flew down the hill, bouncing off the craggy terrain and sowing panic and death among Wulfila's horsemen as they tried to make their way uphill. Other logs crashed into the blazing straw heaps and exploded them into balls of flames that the wind turned into burning clouds.

Aurelius reached out his hand to Romulus so he could climb on to Juba, then they set off through the forest after Livia, who seemed to have some idea of where to go. They followed her at full tilt down a path which wound through the vegetation and ended up at an old branch of via Popilia, now little more than a trail which led into a thicket of brambles and oaklings. Livia jumped to the ground and pointed at a passage through the wood, slightly uphill from where they were. 'Get off your horses and lead them by the reins. The last one to pass must be sure to cover our traces.'

Orosius volunteered for the job; he bundled some branches together and brought up the rear, wiping away all their tracks. Livia had gone around the dense thicket which had interrupted their path until she found herself at the base of a hillock blanketed with creepers and ivy. She dipped her sword into the thick vegetation here and there until it sunk in all the way to the hilt. 'Here we are,' she said. 'I've found it.' She moved aside the creepers and uncovered a passage carved into the sandstone, which led deep inside the hill. Her comrades followed her one by one. Orosius was last, and he rearranged the vines so that the opening of the chamber was camouflaged once again. When he turned around to face the others inside, they were all looking around in astonishment. The light of day filtering through the leaves relieved the darkness, making the outlines of the cavern visible.

'It's an old sanctuary to the god Mithras which hasn't been used for centuries. This Mithraeum was once patronized by sailors from the east who came ashore at Fanum,' explained Livia. 'I used it once before as a hideaway. It's a miracle that I remembered its position. God must be with us if he's shown us the way to salvation like this.'

'If your God is with us he has a strange way of showing it,' commented Vatrenus, 'and if I must be honest with you, I wish he'd forget about us in the future and worry about someone else.'

'Gather all the horses together at the darkest part and try to keep them quiet. Our pursuers will be here any moment, and if they find us this time, it's all over.'

She hadn't finished speaking when the sound of hooves was heard on the road. Livia neared the entrance and peeked outside: Wulfila had arrived at the head of his men and raced by at great speed. Livia breathed a sigh of relief and was about to let the others know that the worst was over when she suddenly had to reconsider. The noise of the galloping stopped all at once and she could now hear the slow shuffling of the horses as they turned back. Livia signalled for the others to remain completely silent and turned to face the entrance. Aurelius joined her after leaving Juba's reins in Batiatus's hands.

Wulfila was no further than twenty paces from the opening to the chamber, his chest and shoulders protruding from the thick brush that hid the original course of the road. He was a horrible sight to see: his face was black with soot, his eyes were red and his scar stood out on his cheek as he sniffed the air like a wolf who has scented his prey. His men were right behind him, fanned out to patrol the forest all around in search of footprints. Inside the cave everyone held his breath, sensing the imminent danger, and gripped the hilt of his sword, ready, as always, to fight to the death with or without a reason – but then the squad dispersed. Wulfila had had to acknowledge the failure of their endeavour and he called them off. They retraced their steps, back to the *mansio*.

*

Livia was finally able to explain to the others what had happened. 'I met Stephanus before dawn,' she said. 'He told me that Antemius has sold us out. I won't have the money I promised you, at least not yet.'

Ambrosinus drew close: 'But . . . I don't understand.'

'It's simple,' replied Livia. 'Emperor Zeno has regained power in the East by ousting Basiliscus and he wants to maintain good relations with Odoacer. Zeno must have learned of Antemius's plotting, leaving him with no alternative but to sacrifice Romulus to the new political situation.'

'What will we do with the boy?' asked Vatrenus.

'We could take him away with us,' proposed Aurelius.

'Wait a moment . . .' Livia attempted to make herself heard.

'Take him where?' retorted Demetrius without letting her speak. 'Odoacer will send every last one of his men after us. We don't have a chance. It's no use fooling ourselves into thinking they're gone. They'll be back all right, when we least expect it, and they'll make us pay. No use pulling the wool over our eyes, is there?'

'Well then, what do you say we should do?' shot back Aurelius. 'Negotiate a reward and turn him over to the barbarians ourselves?'

'Hey! I want to understand what the devil is happening!' protested Batiatus. 'Will someone explain . . .'

'If you would let me say something, confound it . . .' burst out Livia.

Romulus, bewildered and distressed, listened to their arguing, their comments flying back and forth as if he weren't even present: once again his fate rested in someone else's hands. Now that there was no more reward to be had, he was just a burden for these people, a nuisance. Aurelius noticed the dismay and humiliation in the boy's eyes and tried to patch things up: 'Listen, they don't . . .'

Ambrosinus's voice rose loudly above all the others, a voice which had never spoken before with such anger and indignation. 'That's enough!' he exclaimed. 'You listen to me now. All of you! I came to this country from Britannia many many years ago, as part of a delegation sent to speak to the emperor. We were to ask him for help in the name of the people of our island, oppressed by ferocious tyrants and tormented by continuous barbarian onslaughts and plunder. I lost my companions during the journey, to the cold, to disease, to the ambushes of brigands. I arrived alone, and was never received by the emperor. He was nothing but a cowardly puppet in the hands of other barbarians: he simply would not hear me. In no time I was reduced to utter misery and I had to live by my wits for years, using my knowledge of medicine and alchemy, until I became this boy's tutor. I have followed him through good times and bad, in moments of joy and of despair, of humiliation and imprisonment, and I can tell you that there is more courage, compassion and nobility of spirit in him than in any other person I have ever met.'

They all fell silent, dominated by the voice of the improvised orator, who put his hand on Romulus's shoulder and set him at the centre of the group, as if to call everyone's attention upon him. In a quieter but more solemn tone, he continued: 'Now I am asking him to heed the call of his subjects in Britannia, abandoned to their destiny for years, and to succour them in their hour of need. I'm asking him to face more danger with me, and more hardship – with or without your help.'

They all gazed at him in astonishment, and then exchanged glances as if they could not believe their ears.

'I know just what you're thinking, I can read it in your eyes,' persisted Ambrosinus. 'You think I've lost my mind, but you're wrong. Now that you've been deprived of your reward and of the successful completion of your mission, you have but two choices. You can deliver Romulus Augustus to his enemies and perhaps obtain an even bigger reward – you can betray your emperor and stain yourselves with this disgraceful crime – but I am certain that you will not do so. I've come to know you in this brief time we've been together and I've seen something alive in you that I had thought long dead: the bravery, valour and loyalty of the true soldiers of Rome. The choice is yours: you can turn him in, or you may allow us to go on our way as free men.' His gaze fell on the hilt of the sword hanging from Aurelius's side. 'That sword will be our talisman, and we shall be guided by the ancient prophecy that only he and I know.'

Complete silence fell over the vast hidden chamber. They were all overwhelmed by his wise words, and by the dignity and courage of that little sovereign without a kingdom and without an army.

Romulus was the first to speak up: 'I'll come with you, *Ambrosine*. Wherever you take me, with or without the sword, God will help us.' He took his tutor's hand and they started off towards the exit.

Aurelius blocked their way: 'Can I ask you how you think you're going to get all the way up there?'

'On foot,' replied Ambrosinus tersely.

'On foot,' repeated Aurelius, with the tone of someone who isn't sure he can trust his ears.

'That's right.'

'And when you get there,' picked up Vatrenus with a hint of sarcasm, '*if* you get there, how are you going to defeat these bloodthirsty tyrants with all their fearsome barbarians that you were talking about? The two of you, an old man and a . . .'

'Child,' Romulus finished. 'I'm just a boy, right? Well, wasn't Julus, the son of the hero Aeneas, just a boy when he left Troy in flames and came to Italy? Yet he became the founder of one of the greatest nations of all time . . . I have nothing to give you. I have no possessions, nor money to pay my debt to you. I can only thank you for what you've done for me. I can only say that I'll never forget you, and that you'll always be in my heart, even if I live to be a hundred.' His voice trembled with emotion. 'You, Aurelius, and you, Vatrenus, and Demetrius, Batiatus, Orosius, and you too Livia, don't forget me. Farewell.' He turned then to his tutor: 'Come on, *Ambrosine*. Let's get started.'

They reached the entrance of the Mithraeum, pushed aside the vegetation and began walking down the path. Aurelius took Juba by the reins, looked his comrades in the face and said, as if it were the most obvious thing in the world: 'I'm going with them.'

Vatrenus tried to shake off his shock. 'You can't be serious,' he said. 'Wait, blast you! Wait, I said!' He set off after him. Livia smiled, as if she had been waiting for just this, and started walking out herself, pulling her horse behind.

Batiatus scratched his head: 'Is this Britannia very far?' he asked the other two.

'I think so,' replied Orosius. 'I fear it's the farthest of any known land, at least from what I've heard.'

'Then we'd better get moving,' Batiatus concluded, whistling to his horse and moving through the curtain of creepers, towards the light of the sun.

Ambrosinus and Romulus, already walking along the path, heard snapping twigs and scuffling hooves behind them but resolutely continued on their way. Then, seeing that they were all taking the same road after all, Romulus tugged at Ambrosinus's arm to make him stop and turned around slowly to find all six of them before him. 'Where are you going?' he asked, looking at them one by one.

Aurelius took a step towards him. 'Did you really think we would abandon you?' he said. 'From now on, if you'll have us, you can count on an army – small, but valiant and loyal. Hail, Caesar!' He unsheathed his sword and held it out to Romulus. At that very moment a ray of sun emerged from behind a cloud and penetrated the branches of the pines and holm oaks, illuminating the boy and his miraculous sword with a magical, unreal light.

Romulus handed it back to Aurelius with a smile. 'You take care of it for me,' he said.

Aurelius held out his hand and helped Romulus up into the saddle in front of him. The others brought Ambrosinus his mule. 'We have a long and dangerous journey before us,' said Aurelius. 'In two or three days we'll reach the Po river valley; it's all open terrain, and it won't be easy to stay hidden. We'll have to find some way to stay out of sight.'

'We'll have a powerful ally,' replied Ambrosinus.

'We will?'

'Certainly. The fog,' he answered.

'Perhaps Stephanus can still do something for us,' said Livia. 'When he came to warn us, he said he had a boat, and he offered to take us to safety. Maybe he can give us some of the money they promised, or at least some provisions. The Po valley is big, and the days are short and foggy; it won't be that easy to spot us, after all.'

'Agreed,' nodded Aurelius, 'but then we'll have to cross the Alps, in the dead of winter.'

22

Stephanus watched Wulfila's squad regroup at the edge of the forest; there were only half a dozen of them in all. He walked towards them, doing his utmost to appear natural. 'Where are the others?' he asked.

'I've divided them into groups and sent them out to search. I'm sure we'll find them in the vicinity. They can't have got too far with that old man and the boy.'

'Yes, but the weather is worsening, and that won't help matters,' replied Stephanus. A front of dark clouds was coming in from the sea, and a freezing rain mixed with sleet began to fall.

The fire had consumed the stubble and straw and had burnt itself out, leaving behind a blackened, smoking expanse. The tree trunks that hadn't lodged against obstacles had rolled all the way to the coastal plain or into the river.

Stephanus's teeth were chattering from the cold and he was trembling like a leaf, but he found the strength to speak up. 'Odoacer won't like this, and neither will Zeno's emissaries. I wouldn't like to be in your shoes when you have to tell them about it – and don't expect me to come to your defence and put my own position at risk. You let an old man and a boy get away from right under your nose, with seventy guards at your command. It just isn't credible; someone might think that you let yourself be bought out.'

'Shut up!' growled Wulfila. 'If you'd informed me earlier, I would have taken them all.'

'You know that wasn't possible. Antemius's contact in Naples organized their escape so well that I'd lost track of them myself.

What could I tell you? The only certain place of encounter was here, at their appointment with the ship. I had no other information to give you.'

'I don't know whose side you're really on, but you watch out! If I find out that you're double-crossing me, I'll make you curse the day you were born.'

Stephanus didn't have the strength to refute his accusation. 'Give me something to cover myself with,' he said. 'Can't you see I'm freezing to death?'

Wulfila looked him up and down with a sneer of disgust, then took a blanket from his saddle and tossed it on the ground near him. Stephanus picked it up and wrapped himself head to toe.

'What are you planning to do now?' he asked Wulfila when he'd caught his breath.

'Capture them. At any cost. Wherever they're headed.'

'Who knows how long that will take. If you didn't manage to get them when they were right at hand, how do you think you'll succeed now? Time is on their side, and in the meantime, rumours are bound to start leaking out of Capri. That's where your troubles will truly begin.'

'What do you mean by that?' Wulfila asked, deciding to get off his horse. Stephanus's neck finally assumed a more normal position.

'It's simple. If the news gets out that the emperor has escaped, someone may want to take advantage of the fact, with dire consequences.' Wulfila shrugged. 'Odoacer himself expressly willed that the boy spend the rest of his days on that island,' continued Stephanus, 'and he must not be disappointed. No one must realize that the emperor has disappeared.'

'So what am I supposed to do?'

'Send someone you trust to Capri. Have Romulus Augustus replaced by a double, a boy of his age dressed in the same clothing. Make sure no one sees him up close, at least for a few months, until you've had time to replace all the personnel, including his personal bodyguards. For the powers that be – as well as for the common folk – he'll never have left the villa.

They'll assume that he's still on the island, never to leave it. Have I explained myself?'

Wulfila nodded.

'Then you will report to Odoacer. Personally.'

Wulfila nodded again, holding his temper in check. He detested the scheming courtier, but realized that this drenched and shivering excuse for a man, all bundled up in a horse blanket, was certainly in a better position than he was. He signalled for Stephanus to follow him, and they made their way to the *mansio*, which, thanks to its position, had not been touched by the fire. There they waited for the men to return from the hunt.

Stephanus, recalling an episode he'd heard about, beckoned for Wulfila to listen closely. 'Antemius had informers in Capri, even on the ships that went out in pursuit of the fugitives, and one of them told me a strange story . . .' he began. Wulfila eyed him with suspicion. 'It seems that one of those men had a formidable weapon that no one had ever seen the likes of, a sword of immense power and strength. Did you see it by any chance?'

Wulfila avoided his gaze with sufficient embarrassment to make it clear that he was lying when he answered: 'I don't know what you're talking about.'

'Strange. I would have thought that you'd have joined personally in the fight to stop that meagre bunch from carrying off the emperor.'

'People say anything. I know nothing about it. When you're fighting you look your opponent in the eye, you don't look at his sword. That reminds me, I asked you to get some information for me, and I haven't heard a word from you yet.'

'Oh yes, about that legionary. All I was able to find out is that he was part of that division that Mledo wiped out at Dertona, and that his name is Aurelius.'

'Aurelius? Aurelius, you said?'

'Yes, why?'

Wulfila fell into silence, thinking, then said: 'I'm certain I've seen him somewhere before. A long time ago. I never forget a face. Anyway, it's no longer important. That man finished up in the sea that night, probably as fish food.'

'I wouldn't be so sure of that if I were you. My informants tell me he may still be alive – and still have that sword with him.'

*

The first of Wulfila's men arrived some time later, exhausted, horses steaming; it was clear from their dejected expressions that they'd had no success. Wulfila lashed out at them, beside himself with rage: 'You can't tell me that you didn't find them. All those people on horseback don't just vanish into thin air, damn it!'

'We looked everywhere,' one of them said. 'They must have known about some hiding place. They've always lived in this land, and they know it much better than we do. Or perhaps someone gave them shelter.'

'Search the houses, then. Force the peasants to talk. You know how, don't you?'

'We have done already, but many of them don't even understand us.'

'They're faking it!' howled Wulfila. Stephanus observed him without any visible reaction, but in his heart of hearts he gloated, watching that hairy beast in the throes of panic.

More of the groups arrived around midday. 'Maybe those of us who headed further north will have more luck,' said one of the horsemen. 'We've decided to meet in Pisaurum. Whoever arrives first will wait for the others. What are your orders?'

'Resume the hunt,' replied Wulfila. 'Now.'

Stephanus took his leave. 'I'll see you back at Ravenna, I imagine. I'll wait here for the boat that's coming to collect me.' Then he gestured for Wulfila to come close again. 'Is it true the sword had a golden hilt shaped like an eagle's head?'

'I don't know anything about it. I don't know what you're talking about,' repeated Wulfila.

'Maybe – but if it should ever fall into your hands, remember that there's someone who is willing to pay any price to have it, to cover you in gold, literally. Understand? Don't do anything stupid if you do get hold of it. Let me know, and I'll arrange for you to spend the rest of your life in luxury.'

Wulfila didn't answer, staring at him briefly with an inscrutable look. He called his men to order and had them fan out and take off again at a gallop in every direction, personally leading the group headed north. They advanced for days, combing the entire area with no luck, until they finally met up at the gates of Pisaurum with the group that had preceded them. The weather was worsening everywhere, and the light, persistent rain that fell turned the roads into muddy torrents and made the cultivated fields inaccessible. Even the lower slopes of the hills were turning white. The advance guard had already communicated to the garrisons they'd passed that they were looking for a group of five men travelling with a woman, an old man and a boy. Someone was sure to notice them sooner or later. Wulfila proceeded as quickly as possible in the direction of Ravenna, where the most difficult task still awaited him: facing Odoacer.

*

The *magister militum* received him in one of the rooms of the imperial apartments where he had established his quarters. His look made it clear that he already knew about what had happened and that anything that Wulfila said would only serve to worsen his mood. He would have to let his commander's rage run its course before he spoke.

'My best men!' shouted Odoacer. 'My second-in-command, in person, made a fool of by a fistful of spineless Romans: how is that possible?'

'They were not spineless!' burst out Wulfila.

'That's evident. So you were the spineless ones.'

'Beware, Odoacer, not even you can afford to talk to me this way.'

'Are you threatening me? After you've failed this mission so miserably, so shamefully, you dare to threaten me? You will now tell me everything that happened, without leaving out a single detail. I have to know what kind of men I've surrounded myself with; I have to know whether you've become as lily-livered and incompetent as the Romans that we've subjugated!'

'They took us by surprise. It was a stormy night, and they managed to scale the north wall, a sheer cliff we thought to be inaccessible. They escaped through a secret passage that communicated with the sea. I had the waters patrolled by the two ships I had at my disposal, but the very elements were pitted against us: as the storm started to subside, the volcano erupted, and their boat disappeared in the middle of a black cloud of soot. Their commander was swallowed up by the sea: it was the same man who tried to liberate the boy here, in Ravenna. I saw him go under myself, and yet I didn't give up the chase.'

'Are you sure?' interrupted Odoacer in amazement. 'Are you sure it was the same man? How could you tell if it was as dark as you say?'

'I saw him as I'm seeing you now. I'm sure it was him. In any case, I don't find it so surprising: he who tries once and fails is bound to try again. Although encountering him face to face again, so far from here, certainly shocked me.'

'Continue,' said Odoacer, impatient to hear the conclusion of the strange story.

'I could have imagined that they'd been shipwrecked,' Wulfila went on, 'that they had been smashed to bits on the rocks; a logical conclusion, given the conditions they were faced with. Instead I crossed the entire Apennine range – arriving the very day they did, although they were advantaged by their knowledge of the territory – and then, the devil knows how, when they were already within my grasp, they slipped away. Without a trace. We ransacked the entire surrounding countryside, but never found a clue.

'It was evident that they knew where the prisoners were being held in Capri, they knew that the northern wall was undefended and they knew of an escape route that we were totally unaware of. Someone was obviously feeding them information.'

'Who?' demanded Odoacer.

'Someone inside. Almost anyone: a servant, a labourer, a baker or a blacksmith, one of the cooks or the sutlers, or even a prostitute, who knows? But there must have been someone more important behind them; otherwise how could they have known about the secret passage? I limited contact between the villa and the rest of the island as much as possible, but complete prevention was impossible.'

'If there's someone you suspect, say so.'

'Antemius, maybe. He may have known the villa in Capri well; they say he had many contacts in Naples. Even Stephanus himself . . .'

'Stephanus is intelligent and capable; he's a practical man and he is useful to me in maintaining relations with Zeno,' replied Odoacer, but it was obvious that he'd been struck by Wulfila's words. The Romans who had carried this off were courageous and incredibly shrewd. He realized how difficult – if not impossible – it would be to reign over that country by armed force alone, especially with an army that was perceived as foreign, violent and cruel: barbaric, in a single word. He understood that intelligence was more important to him than swords; knowledge more than strength. He felt more exposed, more vulnerable, in that palace surrounded by hundreds of guards than in the middle of a battlefield – and for a moment he felt threatened by a thirteen-year-old boy: free now, protected and unfindable. He mused over the boy's promise for revenge that day he mourned his mother down in the crypt of the basilica. 'So now what do we do?' he sputtered out in irritation.

'I've already taken measures,' replied Wulfila. 'I've had the boy replaced by a double, a boy his age and build, dressed as he was, who will live in the villa but be approached only by people we trust. The others will only see him from afar. I'll replace all the guards and servants as quickly as possible. The new ones won't have anyone to compare him with and will assume he is the true Romulus Augustus.'

'An astute plan. I wouldn't have said you were capable of it. Fine. Now I'd like to know how you plan to capture the boy and the men who are with him.'

'Give me a decree awarding me full powers, and the authority to set a price on his head. They won't get away from me. They're the most mixed bunch you can imagine; it won't be too difficult to spot them. They will have to come out of hiding sooner or later; they have to buy food, seek lodging. They won't be able to sleep outdoors this time of year.'

'You don't even know where they're headed.'

'I'd say north, seeing that they can't go east. Where else? They have to be trying to escape Italy, and they won't be able to get out by ship; the season for navigation is over.'

Odoacer mulled over his words in silence. Wulfila observed him as he never had before. It had just been a few months, and yet the change in the man was striking. His hair was short and neatly styled, he was freshly shaved, he wore a long-sleeved linen dalmatic robe with embroidered strips of silver and gold descending from his shoulders all the way to the hem. His calf-skin boots were decorated with red and yellow wool embroidery, and red leather laces. A silver medallion with a golden cross hung at his neck, and his belt was silver mesh as well. The ring finger on his left hand bore a stunning cameo. Nothing distinguished him from a great Roman dignitary, except for the colour of his hair, a reddish-blond, and all the freckles scattered over his face and hands.

Odoacer realized that Wulfila was studying him and decided to cut the embarrassing inspection short. 'Emperor Zeno has nominated me Roman Patrician,' he said. 'This gives me the right to add "Flavius" before my name and to have full power over the administration of this country and the adjacent regions. I shall give you the decree you've requested. Since that boy's life no longer has any political value, at least as far as our relations with the Eastern Empire are concerned, and given the risk of new turbulence, I order you to find him and kill him. Bring me his head; burn the rest and scatter his ashes. The only Romulus Augustus – or Augustulus, as he was called in derision by his own courtiers behind his back – will be the one in Capri. For everyone, and for all time. As far as you are concerned, Wulfila, do not dare return until you've fulfilled my orders. Follow him to the ends of the earth if need be. If you come back without his head I'll take yours instead. You know I'm capable of doing it.'

Wulfila did not deign to answer this threat. 'You prepare those decrees,' he said. 'I'll leave as soon as I have them.' Before exiting the room, he stopped a moment at the threshold. 'What ever happened to Antemius?' he asked.

'What do you care?'

'I'm trying to figure out how Stephanus got to be so important all of a sudden.'

'Stephanus has made it possible to rebuild relations between the East and West,' replied Odoacer, 'He has been instrumental in stabilizing my position here in Ravenna – a complex and delicate operation that you could never even manage to understand. As far as Antemius is concerned – he met with the end he deserved. He had promised Basiliscus a base in the lagoon in exchange for protecting Romulus. What's more, they were plotting to assassinate me. He was strangled.'

'I see,' said Wulfila, and left the room.

*

From that moment on, Wulfila made sure he would be informed of Stephanus's every move. He'd understood several basic things about him. That sword obsessed him, at least as much as it did Wulfila himself. The reason for such obsession escaped him, but both power and money must be involved, if he was willing to hand over such a huge sum for it. Furthermore, Stephanus must have inherited the network of informers who once worked for Antemius, and had managed to remove the old man from the picture without having to dirty his hands personally. He was the most calculating and dangerous person Wulfila had ever had to deal with. Coming to terms with him would mean playing on his turf, and he would surely lose. The best strategy was to wait until something moved Stephanus away from Ravenna. He had the feeling that this would happen soon enough; and then he'd stick to him like his shadow until Stephanus took him where he wanted to go. In the meantime, Wulfila had already sent couriers everywhere on the look-out for a company of six or seven people travelling with a woman, an old man and a boy.

*

Aurelius's little caravan had managed to elude Wulfila's men by journeying up the sunken, hidden valley of a small torrent. They then stayed high enough on the flanks of the mountainside to ensure their vantage over a vast range of territory. They had separated into three groups, and were marching at about a mile's distance from each other. Batiatus was on foot, wearing a long hooded cloak that covered him completely; he walked alone so that his size would not be as evident as if he were travelling with a group. Romulus was with Livia and Aurelius, seeming a family on the move with their modest belongings. The others were together. They all kept their weapons hidden under their cloaks, except for the shields, which were too bulky. These were loaded on to the back of Ambrosinus's mule and covered by a blanket. It was he who had suggested these stratagems while Livia had chosen the itinerary, showing the expertise of a consummate veteran once again. There was snow almost everywhere, but it wasn't deep enough to impede their passage, and the temperature wasn't too cold, since the sky was always overcast. The first night they prepared a makeshift lodging by chopping down fir branches and building a little hut sheltered against the wind. When they were certain that the enemy wasn't at their heels, they lit a fire in the forest, screened by the thick vegetation.

The next day the sky cleared and the inland temperature dropped; the warmer, more humid air which came from the sea condensed on the lower slopes of the Apennines to create a dense curtain of fog that would keep them completely hidden from any search parties roaming below. As they neared the plain on the evening of the second day they had to decide whether to descend and cross it or to remain on the Apennine ridge which would take them westward. This would have certainly been the easier and perhaps the safer route, but it meant they would be forced to travel along the Ligurian coast towards Gaul, where they would surely find garrisons of Odoacer's men alerted to their possible passage. Wulfila may even have sent someone capable of recognizing the fugitives to man each of the passes; dozens of his warriors knew both Romulus and his tutor quite well, having accompanied them to Capri and guarded the boy's prison. The map that Ambrosinus had providentially copied at the *mansio* in Fanum became precious as night fell and they gathered around the campfire to decide their itinerary and strategy.

'I would refrain from moving to the plain and crossing Aemilia now,' said Ambrosinus. 'We're still too close to Ravenna, and Odoacer's spies will be watching for us. I say we stay in the mountains, continuing westward at mid-slope until we are even with Placentia. At that point we'll have to decide whether to go on until we reach Postumia and from there descend to Gaul, or to turn north towards Lake Verbanus. We'll be close to the pass that puts the Po valley in communication with western Rhaetia, which is now controlled by the Burgundians.'

Ambrosinus also recalled that while journeying to Italy he had found a trail near the pass which wasn't too impracticable and which led through the territory of the Moesians to a Rhaetian village which was practically at the watershed.

'If you want my advice,' he concluded, 'I would reject the first route, because the area is heavily frequented and we would be exposed to constant danger. The northern itinerary is much more arduous, and safer for that very reason.'

Aurelius agreed, as did Batiatus and Vatrenus. Ambrosinus couldn't help but notice the unanimous reaction of the three comrades: they knew that choosing the western route meant passing through Dertona, where the fields still gleamed white with the unburied bones of their fallen mates.

23

'IT'S VERY LONG THAT WAY,' observed Livia, breaking the silence that had suddenly fallen over their little camp. 'We'll need money and we haven't any.'

'That's true,' admitted Ambrosinus. 'To buy food, to pay for passage on the bridges and ferries, forage for the horses on the highlands and lodging for us, when it becomes too cold to sleep in the open.'

'There's only one way,' said Livia. 'Stephanus must be back in Rimini by now, in his villa at the sea. He owes us the reward money for the mission we completed. Even if he can't pay it all, I don't think he'll refuse to help us. I know where the villa is; I once met Antemius there, and it won't be difficult for me to reach it.'

'Can we trust him?' asked Aurelius.

'He was the one who came to Fanum to warn us and offer us a means of escape. Stephanus has to survive, just like the rest of us, and adapt to all these sudden changes in the balance of power, but if Antemius trusted him, it must have been with good reason.'

'That's what worries me. Antemius betrayed us.'

'That's what I thought at first as well, but then I realized that the change of throne in Constantinople must have put him in an impossible situation. Perhaps they found him out, tortured him . . . it's difficult to imagine what really happened. In any case, the rest of you won't risk anything. I'm going alone.'

'No, I'm coming with you,' insisted Aurelius.

'It's better you don't,' Livia replied. 'You're needed here, alongside Romulus. I'll leave before dawn, and if all goes well,

I'll be back the day after, towards evening. If you don't see me, go on without me. You'll manage to survive somehow, even if you never get Stephanus's money. You've been through worse.'

'But are you sure you can go back and forth in so little time?' asked Ambrosinus.

'Certainly. If nothing unexpected happens, I'll be at Stephanus's villa before dark. The next day I'll leave before dawn and I'll be back here to spend the night with you.'

Her comrades looked at each other perplexed.

'What is there to be afraid of?' asked Livia in a reassuring tone. 'Before you met me, you always got along just fine. And you know I'm capable of getting the job done; you've seen me in action, haven't you?'

Ambrosinus lifted his eyes from the map. 'Listen to me, Livia,' he said. 'Splitting up means creating a difficult situation. If the wait lasts longer than expected, those left behind think up the strangest explanations, counting the steps of the missing person, calculating and recalculating how long his return should take, and the conjectures invented to explain a delay never match up with what is really happening. On the other side, an unexpected delay causes no end of worry; the person thinks, if only we'd have agreed upon a few hours more, my friends would be spared all this anguish. So, Livia, my friend, what we need is a second appointment. If we don't see you the day after tomorrow in the evening, we'll remain here all night none the less; we won't leave before dawn the following day. If we still haven't seen you, we'll know that some insurmountable obstacle has placed itself between us. I want to show you where we'll be crossing the Alps. See, here, on the map, the Moesian pass,' he said, pointing at it. 'You can keep this; I'll trace out the route for you. I already know all the details by heart. It will guide you to the pass, so you can join up with us on your own if necessary.'

'Excellent solution,' approved Livia. 'I'm going to prepare for my departure.' She picked up her gear and went towards her horse, who was grazing not too far away.

Aurelius followed her. 'Rimini,' he said, 'is very close to home for you. Just a few hours' boat ride and you'll be in your city on the lagoon. What will you do?'

'I'll come back,' replied Livia. 'As I promised.'

'We're going towards the unknown,' Aurelius insisted, 'following the dreams of an old man, accompanying a boy emperor hunted by fierce enemies. I don't think it's wise for you to continue on this journey. Your city on the water is waiting for you. Your friends will be worried about you, not having seen you in such a long time. You do have people you love there, don't you?'

Livia stared off over the valley, over the sea of fog from which only the tips of the tallest trees emerged, along with a little town perched at the top of a hill. Slender wisps of smoke rose from the chimneys of the houses like evening prayers towards a starry sky, and the barking of the dogs was muted by the cold, dim atmosphere that lay heavily on the plains. Since they'd left the *mansio* at Fanum she and Aurelius had never been alone, leading each to believe that the other was avoiding even the briefest moment of intimacy, as if they feared that there would never be another reason to fall into each other's arms, never another moment as pressing as their farewell in Fanum. It was like watching the sun sink into a foggy horizon and fearing that it would never rise the next day.

'Would you ever have expected such an end to our endeavour?' Aurelius spoke again.

'No,' replied Livia, 'but that's not very important right now.'

'What is important then?'

'Why we're doing what we are. Why are you continuing with them? Why have you decided to follow them?'

'Because I care about the boy. He has no one else to defend him. Half of the world wants him dead, and the other half wouldn't mind it at all if he died. That young boy is carrying a weight on his shoulders that will end up crushing him. Or maybe the answer is even more simple: I don't know where else to go, what else to do.'

'And what makes you think your shoulders are big enough to

carry that weight for him? Like Hercules, holding up the vault of the heavens for Atlas.'

'Your sarcasm is unfair,' replied Aurelius, turning away.

'Aurelius, forgive me,' said Livia. 'I'm sorry. It's myself that I'm angry at: for letting myself be tricked into this, for dragging the rest of you into this crazy adventure without being able to repay you or reward you, for exposing all of you to such mortal danger.'

'And for having lost control of the mission. Now you are no longer leading the others, but following along without knowing where we're going or what awaits us.'

'Of course, you're right,' she admitted. 'I'm used to making plans and carrying them out. I'm upset by the unexpected.'

'Is that why you're avoiding me?'

'It's you who are avoiding me,' shot back Livia.

'We're afraid of our feelings . . . maybe.'

'Feelings . . . you don't know what you're talking about, soldier,' Livia lashed out. 'How many friends have you seen killed on the battlefield, how many towns and villages burnt to the ground, how many women raped? How can you still think that there is any room left for feelings in a world like ours?'

'You haven't always felt that way: when you spoke to me about your homeland, when you covered Romulus with your cloak and held him close on your horse.'

'That was different. The mission was practically concluded. The boy was going to be taken to a place where he would be cared for and respected, you were going to be paid and so was I. The promises for the future were all good, just then.'

'I can't believe that was the only reason.'

'All right. I was just a step away from finding a man I'd been searching for, for years.'

'And that man didn't let himself be found, did he?'

'No, he didn't. Out of fear, cowardice, how am I to know?'

'Think what you like. I can't play the part of someone I'm not. I'm not the hero you're looking for, and not enough of an actor to pretend that I am. I'd say that I'm a good combatant, and that makes me a fairly common man these days. Nothing more than that. You want someone or something that you lost that night you fled from Aquileia. That young man who gave up his place on the boat for you and your mother represents your roots, roots ripped from the ground before you were grown. Something died in you that night, something that you've never managed to revive. Then, suddenly, you find a stranger, a legionary fleeing through the swamps of Ravenna, hunted by a band of barbarians, and you think you've found your ghost. It was just the similarity of the situation, nothing more, that struck up that association in your mind: the legionary, the barbarians, the boat, the lagoon . . . It was like a dream, Livia, understand? It happened like in a dream.'

He gazed into her eyes, damp with tears that she tried fiercely to blink back, gritting her teeth. He continued: 'What did you expect? That I would follow you back to your city on the water? That I would help you to revive Aquileia, lost for ever? You know, that might even have been possible. Anything is possible – just as nothing is possible – for a man in my condition, a man who has lost everything, even his memories. But one thing has remained. It's the only thing that has remained to me: my word as a Roman. The concept is obsolete, I realize that: stuff you just read about in history books. Yet it's an anchor for someone like me, a point of reference if you will, and I gave my word to a dying man. I promised to save his son. I tried to convince myself that a single attempt had exonerated me, that I could give it up even though I'd failed, but no, the one try wasn't enough: I keep hearing his words in my mind, and there's no way I can be free of them. That's why I followed you to Misenum and that's why I'll continue to stay by the boy's side until I know that he is safe somewhere: in Britannia, at the ends of the earth, who knows?'

'What about me?' asked Livia. 'Don't I represent anything to you?'

'You certainly do,' answered Aurelius. 'You represent everything I can't have.'

Livia hurled a look of wounded passion and disappointment

at him, but didn't say a word. She walked away and continued her preparations.

Ambrosinus approached her with the little roll of parchment on which he'd traced their itinerary. 'This is your map,' he said. 'I hope you'll never need to use it and that we'll see each other two days from now.'

'I hope so as well,' replied Livia.

'Perhaps this mission of yours isn't really necessary . . .'

'It's indispensable,' she replied. 'Imagine that one of the horses goes lame, or that one of us falls ill, or that we have to find a boat. If we have money, our journey will proceed much more quickly and smoothly. If we're forced to look for help as we go along, we'll have to come out of hiding and we'll certainly be noticed. Don't fear, Ambrosinus. I'll be back.'

'I'm certain of that, but until you are, we'll all be worried. Especially Aurelius.'

Livia lowered her head without speaking.

'Try to get some rest,' said Ambrosinus, as he left her.

*

Livia awoke before dawn, fitted her horse's bit and took her blanket and weapons.

'Take care, I beg of you,' sounded Aurelius's voice behind her.

'I'll be careful,' replied Livia. 'I can take care of myself.'

Aurelius pulled her towards him and kissed her. Livia gave in to his embrace for a few moments, then leapt on to the saddle. 'You take care of yourself,' she told him. She spurred on her horse and set off at a gallop. She rode through the forest until she reached the valley of the Ariminus river and continued at a steady pace along the bank for several hours, heading resolutely towards her destination. The sky was overcast again; huge puffy black clouds were being pushed in by the sea breeze, and it soon started to rain. Livia covered up as best she could and rode down a lonely path without meeting anyone but a few hurrying farmers or servants surprised by the bad weather on their way to the fields or to work.

She came within sight of Rimini late in the afternoon and turned south, leaving the city on her left. She could see the city walls and the top of the crumbling amphitheatre in the distance. Stephanus's villa appeared after she crossed via Flaminia, its basalt slabs gleaming metallic under the rain. The villa looked like a fortress; two towers flanked the entrance, and a sentry walk topped the perimeter wall. Armed men guarded the entrance and patrolled the walkway and Livia hesitated; she didn't want to be noticed. She encircled the building until she saw a servant leaving through a service door near the stables, and approached him.

'Is your master Stephanus in?'

'What do you want him for?' snapped back the man ungracefully. 'Go to the entrance and have yourself announced.'

'If he is home, tell him that the friend he met in Fanum a couple of days ago is out here and needs to talk with him.' She took one of the few coins she had left and slipped it into his hand.

The man looked at the coin, and then at Livia, dripping wet in the rain. 'Wait here,' he said, and went back into the building. He soon returned in great haste and said, simply: 'Hurry up now, come in.' He secured her horse to an iron ring hanging on the wall under a canopy, and led the way. They walked down a hall to a closed door, where the servant left her alone.

She knocked lightly and the latch immediately flew up. Stephanus greeted her: 'Finally! I'd lost all hope. I've been so worried all this time, not knowing anything about your fate. Come in, please, and dry off. You are soaking!'

Livia entered the vast room at the centre of which a lively fire was burning; she drifted towards it, attracted by its warmth. Stephanus called two maidservants. 'Take care of my guest,' he ordered. 'Prepare a bath and dry clothes for her to change into.'

Livia tried to stop him. 'I can't stay, I have to leave again immediately.'

'How can you say that! Look at the condition you're in. There's nothing more urgent than you taking a warm bath and then joining me at a finely laid table. We must talk, the two of us. You have to tell me everything that's happened and how I can help you.'

Livia felt the warmth of the fire on her face and hands, and the troubles and hardships of the previous days seemed to weigh upon her intolerably. A bath and a hot meal seemed like the most desirable things in the world, and she nodded. 'I'll have a bath and something to eat,' she said, 'but then I must leave.'

Stephanus smiled. 'That's better! Follow these ladies and they'll make a new woman of you!'

She was taken to a little room decorated with ancient mosaics and scented with rare essences, saturated by the steam rising from the huge marble bathtub at the centre of the room, filled to the brim with hot water. Livia undressed and slipped into the water, laying her weapons – a pair of razor-sharp daggers – at the edge of the tub, under the astonished eyes of the maids. She stretched out her stiff limbs and delightedly breathed in the perfume that permeated the atmosphere. She'd never had such an experience in her whole life, she had never enjoyed such pampering. One of the women sponged her shoulders and back, massaging them with great expertise, as the other washed her hair with scented water. Livia let herself sink back into the tub, closing her eyes as she seemed to dissolve in that delicious warmth. When she stepped out they dressed her in an elegant, finely-embroidered Phrygian wool tunic and a pair of soft slippers, while her muddy leather trousers and corselet were handed over to a laundress.

Stephanus awaited her in the dining room and he came towards her with a smile: 'Incredible!' he exclaimed. 'What an astonishing metamorphosis! You are the most beautiful woman I've ever seen.'

Embarrassed by such a new and uncomfortable situation, Livia replied brusquely. 'I didn't come to receive compliments. I came for what you promised me. It's not my fault that things changed: I brought my mission to completion and I must pay my men.'

Stephanus assumed a more detached tone. 'Point well taken,' he replied. 'Unfortunately, the money you were promised was to come from Constantinople, but since the situation has changed so radically, you undoubtedly realize . . . but please, sit down, have something to eat.' He gestured to the steward, who served her roast fish and poured some wine.

'I need the money,' Livia insisted. 'Even if it's not the sum we agreed upon, give me whatever you can. Those men risked their lives and I gave them my word. I can't just say, "Thank you, nice work, you can go now."'

'You don't have to tell them anything. You can stay here as long as you like. It would be a great pleasure for me and no one will come looking for you.'

Livia took a large piece of fish and swallowed down a glass of wine, and then said: 'You don't think so? You forget that those men climbed the cliff of Capri, killed fifteen guards, liberated the emperor and crossed half of Italy without any of Wulfila's ruffians catching up with them. They could be waiting outside this very instant.'

Stephanus backed down. 'That's not what I meant . . . it's just that . . . no one could have foreseen what happened. What do you intend to do with the boy?' he asked.

'Take him to safety.'

'In your city?'

'I can't say. Someone might be listening.'

'Absolutely right,' Stephanus nodded. 'It's best to be prudent. These days, the walls have ears.'

'Well then, what's your answer? I have to leave tomorrow morning at the latest.'

'How much do you need?'

'Two hundred solids will suffice. It's a small part of what we agreed upon.'

'It's a large sum none the less. I don't have that much money here. I can send for it.' He whispered into the ear of a servant, who hurried away. 'If all goes well, you should have your money tomorrow, so at least I'll have the pleasure of having you as my guest tonight. Are you sure you can't remain any longer?'

'I told you. Tomorrow morning at the latest.'

Stephanus seemed resigned, and resumed his dinner without insisting. A little later he poured himself some wine and leaned in close, assuming a confidential tone: 'You know, there's still a way for you to earn that sum we agreed upon. Even much, much more.'

'What are you talking about?' asked Livia.

'I've heard that one of your men had a sword: a very particular sword. The hilt is shaped like an eagle's head, with two open wings as the guard. You know what I'm speaking of, don't you?'

It was evident that Stephanus had very precise information and that it would be useless to refute him. Livia nodded.

'There's someone who would pay an enormous amount of money to have that sword. That would make things much easier on you, wouldn't it? Everything would be so much simpler.'

'I'm afraid it was lost during a sword fight,' she lied.

Stephanus lowered his head with obvious disappointment and did not insist further.

'What has happened to Antemius?' asked Livia to change the subject.

'It was he who sent me to warn you of the danger you were in; his plan had been discovered, and he wanted me to save you. Unfortunately I arrived too late, but at least you managed to escape. I haven't seen Antemius since then and I'm afraid not much can be done for him. If he's still alive, that is.'

'I understand,' replied Livia.

Stephanus stood and approached her, laying his hand on her shoulder. 'Are you really so sure you want to go back to the woods, to be hunted down like an animal? Listen to me. You've already done everything in your power. You're under no obligation to continue to risk your life for that child. Stay with me, I beg of you. I've always admired you, I . . .

Livia stared at him with a firm gaze. 'Stephanus, that's impossible. I could never live in a place like this, in the lap of such luxury, not after all the poverty and suffering I've seen.'

'Where are you directed?' Stephanus persisted. 'Perhaps I can help you, at least.'

'We haven't decided. And now, if you will excuse me, I would like to retire. I haven't really slept for many nights.'

'As you wish,' replied Stephanus, and called the maidservants who would accompany her to the bed chamber.

*

Livia undressed as the women removed the earthenware jar containing ashes and embers that had warmed the bed. She lay down, relishing that marvellous lavender-scented warmth, but couldn't fall asleep. The storm raged outside: rain pounded down on the roof and terraces and lightning penetrated through the cracks in the shutters, casting a livid glow on the ceiling as thunder exploded with such deafening claps that she started under the covers. She thought of her companions, huddled together somewhere in the middle of the forest, sitting in the dark around a smoky campfire, and she felt like crying. She would leave as soon as she had the money.

Absorbed in his own thoughts, Stephanus lingered by the fire on the ground floor, petting a large molossian hound stretched out next to him on a mat. Livia's beauty had disturbed him. The admiration and desire that he'd always felt for her since the first time he'd seen her on the lagoon had become an obsession. The thought that she was in his house, lying there in the bedroom, covered in only a light gown, drove him wild. How could he ever hope to tame such a creature? The luxury and comforts he'd heaped on her seemed to make no impression whatsoever, nor did the promise of a great sum of money. He was certain that she was lying when she'd said that the sword had been lost. That sword . . . he'd give anything to be able to see it, to touch it with his hand. It was the symbol of the power he desired with all his soul, and of the kind of strength that he had always coveted and never had.

One of the women came in, holding something in her hand. 'I found this in your guest's clothes,' she said, giving him a small piece of parchment. 'I didn't want it to be ruined by washing it.'

'You did well to bring it to me,' replied Stephanus, and he

opened it under the light of a lantern burning nearby. Seeing the itinerary, he realized just where they were headed. The fantastic sword was practically in his grasp, and perhaps Livia would be his as well. He turned towards the woman who was walking away. 'Wait,' he said, handing the map back to her. 'Put it back where you found it when the clothes are dry.' The woman nodded and left the room.

Stephanus leant back on his chair to get a little rest. The only sound to be heard in the huge room was the pelting rain and the howl of the wind as the sea heaved up huge breakers which rolled on to the deserted coast.

24

LIVIA AWOKE AT DAWN and found her clothes lying on a carpet, washed and dry. They still felt warm when she put them on: they must have been left in front of the fire all night. She slipped her daggers into the belt under her corselet, pulled on her boots and went down to the ground floor. Stephanus was still sprawled in front of the fire, lying in an armchair that Livia recognized as an antique from the age of the Antoninian emperors; it must have been part of the home's original furnishings. He was roused by Livia's light step descending the stairs and turned towards her: he obviously hadn't been to bed all night.

'You can't have slept very well,' observed the girl.

'I dozed a little in front of the hearth. The noise of the storm would have stopped me from sleeping anyway. Can you hear that? It's still pouring.'

'I can indeed,' replied Livia in a worried tone. A maid came up to her with a cup of warm milk and honey.

'You can't leave with this weather,' said Stephanus. 'Take a look yourself. The floodgates of heaven have opened. If you had only brought your comrades here as I wanted you to, you would all be safe and sound now.'

'You know that's not true,' retorted Livia. 'You could never have hidden us away here. I'm certain this place is full of spies. Odoacer will soon learn that I've been here, as will Wulfila.'

'They'd surely be in no more danger here than where they are now, wherever that is. Not even the most eager spy would feel like leaving my house under this downpour to report on my visitors. Livia, if you'll change your mind, there is still much

I can do for you. I can have the independence of your little city on the lagoon recognized by all, East and West. Hasn't that always been your dream?'

'A dream that we've defended with weapons, and our faith in the future,' replied Livia.

Stephanus sighed. 'Is there nothing I can say or do to convince you to give up this mad adventure? As much as I hate to admit it, there's only one possible explanation: you've fallen in love with that soldier.'

'I'd rather talk about the money you've promised. Where is it?'

'What do you think? With all this rain, there will be vast areas of flooding between here and Ravenna. My messenger may not arrive before evening, or tomorrow at this rate.'

'I can't wait that long,' replied Livia curtly.

'Think about it: it makes no sense for you to leave under these conditions. Your men will wait for you.'

Livia shook her head. 'No they won't. Not any longer than what we decided. They can't afford to take risks, and I'm sure you can understand why.'

Stephanus nodded, but made one last plea: 'Then stay, please, they'll manage without you. You've already done so much for them; you've risked your life! That soldier can't give you anything, but I'm ready to share everything I have with you: dreams, power, wealth. Think it over, while you're still in time.'

'I have thought it over,' replied Livia. 'Last night, lying snug in that perfumed bed, I thought of them sleeping out in the open, under a makeshift shelter, and I felt terrible. My place is with them, Stephanus. If that money isn't here this morning, I'll leave none the less. Please excuse me, now, I have to prepare my horse.'

She walked down the hall she'd entered only the day before and ran in drenching rain across the ground that separated the villa from the stables. Her horse was waiting tranquilly, tied to a post. He had been combed and fed and was ready to face a hard day's journey. She put on his bridle and fastened his saddle, adding on the blanket. Stephanus, accompanied by two servants holding up a canvas sheet to protect him from the rain, joined her as she finished.

'What can I do for you,' he asked, 'seeing that I can't convince you to stay?'

'If you can give me something, whatever you can, I'd be grateful. You know I'd never ask for anything for myself.'

Stephanus handed her a purse. 'This is all I have,' he said. 'No more than twenty or thirty solids, in silver siliques.'

'It will do,' answered Livia. 'I thank you.' She took the money and made to leave.

'Aren't you even going to say goodbye?' asked Stephanus.

He tried to kiss her, but Livia avoided his lips and held out her hand instead. 'A handshake is customary between old comrades in arms, Stephanus.'

He tried to hold her hand between his, but she was too quick. 'I must go,' she repeated. 'It's late.'

Stephanus ordered the servants to give her an oilcloth cloak and a satchel with provisions. Livia thanked him again, mounted her horse and then vanished behind a curtain of rain.

Stephanus returned inside and had his breakfast served in the villa's library. On the large oaken table at the centre of the room was a scroll with a precious illustrated edition of Strabo's *Geography*, open to the description of the Roman Forum. One of the drawings represented an external view of the temple of Mars the Avenger with its altar. Another showed a detail of the interior, with a magnificent statue of Caesar in polychrome marble, donning his armour. At his feet lay a sword: tiny, in the picture, but not so small that one could not distinguish the fine craftsmanship and the hilt, shaped like an eagle's head, with open wings. He contemplated it at length, fascinated, then rolled up the scroll and replaced it on the shelf.

*

Livia was in the meantime riding towards the city, figuring that the bridge on via Aemilia would be the only feasible way to cross the Ariminus river, but she soon found the road completely flooded. In the distance she could barely make out the bridge embankment, nearly submerged under the swirling waters. She felt profoundly discouraged: how would she ever be able to meet up with the others by that evening? Would they still be waiting for her in the same place, or would the fury of the elements have forced them to move elsewhere? The torrential rain had caused the river to overflow its banks and flood a vast territory; further up the situation might be even worse, with cave-ins and landslides.

She mustered up her courage and started travelling along the river to find an upstream passage, but her journey soon turned into a nightmare. The lightning blinded her horse who reared up and neighed, terrified, forcing her to dismount and drag the balking animal by his reins. He would stumble back, slipping on the mud, then start the climb again, step after step. The path she had taken on her way down had turned into a torrent, rife with pointed rocks, and the river below boiled, its silty waters rushing downstream with a roar. At midday, she had covered perhaps three miles, and she realized that nightfall would surprise her on an exposed area of the mountainside, without a shelter to be found. The peaks on high were white with snow and she knew she could be risking her life.

She felt gripped by panic for the first time ever: terror at the thought of dying alone, in a deserted place. Her body would be abandoned to the flooding, muddy waters, dragged away over the sharp river stones. She forced herself to react, to draw upon all her resources and advance as far as possible towards the village that she'd seen emerging from the fog two days before. She finally spotted it when it was nearly dark. As the temperature fell, the rain had turned into sleet that cut into her face like shards of glass. She proceeded none the less, guided by the dim lights of the infrequent cottages near the pastures and the edge of the forest. When she reached the torrent she realized that the only way to cross it was over a makeshift bridge of logs and branches, suspended over the tumultuous water seething with yellow foam.

Her horse backed off in fright, and she had to blindfold him to lead him across, step after step, as the bridge swayed precariously.

When she arrived at the outskirts of the village it was already dark. She wove her way through the houses and huts, dragging herself along with the last of her strength, until she fell on to her knees in the mud, utterly exhausted. She heard a dog barking and then voices. She was lifted and carried inside. The warmth of a fire, then nothing.

*

Aurelius and the others waited at length before deciding to abandon the precarious shelter they'd built to defend them from the elements. They considered the obstacles that Livia must have met on her return journey, and lingered all the following day and night before making their decision. 'If we don't move, the cold will kill us,' said Ambrosinus. 'We have no choice.' He looked over at Romulus wrapped up in his blanket, pale with fatigue and hunger.

'I agree,' approved Vatrenus. 'We have to move while we're still capable of it, and we can't be reduced to killing the horses to nourish ourselves. After all, we can't rule out that Livia was unsuccessful in reaching us and decided to return to her city.'

'That would be perfectly understandable,' admitted Ambrosinus thoughtfully. 'This is no longer her mission, it's not her journey. She has a homeland, and perhaps people who are dear to her there.' He looked at Aurelius as if trying to read his thoughts. 'I know that all of us will miss her. She was a most extraordinary woman, worthy of a place among the shining examples of the past.'

'There's no doubt about that,' added Vatrenus, 'and one of us will miss her more than the others. Why don't you join her, Aurelius, there in her refuge on the lagoon? You're still in time. It's what she wants, trust me. Perhaps she realized that this was the only way to get you to make a choice that otherwise you could never have made. There are enough of us to protect the boy, and we'll meet up again some day. There aren't all that many cities on the water. Hers is the only one I've ever heard of. We'll celebrate when we meet again – and if we don't, let this be our leave-taking, among sincere friends who will never forget the years we spent together.'

'Don't be absurd,' replied Aurelius. 'I'm the one who engaged you in this mission, and I have no intention of leaving now. Let's move, then, shall we? We have a long march ahead of us and we must get on with it: each passing day will make it more difficult to cross the Alps.' He said nothing more, because he was sick at heart and he would have given anything at that moment to see the woman he loved again, even just for an instant. Romulus was hoisted upon a horse, bundled up as well as possible, and the others proceeded on foot down an impervious path, through wild and solitary places, under the snow which fell in large flakes.

*

Livia opened her eyes hours and hours later, and found herself in a little cabin, dimly lit by a tallow lantern and by the flames flickering in the hearth. A man and woman of indefinable age watched her curiously. The woman took a ladleful of hot soup from the pot bubbling on the fire and handed it to her along with a chunk of stale bread, hard as a rock. It was just turnip soup, but Livia felt heartened at the sight of the steaming bowl. She dipped in the bread and began eating avidly.

'Who are you?' asked the man after a little while. 'What were you doing out in this weather? No one ever comes this way.'

'I was travelling with my family and got lost in the storm, but they'll be waiting for me at the clearing near the pass. Could you guide me there, so I don't lose my way again? I can pay you.'

'The pass?' the man repeated. 'The path has been destroyed by a landslide, and it's snowing now, can't you see?'

'Are you sure there's no other way up? I have to reach them! They'll be frantic, they'll think I'm dead. I beg of you, help me!'

'We would do so willingly,' said the woman. 'We are God-fearing Christians, but what you ask is truly impossible. Our two sons, who were trying to take our cattle down into the valley, must have been stranded by the flooding, for we've had no word from them. We are worried as well, but there's nothing we can do but wait.'

'I'll go on my own then,' said Livia. 'I'll find them further along.'

'Why don't you wait until it stops snowing?' said the man. 'You can stay here with us for another day, if you like. We are poor, but you are our welcome guest.'

'I thank you,' replied Livia, 'but I must find the people I love. May God reward you for the shelter and food you have given me. You have saved my life. Farewell, pray for me.' She threw her cape over her shoulders and left.

Livia descended the steep sides of the valley with great difficulty, often investigating the most dangerous passages herself first for fear of laming her horse. When she had finally reached the plain, she got back into the saddle and set off, keeping parallel to via Aemilia on elevated terrain to avoid the vast areas submerged under the flooding river waters. As she advanced, she tried to imagine what her comrades must be thinking; what had Aurelius thought when he didn't see her return? Had they imagined all the obstacles she'd found on her way or had they assumed she'd abandoned them? How would they manage to continue on their route with no money and so few provisions?

She travelled on for three days without stopping, sleeping in hay lofts or in the huts the farmers used on summer nights to guard their harvest. She thought that the only way she could catch up with the others was to arrive at an obligatory point of transit before they did. She'd located a spot on Ambrosinus's map: there was a bridge or ferry crossing on the Trebia river which was marked as if to indicate that they meant to cross there. She had calculated their itinerary time and time again, and became convinced that she would find them at that river passage; she would reach it that very evening, after nightfall. She was so anxious to be there that she had pushed her horse into a gallop without even noticing, but when she heard how short and laboured his breathing was, she slowed him to a lope.

She advanced at that slow pace in the shadows of the long winter night, through a countryside shrouded in fog, amidst skeletal trees and the long laments of stray dogs. She didn't stop, although she was afraid she would collapse with exhaustion, until, like a moth, she was attracted by a light, the only light to be seen in the total darkness of land and sky. As she approached, a dog began to bark furiously, but Livia took no heed. She was bone weary and starving. The cold and damp had numbed her limbs to the point that every movement was excruciating. The light that she had seen was a lantern hanging in front of a rundown building which displayed the sign of an inn: *Ad pontem Trebiae*.

There was no bridge, as claimed by the rusty sign, but perhaps there would be a ferry that crossed the Trebia from shore to shore. The voice of the river rushing between its banks made it clear that there was no other choice for anyone seeking a passage north. Livia entered, and was struck by the dank, oppressive atmosphere. A fire of damp poplar branches in the centre of the room spread more smoke than warmth. A small group of travellers sat around a table of warped planks. They were eating millet soup, with broad beans and turnips from a common platter, dipped in a little salt. The innkeeper was sitting near the oven, peeling live frogs which he tossed writhing into a basket. A thin, rag-clad girl picked them up one by one, chopped off their heads and removed their innards, then threw them into a frying pan full of lard. Livia took a place off to the side, and when the innkeeper approached to see what she wanted to eat, she asked for bread.

'Rye's all we have,' replied the man.

Livia nodded. 'And some hay and a shelter for my horse.'

'Nothing but straw. The horse can sleep with you in the stable.'

'All right. Please cover him in the meantime with the blanket that's on the saddle.'

The innkeeper muttered something to the little girl, who went to fetch some bread. He walked out grumbling to take care of the horse. The newcomer didn't look all that hardy, but he must have money to pay him with, if he owned a horse and wore leather boots. Barely out the door, he was startled to see a group of horsemen who had just reached the bank using the rope ferry. They got off one after another, holding their horses by the reins with one hand and lit torches in the other. They turned the animals over to the tavern-keeper and demanded that he bring them food immediately. 'Meat!' they continued to shout, as they sat down inside. The innkeeper called the stable hand. 'Kill the dog,' he said, 'and cook it up. There's nothing else, and they'll never notice. They're just like beasts themselves. If we don't give them what they want, they'll rip this place apart.'

Livia took a sidelong glance: barbarian mercenaries, probably in the service of the Imperial Army. She felt extremely uncomfortable, but didn't want to make them suspicious by leaving abruptly. She chewed on the hard bread and took a few gulps of a liquid that was more like vinegar than wine, but when she was about to get up, she realized that one of the barbarians was standing right in front of her, looking her over. She instinctively brought her hand to the dagger under her corselet while she poured herself some more wine with the other to appear nonchalant. She drank it slowly, then drew a long breath and pushed away from the table. The barbarian walked away without a word and went over to the kitchen to ask for more wine. Livia paid for her dinner and went to find a nook to sleep in next to her horse in the stable. She didn't notice that the barbarian had turned around to look at her again as she was leaving and had exchanged a look with his chief as if to say: 'Is that her?' The other nodded, then shouted out: 'Man, bring us some wine and the meat we've ordered or I'll have you beaten!'

'Just a bit of patience, my lord,' responded the innkeeper. 'We're roasting a kid we've had butchered just for you, but it will take a little time.'

It took an hour before the dog was roasted, carved and served with bitter greens. The barbarians threw away the greens and flung themselves at the meat, devouring it all the way to the bone under the satisfied gaze of the innkeeper, who had faced only a moment of alarm when the chief ordered: 'Bring me the head, the eyes are the best part.'

He had been quick to respond. 'The head, my lord? Oh, I'm terribly sorry but I can't; you see, we gave the head and the innards . . . to the dog.'

*

Livia, still troubled after her encounter with the barbarians, stayed awake listening to the racket they were making, ready to get on her horse and race away at a moment's notice, but nothing happened, and she finally heard them leaving the inn and heading south. She breathed a sigh of relief and lay down to rest a little, but her mind was assailed by a riot of emotions. She missed Aurelius, his voice and his presence, and she was tormented by not knowing where Romulus was, how he was feeling, what he was thinking. She even missed old Ambrosinus: his wise, tranquil way of having a ready answer for everything, his protective affection for Romulus and his blind faith that the boy's future would be brilliant, despite all the evidence to the contrary. She missed the other men as well: Vatrenus, Batiatus, Orosius and Demetrius, inseparable as the *Dioscuri*, their courage, their abnegation, their incredible strength of character. How could she have separated from them merely to look for money?

Even the memory of her city seemed to be fading from her mind. She realized there was nothing left for her. This horrible world and its abject poverty dispirited her and her only goal was meeting up with her companions again. An acute, painful sense of solitude threatened to overwhelm her, and she knew that finding the others would be incredibly difficult. She had to make a decision. She could perhaps have waited there for another couple of days in the hope that they would show up, but if they didn't, her wait would just have put further time and distance between them, and she'd never find them at that rate. She thought that the only wise plan at this point was the one

Ambrosinus had suggested: she would reach the pass before they did and stay there until they arrived. And then may God's will be done.

She waited for the first glimmer of dawn, saddled her horse and stole away, heading north towards the same road her friends would be travelling, whether they were behind her or ahead of her. She was alone and could cover a great deal of ground, so she'd certainly be able to get to the Moesian pass before them. For a moment she considered the thought that they might have to change their route, forced to do so by conditions on the ground or unforeseen events. If that happened she'd never see them again. She swallowed her panic, remembering that Ambrosinus always made the wisest decision and always maintained it, at any cost.

*

That same evening Stephanus was informed that a person corresponding to Livia's description had been seen at an inn near the Trebia ferry crossing. He decided to set off with an escort, planning to follow at a certain distance so as not to attract attention. He was certain that if he caught up with her on the road to Rhaetia, he'd succeed in taking her back with him in the end – and succeed as well in taking the sword which one of her comrades surely still held. He'd mentioned the wondrous weapon to the emissaries of Emperor Zeno, and he had no doubt that the Caesar of the East would offer any amount, and no end of privileges, to the person who could procure such a precious object for him. Possessing the capital symbol of the power of the Roman Empire would cost the emperor dearly. Stephanus left as soon as the storm had subsided and the river waters had drained off into the sea, inventing a pretext so that Odoacer would assign a group of mercenaries to escort him.

Wulfila left soon after, certain that only Stephanus had the means and the information to set him back on the tracks of his prey. The barbarian had already tried sending out his scouts in every direction on the search for a company of travellers that included a woman, an old man and a boy, but nothing had turned up. Nothing. When he learned that Stephanus was making preparations for a hurried departure, and that he had obtained an armed escort from Odoacer, ostensibly to conduct a diplomatic mission with the governors of the Alpine regions, he smelled a rat.

He mustered his men – sixty warriors ready to make hell – and took off behind him. He was certain that his objective and Stephanus's coincided perfectly. But if he turned out to be wrong, if he had bet all his stakes on a losing game, there would be no return for him. He would have to disappear into the vast inner stretches of the continent; vanish without a trace, because Odoacer would never forgive another failure so close after the first. There was no imagining his reaction. Wulfila, however, was convinced that he was on to something here. Stephanus would lead him to the fugitives, and their long flight would soon be over. He would decapitate the boy with that awesome sword, and cut the face of the Roman who had slashed at his. He would discover the man's identity, once and for all, and then wipe him off the face of the earth.

*

Livia continued in her search for her comrades. Nothing was further from her mind than imagining that she was unsuspectingly leading their fiercest enemies through the damp Insubrian plains to menace them once again and hunt them down like animals on the run.

25

LIVIA HAD HOPED AT first for a second chance at meeting up with the others at the crossing of the Po river. After all, there were very few rope ferries, like the one at the Trebia, still functioning. The pontoon bridges that had once existed at numerous points along the great river, providing stable passage at the main consular roads, such as via Postumia and via Aemilia, had been allowed to fall to pieces over decades of anarchy. After the recent turbulence surrounding the death of Flavius Orestes, any remaining floating pontoons had been stolen piecemeal by the people living along the banks, who used them for transport or fishing.

In much this way, everything that had once contributed to uniting cities, populations, rural and mountain communities – in all the provinces from one end of the empire to the other – had been lost to negligence, plundering and abandon. The public structures like the *mansiones* on the consular roads, the thermal baths, the forums and basilicas, the aqueducts, and even the slabs covering the roads had been dismantled, demolished, sold or reutilized for other purposes. Poverty and degradation had forced people to sack their native land to attempt to survive on a personal level, since collective survival was no longer possible, not to mention any kind of progress. The ancient monuments and the bronze statues that once celebrated the deeds of their ancestors and their common homeland had long been melted down to make coins and other objects of everyday use. Thus the noble metals that had given shape to the effigies of Scipio and Trajan, Augustus and Mark Aurelius, had become pots, used to cook the meals of the new masters, or coins used to pay the mercenaries who bullied their way through this sorry land.

Even the common language, Latin, which had once united dozens of peoples, was now only used by officials, rhetors and priests in its more noble forms. At the commoners' level, the language was breaking up rapidly into new idioms tied closely to the small regional communities, emphasizing the accents of the local peoples who had populated Italy even before the Roman conquest. Although these small communities were becoming increasingly isolated, the cities could still count on some measure of municipal traditions. Many maintained their own magistratures and several of them were still enclosed by walls which allowed for defence, at least against the armed bands who roamed the countryside in search of easy prey.

The temples of the ancient religion had also been abandoned and torn down, accused of harbouring demons. Sometimes their columns and precious marbles had been wisely reused to build the churches of the Christian God and were thus inserted into new and no less majestic architectures and continued to inspire people with their beauty and spirit.

In the end, all these changes contributed to augmenting everything which divided people and forfeiting everything that was meant to unite. The world was shattering to pieces, breaking into splinters which were set adrift on the river of history. Only one force still seemed capable of keeping men united: religion, with its promise of immortality and happiness in another life. Yet even this unity was largely superficial. A number of heresies had taken hold and had begun to unleash bloody conflicts. Curses and reciprocal excommunications were hurled in the name of that single God who should have been the common father of all humanity. Life for most had become so miserable that it would have been impossible to bear, if not for the expectation of happiness without end after death, death which often came at much too early an age.

*

These thoughts drifted through Livia's mind as she advanced across the great Valley of the North, aware of the risk she was running by travelling alone on a magnificent horse that was worth a fortune, whether butchered for his meat or sent off to war. She consciously adopted all of those tricks learned over a lifetime of flight, assault and ambush over land and sea. She could not have imagined that her safety was never less at stake, or that invisible eyes were keeping her every move under control day and night. Any change of direction was immediately reported to Stephanus, who was trailing at a distance to avoid any chance contact. For the moment.

He had foreseen everything. Except being watched and scrutinized in his turn by pursuers far more dangerous than his own mercenaries.

Livia decided to follow the banks of the Po, which were partially elevated with respect to the surrounding terrain; this gave her a better vantage over the territory and was a much more reliable guide line than any road. As she rode along the banks, she realized that it would have been quite imprudent and very dangerous for her comrades to attempt to cross the river on a ferry; her unwanted encounter with the barbarian soldiers at the *Ad pontem Trebiae* inn had been proof enough. On the other hand, how would they manage to get the horses across without a ferry, and without attracting undue attention? Perhaps they'd sell them, and buy new ones on the opposite side, but would Aurelius ever agree to separate from Juba?

She tried not to think about it, and to worry just about herself for the time being. She finally found a way to cross without creating too many problems; just half a mile ahead, on the gravelly river shore, a large barge appeared to be transporting sand and gravel from one side to the other. She negotiated her passage and was able to embark her horse without any difficulty. She was beginning to hope that the worst was over, and that her speed would give her a certain advantage over the others, allowing her to reach the pass a good two days before her comrades. If nothing unexpected happened.

She made straight for Ticinum, keeping at a respectful distance from the city, because she feared the presence of a large garrison of Odoacer's army. Then she headed towards Lake Verbanus, where she managed to join up with a caravan of mules going up towards the Moesian pass with a load of wheat and three carts of hay. The provisions were meant for farms up high in the mountains, where cows and sheep were kept in their sheds all winter. The farmers, she was told, could no longer take them to pasture on the plains, for fear of being plundered.

The accents of the people had changed greatly, and the countryside changed continuously as well, as they ascended higher and higher. The large blue-green lake at their backs was sunken into a deep valley and surrounded by woody hills, pastures, vineyards and even olive groves, while their climb took them up steep slopes, through beech and oak forests to woods of fir trees and bare larches.

On the fourth day of their journey, Livia left her occasional travel companions and followed Ambrosinus's map up a snow-covered trail that led to the pass. The old *cursus publicus* exchange post was still functioning a little further north in a village called Tarussedum. Smoke was spiralling from the chimney and she was tempted to seek shelter there from the pungent cold, but a great number of war horses covered with heavy felt saddle-cloths were outside, tied to the crib under an overhanging shelter. She began to look for a more secluded place, in a position high enough to allow her to keep an eye on the road. On the eastern side of the pass, she noticed a couple of wooden cabins with smoking chimneys. They seemed to belong to woodcutters, because there were stacks of logs all around, some with their bark intact, others already stripped and chopped. She neared one of the doors and knocked repeatedly, until an old woman came to open it. She was wearing heavy coarse wool clothing and felt shoes. Her hair was braided and gathered at her neck with wooden pins.

'Who are you?' asked the woman brusquely. 'What do you want?'

Livia bared her head and smiled. 'My name is Irene. I was travelling towards Rhaetia with my brothers, but a snow storm separated us yesterday, and we had agreed that any one of us who got lost would meet up with the others here at the pass. The post-house is full of soldiers and I'm a girl on my own. I'm sure you understand.'

'I can't offer you lodging or anything to eat,' replied the woman in a slightly more conciliatory tone.

'I'd be happy to sleep in the stable on my travel blanket, and I can pay you for any food you can give me. My father and brothers will be generous with you once they arrive.'

'What if they don't?'

Livia shuddered at her words, considering that her companions might indeed have chosen another road or lost their way, and that she perhaps would never see them again. The woman sensed her thoughts and took pity on her. 'Of course,' she said in a gentler voice, 'if you got here why shouldn't they? And you're right, a girl alone certainly can't sleep in an inn amidst all those barbarians. Are you a virgin?'

Livia nodded with a half smile.

'You shouldn't be, at your age. I meant to say, you should be married with children. You're not bad looking. Not that marriage is all that much fun, you understand. Come on, don't stand there on the threshold! Put your horse in the stable and come in.'

Livia did so and entered the house, standing in front of the fire to warm her numbed hands.

'I could send my husband to sleep in the stables and you could sleep with me, in my bed,' said the woman, her diffidence melting away in the face of the girl's inoffensive appearance. 'He's not much good, anyway . . . in bed, that is.'

'I thank you,' replied Livia, 'but I don't want to put you to any trouble. The stable is fine. I'll be comfortable there and it won't be for long.'

'All right, then, I'll put some straw on the other side of the hearth wall, so you'll stay nice and warm all night. It gets cold after dark here, you know.'

Her husband came home towards dusk. He was a woodsman: an axe on his shoulder and a sack full of iron wedges in his hand. The dog that accompanied him was a beautiful animal with a coat as soft and light as the fleece of a lamb; he obeyed his master's every gesture and always stayed close to him. The man seemed happy to have a guest and asked any number of questions as they were eating, about Ticinum, Milan and the court of Ravenna. Evidently, being located on such an important route of traffic kept him informed on what was happening in the rest of the country, or at least in the great plain.

The couple were called Ursinus and Agatha and they had no children. They had lived alone in that cabin since their marriage, at least forty years, Livia figured. Ursinus insisted that the girl sleep with his wife but Livia politely refused. 'My horse might catch a fright if he doesn't see me, and not let you sleep all night, and I'd die if he were stolen; I wouldn't know what to do without him.'

So Livia settled into the stable with the animals, her back leaning against the outer wall of the hearth which radiated a pleasant warmth, and Agatha gave her more covers. It was a starry night, clearer than any she had ever seen, and the Milky Way stretched across the sky like a silver diadem on God's forehead. She finally fell asleep, overcome by fatigue, but her mind remained alert as she listened for any sound coming from the pass. Every so often she awoke and looked down. What if her comrades passed as she was sleeping? Everything she'd done would have been in vain. She absolutely had to find a way so they wouldn't escape her.

She spoke to Ursinus the next morning as she drank a cup of warm milk. 'I'm terrified that my brothers will cross the pass without me noticing. I don't know what to do; I can't stay awake all night.'

'No, you mustn't worry,' replied Ursinus. 'They'll surely cross during the day. It's too dangerous to travel by night.'

'I'm afraid not. You see, my family has lost our home and our belongings because the barbarians took them from us, and now our only hope is to reach our relatives in Rhaetia who may be able to help us. It's for this very reason that I'm afraid they'll try to cross by night; to avoid the pass and the warriors who guard it.'

Ursinus stared at her in silence: he clearly wasn't convinced by her strange story. Livia started up again, in the hopes of persuading him to help her. 'We are refugees and victims of persecution, hunted by Odoacer's soldiers, who want us dead, but we've done nothing wrong, except for refusing to bend to his tyranny and remaining faithful to our principles.'

'Just what are your principles?' asked Ursinus with a strange expression in his eyes.

'Faith in the traditions of our fathers. Faith in the future of Rome.'

Ursinus sighed, then answered: 'I don't know whether you are telling me the truth about your misadventures, girl, and I understand that you must be wary even of those who offer you hospitality, but let me show you something that may persuade you to confide in me.' Livia tried to object, but Ursinus stopped her with a gesture of his hand. He got up and took a little bronze plate from a drawer and put it on the table in front of her. An *honesta missio*, an honorary discharge, issued to Ursinus, son of Sergius, and signed by Aetius, supreme commander of the Imperial Army at the time of Emperor Valentinianus the Third.

'As you can see, girl,' he said, 'I was a soldier. I fought at the Catalaunian Fields against Attila years ago. Aetius was our commander, and that was the day we gave the barbarians their most disastrous defeat, the day in which we hoped that we'd saved our civilization.'

'I'm sorry,' said Livia. 'I couldn't have imagined.'

'And now you tell me the truth. Is it really your brothers you're waiting for?'

'No. They are friends and . . . comrades in arms. We are trying to leave this country and save an innocent boy from certain death.'

'Who is this boy?'

Livia looked into his eyes: she saw the clear gaze of an honest man. She answered: 'My real name is Livia Prisca. I guided a group of Roman soldiers in an attempt to liberate Emperor Romulus Augustus from his prison, and we succeeded. We were to turn him over to trusted friends, but we were betrayed and we have had to flee. We've been hunted down like animals in every corner of this land. Our only hope is to cross the border and enter Rhaetia and then Gaul, where Odoacer has no power.'

'Almighty Lord!' exclaimed Ursinus. 'Why are you alone? Why have you left your comrades?'

'We were separated by a flood, and I haven't been able to find them since.'

'How do you know that they will be passing through here?'

'That was our agreement.'

'And that's all they said? It's important, you have to tell me exactly what was said.'

'There's an elderly man with us, the boy's tutor, who came through here many years ago, travelling from Britannia. He told me that there's an uphill passage that skirts the control station at the pass. Look, here it is,' she said, showing him Ambrosinus's map.

'I think I understand. There's not a moment to lose. How far ahead of them may you be?'

'I don't know. One day, perhaps two or three, it's difficult to say. Anything might have happened. They may even have changed their minds.'

'I don't think so,' replied Ursinus. 'If they have agreed to meet you here, it's here they'll be. Tell me how many of them there are and what they look like; I have to be able to recognize them.'

'There's no need. I'll come with you.'

'You still don't trust me, do you? You must stay here, in case they do try to cross over the pass. We can't rule that out, because the path you're talking about is covered with snow and won't be easy to distinguish. Do you understand?'

Livia nodded. 'Six men. One of them is a huge black man,

you can't miss him. Another is elderly, close to sixty. He's nearly bald and has a beard. He wears a tunic and walks with a long pilgrim's staff. Then there's a thirteen-year-old boy. He's the emperor. They have horses and are armed.'

'Now listen well. I'm going up. If I see them, I'll send my dog, understand? If you see him come barking, follow him – he'll bring you to me. If you should see them first, try to stop them before they cross the pass and have them hide in the forest. I'll help them across when it's dark. Your signal for me will be white smoke from the chimney. Agatha will throw green branches on the fire.'

'How will you last up there? It's so cold.'

'Don't worry. I have a little log cabin well protected from the wind. I'll manage; I'm used to this cold, remember.' He started off, followed by the dog merrily wagging his tail.

Livia called him: 'Ursinus!'

'Yes?'

'Thank you for what you're doing for me.'

Ursinus smiled. 'I'm doing it for myself as well, girl. It's like being in the service again. Being young again, right?'

He walked off before she could answer, and some time later Livia saw him climbing the other versant, up a snowy slope that led to the top of the hill. Several hours went by, and it seemed to Livia that strange things were going on down at the pass; a coming and going of armed soldiers on horseback that seemed unusual, given the time of year. The situation soon returned to normal, with a pair of mounted guards patrolling back and forth along the road. Livia was gripped by doubt again. How could she ever have hoped to intercept a tiny group travelling through an immense territory, amidst forests, ravines and labyrinthine valleys? As she was immersed in those melancholy thoughts, she was startled by the sudden barking of the dog, who she hadn't seen, white as he was against the snow. She looked up and thought she saw Ursinus waving at her. Almighty God! Could her prayers have been answered? Could such a miracle have truly happened? She covered herself with her cape and followed the dog down the slope and then up the opposite side of the valley, a route that kept her out of the line of vision of the men at the pass. She felt seized by irrepressible excitement, and yet she dared not believe it was true, dared not hope that she would see them again. Perhaps Ursinus had misjudged the situation, perhaps the dog was just playing with her. Violent, contrasting emotions stormed within her. She finally caught up with the old man, who didn't even turn, wouldn't take his eyes off something moving at a great distance along the path that branched off from the main road and wound its way up to the top of the hill.

'Do you think it could be them?' he asked. 'Take a look, my sight isn't as sharp as it used to be.'

Livia looked down and her heart skipped a beat: they were far away, tiny, but there were seven of them, with six horses, one of them was much bigger than the others and another was much smaller. They were trudging along slowly on foot, leading their horses by the reins. She wanted to scream, cry, call them with all the breath she had in her, and yet she had to bite her tongue. Best to wait, and to prepare for new risks, new danger, but what did it matter? She'd found them again and nothing else in the world mattered.

She threw her arms around Ursinus's neck. 'It's them, my friend! It's them, I'm sure of it.'

'See? I told you not to worry.'

'I'll go and get my horse,' replied Livia. 'Wait here, I'll be right back.'

'There's no hurry, girl,' he answered. 'They've got quite a stretch of road ahead of them. Distance can deceive you in the mountains, and as if that weren't enough,' he said, looking up at the clouds gathering in the sky, 'the weather's changing, and certainly not for the better.'

Livia took another long look at the little band struggling up the snowy slope, and then began to make her way downhill. She reached the house and entered to say goodbye. 'Agatha! I'm leaving; my brothers are here and . . .' But Agatha was stiff and pale, and looked terrified.

'What good news!' exclaimed a voice behind Livia, a voice she knew well: Stephanus! 'This poor woman is not in her usual good humour, as you can see, because one of my men is pointing a spear at her back. Now, my dear, let me look at you! It's been ages!'

'You damned bastard!' cursed Livia, spinning around. 'I should have expected this!'

'You pay for your mistakes,' replied Stephanus without betraying any emotion at all, 'but thankfully, there's a remedy for everything. We just need to come to an agreement.'

Livia would have liked to nail him to the wall with the dagger she was gripping spasmodically in her fist, but Stephanus seemed to read her thoughts. 'Don't let your feelings get the better of you; emotion is a poor counsellor.'

'How did you find me?' asked Livia, gritting her teeth.

'Oh, how true it is that curiosity is female!' mocked Stephanus. 'Allow me to explain, then, it certainly won't cost me anything. My maid found a map in your clothes before she washed them and so I was informed of your exact itinerary. That medal you wear at your neck betrayed you as well.' Livia clasped it instinctively as if to protect it. 'An object of no value whatsoever, but quite rare. One of my men noticed it in a tavern one night near the Trebia ferry crossing. Not only did that good man realize you were a woman, by the harmony of your movements and your tiny maiden's feet, but he also recognized that worthless trinket, that I had thought to include among your distinguishing characteristics. He had orders not to react if he located you, but simply to report to me. That is exactly what he did.'

'What do you want?' asked Livia without looking him in the eye. 'Isn't what you've done enough?'

'The area is surrounded by my men. What's more, there is a garrison of forty Goth auxiliaries at the pass awaiting my orders. They've already been alerted. Wherever they are, your friends have no way out. I'm a civilized person, however. I don't want their blood. I only want what interests me: I want that sword and I want you. It will make me so rich that one life won't suffice to spend so much money, and I want to share that life with you. You'll see, wealth and comfort have a way of growing on you. Forget about that boorish friend of yours. If you care for him at all, you'd better do as I say.'

'But I've already told you! That sword was lost.'

'Don't lie to me, or I'll have this good woman killed immediately.' He raised his hand.

'No, stop,' said Livia. 'Leave her alone. I'll tell you everything I know. It's true, that sword did exist, but I haven't seen my comrades for quite a long time. They may have sold it in the meantime, or lost it.'

'We'll find that out immediately; you can ask them yourself. You'll be my negotiator. If I get that sword, I'm willing to let them all go, including the boy. Everyone but you, obviously. It's a generous offer. You must know that Odoacer wants you all dead. Well then, what is your answer?'

Livia nodded her head. 'All right, but how can I be sure you won't betray us none the less?'

'First of all, the fact that I've said nothing to Wulfila. He's looking for you as well, and it's a good thing I got here first or none of you would have survived. Second, I'm no bloodthirsty monster. I see no need for slaughter when kindness does the trick. And third, you have no alternative.'

'All right,' said Livia. 'Let's go – but remember, if you've lied to me I'll kill you like a dog, even if it takes me my whole life, and before you die you'll be sorry you were ever born.'

Stephanus did not react. He said only: 'Shall we go, then? All of you, come with me,' he added, turning to the stables where twenty or so guards were waiting. They followed at a few paces.

'If you try anything, my men have been ordered to kill you, and to sound the alarm with all the others posted in the woods as well as the garrison. Your friends would be cut down instantly.'

'Then let me get my horse, and tell your mercenaries to hang back, by the woods. There's a man waiting for me up there, this woman's husband. If he sees anything suspicious, he's likely to become alarmed.'

Stephanus ordered his men to hide behind the trees in the wood which extended all the way to the first snowy clearing. Livia took her horse by the reins and began a slow ascent up the hill.

'You keep back as well,' said Livia to Stephanus. 'There's no telling how he'll react.'

Stephanus slowed his step while Livia approached Ursinus. At that moment, Aurelius, Vatrenus and the others appeared from behind a large boulder, just paces away.

'Livia!' shouted Romulus as soon as he saw her.

'Romulus!' exclaimed Livia. She turned immediately towards Aurelius. 'Aurelius, listen!' she burst out, but didn't have time to finish. She saw the expression of joy and surprise in her companion's eyes turn into an angry grimace. She saw Aurelius draw his sword as he shouted: 'Damn you! You've betrayed us!'

PART THREE

26

Wulfila and his men had just appeared at Livia's back: fanned out in a wide arc, they were rushing at Aurelius from the top of the hill.

Livia wheeled around, saw them and understood. 'I did not betray you!' she shouted. 'You must believe me! If you can make it up here, you can mount your horses! Fast!'

'It's true,' shouted Ursinus. 'This girl is trying to help you. Hurry, quickly, come up this way.'

Aurelius and the others could not fathom what had happened, nor how Livia had suddenly shown up surrounded by their most implacable enemies. They climbed up the last rise and found themselves on flat ground some distance below the top of the hill from which Wulfila's warriors still descended, their horses foundering in the deep snow. There were at least fifty of them. 'There are more at the pass!' shouted Ursinus. 'Don't attempt to cross at the road!'

'Stephanus's mercenaries are posted down there,' shouted Livia. 'He had me followed without my knowing!'

Stephanus, given the ominous turn of events, had turned back towards the road to regroup with his men. Livia pulled the bow from her saddle, aimed and hit him full in the back, at just one hundred paces. Then she turned her attention to his men, who were trying to seek shelter behind the trees: they had seen their leader fall and were thrown into utter confusion by the arrows flying around them.

Ursinus pointed to the western side of the hill. 'That's the only way out!' he shouted, 'but it ends up in a precipice, and the snow may be icy, so you'll have to be very careful. Quickly, quickly, that way!'

Livia took the lead but Wulfila realized what was happening from his vantage point at the top of the hill and diverted some of his horsemen in that direction. 'Don't forget!' he roared. 'I want the boy's head and I want the sword, at any cost! And that soldier down there as well, the one with the red belt.'

Vatrenus was already racing after Livia, as were Aurelius, Batiatus and the others. Their way seemed clear and they all spurred on their mounts to make it across the most dangerous stretch as quickly as they could; further to the west, they would be forced to ride on the brink of a chasm. They kept at mid-slope as far as possible, as Ambrosinus urged on his mule behind them. Aurelius realized how vulnerable they were in that position and he drove Juba upwards, the better to survey the situation. Just at that moment Wulfila and his men burst from behind a ridge in a cloud of powdery snow, brandishing their swords.

The barbarian was upon him in a flash; he rammed his horse into Aurelius's mount and sent him flying to the ground. Wulfila leapt at him and the two of them began to fall headlong down the slope, clutching at each other in an inextricable jumble of limbs stiffened by hate and the icy snow. In their wild tumble downhill, Aurelius's sword slipped out of its sheath and began to slide towards the precipice. A rocky outcropping that rose up over the thick blanket of snow finally stopped their fall. Their hands gripped hard at each other's wrists as they gasped for breath. Wulfila was on top of Aurelius, staring straight into his eyes, and the barbarian was struck by the realization that he had been seeking for so long: 'I know you now, Roman! Time has passed, but you haven't changed enough. You're the one who opened the gates of Aquileia to me!'

Aurelius's face twisted into a mask of pain. 'No!' he shouted. 'No! Noooo!' and his cry echoed again and again off the icy walls of the Alps. He reacted as if possessed by a fearsome force; he braced his knees against his enemy's chest and pushed him off hard, sending him rolling.

As he twisted to his side to get to his feet, he saw Ambrosinus slipping by on the snow not far from where he lay; the old man had fallen from his mount and was trying to break his slide towards the precipice. Their eyes met for the briefest instant, but long enough for Aurelius to realize that he had heard. Shaken, he began clambering back up the slope towards his comrades who were engaged in furious combat. He could hear Batiatus roar as he grabbed his enemies, lifted them over his head and hurled them down towards the gorge, and Vatrenus curse as he faced off against two men at once, a sword in each hand, knee-deep in snow.

Aurelius finally managed to get to his feet and put his hand to his sword to join in the brawl, seeking, perhaps, death. He couldn't believe that the scabbard was empty. Just then, another squad of horsemen, those who had been guarding the pass, hurtled over the top of the hill and crossed the entire clearing, then changed direction and cut across the slope again obliquely instead of taking the steep descent head-on. That sharp transverse movement loosened a great mass of snow, which began to slide swiftly downhill, growing as it descended. The first to be hit were Vatrenus and Batiatus, fighting in the fore, and then all the others, including Romulus, full force.

Demetrius and Orosius had been trying to protect the boy with their shields from the rain of enemy arrows and javelins trying for the kill. The impact of the avalanche knocked them backwards before they could help Romulus in any way. Even the horses, large as they were, were swept away and dragged towards the chasm.

Wulfila was still slipping downhill, trying in every way possible to slow his fall; sinking his hands in the snow, breaking his nails and skinning his hands, until he finally managed to stop by closing his fingers around a rocky protuberance. He found himself dangling half over the void. His hands were stiff with the cold and no longer obeyed his will to survive, refusing to hoist him up over the ridge. As he struggled against the moment in which the frost would force him to loosen his grip he suddenly saw, not ten paces away, the magnificent sword as it, too, slipped towards the abyss. It had lost its impetus, but continued to slide down, further down, ever more slowly but ever closer to the edge of the precipice. The blade shivered at the brink, slipped over for more than half of its length, wobbled and swayed, and then, miraculously, stopped. The weight of the massive gold hilt had anchored it to the ground at the last moment.

The vision was like a whiplash for Wulfila: he arched his back and, with a savage cry, mustered all his strength and pulled up until his elbows were resting on the icy edge, then one knee and then the other. He was safe. And on his feet. He approached the sword slowly, painfully aware that any vibration of the ground, or even the air, could cause it to fall. When he was just a few steps away, he stretched out on the snow, legs wide, and dug his boot nails into the ice. He eased his hand forward until he managed to seize the hilt of the sword and grip it triumphantly in his fist. He rose to his feet and lifted it high towards the stormy sky, his cry of victory piercing the clouds and smiting the ice-encrusted peaks, resounding at length in the wooded valleys. He climbed the slope until he reached the men who had provoked the avalanche, one of whom immediately turned his own horse over to Wulfila. The weather was worsening as the daylight quickly waned.

'It's getting dark,' he said to his men. 'We'll come back in the morning. They've lost their horses, and if any of them have survived they won't get far. Tomorrow we'll close all the roads that lead to the valley, both north and south of the pass: no one will escape us. It will be easier to search for the bodies by the light of day. I want the boy's head: whichever of you brings it to me will have a sizeable reward.' His men followed him down to the rest station at the pass.

It was beginning to snow, sharp tiny crystals that pierced their faces and hands. The stinging sleet soon turned into large, dense flakes that swirled around the horses who descended, ghost-like, on the hillside scattered with dead bodies and patches of blood. Wulfila was surprised to see Stephanus among them, run through by an arrow that he'd tried to rip out in his last spasms of agony. 'Just what you deserved,' he muttered, and rode on, lowering his head and gripping his cloak tight to defend himself from the blizzard.

They entered the *mansio* which was heated by a big crackling pinewood fire and sprawled out on benches as the innkeeper spit-roasted mutton and served jugs of beer and loaves of bread. Wulfila was euphoric, despite the pain of his injuries. The most wondrous weapon he'd ever laid eyes on hung at his side, and his enemies slept stiff under a deep blanket of snow. Chopping off the boy's head would be as easy as snapping an icicle.

'You,' he said, pointing at the group sitting in front of him, 'as soon as day breaks, you'll go down the road until you reach the river at the bottom of the valley. You'll block the bridge, which is the only passage to Rhaetia. And you,' he said, turning to another group seated at his right, 'turn back on this road until you come to a path that leads to the same bridge, approaching from the west. You'll have a guide with you, so you won't get lost. This way no one will get by us. And the rest of you,' he said to those sitting on his left, 'you'll come up with me to search for the bodies. As I told you, there's a purseful of silver for the first man to find the boy's corpse and sever his head. Now let us eat and drink and make merry, for fortune has been good to us!' He raised a full tankard and the others all cheered. Exultant over their victory, they gulped down massive quantities of beer, punctuating each draught with thunderous burps.

*

Juba got back on to his feet with tremendous effort, shaking off the snow and blowing a dense cloud of steam from his frosty nostrils. He snorted, shook his mane and neighed loudly, calling to his master, but the slopes were deserted and darkness was descending silently over the vast field of snow covered by the avalanche. Juba began to lope across, still whinnying and whipping his tail back and forth; he stopped at a certain spot and began scraping with his hooves, slowly pushing aside a little snow at a time, until his master's back appeared and then his neck. The horse nuzzled him, snorting hot steam on to the semi-conscious man's nape. That warm, gentle touch infused a little life into Aurelius's frost-stiffened body. He slowly, laboriously pushed up on his hands and then his elbows, getting to his knees as Juba neighed softly to encourage his efforts. He finally got to his feet and embraced his horse. 'Good boy, good Juba, I know you're good, I know you are. Now help me to find the others, come on now.' A little way off Ambrosinus's mule had appeared as if out of nowhere, and Aurelius thought of the shields hanging from his saddle. He took one and began using it as a shovel to lift the snow, soon hitting the chest of Vatrenus, who let out a moan.

'Are you all in one piece?' asked Aurelius.

'I was until you started digging into my stomach with that thing,' grumbled Vatrenus.

A whimpering reached their ears, coming from the other side of the slope: it was Ursinus's dog, accompanying his master who was clambering towards them with considerable difficulty. The man met up with the two soldiers and said: 'I'm the one who took Livia in and I can help you. My dog is trained to find people buried by avalanches. We don't have much time; when night falls, there will be nothing more we can do.'

'I thank you,' said Aurelius. 'Please help us.'

The man nodded and set his dog off on the trail. 'Go on, Argus, there you go, boy, find our friends for us. His name is Argus,' he said, turning to Aurelius. 'Like Ulysses' dog. It's a good name, isn't it?'

'It certainly is,' commented Vatrenus. 'Let's hope he's as good as his name.'

The dog had already sniffed something out and was digging frenetically with his front paws. 'Dig where he shows you,' ordered Ursinus. Aurelius and Vatrenus obeyed and pulled out Ambrosinus, livid and half frozen.

'Help us, quickly!' called out a voice on their right, from the rocky brink of the cliff. Aurelius rushed over, taking care not to slip. The scene he found was shocking: Orosius was hanging over the abyss, holding on to a pine tree which dangled over the void. Demetrius gripped the hilt of his dagger, which he'd planted into the ice and Livia was sliding down the length of his body until her legs were stretching out towards Orosius's arms. He grabbed on, and Livia started pulling herself back up, hanging on to Demetrius's belt as he desperately clutched his dagger. It seemed to Aurelius that he might let go at any moment. Aurelius plunged his own dagger into the ice and stretched out his other hand until he could grasp Demetrius's and enable him to secure a better hold and drag himself slightly forward, where he could stick his weapon into a more compact layer of ice. The improved resistance of the new anchor and the fresh energy supplied by Aurelius gave the human chain new impetus and the strength to drag itself to safety.

'Batiatus?' gasped Aurelius.

'The last time I saw him, he was rolling down that slope, in a clinch with two or three of the enemy. He'll be back,' replied Demetrius.

'If they haven't killed him,' objected Aurelius.

'If they haven't killed him,' echoed Demetrius, 'but somehow I don't think they will have.'

They were startled by a groan, and a barbarian soldier rose up just behind Livia, who wheeled around and knocked him over with a kick to the face, sending him tumbling into the precipice.

'Where's Romulus?' she asked, not seeing him anywhere, just as Ambrosinus's anguished voice reached them.

'Run!' he was shouting. 'Run, for the love of God, this way!'

Batiatus's bulky shape appeared just then at the edge of the slope facing east, and the Ethiopian rushed over as fast as he could. 'What's happened?' he asked.

'I think they've found the boy,' replied Aurelius, with a voice that reserved no hope.

They neared the point where the dog was yelping and saw

Vatrenus lifting Romulus's lifeless body in his arms. The veteran's face, whipped by the wind, was a mask of stone. Livia touched the boy's frozen limbs and burst into tears. 'Oh, my God! No!'

Aurelius got closer and looked questioningly into Vatrenus's eyes.

'He's dead,' announced his comrade. 'There's no pulse, and his heart has stopped beating.' They all looked at each other, appalled. Batiatus was weeping, and drying his tears with the back of the hand still holding his sword. Only Ambrosinus seemed to remain in possession of his faculties in that storm of wind and despair. 'We must find a shelter, quickly,' he said, taking control of the bewildered group. 'There's not a moment to lose. If night falls upon us we shall be ruined.'

'Follow me, then,' said Ursinus. 'There's one not far from here. Stay close; it's easy to get lost.' He walked at mid-slope, circling the hill to its northern face, and pointed at a slab of rock jutting from the mountainside. A palisade of fir trunks reached up from the ground, creating a sort of enclosure fenced in on three sides. He slipped in and had the others enter as well. At the back was a thick layer of dry leaves and slender pine branches, while the inside of the palisade was lined with tanned goatskins. 'They bring the sheep here when they are lambing,' he said. 'It's the best I can offer.'

Vatrenus laid the boy's body on the ground and Livia wept her heart out, hiding her face against the wall. Ambrosinus seemed neither to hear nor feel a thing. Distant, never forgotten images passed through his mind: a little boy who lay dying in a tent in the Apennine forest so many years before, a woman crying, overcome with grief. He would never give up. Never. He gave the boy a long caress, then began to undress him.

'What are you doing?' gasped Aurelius.

Ambrosinus placed his hand on the boy's bare chest and closed his eyes. 'There's still a spark of life in him,' he said calmly. 'We have to feed it.'

Aurelius shook his head incredulously. 'He's dead, can't you see? Dead, Ambrosinus.'

'He cannot be dead,' replied Ambrosinus, completely sure of himself. 'The prophecy cannot be wrong.'

It was totally dark now, and the only reply to his words was the furious raging of the wind which whipped the mountainside. Ambrosinus had undressed the boy to his waist and had laid him on the blanket of leaves. His white skin stood out against that utter darkness. Ambrosinus turned to Batiatus: 'You give off more warmth than anyone,' he said, 'because you have accumulated all the heat of Africa within you. Bare your chest and hold him tight; let your heart beat against his until it awakens again. I will try to light a fire.'

Batiatus did as he was asked, lifting the lifeless boy like a twig and clasping him close. Livia covered them both with a blanket so no heat would be lost. Aurelius and Vatrenus shook their heads, inconsolable and unbelieving.

Ambrosinus groped along the wall until he found a little dry moss, which he arranged carefully in a little pile, adding a few dry leaves. He then took the flints from his satchel and began to rub them one against the other with an expert hand. Large sparks sprayed up from the base of the little hearth and then a minuscule red spot appeared, barely visible at first. Ambrosinus got down on his knees and started to blow. The others watched with scepticism, unable to believe that he might succeed, but the little red spot slowly began to spread and the old man never stopped blowing at it, as if in doing so he could infuse life into the spent spirit of his boy.

Suddenly a little flame glittered in the dark, so small that it could scarcely be seen, but it soon grew in size and the moss caught fire and fed the flames which became brighter and more vigorous. Ambrosinus blew and blew, adding strips of moss, a leaf or two, a twig, until the flame became fire, and light. Little by little it conquered the darkness of that wretched shelter, illuminating the bodies huddled inside that tiny space, revealing Ambrosinus's haunted expression and the broad face of the Ethiopian giant. Batiatus's eyes were wide open in the dark, and filled with tears. Of joy.

'He's breathing!' he whispered.

Ambrosinus had a shaken look, the look of a man who has startled awake in the dead of night, escaping a frightful nightmare.

They all gathered around Romulus, eager to hug him, each wanting to hold him close, while Ambrosinus warned: 'Careful! The boy is still very weak. Let him catch his breath and gain back a little strength.' Ursinus left the shelter to collect what dry branches he could find and added them to the fire, then rearranged the goatskins around the entrance to keep out the cold. A little warmth had begun to spread through the enclosure, and Romulus held his numb hands over the fire.

'It was Batiatus who brought you back to life,' Ambrosinus told him. Romulus got up and hugged the big Ethiopian close. Batiatus hugged him back, gently, so as not to crush him. Aurelius said, 'I'm going out to cover my horse; he's the only means of transport we've got left, apart from Ambrosinus's mule, who won't do us much good. It's going to get very cold tonight.'

Ambrosinus saw the sadness in his gaze, which contrasted with everyone else's joy. He waited a little while, then threw his cloak over his shoulders, saying: 'I'd better go all the same and take care of my mule.'

He found Aurelius outside near Juba, grasping his cloak tight around him. He seemed to be looking out over the valley and the river, and Ambrosinus's voice startled him: 'Two truths. Two diverse and contrasting versions of your past, Livia's and Wulfila's. Who to believe?'

Aurelius didn't even turn. He just pulled his cloak closer, as if the chill had penetrated all the way to his soul. 'You know both of them. Why don't you tell me?'

'It's true, I did hear the words of that barbarian, but you're asking too much from a simple tutor. A vision has emerged from the past, forcing you to face a blot on your conscience that you didn't know you had.'

Aurelius didn't answer.

'It hurts, I know,' continued Ambrosinus, 'but it's better this way. A hidden ill devours us slowly without allowing any remedy, and can take us by surprise at any moment. Now at least you know.'

'I don't know anything.'

'That's not possible. You must remember something.'

Aurelius sighed. He felt a great desire to talk, to confide with someone who could lift the millstone crushing his heart. 'Just fragments of memories,' he muttered, 'and a nightmare that haunts me.'

'What nightmare?' prompted Ambrosinus.

Aurelius's voice began to tremble. 'It's night. Two old people, each hanging from a stake, tied by the wrists. Their bodies are horribly mutilated, and then . . .'

'Continue, you must continue.'

'And then . . . a barbarian soldier advances with a drawn sword and runs them through, first one and then the other.' He let out a long shudder, as if his words had required an immense effort.

'Who are they?' asked Ambrosinus. 'Perhaps it is there that the secret to your identity lies.'

'I don't know,' answered Aurelius, covering his eyes with his hands. 'I just don't know.'

Ambrosinus could feel the torment that racked his soul, and he placed a hand on his shoulder. 'Don't let it vex you so,' he said. 'Whoever it was makes no difference now. Only the present exists, and it does you honour. The boy, perhaps, can give you a future. You've seen for yourself that his life force can't be snuffed out.'

'I've lost the sword,' said Aurelius.

'Don't think about it. We'll find it again, I'm certain of it. And you'll find your past, but you'll have to go through hell, like that innocent boy has already done.'

27

An hour before dawn, when it was still dark, Demetrius finished the last shift of guard duty and woke his companions. They were all stiff despite the little fire they'd managed to keep burning all night inside their shelter. Even the horse and mule, who had spent the night out in the open, had drawn close to the enclosure to find some respite from the bitter cold. After their immense joy at the unexpected salvation of Romulus, the group had to face a harsh, if not desperate, reality. All they had left to them was one horse and a mule, and Aurelius's sword was now in the hands of Wulfila, who certainly could not wait to test its devastating power. How could they continue their journey? More importantly, how could they hope to escape Wulfila and his men if they were discovered? Their enemies would undoubtedly return to the hill to search for their corpses, and would find the evident signs of their escape, which the night's snowfall had not completely erased.

They all decided after consulting briefly that it was necessary to leave that place as soon as possible, descend to the valley and cross the border. Ursinus urged them to make the river crossing as soon as possible, before their enemies became aware of their presence. Then he bid each of them farewell, choked with emotion. 'The river is straight ahead of you. You'll find a pontoon bridge, you can't miss it. If I weren't so old, I'd join you. It would be a great honour for me to fight for my emperor, but I'm afraid I would be more of a nuisance than anything else, seeing the task you have before you. Also, I must see how my wife is faring; she will be frightened to death.'

He approached Romulus and kissed his hand respectfully. 'May the Lord God protect you, Caesar, wherever you go, and may Rome continue to exist through you and your descendants for centuries to come.' Then he walked off with his dog so he would reach his home before daybreak. They watched him go, just as moved as he was, and worried about what might befall him for the help he had given them.

'We must go now,' said Ambrosinus. 'It won't be long before daylight.'

They began to make their way slowly down towards the valley. Aurelius was last, leading Juba by the reins, while Vatrenus led the column, probing out the safest terrain. He suddenly raised his arm: 'Stop!'

Aurelius rushed to his side: 'What's wrong?'

'Look for yourself,' replied Vatrenus.

At the bottom of the slope there was an area of level ground, perhaps two or three hundred feet wide, crossed to the north by a torrent that glittered in the dark valley. The banks were joined by a bridge of boats held together by a pair of ropes anchored to the shores. At a distance of perhaps one hundred feet beyond the river they could see the dark mass of a dense forest of fir trees, contrasting with the snowy white bank.

'The bridge! If we manage to cross, we're saved. They'll never find us, once we get into the woods. At least I hope not.'

'That's not what I'm talking about,' retorted Vatrenus. 'Down there, to your left. You don't see anything?'

Aurelius cursed: 'Damned sons of bitches! What do we do now?' A column of armed men proceeded towards the river, barely visible in the dim light reflecting off the snow.

'And more are coming from that direction,' said Demetrius, pointing at another group closing in on the right. 'We're trapped.'

'Wait, there's still hope,' interrupted Livia. 'You still have your horse, Aurelius. Take Romulus with you; as soon as you are past the steepest part of the slope head towards the bridge at full speed. The barbarians are advancing through deep snow, which is slowing them down. You'll take them unawares, and they won't be able to catch up with you. We'll find a place to hide and we'll join up with you in the forest, later tonight, on foot.'

'That won't be possible,' objected Ambrosinus. 'They have certainly been ordered to garrison the bridge, and we'll never get past them. We'll be separated forever.' He looked over at the mule and the shields still hanging from his saddle, and a sudden idea struck him. 'Listen, I know what we can do. Six centuries ago, a group of Cimbrian warriors managed to avoid being encircled by the troops of consul Lutatius Catulus on the Alps. What they did took their opponents completely by surprise: they slid down the snowy slope on their shields.'

'On their shields?' repeated Vatrenus incredulously.

'Yes, that's right, holding on to the inside straps. Plutarch tells the stories in his *Lives*. We haven't a moment to lose.'

A pause of uncertainty greeted his proposal, apparently so absurd. Then, one by one, they untied their shields and set them down on the ground.

'That's right,' approved Ambrosinus. 'Sit inside and hold tight to the straps, like this. By shifting the weight of your body to the right or to the left and by pulling on the straps you should be able to stay on route. Is that clear?'

They all nodded, even Batiatus, who was looking terrified at the steep descent that separated them from the bridge. Aurelius helped Romulus on to the saddle in front of him and began to cross the slope at oblique angles, first in one direction and then in the other. When he reached the level ground, he dug in his heels, urging Juba into a fast trot and then into a gallop, across the snowy plain. The barbarians on both sides soon realized what was happening and spurred on their horses, but they were hindered by the snow which had accumulated in the hollows on the sides of the hill, so that Aurelius managed to stay ahead of them.

'Go, Juba!' he pressed on his steed, as Romulus looked back and forth to measure the advance of their enemies, and then twisted around to see if Ambrosinus had succeeded in his mad plan. What he saw left him nearly speechless: 'Look, Aurelius!' he shouted. 'They're coming down!'

One after another, darting to the left and right, they shot down on their shields, each one driven by its occupant: Demetrius, Vatrenus, Orosius, Livia, Ambrosinus himself with his long white hair flying out behind him and finally Batiatus, who was struggling to keep his balance on that precarious nutshell.

Aurelius sped on and crossed the bridge at a gallop, proceeding straight to the edge of the forest. He turned to see how his comrades were faring and saw that the human avalanche had hit rough terrain on the level ground near the bank and concluded its descent with a ruinous fall. What happened next was a question of mere moments. Vatrenus got to his feet first and saw the barbarians converging on them, very close now, from both sides. He looked towards the bridge and realized that they had one last chance. 'On the bridge, everyone!' he shouted. 'The bridge will take us down the river!' The others stumbled to their feet as quickly as they could and ran after him on to the pontoons. Vatrenus ordered: 'Batiatus, you and Demetrius, cut the ropes on that side, Orosius and I on this side. At my signal. Now!'

Aurelius tried to draw up on the other side, but their axes and swords were already coming down on the anchor ropes and the entire pontoon bridge, cut loose, slipped off on the current at great speed, leaving the furious barbarians at the shore. Wulfila himself had just arrived and he shouted at Aurelius: 'I'll find you, you coward! I'll find you wherever you hide! I'll follow you to the ends of the earth!'

Aurelius was seething: for the first time in his life he couldn't react to such an arrogant challenge. He said not a word, but turned his horse and galloped away.

*

After not even a mile, Romulus, who hadn't lost sight of the river for an instant, spotted the convoy of boats gliding swiftly over the waters, and it looked to him as if everyone was there. They were gripping the ropes at the rail and holding fast to each other so they would not slip into the whirlpools of the impetuous current. Then the strange vessel disappeared behind a wooded thicket which cut them off from his view. He had barely had time to shout: 'There they are,' when they had already vanished.

Aurelius let his horse slow to a walk.

'Now we'll never catch up with them!' complained Romulus.

'There's no horse that can keep pace with a mountain river. The slope is steep and the water rushes very swiftly downstream. Juba is tired, you know: he has to carry both of us, we can't ask him for more than he can give. Don't worry, Romulus, we'll continue to follow the current; I wager that we soon find them run aground on some sandbank, you'll see. Otherwise they'll go to shore as soon as the river slows down, at a port down on the plain. They'll wait for us there.'

'But why did they do it?' fretted Romulus. 'They could have crossed the bridge and cut the ropes on this side.'

'That's true, but Vatrenus made the wisest decision, like the true strategist and great soldier that he is. Think about it a moment: if he had done as you suggest, we would have been all together again, true, but on foot. Our progress would have been so slow that the barbarians would have had plenty of time to improvise a makeshift footbridge, or ford the river upstream, and overtake us easily within our first day's march. Instead, our companions now have the possibility of putting a considerable distance between themselves and their pursuers, and the two of us are free to move along much more rapidly. We can hide if need be, change itinerary or even perhaps find another horse on our way, which would allow us to move even faster.'

Romulus pondered over his words, then said: 'I'm sure you're right, but I'm just wondering what Ambrosinus can be thinking, and what he's feeling now that we're separated.'

'Ambrosinus can take good care of himself, and his advice will be precious for our comrades.'

'That's true, but this is the first time we've been separated since I was five years old'

'Do you mean that he's always been at your side in all the years you've known him?'

'Oh, yes. Much more than my mother and father. More than anyone else. He is the wisest and the most clever person that I know. He never ceases to surprise me: I've seen him do things, in this time since Odoacer imprisoned me, that I could never have imagined. Who knows how many other secrets he has in store!'

'You must care for him deeply,' said Aurelius.

The boy smiled, recalling certain moments they'd lived through together. 'He's a little crazy at times,' he said, 'but he's the dearest person in the world to me.'

Aurelius fell silent. He spurred his horse into a faster gait again so as not to put too much distance between them and the boats, which he imagined must be travelling swiftly down the river. Nor did he want their pursuers to gain an advantage; he was convinced that they hadn't given up the chase and were trying somehow to cross over. Their journey continued without difficulty through an enchanting landscape of rocky peaks coloured purple by the sun as it descended towards the horizon. The mountain lakes were incredibly translucent, shiny as mirrors as they reflected the deep green of the forests, the blinding white of the snow and the intense blue of the sky. Romulus was struck by such beauty, breathlessly taking in every change of perspective, every variation of light.

Aurelius once again gave Juba a rest and let him walk for a while.

'I've never seen anything like this!' said Romulus. 'Whose land is it?'

'It was once the land of the Helvetians, a people belonging to the Celtic nation who dared to challenge the great Caesar.'

'I know about that episode,' replied Romulus. 'I've read *De Bello Gallico* several times. Why would they ever choose to leave such a delightful place?'

'Men are never happy with what they have,' replied Aurelius. 'We are always condemned to seek new lands, new horizons, new riches. Just as individuals want to emerge over others, and excel in terms of wealth or bravery or wisdom, so do peoples and nations. On the one hand, this means continuous progress in research, exploration, the trades and other human activities, while on the other it produces conflicts which are often bloody. Huge efforts are demanded, but they are often futile, I'm afraid, and we have to pay dearly for everything that we've attained at the cost of such exertion. In the end, the losses suffered are greater than the advantages won. The Helvetians had the mountains but perhaps they desired the vast, fertile plains. Or perhaps their numbers had multiplied so that these narrow valleys could no longer contain them. They imagined that by expanding into the plains they would become a stronger, more populous nation and thus more powerful. What they obtained, instead, was their own annihilation.'

'What about you, Aurelius?' asked Romulus. 'What do you want for yourself? What do you aspire to?'

'I want . . . peace.'

'Peace! I can't believe that: you're a warrior, the strongest and bravest that I've ever met.'

'I'm not a warrior, I'm a soldier. It's different. I only fight when fighting becomes necessary to defend what I believe in. No one knows how horrible war is more than a *miles*, a combatant. Do you know what I'd really like? I would like, one day, to live in a secluded, tranquil place, cultivating the fields and raising animals. I'd like to sleep without having to jump to my feet at any moment of the night, at any sudden sound, my sword already in fist. I'd like to awaken to the cock's crow and not to a trumpet sounding an alarm. But what I'd really like is the peace of mind that I've never had. That doesn't seem all that difficult, now does it Romulus? Yet it's impossible. We live in a world where no one is sure of anything any more.'

The sun was sinking below the horizon, spreading its last rosy glow on the majestic peaks that crowned the immense range. Aurelius was eager not to lose contact with his only link to his companions, and had tried to get as close as possible to the river, but he was also afraid of running the risk of being spotted by Wulfila's men, who couldn't be far away now.

'We'll rest just a little,' he said, 'and then we'll resume our journey.'

'Where will they be now?' asked Romulus.

'Ahead of us, certainly, by at least a day's journey I'd guess. The river never rests, it flows day and night, and they'll flow with the river. We have steep, narrow, rocky paths to contend with, we'll have to cross forests and ford streams.'

Romulus took the blankets from the saddle and prepared a resting place for the night in a niche in the rock, which would do fine as a look-out as well, as Aurelius removed the horse's bit and put on his halter.

'Aurelius?'

'Yes, Caesar.'

Romulus broke off a moment, peeved by Aurelius's use of that title, then asked: 'Is there a chance we'll never see them again?'

'I think you know the answer to that question: yes. There may be rapids on the river, waterfalls or sharp rocks that could break the boats to pieces. There's nothing but ice and snow all around, and the water is freezing; if they fall in they won't be able to last more than a few moments. No environment is more hostile than the mountains in the wintertime. They may be attacked by bands of brigands, derelict soldiers looking to plunder them. Dangers never end in this world of ours.'

Romulus lay down in silence, pulling the blanket up over his shoulders.

'Sleep now,' said Aurelius. 'Juba is a good guard. He'll let us know if anyone approaches and we'll be able to slip away in time. I always sleep with one eye open anyway.'

'What about them? How close might they be?'

'Our pursuers? I don't know. A couple of hours, maybe half a day or more. I don't think they're too far away, and the traces we're leaving in the snow are so evident that even a child could follow them.'

Romulus was quiet for a little while, then asked: 'What happens if they catch up with us?'

Aurelius hesitated for a moment before answering. 'Danger is something that must be faced when it comes. Imagining it ahead of time can only make the situation worse. Fear can only magnify what threatens us. When you do find yourself suddenly faced with a dangerous situation, your mind calls up all its resources and your body is flooded with a powerful flow of energy. Your heart beats faster, your muscles expand and become harder, the enemy becomes a target to bring down, to crush, to annihilate . . .'

Romulus looked at him in admiration. 'You're not just a soldier, Aurelius. You are a warrior.'

'That happens when you've had to live in the midst of horror and destruction for years. There's a beast slumbering in each one of us: war awakens him.'

'Can I ask you one last thing?'

'Certainly.'

'What are you thinking about when you are silent for hours and hours, and you don't even hear me when I say something to you?'

'Do I do that?'

'Yes. Maybe my conversation annoys you or bothers you.'

'No, Caesar, no . . . it's just that I'm trying . . .'

'Trying to do what?'

'To remember.'

*

The pontoon bridge, freed from its anchors, had been swept away by the current at great speed. It had held together horizontally at first, foreboding a catastrophe. A huge boulder sat in the middle of the river not half a mile away; it would certainly break the fragile convoy in two. Ambrosinus immediately foresaw the danger and shouted: 'To the outermost boat, hurry!' He was the first to crawl over, grabbing on where he could to avoid falling into the water. The others followed him, and as their weight accumulated on the pontoon furthest to the left, it picked up speed and edged forward, assuming the head position. The other floats shifted rapidly behind it. Thus stabilized, the convoy passed to the right of the rock, skimming it but avoiding impact, and they all breathed a sigh of relief.

'We need poles to use as oars,' said Ambrosinus. 'Try to fish some branches out of the current.'

'We can dismantle part of the boats,' proposed Vatrenus.

'No, that would just make us go faster and we'd lose stability; the floats trailing behind us are keeping us in trim. We need something to row with, quickly.'

There were no big branches in the water, just lightweight sticks that wouldn't serve their purpose. Batiatus looked towards the rail. 'Will this do?' he shouted to be heard over the rushing waters. Ambrosinus nodded and the giant easily pulled out the left railing, a long, roughly-squared pole, and took a stance near Ambrosinus who had become the helmsman of that strange vessel. The speed of the current was increasing and there were rapids up ahead: the water was seething and foaming from the middle of the river almost all the way to the right bank. Ambrosinus ordered Batiatus to drive the pole down on the left, as deep as he could and with all the strength he had. Batiatus carried out the task with unsuspected expertise and the pontoon veered to the left, skirting the rapids, but the tail had not adjusted so quickly to the rapid change of direction of the front floats, and the last boat crashed violently against the rocks and flew into pieces.

The men turned to watch the shattered bits of the wreck being carried away by the whirling rapids, then immediately turned their attention to how they could maintain an equilibrium so continuously threatened by the jarring impact with rocks and waves. It felt something like being in the saddle of an untamed horse, as the boats bounced and jerked their way down the river. The bottom and banks were irregular and the rocky outcrops jutting towards the centre created sudden whirlpools and vortexes. The river bed would widen and they would slow down unexpectedly, only to pick up speed just as suddenly as the river took a turn downhill. The occupants of the bizarre craft were under continuous stress in the mere attempt to maintain their balance.

At a certain point, the torrent slowed and the rough bottom seemed to level out so that they thought they were out of danger, but large gravel beds began to appear, along with the no less devastating risk of running aground. In one of their sudden turns, Orosius lost his balance, rolled over the planks and fell into the water.

'Orosius has fallen overboard!' cried Demetrius in distress. 'Hurry, help me, the current is pulling him under!' Vatrenus used his sword to cut one of the ropes which served as a stay and he threw it out repeatedly, but Orosius couldn't manage to grab it.

'If we don't get him out, the cold will kill him,' shouted Ambrosinus.

Without saying a word, Livia took one end of the rope and tied it to her waist, and gave the other end to Vatrenus. 'Hold on tight!' she said, and dived into the water, swimming energetically towards Orosius who was at the mercy of the current and fast losing his capacity to react. She reached him and grabbed him by the belt, shouting: 'I've got him! Pull me in!' Vatrenus and the others pulled on the rope with everything they had as Batiatus tried to keep the bow as straight as possible, until first Livia, then Orosius, were hoisted on board. They were completely soaked through and freezing and Orosius was practically unconscious. Their comrades covered them with their blankets, so they could remove their wet clothes and try to dry off somehow. Their teeth were chattering and both were deathly pale. Orosius barely had the time to stammer out 'Thank you,' before he fainted.

Vatrenus approached Livia and lay a hand on her shoulder. 'And to think I didn't want you with us. You are strong and generous, girl. Happy is the man who will someday join his life with yours.' Livia responded with a tired smile and went to curl up near Ambrosinus.

The current finally slowed towards evening and the river became wider and wider as they reached the high plains, but they still found no place to anchor and wait for Aurelius, who everyone imagined was following them as fast as he could. The next morning they found themselves at a confluence with another course of water on their left, and yet it wasn't until the next day, towards evening, when the river had finally reached the plains, that they succeeded in taking the craft ashore and tying it with a rope to a stake. Their great river journey had come to an end for the moment. Now they would wait patiently for the group to reunite, for the little army to find its leader and its emperor.

Ambrosinus, perhaps the most worried among them, tried none the less to inspire the others with confidence and tranquillity, and the peace that reigned in that place did much towards convincing them; the shepherds bringing home their flocks, the red line left by the sun on the clouds as it disappeared over the distant horizon, the gentle bends of the river and the slow rowing of boatmen descending the current to find a shelter for the night. 'God has assisted us,' he said, 'and He will continue to do so, for we are in the right and we are persecuted. I am certain that we will soon be joined with our companions.'

'It's been mostly thanks to you,' said Vatrenus. 'I don't know how you managed to steer this wreck through rapids, shallows and whirlpools. I think that you, in reality, are a magician, *magister*.'

'Just the principle of Archimedes, my good friend,' replied Ambrosinus. 'A vessel deeply immersed in the water becomes faster, and will tow lighter ones along if the current is strong, whereas if the current is slow, the vessel offers greater resistance. All that was needed was to rearrange the weight as soon as we arrived in tranquil waters: it was sufficient to move Batiatus to the end pontoon. Now I would like to go ashore with Livia, who has some money, if I'm not mistaken, and buy a little food for us: milk and cheese should be abundant around these parts, and perhaps bread as well.'

They found a village just a little way off called Magia, where the people spoke a Celtic dialect not too different from Ambrosinus's native language, but the presbyter officiating over Christian rites in the small church there spoke surprisingly good Latin as well. They learned that the river they had travelled on was the Rhine, the largest river in Europe and one of the biggest of the world, second not even to the Tigris and Euphrates which flowed through the garden of Eden. Had they continued they would have soon encountered a large lake, followed by impassable rapids; the only way to get by them was over land at that point, after which the river ran free once again. Ambrosinus nodded. 'That will be our way: descending the current we will avoid any number of dangers and perhaps even reach the Ocean, but first we must find a boat worthy of that name. On a bridge of boats tossed this way and that by the current, it's already a miracle we arrived this far safe and sound!'

He considered the situation further north as well. The Franks had occupied vast territories in what was once Gaul, the richest and most faithful province of the empire. The central part had remained an island of Romanity, governed by a general named Siagrius who had proclaimed himself king of the Romans.

'I would say that eventually it will be best for us to go ashore on the river's west bank,' he concluded, 'and continue by land until we reach the channel of Britannia: there we will be at less than one day's navigation from my homeland. Lord God! How much time has passed! Who knows how many things have changed, how many of the people I once knew are now gone . . . how many friends have forgotten me.'

'You speak as though we were already in view of the coast!' said Livia. 'Yet our journey is still long, and no less fraught with danger than the road we have already travelled.'

'You are right,' replied Ambrosinus, 'but our heart is swifter than our feet, swifter than the swiftest of steeds, and is afraid of nothing. Is that not so?'

'It is,' admitted Livia.

'Don't you ever think of your city on the sea? Don't you miss it?'

'Terribly, and yet I would never have left Romulus.'

'And Aurelius, if I'm not mistaken.'

'I suppose so, but, in all this time we've spent together, only once did he admit that he had anything like feelings for me. It was that night at Fanum, when we knew that the next day we'd be taking our separate ways and that we'd never see each other again. Not even I had the courage then to pronounce the words that perhaps he expected from me.'

Ambrosinus took on a serious expression. 'Aurelius is tormented by a painful doubt that occupies his mind. Until he resolves his enigma there is no room for anything else in his soul. You can be certain of that.'

They had returned within sight of the river and Ambrosinus suddenly changed the subject. 'We must find a boat,' he said. 'It is absolutely essential. If Aurelius has managed to escape Wulfila, he might be here in a couple of days' time and we must be ready to set sail. You prepare dinner; I hope to return soon with some good news.'

He left her and headed over to the wharf, where several boats were moored for the night. Some fishermen had laid out the day's catch on wooden benches, drawing a number of buyers. The lanterns which began to glimmer on board the boats shone their flickering light on the surface of the great river.

28

AMBROSINUS RETURNED LATE THAT night with a couple of porters carrying a heap of sheepskins, covers and blankets, and announced that he had come to an agreement with a boatman whose job it was to transport loads of rock-salt towards the north by descending the current of the Rhine. He was willing to take them along, all the way to Argentoratum, for a slight fee; if all went well, they'd be there within the week. What's more, the boatman had sold him this wealth of bedstuffs for a pittance, ensuring them a warm night's sleep under these cold, damp skies.

However, the old man's hearty good cheer contrasted acutely with the sense of uncertainty and anxiety about the fate of Aurelius and Romulus that none of them could shake off. They'd had no contact with them, and realized that all the hardship and danger they'd faced together had no sense at all without the boy. They'd bound their own destinies to his, and his fate depended on them and them alone. The very meaning of their existence seemed to have slipped away without him.

Ambrosinus sat on the deck with his legs crossed, took a little bread and cheese from one of the shields which served as their table, and started to eat listlessly.

'I've checked and re-checked my calculations,' said Vatrenus. 'Considering the type of terrain the river crosses, we should have at least two days' march on them.'

'You mean to say that we'll have to wait all night, all tomorrow and all the next day?' asked Orosius.

'It might take that long, but I wouldn't be so sure. Aurelius will try to put as much space as possible between him and his pursuers, and Juba's a strong, fast horse. They'll be resting as little as possible and trying to make good time,' offered Demetrius.

'Trying,' objected Batiatus, 'but the days are awfully short now, and it's impossible, or damned dangerous, to travel at night in the mountains. I know Aurelius doesn't want to risk falling into a precipice, or laming his horse. I'd recalculate, keeping in mind that they'll only be able to take on short distances at a time.'

Each expressed his own point of view, and it soon became clear that none of their estimates matched up.

'They might be way up there, on those high peaks, right now,' said Livia, gazing at the mountains. 'They'll be cold and hungry and completely worn out. We've been much luckier, even though our journey was so eventful.'

Vatrenus tried to inject a note of optimism. 'Perhaps we're worrying over nothing. Wulfila may not have succeeded in crossing the torrent, or he may have lost a great deal of time travelling up and down its length looking for a ford. Perhaps Aurelius can afford to take his time and get here when he gets here. He knows that we'll be waiting for him in a visible position, and that we won't leave this floating convoy of ours until he meets up with us.'

'Couldn't we try to set up a light signal of some sort?' suggested Demetrius. 'If they were up there, they'd see it, and it would give them heart. They'd know we're here waiting for them. My shield is made of metal; if we polished it . . .'

'No, better not,' objected Ambrosinus. 'They know we're here anyway, and they'll find us because they'll keep to the river. A light signal would attract Wulfila as well; you can be sure that he hasn't given up the chase. He'll have no peace until he's got rid of every last one of us, mark my words. Try to rest now, all of you. It's been a most tiring day, and we have no idea of what awaits us tomorrow.'

'I'll take the first shift,' said Livia. 'I'm not tired.' She sat at the bow, on the edge of the boat, with her legs dangling over the side. The others laid out Ambrosinus's sheepskins on the deck, stretching out close together to stay warm and covering up with the blankets. Ambrosinus sat off to one side, his eyes piercing through the darkness, then he stood and joined Livia.

'You should get some sleep yourself. This place seems safe enough to me. Maybe even an old pedagogue will do to stand guard.'

'I told you. I'm not tired.'

'Neither am I. Perhaps I could keep you company for a while . . . if you like.'

'I'd like that very much. We never finished what we were saying, remember?'

'Yes, of course.'

'You were speaking to me of some enigma in Aurelius's life.'

'Yes, that's right: words I heard without meaning to, that night at Fanum and the other night at the pass, while I was trying to stop myself from slipping down into the chasm.'

'What did you hear?' asked Livia, troubled.

'Perhaps you should tell me everything you know about him first.'

'I know so little.'

'Or what you think you know.'

'I . . . I think he is the young officer who so heroically defended Aquileia for nine months against Attila's Huns. I think he was the one who helped me and my mother to escape by letting us take his place on a boat on the night the city fell, at the hand of a traitor.'

'How can you be sure?'

'I feel it. I know I'm not wrong.'

Ambrosinus sought out Livia's eyes in the darkness. 'In truth, you've lied to him . . . haven't you? You needed a man who was capable of carrying out the impossible, and you thought you could inject the memory of a hero, of someone who perhaps no longer exists.'

'No!' objected Livia. 'Well, maybe a little, at first; but then the more I saw him fighting, risking his life again and again to save the life of another, I had no doubts. He is the hero of Aquileia, and even if he wasn't, this is the truth for me.'

'A truth that he denies. This is the cause of your discord, the ghost that stands between you and makes you strangers to each other. Listen to me: no memory, no recollection, can take root in his mind if there's nothing beneath. You can't build on water.'

'You say not? I've seen it done.'

'Yes, your city on the lagoon. But this is different; here we're talking about the soul of a man, his wounded mind, his feelings; and as if that weren't enough, another truth has emerged from his past and threatens to crush him.'

'What are you talking about? Tell me, I beg of you.'

'I can't. I don't have the right.'

'I understand,' said Livia, resigned, 'but is there nothing I can do for him?'

Ambrosinus sighed. 'The truth, the only truth, must be forced to emerge from his mind, where it has lain buried so long. I know a way, perhaps, but it is terrible, terrible . . . he might not survive it.'

'Where might he be now, *Ambrosine*?'

She noticed him stiffen at her question. His eyes clouded and his entire being seemed centred on some immense effort.

'Perhaps . . . in danger,' he said, with a strange, metallic voice.

Livia got closer and looked at him in amazement. All at once, she became aware that he was no longer with her: his mind, and perhaps his soul, were elsewhere, scouring mysterious paths, exploring remote territory, snowy expanses . . . wandering the mountainside, carried by the wind over fir woods and icy peaks, flying over the surface of frozen lakes, silent and invisible as a midnight bird of prey.

Livia said nothing, and sat absorbed in her own thoughts, listening to the soft lapping of the waves against the boat's planks. A cold north wind tore into the clouds, uncovering the disc of the moon for a moment. Ambrosinus's face, illuminated by that pale light, seemed a waxen mask. His eyes were white, empty, unblinking, like a statue's. Only his mouth was open, as if he were screaming, but no sound came out, nor did his breath vaporize in the air like the others'. It was as if he were not breathing at all.

*

The shrill shriek of a bird of prey fractured the deep silence of the forest and Aurelius jerked awake, eyes darting as he strained to perceive the slightest sound. He shook Romulus who was sleeping curled up next to him. 'We have to go,' he said. 'Wulfila's here.'

Romulus scanned the woods around him in terror, but everything was quiet and calm and the moon was peeking out from behind the clouds, over the tips of the fir trees.

'Hurry!' insisted Aurelius. 'We haven't a moment to lose!' He adjusted the horse's bit and led Juba by the bridle down the path through the forest as quickly as he could, Romulus running alongside.

'What did you see?' gasped the boy.

'Nothing. A cry woke me; a cry of alarm. It's my instinct. 1I can feel a threat, after so many years of war. Run, Romulus, we have to move faster. As fast as we can.'

They left the forest behind them and found themselves on a clearing blanketed with snow. The moon diffused a soft glow that reflected off the white countryside, and Aurelius could make out the tracks of a couple of wheels crossing the clearing and heading down the valley.

'That way,' he pointed. 'If a cart can get through, it means the terrain is solid underneath. We can mount the horse now, finally. Come on, quick now, up you go!'

'But Aurelius, there's no one . . .'

Aurelius didn't even answer. He grabbed the boy's arm and hoisted him up on to the saddle in front of him. He touched the spurs and Juba broke into a gallop, following the traces of the cart over the snow-covered meadow. Off in the distance the dark shape of a village could be seen, and Aurelius spurred the horse on even faster. They were greeted by a chorus of barks as they neared the first home, so Aurelius veered towards the bottom of the valley, reaching a slightly raised area from which he could see the whole river bed. He breathed a sigh of relief and slowed Juba to a walk so he could catch his breath as well. The untiring animal, steaming with sweat, blew great clouds of vapour from his nostrils and snorted impatiently, champing at the bit as if eager to get on with it. Perhaps he, too, could feel danger looming.

*

Wulfila and his men reached the end of the fir woods and immediately noticed the trail on the candid white blanket of snow: horse tracks, mixing into those of a cart, descending the slope.

One of them jumped to the ground and poked at the marks. 'The left rear horseshoe has only three nails and the front prints are deeper than the back ones. That means the horse is carrying weight between the saddle and his neck. It's them.'

'Finally!' exclaimed Wulfila. 'We've got them now; they can't escape.' He raised his hand and signalled to the others to follow him at a gallop down the mountain side. There were over seventy of them, and their passage raised a white cloud, a halo of silvery powder that glimmered in the moonlight like a magical nocturnal rainbow. Awakened by the furious barking of their dogs, the men of the village beheld that phantasmagoric ride across the wide clearing above their houses, and swiftly made the sign of the cross. Those could be nothing else but the damned souls that escaped from hell by night in search of victims to drag down with them into the fiery pit. They barred their windows, and kept their ears to the doors, trembling with fear, until the sound of that galloping vanished off into the distance and the howling of their guard dogs settled into a soft whimper.

*

The cold light of dawn slowly began to permeate the thin layer of clouds that covered the sky and to awaken the men who were sleeping curled up under their blankets. Livia got up as well, touching her hands to her forehead and temples. She felt as if she'd dreamed it all, as if Ambrosinus had never really spoken to her. There he was, stretched out with the others, sleeping on the sheepskins. Demetrius was standing guard; he appeared to be scanning the snow-covered hills. Ambrosinus proposed that they move on to the boat that would take them north, so that they'd be ready to deport as soon as possible. They had decided to leave the pontoons in a barter agreement with the boatman, who planned to use them as tows.

He was a man of about fifty, heavyset and sturdy, with a thick head of grey hair, dressed in a felt tunic and a leather apron. His manner was brusque and resolute.

'I can't wait much longer,' he told them as soon as they appeared. 'People are starting to butcher their pigs and they'll need salt to conserve the meat. But there's another reason we must set off soon, a much more important one. The colder it gets, the greater our risk of being blocked as we travel north. The river may freeze up and I don't want my boat getting stuck, and crushed by the ice.'

'You said we could wait until this evening. A few more hours surely won't change the situation much!' objected Ambrosinus. Livia noticed how weak his voice had become, how hoarse. His face was ashen and deep wrinkles furrowed his brow, as if he hadn't slept all night.

'Sorry,' insisted the boatman, 'but the weather's changing, as you can see. There's a thick fog coming up and it's a risk navigating under these conditions. Not my fault if the weather is turning bad on us.'

Ambrosinus entreated him: 'We've left you the pontoons and you still stand to make a profit on your load. I've promised you more money for our passage; consent to our request, if you can. The friends we are waiting for will arrive soon, I assure you.'

The boatman wouldn't budge. 'I have to weigh anchor,' he answered. 'There's no more to be said.'

Vatrenus approached. 'I'm afraid there is, old man. Listen:

either you do as we ask nicely, or we have ways to persuade you. We're all armed and you'll weigh anchor when we tell you to.'

The boatman huffed off in a fury and went aft to consult with his crew.

'You shouldn't have done that,' said Ambrosinus. 'It's always wiser to negotiate; always prefer reasoning over force.'

'That may be,' replied Vatrenus, 'but for the time being we're still at anchor, so my reasoning must have been more convincing than yours.'

He hadn't finished speaking when Livia shouted: 'There they are!'

Aurelius and Romulus were racing headlong down the hillside, with the barbarian squad in close pursuit. Wulfila was at their head, brandishing his sword and screaming out savagely. The boatman took one look and immediately pictured his precious vessel turned into a battlefield or, worse yet, burned to a crisp in retaliation by those screaming demons. Perhaps this bunch here were fugitives; they must have committed some crime. He yelled out with everything he had: 'Cast off! Now!' A couple of the crewmen freed the moorings in a flash while another pushed off with an oar.

Vatrenus shouted: 'Nooo! You damned bastards!'

It was too late: the boat had already detached from the wooden pier and was slowly moving away. Livia saw a moment of indecision in Aurelius's eyes: he had been heading towards the pontoons, but must have seen that they were empty. She shouted as loudly as she could: 'This way! We're here! Hurry, Aurelius, hurry!' and started waving her cape in the air, as the others jumped up and down, yelling: 'Over here! Quickly!'

Aurelius spotted them, clenched his knees into Juba's flanks and yanked on the bit, making the horse veer sharply. He then urged him into a fast gallop, shouting: 'Go, Juba, go, jump!' pulling up on the reins at his bit and neck. The boat was parallel to the shore now and was moving past the end of the pier. Aurelius swiftly covered the entire length of the pier, then launched Juba into an incredible leap that landed them on the pile of rock-salt. The horse sank in up to his knees as Aurelius and Romulus jumped free, tumbling sideways into the white mound that broke their fall.

Batiatus, seeing the sudden change in the situation, yanked free the two stern rudders, stuck them in the oarlocks and started rowing to help the boat pick up speed. Wulfila galloped down the pier after them, wild with the fury of the chase, but he had to draw up his stallion at the last minute to stop him from plunging into the water. His comrades crowding behind him, he was left behind once again in a frenzy, powerless to stop his prey.

Vatrenus raised his arm in an obscene gesture, shouting out an insult that Romulus couldn't understand. The boy brushed off the salt he was completely covered with and drew closer. 'What does *temetfutue* mean?' he asked him innocently.

'Caesar!' scolded Ambrosinus. 'You mustn't repeat such words!'

'It means "Fuck you!"' replied Vatrenus calmly, and he lifted the boy and raised him high, over everyone's heads as they all shouted: 'Welcome back, Caesar!' in an explosion of irrepressible joy that their tension had suffocated until that very instant. They were all embracing each other and even Juba got a few well-deserved hugs. The heroic steed had brought Romulus and Aurelius to safety with incredible valour. Batiatus handed the rudders back to the crew and joined his rejoicing companions.

Wulfila continued to follow the boat, galloping along the shore with the sword of Caesar held high like an implacable threat. Aurelius hung over the starboard railing, exposing himself to the waves of his enemy's hate, like an icy wind that burned into his skin. He couldn't help but stare at the shining sword the barbarian grasped in his fist. The horsemen sent swarms of arrows at them, which fell into the water with soft splashes. One had been shot in such a high arc that it landed on the deck, but Demetrius promptly raised his shield to stop it from striking Livia. The distance between them was increasing with each passing instant until the boat was completely out of reach.

Romulus went to Aurelius and touched his arm: 'Don't think

about that sword any more,' he said. 'It doesn't matter that you've lost it. Other things are more important.'

'Which things?' asked Aurelius bitterly.

'That we're all here, all together again. All that matters to me is that everyone cares about me. You too, I hope.'

'Of course I care, Caesar,' replied Aurelius without turning.

'Don't call me Caesar.'

'I do care about you, my boy,' answered Aurelius, and he finally turned and hugged him close, eyes hot with tears.

Just then the thick cloud bank opened, the fog creeping through the air dissipated and the sun set the surface of the great river aflame, illuminating the snowy expanses that lined its shores and making them glitter like a silver cloak. They were all enchanted by that sight, as if a vision of hope had been offered them. From the small group of veterans at the stern, the husky voice of Rufius Aelius Vatrenus slowly and solemnly struck up the Hymn to the Sun, Horace's age-old *Carmen Saeculare*:

Alme Sol curru nitido diem qui
promis et celas . . .

His voice was joined by a second and then a third and a fourth, then by Livia's voice and by Aurelius's too:

aliusque et idem
nasceris, possis nihil Roma
visere maius . . .

Romulus hesitated, looking at Ambrosinus. 'It's a pagan song . . .' he said.

'It's the hymn to the greatness of Rome, my son, which would never have achieved such splendour had God not allowed it. Now that Rome's sun is setting, it is only right that we raise this song of glory,' and his voice united with the others.

And Romulus sang as well. He lifted his clear, sweet voice as he had never done before, dominating the deep, strong voices of his companions, joining Livia's throbbing notes. The boatman himself was so taken by their intensity that he joined in, following the melody although he knew not the words.

The song finally faded as the sun, having vanquished the clouds and the fog, shone in triumph in that winter sky.

Romulus approached the boatman who had fallen silent and had a strange, moved look in his eye. 'Are you Roman too?' he asked.

'No,' replied the boatman, 'but I'd like to be.'

29

The lake of Brigantium materialized before them like a huge resplendent mirror surrounded by woods and pastures dotted with isolated houses and villages. It took an entire day of navigation to cross it from one side to the other, before they reached a promontory that separated two long, narrow inlets, like the tines of a fork. The boat entered the one on the left and dropped anchor for the night near a small city called Tasgaetium.

'Here we are on the Rhine again,' announced the boatman the next day, as the vessel turned into the current where the river resumed its northerly flow. 'We'll be making our way down for about a week, and then we'll reach Argentoratum, but before that, you'll see a sight that you never have seen nor will see again in all your lives: the grand rapids.'

'Rapids?' repeated Orosius, still terrified over their last fluvial adventure. 'But rapids are dangerous . . .'

'That they are!' agreed the boatman. 'These are over fifty feet high and five hundred feet wide, and they crash foaming into the valley with a roar like thunder. If you are very quiet and listen hard, you can even hear them from here, if the wind is in our favour as I'd say it is.'

They all fell silent, looking at one another with apprehension, unable to understand what effects the boatman meant his warning to have. They could in fact hear, or so they imagined, a deep rumble – mixing with the other sounds of nature – which might be the voice of the rapids.

Ambrosinus approached the boatman: 'I suppose you must

have an alternative route in mind: a fall of fifty feet seems excessive, even for a solid boat like yours.'

'You're absolutely right,' he replied, luffing the sheets and putting about with the rudder. 'We're going ashore and crossing over land. There's a special service with oxen-towed slides that will take us over to the valley of the cascades.'

'Great gods!' exclaimed Ambrosinus. 'A *diolkos*! Who would ever have guessed such a thing, in these barbarian lands?'

'What did you say?' asked Vatrenus.

'A *diolkos*: a system for allowing passage over land for ships that have to overcome a natural obstacle. There was one at the isthmus of Corinth in antiquity – truly spectacular, they say.'

The boat was just drawing alongside the dock. It was hooked on to a haulage system and was pulled on to a slip on wheels, as the boatman negotiated a price for passage. The driver called out to the oxen and the massive train was set into motion. Juba was allowed ashore so that he could stretch his legs on a long walk. It took nearly two days, with frequent replacements of the oxen, before the boat reached flat land. As they passed under the rapids, they all stopped to admire the immense wall of foaming water, as a rainbow spanned it like a bridge from one shore to the other. Beneath, the waters boiled and seethed with whirlpools and vortices at the point where the river resumed its westward flow.

'What a wonder!' exclaimed Romulus. 'It reminds me of the Nera waterfall, but this is ever so much bigger!'

'Thank Wulfila!' laughed Demetrius. 'If it hadn't been for him, you never would have seen this.'

The others started laughing as well, as the boat was launched back into the river. They were all giddy, as if they were starting out on some playful adventure, except for Ambrosinus.

'What's wrong, *Ambrosine*?' asked Livia.

The old man's forehead creased: 'Wulfila. This journey over land will have cost us the lead we had over him. He could be anywhere on those hills, right now.' Their laughter died out into hushed whispers. Several of them began to scan the hillsides all around, others leaned over the railing to watch the placid flow of the waters.

'The river current is slower now,' continued Ambrosinus, 'and when we turn north, we'll have the wind against us as well. What's more, this boat is easily recognizable, with all this salt and a horse on board.' No one felt like laughing any more, or even like talking.

'What are we going to do when we get to Argentoratum?' asked Livia to change the subject.

'I think we should go to Gaul, where we won't be so easy to spot,' replied Ambrosinus. He took the map he had drawn at the *mansio* in Fanum, returned to him by Livia after they'd met up at the pass. He laid it out on a bench and gestured for his companions to gather around. 'Look,' he said, 'let me show you the situation, more or less. Here, the central south of the country is settled by the Visigoths, friends and confederates of the Romans for many years. They fought at the Catalaunian fields against Attila under the command of Aetius, who was a personal friend of the Visigoth king. The king paid for this loyalty and friendship with his life: he fell in battle as he valiantly led the right wing of the confederate battle line.'

'So not all barbarians are cruel and wild,' commented Romulus.

'I've never said that,' replied Ambrosinus. 'On the contrary. Many of them are extraordinarily courageous, loyal and sincere: values which unfortunately no longer appertain to our own so-called civilized customs.'

'Yet they've brought about the destruction of our empire, of our world.'

'Not through any fault of mine,' said Batiatus. 'I've killed so many of them that I've lost count.'

Ambrosinus returned to the heart of the matter. 'My son, it's not a question here of distinguishing between good barbarians and bad ones. Those whom we call "barbarians" were peoples who lived from time immemorial as nomads on the vast

Sarmatian steppes. They had their traditions, their customs, their way of life. Then, for some reason, they began to push at our borders. Perhaps their territories suffered from drought, or from epidemics that wiped out their livestock. Perhaps they were pushed by yet other peoples fleeing in turn from their own homelands. It's hard to say. Perhaps they realized how poor they were with respect to our riches, how wretched their tents of animal hides were, compared to our houses of brick and marble, our villas, our palaces. Those who lived at the borderline and traded with us saw the enormous differences between their frugal lives and our wasteful ones. They beheld our profusion of bronze, of gold and silver, the beauty of our monuments, the abundance and refinement of our foods and our wines, the sumptuousness of our clothing and jewels, the fertility of our fields. They were dazzled and fascinated; they too wanted to live as we did, and so the attacks began. They attempted to storm our defences or, in other cases, kept up constant pressure, slow infiltration. This conflict has gone on for three hundred years, and it's still not over.'

'What are you saying? It *is* all over. Our world no longer exists.'

'You're wrong. Rome cannot be identified with a race, or a people, or an ethnic group. Rome is an ideal, and ideals cannot be destroyed.'

Romulus shook his head, incredulously. How could that man still cherish such faith in the face of desolation and decline?

Ambrosinus pointed his finger at his map again. 'Here, between the Rhine and Belgica, are the Franks, who I've already told you about in part. They used to live in the forests of Germany, but now they occupy the best land of Gaul, west of the Rhine, and do you know how they crossed over? The cold. One night, the air temperature dropped so low that the Rhine froze over, and our soldiers awoke the next morning to a spectral vision: an immense army on horseback emerging from the fog as if they were walking on the waters. They were advancing on a sheet of ice. Our men fought valiantly, but they were overwhelmed.'

'It's true,' nodded Orosius. 'I once heard a veteran on the Danube telling the story. His teeth had all fallen out, and he had more scars than skin, but his memory was still fine, and the vision of those warriors crossing the river on horseback was still a nightmare for him. He'd jerk awake in his sleep yelling: "Alarm! Sound the alarm! They're upon us!" Some of us thought he'd lost his mind, but no one dared mock him.'

'To the northeast,' continued Ambrosinus, 'there's what remains of the Roman province of Gaul which has claimed independence. It is ruled by Siagrius, the Roman general who has had himself recognized as *Rex Romanorum*. Only an uncultured soldier could aspire to a title at once so antiquated and so high-sounding.'

'Hey, *magister*,' objected Batiatus. 'We're uncultured soldiers ourselves, but we've got our good points. I kind of like this Siagrius.'

'Yes, perhaps you're right. It will be best for us to travel through his kingdom; the territory is still well organized and sufficiently under control. We could head for the Seine and go down the river to Parisii; we can reach the channel of Britannia from there. It's a long, difficult journey, but we should be able to make it, and hopefully shake off our pursuers. Once we reach the channel, it won't be difficult to find passage. Many of our merchants come to sell sheep's wool in Gaul, where it is woven, and to buy goods that can't be found in Britannia.'

'What then? When we've finally arrived in your Britannia? Will things be better? Will life be any easier?' asked Vatrenus, expressing everyone's unspoken doubts.

'I'm afraid not,' answered Ambrosinus. 'I've been gone for many years and I don't nurture any vain hopes. The island has been abandoned to its fate for half a century, as you know, and many local chieftains continue to wage war. What I do hope is that the institutions of civilization have survived in the most important cities, especially in the city that led the resistance against the invasions of the north: Carvetia. That's where we shall go, and to get there we will have to cross nearly the entire island, from south to north.'

No one said another word. Those men had come from the Mediterranean, and here the entire continent around them was in the grip of this bitter cold. The snow covered everything with its white shroud, wiping out every natural feature, every border. It was nature who imposed her rules here, and her limits – limits made of rivers, mountains and boundless forests.

*

Their journey continued for long days, and even nights, when the faint light of the moon permitted it. They descended the current of the great river and as they got further and further north, the sky was increasingly clear and cold, the wind more cutting. Aurelius and his companions had crafted rough tunics for themselves out of sheepskins; their beards grew long and unkempt, as did their hair. Day after day, they had begun to resemble the barbarians who inhabited those lands. Romulus watched the landscape with a mix of wonder and fear; that endless desolation filled his heart with dread. Sometimes he even regretted leaving Capri: the island colours, the sea, the scent of pine and broom, an autumn so mild it seemed like spring. He tried hard never to let his low spirits show, aware of the sacrifices and dangers his friends were facing for him. It was just that those sacrifices were becoming too much for him to bear. With every passing day he felt that the price they'd paid was too high, out of proportion to the goal that could be achieved, a goal that wasn't clear to any of them, in the boy's eyes, except Ambrosinus. The old man's wisdom and his knowledge of the world and nature never ceased to amaze him, but the mysterious depths of his personality left Romulus feeling uneasy. When the giddy enthusiasm of being freed, and then rejoined with his companions, had died down, he was left with a sense of apprehension and even guilt towards these men who had tied their own destiny to the fate of a sovereign without a land and without a people, a poor boy, who could never begin to pay them back for what they had done.

Vatrenus, Batiatus and the others in truth felt increasingly united with one another, not so much in view of a goal to be achieved or a plan to be carried out, but for the very fact of finding themselves together, armed again and on the march. It was the restlessness of their leader that had them worried; they couldn't understand Aurelius's absent looks and pensive expression, and didn't know how it would all end up. Livia was troubled as well, but for much more personal, intimate reasons.

One evening she approached him as he was leaning over the boat's railing, alone, standing guard, staring at the grey waters of the Rhine.

'Are you worried?' she asked him.

'Like always. We're heading for a completely unknown territory.'

'Don't think about it. We're all together, and we'll face whatever awaits us. Isn't that a comfort to you? When you and Romulus were up in the mountains, I was so distraught. I kept trying, in my mind's eye, to follow your every step; I imagined the two of you alone, exposed to all the perils of the forest, hunted down by your worst enemy . . .'

'As I was thinking of all of you. You, especially. I couldn't get you out of my mind, Livia.'

'Me?' Livia repeated, searching out his eyes.

'I've always thought of you, I've always desired you, since I saw you bathing in that spring on the Apennines; you were like some woodland divinity. I've always suffered, every moment I've been separated from you.'

Livia felt a shiver under her skin, and it wasn't the northern wind: it was this sudden, unexpected glimpse into Aurelius's soul as he bared his emotions in such a seemingly casual way.

'Why couldn't you open up to me?' she asked. 'Why haven't you ever let me know how you feel? Why did you always push me away when I tried to talk to you about my feelings, closing me out of your heart? My life has no meaning apart from you, Aurelius. I know, I've made my mistakes, too. I've loved you since the first moment I saw you, and yet I tried to deny it. I wanted to be strong, to resist, to hide my emotions, even from myself. I thought my love made me weak and vulnerable, and if there's one thing that life has taught me it's never, ever show any kind of weakness.'

'I didn't want to reject you,' said Aurelius. 'I wasn't afraid of opening up to you. I was afraid of what you might have seen inside me. You don't know what goes through my mind, what kind of hell I suffer, how I have to fight off the ghosts. How can I tie myself to another person if I'm divided inside? If I'm terrified that at any instant I could remember something that would change me completely, make me a stranger to myself, a hateful, despicable stranger. Can you understand what I'm trying to say?'

Livia lay her head on his shoulder and felt for his hand. 'It won't happen: you are the man here with me now, the man I've come to love. I look into your eyes and I see a good, generous person. It doesn't matter to me any more whether you are truly who I think you are; the man that little girl swore always to remember. I don't care what might be hidden in your past, no matter what it is.'

Aurelius straightened up and stared into her eyes with a mournful expression. 'No matter what it is? Do you know what you're saying?'

'I'm saying that I love you, soldier, and that I'll always love you, no matter what destiny has in store for us. Love is fearless. It gives us the courage to face any obstacle on our path, to overcome pain, and disappointment. Stop tormenting yourself. The only thing I want to know about you is if you feel for me what I feel for you.'

Aurelius held her close and kissed her, searching out her mouth with thirsting lips. He embraced her as if his body could express the emotion that he couldn't find words for. 'I love you, Livia,' he said, 'more than you can imagine. The heat that I feel in my soul right now could melt all the snow and ice that surrounds us. Even if everything is against us, even if my future is a mystery no less agonizing than my past, I love you as no one could ever love you, in this world or in the next.'

'Why now?' asked Livia. 'Why did you choose this moment to tell me?'

'Because you're here close to me and because my solitude – on these frozen waters, in this suffocating fog – is unbearable. Hold me, Livia, give me the strength to believe that nothing will ever separate us.' Livia threw her arms around his neck and they held each other close, as the wind tousled their hair into a single dark cloud in the pale light of winter.

*

As their last day of navigation approached, the boatman anxiously watched the clumps of ice floating on the surface of the river.

'Your fears were well founded,' observed Ambrosinus, drawing closer. 'The river is icing up.'

'It seems so,' nodded the boatman, 'but luck has it that we're almost there. Tomorrow, towards evening, we'll cast anchor. I know a tradesman from the Germanic port on the eastern bank who could have taken you as far as the river's mouth, but I'm afraid all navigation will be suspended until the waters start to flow freely again.'

'That won't be until the spring, will it?'

'Not necessarily. The temperature can change during the winter as well. You could find a place to stay for a while and wait. Who knows, this ice may be short-lived; you may be able to continue your journey soon on another vessel, all the way to the Ocean. The first day of clear sailing you'll be on your way to Britannia.'

They dropped anchor on the right bank, opposite Argentoratum, just in time. The northwest wind had picked up, strong and very cold, and ice floes pushed up against the side of the boat with an ominous thud. The boatman looked at the haggard band of fugitives and felt sorry for them. Where would they go, without knowing the territory, the roads, the safest routes, in the very heart of winter, with its blizzards and storms, ice and hunger? He said, as Ambrosinus reached for his bag to pay him, 'Forget it. I'm lucky that my load arrived in such good condition, and this northern wind will take me home much quicker than I expected. Keep that money for yourselves. You'll need it. Tonight you can stay on the boat; it's surely safer and more comfortable than any tavern in town, and you don't want to show your faces around just yet. Your enemies may be here waiting for you.'

'I thank you,' replied Ambrosinus, 'in the name of all my companions. Given the circumstances, a friend is the most precious thing we could wish for.'

'What will you do tomorrow?'

'I thought we'd cross to the other side. Our enemies won't have anyone to count on there, and perhaps we'll be able to find help. We'll head towards the Seine and travel by boat to the channel of Britannia.'

'Seems like a good plan.'

'Why won't you take us across to Argentoratum now?'

'I can't, for a number of reasons. I have to wait here for a load of skins from the interior, but what's more, the wind is against us, and the floes of ice carried by the current could easily sink us. You're better off travelling along the shore and looking for a passage further on. If the temperature rises tomorrow, you may even find a ferry willing to take you across.'

'I suppose you're right.'

Ambrosinus gathered his companions and shared his plans for the following day. They decided that one of them would stand guard that night in any case. Vatrenus offered to take the first shift and Demetrius the second. 'I mounted guard many a snowy, frozen night on the Danube,' said Demetrius. 'I'm used to this weather.'

As darkness fell, the boatman went ashore and didn't return until late that night, calling out to Vatrenus who was on guard. Juba, fettered and tied to the bow railing, snorted softly. Livia was just arriving with a steaming bowl of soup for Vatrenus; she took a handful of barley from a bag and fed it to the horse.

'Where are the others?' asked the boatman.

'Below deck. Any news?'

'Yes, unfortunately,' he said. 'Come below as soon as you can.' He went down to join the others, holding a lantern.

Livia followed him and he began to speak: 'The news I have is not very reassuring, I'm afraid. Strangers have recently arrived in town, and from their description and their behaviour they may be your pursuers. They're enquiring about a group of foreigners who they expected to come ashore this evening, and there's no doubt it's you they're looking for. If you go into town, you'll be quickly identified. They've promised a reward to anyone offering information, and there are people in this town who would sell their mother for a handful of coins, believe me. What's more, I heard from a man coming from the north that the river is completely frozen over at just twenty miles from here. Even if I wanted to take you further, it wouldn't be possible.'

'Is that all?' asked Ambrosinus.

'Seems like enough to me,' observed Batiatus.

'Yes, that's everything,' confirmed the boatman, 'but we have to keep in mind that they'll recognize this boat: they saw us close up, and there's no mistaking the heap of rock-salt at the centre of the deck. It's pitch dark now, so they can't see anything, but they'll find us at first light. I intend to unload the salt and load up my skins before dawn and to set sail as soon as I've finished. I don't want them setting my boat on fire. I never would have believed that they could get here before us. They must have ridden day and night without stopping, or maybe they found passage on a faster boat than this barge. One day, if we ever meet up again somewhere in the world, I'd be curious to know where all their tenacity comes from, but there are more important things to be decided now. That is, how to save your skin.'

'Do you have any suggestions for us?' asked Aurelius. 'You know these places and these people much better than we do.'

The boatman shrugged.

'Maybe I have an idea,' said Ambrosinus, 'but we need a cart, immediately.'

'A cart? That's no easy matter at this time of night, but I do know a place where they have them for hire. In theory you have to return it twenty miles from here, but they certainly won't be bothered by the loss of a cart. They earn enough to pay off the cost after two or three trips, so you needn't have any qualms. I'll go and look into it; you get ready. Can I ask you what you're planning to do with a cart?'

Ambrosinus lowered his head with an embarrassed look: 'You'd be better off not knowing; I'm sure you understand.' The boatman nodded and went above deck. He soon disappeared into the maze of roads that stretched out from the port.

'What are you thinking?' asked Aurelius.

'We'll do as the Franks did thirty years ago. We'll cross on the ice.'

'At night, without knowing whether it will hold us?' asked Batiatus, eyes wide with apprehension.

'If someone has a better idea, let's hear it,' said Ambrosinus.

No one spoke.

'Then we're decided,' concluded Ambrosinus. 'Prepare your things, and someone go above to let Vatrenus know.' Demetrius volunteered, but Romulus jumped up first. 'I'll go,' the boy said. 'I'll take him some more soup.'

Romulus had just gone above deck when they heard scuffling noises, and then Vatrenus's voice shouting: 'Stop! Stop, where do you think you're going?'

Ambrosinus immediately realized what was happening and called out: 'Run after him, for the love of God!' Aurelius took off and bounded up the stairs, followed by Livia and Demetrius. Vatrenus was already on the pier, running and shouting: 'Stop right now! Stop I say!'

The others dashed off after him and found themselves at the junction of three roads, each leading in a different direction.

'Vatrenus went down the middle,' said Demetrius. 'I'll go right, you and Livia go left: we'll meet back here as soon as we can.' They could still hear the faint sound of impetuous running in the distance, along with the call of Vatrenus's voice. They all flew off in swift pursuit. Aurelius and Livia soon reached a fork in the road and were forced to separate. Demetrius was running uphill along a road that he imagined to be parallel to the one Vatrenus had taken. He looked everywhere, searching every corner, but the night was very dark and it was like looking for a needle in a haystack. Livia and Aurelius had no better fortune. They met up, panting, at a crossroad.

'Why did he do it?' demanded Livia.

'Can't you understand? He didn't want us to have to go to all this trouble for him. He feels we're risking too much for him and wanted to relieve us of the burden.'

'My God, no!' exclaimed Livia, trying to hold back her tears.

'Let's keep looking,' said Aurelius. 'He can't have got far.'

*

Romulus had reached a little square with a tavern, and he stopped. He thought he could go in and offer his services, cleaning and washing dishes in exchange for room and board. He had never felt so alone and anxious, and the future scared him, but he was sure he'd done the right thing. He took a deep breath and was about to walk in when the tavern door swung open and one of Wulfila's barbarians walked out holding a lantern. Three more followed and they all started walking in his direction. Terrified, he spun around to run the other way, but bumped up against someone standing behind him. A hand grabbed his shoulder and another covered his mouth. He tried to wriggle away, ever so frightened, but a familiar voice said: 'Ssh! It's Demetrius. Quiet. If they see us we're dead.'

They backed up without making a sound and then Demetrius set off at a run, pulling the boy after him, towards the port. Ambrosinus was waiting for them, his face a mask of anguish as he gripped the boat's railing, flanked by the other two men.

'What have you done!' he cried as soon as he saw the boy. He raised his hand as if to slap him, but Romulus didn't blink and looked him straight in the eye. Ambrosinus perceived the dignity and the majesty of his sovereign in that gaze, and he dropped his hand. 'You put everyone's life in danger. Livia, Vatrenus and Aurelius are still searching for you and running a deadly risk.'

'It's true,' confirmed Demetrius. 'We nearly ran into Wulfila's men. They're roaming the town, out looking for us, evidently.'

Romulus burst into tears and rushed to hide below deck.

'Don't be too hard on him,' said Demetrius. 'He's just a boy, forced to face emotions and decisions that are much bigger than he is.'

Ambrosinus sighed and returned to the railing to watch for the others. He heard the boatman's voice instead. 'I found a cart for you,' he said, walking up the gangplank. 'You're lucky, but you have to go and fetch it now. The owner wants to close up and go to bed.'

'We've had a problem,' answered Demetrius. 'Some of us are still stranded in town.'

'A problem? What kind of a problem?'

'I'll go with him,' said Ambrosinus. 'You wait here and no one move, for the love of heaven, until we come back.'

Demetrius nodded and remained on the look-out to await the others, along with Orosius and Batiatus. Vatrenus showed up first, and was soon joined by Livia and then Aurelius. They were frantic.

'Don't worry,' said Demetrius, 'I found him, what a miracle! I think he was about to enter a tavern. Another step and both of us would have finished in the hands of Wulfila's cut-throats.'

'He wanted to enter a tavern?' asked Aurelius. 'Where is he now?'

'Below. Ambrosinus chewed him out.'

'Let me go,' said Livia, going below deck.

Romulus was curled into a corner, crying softly, with his head on his knees. Livia approached him and touched him gently. 'You had us scared to death!' she said. 'Don't ever run away again, please. It's not you who needs us. It's us who need you, can't you understand that?'

Romulus lifted his face and dried his tears with the sleeve of his tunic. Then he stood up and hugged her tight, without saying a word. They could hear the sound of wheels on the cobblestones outside.

'Come on, now,' urged Livia, 'get your things. It's time to go.'

30

THE CART WAS ALREADY on the wharf and Ambrosinus was busy paying the driver, subtracting the price of the horse. 'We've already got one,' he said, 'as you can see.' Aurelius was leading Juba by the bridle down the gangplank, to replace the skinny nag in the shafts.

'By all the saints in heaven!' said the cart driver. 'It's a waste putting him to the cart! I'll give you two of mine, what do you say?'

Aurelius didn't even look his way as he began to adjust the towing harness around Juba's neck.

'He's like a brother for him,' said Demetrius to the driver. 'Would you exchange your brother for two of these nags?'

The cart driver scratched his head. 'If you knew my brother, you'd give him away for a donkey,' he said.

'Let's get going,' urged Ambrosinus. 'The sooner we leave the better.' The others climbed on to the cart after having thanked the boatman and taken their farewell. They sat on some boxes pushed up against the sides. An oilcloth was draped over the hoops formed by several curved willow branches, providing a little shelter and hiding them from view. Livia curled up under a blanket with Romulus. Aurelius came around to the back. 'I'll walk,' he said. 'Juba's not used to pulling a cart, he might become restive. You try to get some sleep.'

Ambrosinus clasped the boatman's hand. 'We are very grateful,' he told him. 'We owe our lives to you and we don't even know your name.'

'That's all right, one less thing to remember. It was a good crossing, and I enjoyed your company. I'm usually all alone for the whole voyage. I believe you're going to try to cross over the ice?'

'Not much choice, I'd say,' admitted Ambrosinus.

'I think you're right, but be very careful. The ice is thicker where the river current is slower. So on the straight stretches, the danger lies in the centre, while on the river bends, the ice is thinnest at the outer part of the curve. Cross one by one, leaving the horse for last with the empty cart. Once on the other side, head northwest. In a week's time you should reach the Seine, if the weather's not too bad. It will all be much easier from there on, at least I hope so. May God assist you.'

'You too, my friend. One day you'll hear tell of this boy, who you've seen so tattered and tormented, and you'll be proud that you met him and that you helped him. Good luck for your return.'

A last hand shake and Ambrosinus stepped up into the cart with the help of Orosius. They pulled up the board at the back and fastened it to the sides. Demetrius shouted to Aurelius: 'We're all in.' The cart started off, creaking and clattering over the cobblestone wharf, and disappeared into the darkness.

They drove on all night, covering about fifteen miles and taking turns at leading Juba by the bridle. When the horse had got accustomed to pulling the cart, Aurelius sat on the driver's bench and guided Juba with the reins and his voice. To their left, the river's surface was becoming increasingly white and compact, until it was a uniform sheet of ice from one shore to the other. The cold chilled them to the bone and the fog had frozen overnight, cloaking the shrubs and canes, the grass and bushes with lacy hoar frost. The sky was veiled by high, thin clouds which sometimes let through a little of the sun's first light as a wide white halo just above the horizon.

Not one of them was tranquil. The covered cart hid them well enough from sight, but it was slow and vulnerable, and the most difficult moment was yet to come: crossing the river. Their relief at the visibility brought by the morning light was short-lived; they soon realized that the brightness given off equally by the sky, the snow and the ice made outlines indistinct and blurred volume, flooding the entire landscape in its milky glow. People and animals were the only things to stand out, making their own presence even more conspicuous. In fact, passers-by were few and far between: peasants with pack animals loaded with branches and wood for burning, or some solitary wayfarer, mostly beggars covered with rags. The cock's cry rose to announce the new day for the farms scattered throughout the countryside. Every so often they would hear the whining of a dog, transformed into a mournful lament in the immensity of that empty, cold space.

They went on for another couple of miles and then stopped at a point where the river was narrow and the bank was low to the bed, providing easy access. They decided that two of them would go on foot to test the solidity of the ice, tied together with a rope so that if one sank into the water, the other could pull him to safety. Batiatus volunteered to accompany Aurelius; his strength and size would guarantee a secure anchor. Under the worried gaze of the others, they advanced over the icy crust, tapping the surface with the tip of a javelin in order to gauge the thickness of the ice from the sound. They grew smaller and smaller to their companions' eyes as they rapidly neared the middle of the river. That was the critical point, the place where the ice had solidified last, and Aurelius decided to test it with his sword. Manoeuvring it with both hands, he twisted it forcefully into the ice, scattering crystal bright splinters. He succeeding in nudging it one foot down, before his last blow landed the tip in the water beneath.

'One foot!' he shouted to Batiatus.

'Is that enough?' the other shot back.

'It has to be. We can't stay here any longer; it's too great a risk. We've already been noticed, look!' He pointed at a couple of bystanders along the shore who had stopped to observe the strange operation, then turned back to confer with the others and the crossing began, one after another, at a few steps' distance.

'Hurry!' urged Ambrosinus. 'We're too visible. Whoever's heard of us will recognize us.'

*

The boatman, who had hoped to be sailing south by that time, was unhappily in a completely different situation. Unloading the salt had required much longer than he'd expected, because sitting in the damp for so long had clotted the crystals into huge lumps. He hadn't finished when Wulfila's men burst on to the wharf on horseback and began to inspect all the boats still at anchor. It hadn't taken them very long to identify the one with the load of rock-salt, even though very little remained on the deck, and they rushed on board with their swords drawn.

'Stop! Who are you?' shouted the boatman. 'You have no right to storm on to my boat like that!'

Wulfila himself appeared and ordered his warriors to shut the man up and take him below deck.

'Don't pretend you don't know who we are!' he started. 'It was just ten days ago, and I'm sure you're not a man to forget a face, are you?' he demanded, twisting his deformed features into a grimace. 'We're following a deserter wanted for murder who jumped aboard your boat on his horse. He had a boy with him, didn't he?'

The boatman felt faint: he couldn't deny any of those allegations. 'His friends had been waiting for him,' he stammered. 'They'd already paid their passage and I had no complaint with them. I couldn't have known . . .'

'Shut up! Those men are wanted for crimes of blood that they committed in the territory of the empire. They kidnapped that boy and we must free him and return him to his parents. Understand?'

The boatman had the momentary sensation that scarface was telling the truth: hadn't the boy tried to run away last night, and hadn't they chased after him like mad? Then he remembered the continuous gestures of affection that all his travel companions had showered on the boy, and how affectionate he had been with them as well. He bit his tongue, and said: 'How am I supposed to know the life and hard times of everyone who gets on my boat? I don't care, as long as they pay; they don't bother me, and I don't bother them, and that's what happened. Now I have to get home, so if you don't mind . . .'

'You'll go when I say so,' roared Wulfila, slapping him with the back of his hand, 'and now you'll tell me where they went, if you don't want me to make you sorry you were ever born!'

Terrified and smarting, the boatman tried to convince his persecutor that he knew nothing, but he was certainly not ready to face any kind of torture. He tried to hold out through the kicks and punches, gritting his teeth when they twisted his arm behind his back so hard he thought they would break it and stifling his cries even as the blood poured from his split lip and crushed nose, but when he saw Wulfila pull out his dagger he gave up all at once, overwhelmed by panic. He gasped: 'They left last night, on a cart, headed north . . .'

Wulfila tumbled him on to the floor with a last kick and sheathed his dagger. 'Pray to your God that we find them, otherwise I'll come back and I'll burn you alive inside this boat of yours.'

He left two of his men to keep an eye on the sorry wretch, then went down to the wharf and mounted his horse. He galloped off northwards, followed by his men.

'Look, traces of a cart and a horse,' noticed one of his warriors as soon as they had left the city. 'We'll be able to tell straight away if it's them.' He dropped to the ground and examined Juba's tracks in the snow, recognizing them immediately. He turned to his leader with a satisfied sneer: 'It is them! That pig was telling the truth.'

'Finally!' exclaimed Wulfila. He drew his sword and raised it high. It glittered in his fist, amidst the cheers of his men. He spurred on his horse and set off at a gallop down the snow-covered road.

*

Meanwhile Aurelius, after having helped all the others cross to the opposite side, had gone back for Juba and the cart. He led the horse by his bridle, advancing on foot in front of him. He kept up a continuous patter to soothe and reassure him about the strange, new experience, the passage across a glassy surface that didn't give way under the pressure of his hooves. 'Slow now, attaboy, Juba. Slowly . . . see? Nothing's wrong. We just want to reach Romulus, he's waiting for us. See him down there? He's waving at us.'

They had nearly reached the middle of the river and Aurelius was worried about Juba's considerable size and the weight of the cart, which rested entirely on the narrow iron bands encircling the wheel rims. He strained his ears to pick up the slightest sound, dreading that crack that would swallow him and his horse up into the icy water, a death that struck terror and panic into his heart. Every now and then he would turn towards the others, and he could feel the tension that gripped them as they waited for him to cross.

'Now! Come on, now!' shouted Batiatus all at once. 'You're past the thinnest part: get moving!'

Aurelius accelerated his pace immediately, but he couldn't understand why his friends' shouts seemed to be increasingly excited and urgent. A blood-chilling thought crossed his mind, and he looked back to find, at less than a mile's distance, a pack of horsemen galloping along the river's bank. Wulfila! Again! How was it possible? How could those beasts emerge again and again out of nowhere like spirits from hell? He ran across to the opposite shore, practically dragging the horse behind him, and drew his sword, ready for the death match.

His companions were lined up as well, weapons in hand, ready to cover Romulus' flight.

'Aurelius!' shouted Vatrenus. 'Untie the horse from the cart and escape with the boy! We'll resist here as long as we can. Go, go now while you still can. Get the devil out of here!'

But Romulus was clutching the spokes of one of the cart's

wheels, shouting: 'No! I won't go! I won't go without the rest of you! I don't want to run any more!'

'Grab him and get going! Now!' Vatrenus continued to shout, cursing all the gods and demons he knew. The enemy horsemen had reached the other side, directly opposite them, and were galloping on to the ice. Wulfila tried to hold them back, sensing the danger, but the heat of the chase and their desire to put an end to this unnerving hunt had unleashed their charge across the frozen surface of the river.

Demetrius excitedly turned to the others: 'Look! They're advancing all at once, the ice will never hold! We still have a chance, if we get out of here immediately. Come on boys, on the cart!' He hadn't finished speaking when a crack snaked open under the steeds' hooves, widening as the second wave of horsemen hammered down hard. Water surged over the breaking ice, sending some of them into ruinous falls while others slipped and slid. A huge floe sank beneath the surface as Wulfila ordered: 'Stop! Turn back! The ice won't hold! Get back!'

'Let's get out of here,' shouted Aurelius at the sight. 'We can make it!' They all scrambled into the cart, Ambrosinus lashed Juba's back with the reins and off they went at full speed.

Their relief was short-lived: Wulfila managed to regroup and have his men cross a little further upstream, one at a time. They once again took up the chase, rapidly gaining on the overloaded cart. Aurelius handed out the men's javelins while Livia nocked an arrow into her bow, taking aim, but as the warriors came within range, they slowed down and then abruptly stopped.

'What's happening?' asked Vatrenus.

'I have no idea,' replied Aurelius, feeling that the cart's speed was diminishing as well, 'but don't slow down, don't stop!'

'What's happened is that we're saved!' yelled Ambrosinus. 'Look!'

A group of armed men on horseback appeared before them, backed by a large infantry unit, emerging out of the fog. They were advancing at a march, spread out over a wide front, with their weapons in hand. Wulfila, dumbstruck, called his men to a halt and stopped at a respectful distance.

The infantry stopped as well. Their armour and their banners left no doubt: they were Roman soldiers!

An officer came forward. 'Who are you?' he asked, 'and who are those men following you?'

'May God bless you!' exclaimed Ambrosinus. 'We owe you our lives!'

Aurelius stiffened into a military salute. 'Aurelianus Ambrosius Ventidius,' he said. 'First cohort, Nova Invicta Legion.'

'Rufius Aelius Vatrenus, Nova Invicta Legion,' his comrade echoed.

'Cornelius Batiatus . . .' began the gigantic Ethiopian.

'Legion?' repeated the officer, shocked. 'There have been no legions for half a century. Where do you come from, soldier?'

'You can believe him, commander,' said Demetrius, 'and if you have a bowl of hot soup and a glass of wine for us, we have some fine stories to tell!'

'All right,' replied the officer. 'Follow me.'

They advanced for about a mile, circling a hill, until they found themselves in front of a fieldcamp which looked as if it could accommodate at least a thousand men. The commander had them leave the cart and brought them to his quarters, where his attendants hastened to unfasten his sword belt and to take his helmet and place it on a field stool. An orderly served them the same rations he was distributing to the troops and they all began to eat. Romulus, who was finally recovering from his fear and the numbing cold, would have liked to wolf down the food joyously, but he dutifully imitated his tutor, who was sipping the soup in small spoonfuls and sitting with his back perfectly straight.

'A well-assorted bunch, I'd say,' began the officer. 'Three legionaries, if I'm to believe your words, a philosopher, to judge from his beard, a pair of deserters, if my eyes do not betray me, a lady with a bearing too haughty and legs too slender to be a bedtime companion, and a young man without even the shadow of whiskers beneath his nose, but with enough presumption to be a personage out of the ancient Republic. Not to mention that nasty swarm of cut-throats you had at your heels. What am I to make of you?'

Ambrosinus had already predicted those questions and was ready with an answer. 'You have an acute sense of observation, commander. I realize that the condition we find ourselves in may engender suspicion, but we have nothing to hide and will gladly explain everything. This boy has been the victim of terrible persecution. He is the scion of a very noble family, and the arrogance of a barbarian at the service of the Imperial Army has deprived him of his rightful inheritance. Not content with having stripped this child of all his belongings, he has attempted in every way possible to kill the poor lad, so that he may never claim his birthright. He has had us pursued by a group of fierce hired assassins who today would have succeeded in their vile intent had it not been for you.

'This girl is the boy's older sister. She has grown up like a virago, emulating Camilla and Pentesilea, and can fight with a bow and a javelin with incredible mastery. She has been the foremost defender of her unlucky brother. As for myself, I am the boy's tutor, and with some money that I had hidden away, I recruited these valiant warriors, who have survived the destruction of their division at the hands of other barbarians, and thus we have united our destinies.

'Beholding your army decked in their splendid armour, seeing the Roman banners fluttering in the wind and hearing the Latin language sound on your lips have all been, for us, the greatest consolation. We are profoundly grateful to you for having rescued us.'

Everyone fell silent, stunned by such a display of polished eloquence, but the commander was a tough veteran and he was not overly impressed. He answered: 'My name is Sergius Volusianus, *comes regis et magister militum*. We were sent on a mission of war in support of our allies in central Gaul and we are returning to Parisii where I am to report to our leader, Siagrius,

King of the Romans. I will include you in my report, as well as the circumstances involved in our meeting. You will not for any reason stray from our division from this moment forwards. This is for your own safety: the territory we will be crossing is extremely dangerous and subject to sudden incursions by the Franks. You will be treated as Romans. Please allow me to take my leave of you now; our departure is imminent.' He tossed down a cup of wine, reclaimed his sword and helmet and left, followed by his attendants and his field adjutant.

'What do you think?' asked Ambrosinus.

'I don't know,' replied Aurelius. 'I can't say he seemed entirely convinced by that story you told.'

'Well, it's nearly the truth.'

'The problems lies in that "nearly". Let's hope all goes well. In any case, our situation is now greatly improved, and we can consider ourselves safe for the time being. The commander is certainly an excellent soldier and most probably a man of his word.'

'What about Wulfila?' asked Orosius. 'Do you think he'll give up? There's no way he can get at us now: we're protected by a numerous division in full battle gear, and he's the one who'd better look out for himself on this side of the Rhine.'

'Don't be fooled,' answered Aurelius. 'He can get help from the Franks. We've seen just how determined he is; he's forced us to flee to the very ends of the earth! Anyone else in his place would have given up long ago, but not him: each time he shows up again, he seems fiercer and more aggressive, like a demon out of hell – *and* he has the sword of Caesar in his hands.'

'Sometimes I think he really is a demon,' said Orosius, the expression in his eyes more eloquent than his words.

'Aurelius is the one who slashed his face; he can tell you Wulfila's made out of flesh and blood,' shot back Demetrius, 'but I still can't explain this implacable, relentless hate. He's gone beyond every imaginable limit.'

'I can explain it,' mused Ambrosinus. 'Aurelius has disfigured him; he's made him unrecognizable compared with his former self. In this state, he can never hope to enter the warriors' paradise, and that's absolutely intolerable for someone like him. Wulfila comes from a tribe of eastern Goths who profess a fanatical faith in military valour and in the destiny that awaits combatants in the next world. To redeem himself, he must inflict on you what you have inflicted on him, Aurelius. He has to cut your face to the bone, and then he must offer a libation to the god of war inside your skull, whittled into a cup. We won't be free of him until the day he's dead.'

'Can't say I envy you that fate,' commented Vatrenus, but Aurelius seemed to have taken Ambrosinus's words very seriously. 'Then it's me he wants. Why did you wait so long to tell me that?'

'Because you would have done something foolish, like challenge him to a duel.'

'That may be a solution,' replied Aurelius.

'It most certainly would not. With that sword in his hands, you wouldn't have a chance. He wants Romulus as well, there's no doubt about that, otherwise he wouldn't have shown up at the *mansio* in Fanum. All we can do, Aurelius, is stay together. It's the only way we can survive. Keep one thing in mind, above all: Romulus must reach Britannia, at any cost. There everything we've fought for will come to pass and we will no longer need to fear anything. No more fear, can you understand that?'

They all looked at each other because in truth they didn't understand, not yet, but they felt that somehow he was right, that the inspired light in his eye was true. Each and every time that he referred to their future destiny, so clear for him and so confused for the rest of them, he spoke like the man posted on a look-out tower at dawn who is the first to see the light of the rising sun.

31

Sergius Volusianus's column set off later that day, heading northwest. They marched for six days, covering twenty miles a day, until they reached the kingdom of Siagrius. The *rex Romanorum*'s territory was marked off by a line of defence with a palisade and trench, overseen by guard towers spaced one every mile. The men at the garrison wore heavy coats of mail and conical iron helmets with cheek- and nose-pieces like those worn by the Franks, and they carried long double-edged swords.

They entered through a fortified gate, were welcomed by long trumpet blasts, and continued their march until they reached the first river port on the Seine. There, they took ship and descended the river towards the capital, the ancient colony of *Lutetia Parisiorum* which everyone had become accustomed to calling simply by the name of its inhabitants, Parisii. The long, substantially tranquil voyage gave everyone the sensation that the threat that had loomed over their heads for so long had vanished, or that it was so far away that it wasn't worth their while to worry about it. Each day of their journey brought them closer to their destination, and Ambrosinus was affected by a strange excitement, which not even he could explain. Their only cause for apprehension was their lack of contact with commander Volusianus, who they saw very rarely and fleetingly. He usually remained in his quarters, at the stern, and when going about the ship he was always surrounded by his staff, so he was practically unapproachable. Only Aurelius, one evening, had the chance to speak with him. He noticed the commander standing at the bow, watching the sun go down over the plains, and approached him.

'Hail, commander,' he said.

'Hail, soldier,' replied Volusianus.

'A quiet journey, this.'

'So far.'

'May I ask you a question?'

'You may, but don't be certain you'll receive an answer.'

'I fought for years at the orders of Manilius Claudianus and I commanded his personal guard. Does this mean anything to you? Does it perhaps make me worthy of your consideration?'

'Claudianus was a great soldier and an upright man, a Roman the like of whom no longer exists. If he trusted you this means that you were worthy of his consideration.'

'You met him, then.'

'Personally, and it was a great honour. I earned the vallar crown that you see on my standard under his command and he himself awarded it to me at the walls of Augusta Raurica.'

'Commander Claudianus is dead, betrayed and attacked by Odoacer's troops. My comrades and I are among the only survivors of the massacre, not one of us by way of cowardice or desertion.'

Volusianus stared at him with his penetrating gaze. His grey eyes looked like a hawk's and his face was creased by deep wrinkles. He wore his hair very short, and hadn't shaved for several days. His fatigue was evident in all his features, as was his ability to size up men.

'I believe you,' he said after a few moments of silence. 'What do you want to know?'

'If we are under your protection or in your custody.'

'Both.'

'Why?'

'News regarding important changes in the balance of power travel much more quickly than you can imagine.'

'I realize that. I'm not surprised that your *rex* knows about Odoacer and the assassination of Flavius Orestes and that you have been informed as well. What else have you heard, if I may ask?'

'That Odoacer is searching over land and sea for a thirteen-year-old boy defended by a handful of deserters and accompanied by other . . . picturesque individuals.'

Aurelius lowered his head.

'No one in a governing position,' continued Volusianus, 'is unaware that that is the age of the last emperor of the West, Romulus Augustus, who many call Augustulus. You will admit that the coincidence is too singular to be ignored.'

'Certainly,' replied Aurelius.

'Is it him?'

Aurelius hesitated, then nodded, and added, staring the commander straight in the eyes: 'From one Roman soldier to another.'

Volusianus nodded solemnly.

'We don't want to interfere, or create problems for you,' Aurelius went on with a distressed look. 'We just want to find a distant land where this unfortunate lad can live in peace, sheltered from the persecution he's suffered. He aspires to no power and claims no title for himself, no public position. He desires only oblivion and silence, to begin his life anew as a young boy just like any other – and we want to stay with him. We've given everything we have. We've shed blood and sweat for Rome, and risked our lives every time it was necessary, without a thought for ourselves. We've left only because we refused to obey the barbarians: this is dignity, not desertion. We are exhausted and disheartened. Let us go, general.'

Volusianus looked back out towards the horizon, at the long bloody strip that edged the desert of snow to the west. His words came out with difficulty, as if the wind that chilled his limbs had entered his heart: 'I cannot,' he answered. 'The men that Siagrius has put at my side would like nothing better than to succeed me and replace me; he has done so deliberately to offset my ascendancy over the troops. He'll have learned about your presence from them, and my silence would appear suspect and incomprehensible. It's best that I inform him personally.'

'What will become of us?'

Volusianus met his stare: 'It won't be me who reveals the boy's identity. I don't know whether the others have understood. At best, Siagrius won't catch on himself, and won't care what happens to you. He may order me to deal with the situation myself. In that case—'

'But what if he realizes the truth?'

'At that point, you'd do well to face up to reality. The boy is worth a lot, too much, both in terms of money and of political influence. Siagrius cannot ignore the fact that it's Odoacer who's in charge now in Italy; he is the true *rex Romanorum*. For the rest of you, it will be easier. I could have you sign on with our army: we need good soldiers, and we're not overly particular.'

'I understand,' replied Aurelius with death in his heart, and he turned to go.

'Soldier!'

Aurelius stopped.

'Why do you care so much about that boy?'

'Because I love him,' he replied, 'and because he's our emperor.'

*

Aurelius did not have the heart to tell Ambrosinus about his conversation, nor Livia. He continued to hope that Romulus's identity might remain a secret, trusting in Volusianus's words. A man of honour. He kept his gnawing worries to himself, forcing himself to seem calm and even to joke with Romulus and his friends.

They reached the city on their fifth day of navigation, towards sunset, all lined up at the railing to admire the spectacle opening up before them. Parisii stood on an island in the middle of the Seine, surrounded by a fortification partly in *opus cementicium* walls and partly in wooden palisades. They could see the roofs of the tallest buildings inside, some covered with brick tiles in the Roman manner and others in wood and straw, like the old Celtic constructions.

Ambrosinus drew close to Romulus: 'On the other side of the

river, opposite the western shore of the island, is where Saint Germanus is buried. Many come to venerate his memory.'

'Isn't he the hero who led the Romans of Britannia against the northern barbarians? The one you talk about in your diary?'

'Certainly. He had no army of his own, but he trained ours. He organized them in a military structure based on the ancient Roman legions, but he was mortally wounded in a battle, and died. As you know, I alone know his last words, his prophecy . . . As soon as we set ashore we'll find his tomb so I can invoke his protection and his blessing for your future, Caesar.'

Meanwhile the sailors were calling out orders, preparing to dock. The river port of Parisii had been built at the time of the first Roman settlement after Caesar's occupation, and had not changed much since then. The lead boat drew up alongside the first of the three mooring wharves, tossing a couple of lines from stern and stem, while the rowers pulled their oars into the ship, at an order from their helmsman. Volusianus disembarked with his attendants, and gave orders for the foreigners to follow him. The horses were being unloaded from the barge in the ship's tow, including Juba, who kicked and bucked, refusing to follow the grooms. Ambrosinus, bewildered, tried to approach the commander. 'General,' he said, 'we would like to thank you once again before taking our leave, and to ask you if we could reclaim our horse. We'll have to depart first thing in the morning and—'

Volusianus turned: 'You can't leave. You'll stay here for as long as necessary.'

'General!' pleaded Ambrosinus, but Volusianus had already turned his back and was heading towards the forum. A picket of numerous soldiers surrounded Ambrosinus and his companions and an officer ordered them to follow. Aurelius gestured to the others not to put up any resistance as Ambrosinus wrung his hands in despair. 'What does this mean? Why are they detaining us? We haven't done anything, we're simple wayfarers who . . .' He soon realized that no one was listening, and he dismally followed the others.

Romulus neared Aurelius: 'Why are they doing this?' he asked 'Aren't they Romans like us?'

'Maybe they've mistaken us for someone else,' Aurelius tried to reassure him. 'It happens sometimes. We'll clear everything up, you'll see. Don't worry.'

The soldiers stopped in front of a square stone building with a bleak appearance. The officer ordered the door opened and they were led into a large, bare room. Small iron doors lined the walls. A prison.

'Your arms,' enjoined the officer. A moment of fierce tension ensued; Aurelius considered the large number of soldiers surrounding them, evaluating all the possible consequences of any action he might take. He unsheathed his sword and handed it to one of the jailers. His companions, overwhelmed by this unexpected epilogue to their journey, resignedly did the same. The weapons were locked into an ironclad cabinet near the back wall. The officer exchanged a few whispered words with the jailer, then lined up his soldiers, weapons menacing the prisoners as they were closed up one by one. Romulus cast a despairing look at Aurelius, then followed Ambrosinus meekly into the cell assigned to them.

The sound of the heavy outside door clanging shut echoed loudly through the vast, empty atrium, and the measured step of the soldiers faded off down the road into the distance. Naught but silence remained.

*

Livia sat on her filthy cot. Incapable of sleep, she mused over all the recent happenings and, despite the anguish of their imprisonment, she thought that Aurelius had made a wise decision, avoiding a rash reaction with no hope of success. 'As long as there's a will . . .' she told herself, but she was very worried for Romulus. She was struck by the expression in his eyes at the moment that they locked him up, and she realized that the boy was at the very end of his rope. The constant swing between hope and terror, illusion and despair, was destroying him. His reckless escape attempt at Argentoratum revealed just how shaken and confused he was, and this situation could only make things worse. Her sole consolation was that Ambrosinus was with him; he'd be able to soothe the boy's ragged nerves and give him a little hope.

She was deep in thought when she heard a rattling noise at the door to her cell. She flattened herself against the wall, straining to hear and holding her breath. Her fighting instinct, keened by years of attacks, escapes and ambushes, was immediately reawakened. She steeled her body and her mind and was ready to spring.

She heard the bolt turn, the low muttering of voices and snickering laughter, and she understood immediately. Volusianus had promised that they'd be treated well, but the presence of a young, attractive girl was certainly not an everyday event in that stinking hole, and a couple of libations had been sufficient to tempt the guards into forgetting the punishment they were risking.

The door opened and two jailers appeared at the threshold, holding a lantern. 'Where are you, turtle dove?' called one. 'Come out, don't be afraid. We're just looking for a little company.'

Livia pretended to be terrified, as she slipped her left hand along her leg until she reached her boot laces. She extracted a razor sharp stiletto, shaped like an awl with a rounded handle so she could grip it in her fist with only the point protruding between her index and middle fingers. 'Please, don't hurt me,' she whimpered, knowing that her pleading could only further excite the two guards.

'Calm down, darling, we won't hurt you. We'll be real nice, and later you can offer a libation to old Priapus himself, who gave us the nice big tools we use to make little whores like you happy.' He started to undo his trousers while the other threatened her with a knife. Livia pretended to be even more frightened as she shrank back on the cot, her back to the wall.

'Good girl,' approved the first, turning to his cohort. 'A little bit each. First me, then my friend. Then you'll tell us who was better and who was bigger. Isn't this fun?'

He had completely stripped off his trousers and his knees were against the edge of the cot. Livia readied the claw she held tight in her hand and as he leaned forward to grab her, she twisted sideways and sprang at the second man, sticking the blade deep into his breast bone, as the first tumbled forward on to the cot. She tossed the stiletto lightly from her left hand to her right and plunged it cleanly into his neck, fracturing his spinal cord. One fell on the bed, the other on the floor, without a moan and practically at the same time.

The die was cast: Livia took their keys and went to open the doors to her companions' cells. She appeared suddenly, a vision of hope, smiling and calm: 'Wake up boys. Time to get moving.'

'How . . .' Aurelius muttered in shock as she threw herself into his arms.

She pulled out the stiletto. *'In calceo venenum!'* she laughed, modifying the old proverb. 'They forgot to look in my shoes!' Romulus ran towards her and clung to her neck, squeezing her so hard she thought she would suffocate. Livia found the key to the cabinet which contained their weapons and they all headed towards the exit, but just then they heard the sound of footsteps outside, and the bolt turned. Volusianus appeared at the open threshold, escorted by his fully-armed guard.

Livia exchanged looks with Aurelius. 'They're not taking me again,' she said simply, and it was immediately clear that all the others felt the same by the way they had raised their arms.

Volusianus lifted his hand. 'Stop,' he said. 'Listen to me, there's not much time. Odoacer's barbarians have asked to be received by Siagrius and they surely plan to request that you be turned over to them. There's no time to explain, you must hurry. Your horse is out here, along with some others. Take this road to the western gate, where there's a bridge of boats in the river that connects the island to the mainland. The guards have my instructions to let you pass. Follow the river to the coast; there you'll find a fishing village called Brixate. Ask for a man named

Teutasius and tell him I sent you. He can ferry you to Frisia or Armorica, where no one should bother you. Whatever you do, avoid Britannia: the island is fraught with civil strife and warring tribes, and crawling with brigands and outlaws from north to south. I'll soon have to sound the alarm, and I may have to send my own troops after you, if I'm ordered to do so. If they should overtake you, there will be nothing I can do. Go now, as fast as you can!'

Aurelius came close: 'I knew you wouldn't deliver us to the barbarians. Thank you, general, and may the gods protect you.'

'May God protect you, soldier, and that boy of yours.'

Romulus approached him as well, and with a tone of great dignity, said: 'Thank you for all you've done for us: I won't forget you.'

'I did my duty . . . Caesar,' replied Volusianus, stiffening into a military salute. He bowed his head respectfully and said: 'Go, now, ride to safety.'

They mounted the horses and raced down the deserted city roads towards the gate, reaching the start of the bridge. The guards nodded their permission to proceed, and Aurelius led them to the opposite shore. Here they turned north, following the road that flanked the river. They spurred on their steeds and soon disappeared into the darkness.

*

Volusianus rode back to the winter quarters, not far from the river port, followed by half a dozen men from his personal guard and his field adjutant. One of the servants rushed over to take his horse's reins, and another held a lantern to light their way. Volusianus turned to his adjutant. 'Wait a little longer,' he ordered, 'and then run to the palace and give the alarm. Say that they fled after killing the guards, which is the pure truth. You will say, obviously, that you have no idea where they were headed.'

'Obviously, general,' replied his assistant.

*

'If your generals hadn't protected them,' roared Wulfila, enraged, 'we'd already have captured them and taken them away!'

Siagrius was seated on his throne, a chair that somewhat resembled the *sella curulis* of the ancient magistrates. Wrapped in a fox fur to stave off the biting cold, he was visibly irritated by being rudely awaked in the middle of the night by that unmannered savage with his scarred face.

'My *magister militum* did what he had to do,' he replied, vexed. 'This is territory of the Romans and its jurisdiction is in my hands, along with my officers and magistrates, and no one else! Now that these men have stained themselves with a crime and have escaped from my prison, they have become fugitives, and it won't be difficult to catch them. They know that if they remain within our confines, they won't be able to elude us, and so they'll surely try to flee by sea, from the nearest port. We'll stop them there.'

'And what if they manage to take ship?' screamed the barbarian.

The *rex Romanorum* shrugged. 'They wouldn't get far,' he said. 'No boat can compete with my galleys, and we know they'd be headed for Frisia or Armorica; no one would be crazy enough these days to choose Britannia. However, *my* men will be the ones to capture them, not you.'

'Listen to me,' said Wulfila in a slightly more conciliatory tone, approaching Siagrius's throne, 'you don't know them. They are the most formidable of fighters, the most cunning of scoundrels, as demonstrated by the fact that they broke out of your prison just hours after they'd been locked up. I've been hunting them down for months, and I know all their tricks. Let me go with my men as well. I promise you that you won't regret it. I've been authorized to offer a large sum of money in exchange for the boy. Most importantly, Odoacer is ready to demonstrate his gratitude with a treaty of alliance. He is now the custodian and protector of Italy, and the natural intermediary with the Eastern Empire.'

'You can go as well,' assented Siagrius, 'but don't take any initiatives, of any kind, without the approval of my representative.' He gave a nod to his second-in-command, a Romanized Visigoth named Gennadius. 'This one's for you,' he ordered. 'Take as many men as you need. Leave at dawn.'

'No!' insisted Wulfila. 'If we leave at dawn they'll get away. They already have a considerable advantage over us. We have to leave immediately.'

Siagrius meditated a few moments and then nodded: 'All right,' he said, 'but when you've taken them, bring them to me. The jurisdiction is mine, and anyone who violates it becomes my enemy. Dismissed!'

Gennadius saluted and walked out, followed by Wulfila, and their ship was ready to set sail soon afterwards: a huge galley built of oak, in the Celtic tradition, capable of transporting men and horses over the open sea.

'What's the nearest port?' asked Wulfila as soon as he was on board.

'Brixate,' Gennadius replied, 'at the mouth of the Seine. It won't be difficult to discover if a ship has put out to sea: practically no one sails this time of year.'

They moved along quickly, pushed by the river current, and when the wind shifted from northeast to east, they raised the sail, which further increased their speed. A few hours before dawn the clouds scattered and the temperature dropped, as they saw the lights of the port appear in the distance.

The helmsman turned a worried gaze seaward. 'Fog,' he said. 'The fog is rising.'

Wulfila wasn't even listening, as he scanned the great estuary of the Seine and the open sea beyond. He could smell his prey, and was determined not to let them slip from his hands this time.

'Ship dead ahead!' sounded the voice of the sailor up in the crow's nest.

'It's them!' exclaimed Wulfila. 'I'm sure of it. Look: there are no other ships at sea.'

The helmsman had seen the other vessel as well. 'How strange,' he said. 'They're headed towards the fog, as if they wanted to cross the channel and land in Britannia.'

'Increase to full speed, quickly!' ordered the barbarian. 'We can overtake them!'

'The fog is getting thicker,' answered the helmsman. 'We have to wait until it disperses, when the sun is higher.'

'Now!' bellowed Wulfila, practically out of his mind. 'We have to get them now!'

'I'll give the orders here,' replied Gennadius. 'I don't want to lose the ship. If they want to get themselves killed, they're free to do so, but I'll have none of it. I won't enter that fog bank, and I don't think they will either.'

Wulfila drew his sword with lightning speed and pointed it at the commander's throat. 'Order your men to drop their weapons,' he said, 'Or I'll cut your head off. I'm taking over this ship.'

Gennadius had no choice, and his men grudgingly obeyed, awed by the sight of the barbarian's incredible sword.

'Throw the crew into the sea,' Wulfila ordered his men. 'Thank destiny that I'm not killing you.' He turned to Gennadius. 'The same holds for you.' He pushed the commander to the railing and forced him to jump into the waters of the Ocean, where his men were already floundering in the waves. Nearly all of them went under, dragged down by the weight of their armour and the chilling cold that paralysed their limbs. Master now of the ship, Wulfila ordered the terrified helmsman to turn the bow north, in the direction of the other ship they could now see distinctly, about one mile away. It stood out against the fog bank, which advanced compact as a wall.

*

On board the fugitive ship, faced with that dense cloud that spread over the sea like spiralling smoke, consternation reigned. Teutasius, at the helm, struck the sail because the wind had died down and the ship almost came to a stop.

'It is madness to go forward under these conditions,' he said. 'No one would ever dare follow us.'

'That's what you think,' replied Vatrenus. 'Take a look at that ship down there. They're laying on the oars and heading straight in this direction. I'm afraid it's us they're out for.'

'If we wait to be sure it's them, we'll have to be ready for a fight,' observed Orosius.

'If it's up to me,' said Batiatus, 'I'd rather fight those freckled bastards than be swallowed up . . . in there. It feels like we're descending into the Underworld.'

'We managed it at Misenus,' Vatrenus reminded them.

'Yes, but we knew it would only be for a very short time,' objected Aurelius. 'Here we're talking about hours and hours of navigation.'

'It's them!' shouted Demetrius, who had shimmied up the masthead.

'Are you sure?' called out Aurelius.

'Absolutely! They'll be on us in half an hour.'

Ambrosinus, who seemed to be absorbed in his own thoughts, abruptly came round. 'Is there any oil on board?'

'Oil?' repeated the surprised helmsman. 'I think . . . I think so, but it can't be much. The men use it for the lanterns.'

'Bring it here immediately in a bowl, the widest you've got, and get ready to depart again. We'll use the oars.'

'Give him what he needs,' said Aurelius. 'He knows what he's doing.'

The man went below deck and then came back up with a clay bowl, half full of oil. 'It's all I could find,' he said.

'They're getting closer!' shouted Demetrius from the top of the mast.

'That's all right,' said Ambrosinus. 'It's fine. Place it here, on the deck, return to the helm and, when I say so, everyone who's fit to do so will take up the oars.' He then took the tablet he used for writing, removed the parchment lining and, under the astonished gaze of the onlookers, extracted a little metal leaf shaped like an arrow, so thin that the wind could have carried it away. He placed it on the surface of the oil.

'Have you ever heard of Aristeas of Proconnesus?' he asked. 'No, of course not. Well, the ancients said that he had an arrow that led him, every year, to the land of the Hyperboreans, that is, the far north. This is that arrow, and she will tell us the way to Britannia. We'll follow her.'

Under the ever more astonished gaze of those present, the arrow came to life and began to rotate on the surface of the oil, coming to a stop in a fixed direction.

'That's North,' proclaimed Ambrosinus solemnly. 'To your oars, men!'

They all obeyed and the ship moved, slipping slowly into the milky cloud.

Romulus approached his tutor, who had carved a notch into the bowl at the point that coincided with the direction indicated by the arrow.

'How can this be?' asked Romulus. 'That arrow is magic!'

'I think you're right,' answered Ambrosinus. 'I can't think of any other explanation myself.'

'Where did you find it?'

'Years ago, in the underground chambers of the temple of Portunus in Rome, inside an urn made of tufa. A Greek inscription said that it was the arrow of Aristeas of Proconnesus, and that Pitheas of Marseilles had also used it to reach Ultima Thule. Isn't it marvellous?'

'That it is,' replied Romulus, and he added: 'Do you think they'll follow us?'

'I don't think so. They won't be able to stay on course, and what's more . . .'

'Yes?' urged Romulus.

'The crew are local people, and they will surely be too terrified to continue. There's a story, you see, that they tell around these parts . . .'

'What story?'

'That when the fog rises so thick here, it is to hide a boat making its return journey from the island of the dead, where it has deposited the souls of the deceased.'

Romulus looked all around, trying to penetrate the dense blanket of fog, as a shiver ran down his spine.

32

ROMULUS PULLED HIS CAPE around his shoulders, keeping his eyes fixed on the tiny oscillations of the arrow floating on the oil, as it mysteriously pointed to the pole of the Small Bear.

'The island of the dead, you said?' he asked suddenly.

Ambrosinus smiled. 'That's what I said. People here are quite afraid of it.'

'I don't understand. I thought the dead live in the afterworld.'

'That's what we all believe, but you see, since no one has ever returned from the kingdom of the dead to tell us about it, every people has come up with their own ideas about that mysterious world. Around here they say that there's a fishing village on the coast of Armorica whose inhabitants pay no taxes or any form of tribute whatsoever, because they are in charge of a very important task: ferrying the souls of the dead to a mysterious island shrouded by eternal fog. The name of this island is Avalon. Every night, there is a knock at the door of one of the village houses and a voice softly says: "We're ready." The fisherman gets out of his bed and goes to the beach where he finds his boat apparently empty, although it sinks into the water as if it carried a full load. The same voice he heard at his doorstep calls each of the dead by name, mentioning the name of the husband or father of each of the women as well. Then the fisherman takes the helm and hoists the sail. In the darkness and in the fog, he covers – in the space of a single night – a journey which would take an entire week of navigation to cross just one way. The next night, another fisherman hears a knock at his door and the same voice calls out: "We're ready . . ."'

'My God!' gasped Romulus. 'That is a frightening story. Is it true?'

'Who can say? In a certain sense, everything we believe is true. There must certainly be some truth to the story. Perhaps the people of that village are given to ancient practices of conjuring up the dead, and the sensations they experience are so intense that they seem real . . .' he interrupted himself to give instructions to the helmsman: 'A little starboard, slowly . . . yes, that's it.'

'And where is the island of Avalon found?'

'No one knows. Somewhere along the western coast of Britannia, perhaps, or so I heard once from an old Druid who came from the island of Mona. Others say it is further north, and it is the place where heroes go after their deaths, like the Fortunate Islands that Hesiod spoke of, remember? Perhaps one would have to get into that boat one night, at that fishing village in Armorica, to unravel the mystery . . . All is hypothesis, speculation: the fact is, my son, that we are surrounded by the unknown.'

Romulus nodded his head slowly as if to agree with such a serious assertion, then pulled his cloak up over his head and went below deck. Ambrosinus remained alone with his arrow to govern the ship through the spreading dark, while the others rowed unceasingly, filled with wonder, suspended in a dismal atmosphere without dimension and without time, where their only contact with reality was the lapping of the waves against the keel.

All at once, Aurelius asked: 'Do you think we'll see him again?'

Ambrosinus sat down beside him on the thwart. 'Wulfila?' he replied. 'Yes, until someone manages to kill him.'

'Volusianus advised us to go anywhere but Britannia. Seems like it's a real snakes' nest.'

'I don't think that any single place is better than another in this world of ours. We're going to Britannia because there's someone waiting for us there.'

'How do you know that? It's that prophecy of yours that makes you so sure, isn't it?'

'Does that surprise you?'

'I don't know. You know Pliny and Varro, Archimedes and Eratosthenes. You've read Strabo and Tacitus . . .'

'So have you, I see,' observed Ambrosinus, not without a bit of surprise.

'You're a man of science,' concluded Aurelius as if he hadn't heard.

'And a man of science doesn't believe in prophecies; it's not rational, is it?'

'No, it's not.'

'Is there anything rational in what you've done? Is there anything logical in the events we've experienced over the past few months?'

'Not much, I'd say.'

'And do you know why? Because there's another world, beyond the world we know. It's the world of dreams, the world of monsters and chimeras, the world of delirium, of passion and of mystery. It's a world that comes to the surface in certain moments and induces us to act in a way which makes no sense, or simply causes us to shiver, like a breath of icy air in the night, or the nightingale's warble at dusk. We do not know how far this world reaches, if it ends or is infinite, if it is within us or outside us, if it takes on the semblance of reality to reveal itself to us or to hide from us. Prophecies are like those words that a sleeping man pronounces in his slumber. They apparently don't make sense, but in reality they come from the most hidden abysses of the universal soul.'

'I thought you were Christian.'

'What difference does it make? You could be Christian as well, judging from the manifestations of your soul, and yet you are pagan.'

'If being pagan means being faithful to the traditions of our ancestors and the beliefs of our fathers, if it means seeing God in all things and all things in God, if it means bitterly mourning a greatness that will never come back, then yes, I am pagan.'

'As am I. Do you see this little twig of mistletoe I wear at my neck? It represents my ties with the world I was born in, with that ancient knowledge. Don't we change clothing when we go from a cold clime to a hot one? Our vision of the world is much the same. Religion is the colour our soul takes on, depending on the light it is exposed to. You have seen me under the bright Mediterranean sun, but when you see me in the light-starved forests of Britannia, I will be another man and yet, remember this, the same. It is inevitable and thus it must be. Do you remember when we were on the Rhine and you began singing the hymn to the sun? We sang all together, Christians and pagans, because in the splendour of the sun rising after the night we see the face of God, the glory of Christ who brings light to the world.'

Thus the whole night passed. They would call out to each other now and then, to pluck up their courage, or they would row in silence, until the wind picked up and the fog finally began to clear. Demetrius hoisted the sail and his companions, exhausted by their prolonged effort, could rest at last.

As as soon as the glimmer of daybreak began to spread, Ambrosinus's voice rang out: 'Look! Look, everyone!' he shouted.

Aurelius raised his head, Romulus and Livia ran to the forward railing, and Batiatus, Orosius and Demetrius left the sheets to admire the vision that was slowly unfolding before their eyes. In dawn's first light, a land was emerging from the fog: a land green with meadows and white with cliffs, blue with the sky and the sea, encircled by swirling foam, caressed by the breeze, ringing with the cries of millions of birds.

'Britannia!' shouted Ambrosinus. 'My Britannia!' He opened his arms as if to greet a dear and long-missed friend. He was crying: hot tears lined his mystic's face, making his eyes glow with a new light. Then he fell to his knees and covered his face, hiding it between his hands. He immersed himself in prayer and meditation before the Genius of his native land, before the wind carrying lost yet never forgotten scents.

The others watched him in silence, deeply moved, and soon they were startled by the sound of the keel dragging over the clean gravel of the beach.

*

Only Juba had accompanied them over the channel of Britannia, because the other horses had been left for Teutasius in payment for their passage. Aurelius led his horse down the narrow gangplank, stroking him to keep him calm. He couldn't help but admire him, black and gleaming as a crow's wing in that bright light that seemed a harbinger of springtime. All the others followed, Batiatus last, carrying Romulus on his shoulders in triumph.

They started walking north, across green fields dotted by patches of snow through which purple crocuses pushed up. The robins perching on red-berried hedges seemed to pause and watch curiously as the little procession passed along the path. Now and then colossal oaks rose in the middle of vast pastures. Golden mistletoe berries glittered on their bare branches.

'See?' Ambrosinus pointed them out to his pupil. 'That's mistletoe, a plant sacred to our ancient religion because it was thought to rain from the skies. The oak is sacred as well, giving its name to the wise men of the Celtic religion, the Druids.'

'I know,' replied Romulus. 'From the Greek word *drys*, which means "oak".'

Aurelius called them back to reality. 'We'll have to procure horses as soon as possible; we're too vulnerable on foot.'

'As soon as possible,' promised Ambrosinus. 'As soon as possible.' And they carried on, walking all day through fields scattered with wooden farmhouses covered by thatch roofing. The villages were small, clusters of little houses built close together, and as the evening of that short winter day approached, they could see smoke rising from the chimneys and Romulus imagined families gathered around frugal tables, around the dim light of a lantern, consuming the fruits of their labour. He envied them their simple, humble lives, sheltered from the greed of powerful men.

Before night fell, Ambrosinus, holding Romulus by the hand, walked up to one of the houses and knocked on the door. It was isolated, bigger and clearly more prosperous than those they had seen until that moment. A large pen alongside held a flock of sheep with thick woolly coats, while another enclosed a small herd of horses. The robust man who opened the door wore a grey wool cloak and his face was framed by a black beard run through with silver threads.

'We are wayfarers,' said Ambrosinus. 'Other companions of ours are down by the hedge. We have come from beyond the sea and must reach the lands of the north, which I left many years ago. My name is Myrdin Emreis.'

'How many of you are there?' asked the man.

'Eight in all. We need horses, if you can sell them to us.'

'My name's Wilneyr,' said the man, 'and I have five sons, all strapping lads good at using their weapons. If you come in peace you'll be welcomed as our guests. If your intentions are otherwise, be advised that we'll shear you like sheep.'

'We come in peace, my friend, in the name of God who will judge us one day. We carry arms of necessity, but we will leave our weapons outside the door if we enter under your roof.'

'Come on then. If you want to spend the night, you can sleep in the stables.'

'Thank you,' replied Ambrosinus. 'You won't regret this.' He sent Romulus to call the others.

When Batiatus appeared, the man widened his eyes in wonder and backed up as if taken by a sudden fright. His sons gathered round him.

'Don't be afraid,' said Ambrosinus. 'He's only a black man. In his land, everyone is as black as he is, and if a white man goes that far, he arouses the same wonder and the same surprise that you are feeling now. He's a good man, and quite peaceful, although he's very strong. We'll pay double for his dinner, because he eats enough for two.'

Wilneyr had them sit around the fire and gave them some bread with cheese and beer, which put them all in good spirits.

'Who do you raise those horses for?' asked Ambrosinus. 'The ones I saw are war stallions.'

'You're right, and they're always in great demand, because there's no peace in this land, anywhere, as far as I've travelled, at least. That's why there's always bread on my table, and mutton and beer. You, who say you come in peace: why are you accompanied by armed men wanting to buy horses?'

'My story is a long one, and quite sad, in truth,' replied the old man. 'The entire night would not suffice to tell it, but if you would like to listen, I'll tell you all I can, because I have nothing to hide, except from the enemies who pursue us. As I've already told you, I'm not a foreigner. I come from this land originally, from the city of Carvetia, and I was raised by the wise men of the sacred wood of Gleva.'

'I realized that when I saw what you wear at your neck,' Wilneyr said, 'and that's why I let you in.'

'I might have stolen it,' observed Ambrosinus with a wry smile.

'I don't believe so. Your person, your words and your eyes tell me that you do not wear that symbol unworthily. Tell us your story, then, if you are not too tired. The night is long and we don't often receive guests from so far away,' he said, looking again at Batiatus with amazement: his pitch-dark eyes, his huge lips, his flat nose and bull's neck, and the enormous hands he held folded between his powerful thighs.

So Ambrosinus told of how he had left his city and his wood so many years before to ask the emperor of the Romans for help, as he had been ordered by the heroic Germanus and by General Paullinus, the last defender of the Great Wall. He told of his wanderings and of his misadventures, of happy days and of long suffering. Wilneyr and his sons listened as if enchanted because that story was the best they'd ever heard; not even the bards who went from city to city, from house to house, to narrate the adventures of the heroes of Britannia, had such tales to tell.

However, Ambrosinus did not reveal the identity of Romulus, nor did he speak of the boy's destiny, because the time had not yet come. When he finished it was the dead of night, and the flames in the hearth had begun to languish.

'Now you tell me,' asked Ambrosinus, 'how is power divided on the island? Who among the lords of war is the strongest and most feared? What has happened in the cities that were still proud and flourishing when I left?'

'Ours is an age of tyranny,' answered Wilneyr gravely. 'No one cares about the good of the people. The law of the strongest rules, and there is no mercy for those who fall, but certainly the most famous and most terrible of the tyrants is Wortigern. The cities once turned to him for protection against the attacks of the northern barbarians, but he, instead, subjugated them and imposed heavy tributes. Although the councils of the elders have survived in some of the cities, they no longer have any real power. The merchants who populated the cities were eager for peace, so they could prosper and grow rich through trade and barter. They ended up exchanging their freedom for the promise of security.

'Wortigern himself gradually lost the vigour of his youth, and was no longer able to carry out the task for which he had been given such great powers, and so he decided to call upon the Saxon tribes who live on the continent, on the peninsula of Kymre, but the remedy proved to be worse than the disease. Instead of abating, oppression doubled. The Saxons were only concerned with accumulating wealth by robbing it from the citizens, and certainly not with stopping the raids of the Scots and the Picts from the north. Like dogs over a bone, these barbarians fought each other for the meagre spoils of that which was once a prosperous and lively country and which is now just a shadow of its prior self. We've escaped this fate only here in the countryside, as you can see, but perhaps even this won't last long.'

Aurelius, dismayed, sought out Ambrosinus's gaze: was this the land so long dreamed of? In what way was it any better than the bloody chaos they'd just escaped from? The wise man's mind was elsewhere, however, seeking distant images left behind when he had abandoned his country. He was readying himself to mend a tear in time, an open wound in the history of man and of his people.

They were accompanied by one of Wilneyr's sons to the stable, where they stretched out exhausted on a bed of hay near the oxen who ruminated tranquilly. They abandoned themselves to sleep, guarded by the dogs that had been freed from their cages. They were huge mastiffs with iron spiked collars, used to fighting off wolves or even more fearful beasts.

They woke at dawn and drank the warm milk that Wilneyr's wife poured from a bucket, then prepared for their journey. They bought a mule for Ambrosinus and seven horses, one much smaller than the others and one a great deal bigger: a massive stallion from Armorica, used to cover the Britannic mares. When Batiatus mounted on his back he looked like a bronze equestrian statue, one of those that had once adorned the forums and arches of the world's capital.

Wilneyr counted up the money; Livia had given him everything she had left. Satisfied with doing such good business so early in the day, he rested against the threshold and watched them leave. They had taken up their arms, suspended their swords from their belts, and in the first light of the morning they looked like legendary warriors. Even the pale youth who rode in front on his pony seemed like their young leader, and the girl a woodland dryad. What exploits awaited such a tiny army? He didn't even know their names, and yet it seemed that he had always known them. He raised his arm to bid them farewell and they did the same from the top of the hill as they wound their way at a steady pace, dark shapes against the pearly dawn.

*

This land, so fraught with danger, held no secrets from Ambrosinus, as though he had been gone for a couple of days instead of years and years. He knew the language, the countryside, the character of the inhabitants, he knew how to cross the forests without losing his way and without ending up in the dark corners where outlaws might lie in wait. He knew the depths of the rivers and the length of the days and the nights. From the colour of the sky he could tell if a storm was approaching, or if they could expect good weather. The voices of the birds were precise messages of alarm or peace for him, and even the knotty trunks of the trees spoke to him. They told him stories of long snowy winters or fertile springs, of incessant rains, of lightning bolts fallen from the sky.

Only once did they have to face a threat: they were ambushed one evening by a band of brigands, but the overwhelming impact of Batiatus on his Armorican stallion, the deadly force of Aurelius and Vatrenus, Livia's arrows, Demetrius's swift reactions and Orosius's quiet power soon triumphed over their aggressors, who for years had fought only as marauders and no longer as soldiers.

So, in just over two weeks of journeying, the little caravan had crossed almost a third of the country, and were camped not far from a city called Caerleon.

'What a strange name,' said Romulus, considering the place from a distance, struck by the strange mix of imposing ancient architecture and wretched huts.

'It's just the local deformation of *Castra Legionum*,' explained Ambrosinus. 'The legions of the south once pitched their camps here, and that structure down there is what remains of the amphitheatre.'

Aurelius and the others observed the city as well, and it had a strange effect on them to see the vestiges of Rome, still so imposing and yet already in ruin, bound for complete dissolution.

They continued on for two more weeks, reaching the base of the high lands and the edge of the vast forests. One night, as they were sitting around their campfire, Aurelius thought that it was time to establish the ultimate purpose of their long march, the future that awaited them in that far-flung corner of the world.

'Where are we going, *magister*?' he asked abruptly. 'Don't you think the time has come to let us know?'

'Yes, Aurelius, you're right. We're going to Carvetia, the city I left many years ago. I had promised then to return with an imperial army to liberate this land from the barbarians of the north and from Wortigern. He was an oppressive tyrant at that time, and remains one now, although as we have heard he's become old and weak. Lust for power is the most potent medicine: it keeps even dying men alive.'

They all looked at each other, stunned.

'You promised to return with an army and you're bringing us?' said Vatrenus, pointing at himself and his companions. 'We'll be greeted by hoots of laughter! I thought you'd be taking us to a tranquil place, where we would be able to live a normal existence, in peace. I'd say we deserve it.'

'In all truth,' spoke up Demetrius, 'I expected much the same: somewhere far from the madness of the world, in the country, where we could raise families, and use our swords to cut cheese, or bread.'

'I'd like somewhere like that myself,' piped up Orosius. 'We could set up a little village and get together every now and then to enjoy a meal and reminisce about the trials and tribulations we went through. Wouldn't that be beautiful?'

Batiatus nodded in swift agreement. 'No one around here has ever seen a black man, but I think they'd get accustomed to me soon enough. Maybe even I could find a girl who wouldn't mind living with me, what do you think?'

Ambrosinus raised his arm to cut off their rambling. 'In the north, there is still an armed legion that awaits its emperor. It is known as the Legion of the Dragon, because its emblem is a silver dragon with a purple tail that swells up and moves as if it were alive, when the wind blows.'

'You're mad,' Aurelius broke in. 'The only legion, the last legion, was ours, and as you know, we're the last survivors.'

'That's not true!' objected Ambrosinus. 'This legion does exist, and it was Germanus himself who founded it. He made my people promise, on his dying day, that they would keep it armed, in defence of the liberty of the country, until I returned. They would never break a promise made to a hero and a saint! I know that my words seem like ravings, but have I ever led you astray, have I ever deluded you, in all this time we've been together?'

Vatrenus shook his head, increasingly perplexed. 'Do you realize what you're saying? Even if it were true, they'd all be old men now: they'll have white beards, and have lost all their teeth!'

'You say so?' challenged Ambrosinus. 'They're as old as you are, Vatrenus, or you, Aurelius. The age of hardened, indomitable veterans. I understand that all this must seem absurd to you, but listen to me, for the love of God! You'll have what you are longing for. You'll be able to enjoy a peaceful existence in a place that I'll show you: a fertile, secluded valley, a little paradise watered by a crystal-clear spring, a place where you can live by hunting or fishing, where you can find women for yourselves among the nomad tribes that pass though every year with their flocks. But first you must complete your task, as you've promised me, and as you've promised this boy. I won't ask for anything else. Escort us as far as the fortified camp that is our final destination, and then decide what you must. I will do everything in my power to assist you.'

Aurelius turned to the others: 'You've all heard Ambrosinus's words: our task is to present the emperor to his legion, granting that it still exists, and then we will have fulfilled our pledge. We may continue to serve at his orders, or be discharged with honour.'

'But what if there is no legion?' asked Livia, who had been silent up to then. 'What will we do? Abandon him to his destiny? Will we split apart, each going his own way, or will we live together in this beautiful place that Ambrosinus has described?'

'If it no longer exists, you will be free to do as you wish. That holds for you as well, my son,' said Ambrosinus, turning to Romulus. 'You can live with them if they choose to remain, as I so ardently hope, and grow up in peace. You'll become a man:

a shepherd, perhaps, or a hunter, or a farmer, as you like. However, I am certain that God has set aside quite a different destiny for you, and that these men and this young woman will be the instruments of your destiny, as I have been. This long journey of ours has not been governed by chance, and it was not human valour alone that permitted us to win over so many seemingly impossible challenges. The hand of God, whatever God you believe in, has guided us and will continue to guide us, until we have carried out his will.'

Aurelius examined his companions' faces, one by one. He gave Livia a deeply moving look, as if to communicate all the long-suffocated passion and fears that tormented him. From all he had the same silent response, unequivocal.

'We will not abandon you,' he said then. 'Not before nor after this mad expedition. We will find a way to stay united. If it's true that death has so often spared us, the day will surely come in which we can finally enjoy what remains of our lives, long or short as they may be.' He rose to his feet and walked away, because he felt he could no longer control the tumultuous feelings that crowded his soul.

There was more to it than that. His nightmares had been coming back, the same that had tortured him all these years, and the stabbing pains in his head were getting worse, and more frequent, preventing him from expressing himself and showing his emotions, especially with Livia. He felt as though the circle of his life was drawing to a close. Something was waiting for him there, at the end of the world: a final settling of accounts, with himself and his destiny.

Ambrosinus waited until the fire had gone out and everyone was asleep before he approached him. 'Don't lose heart, I beg of you,' he said. 'Have faith, and remember that the greatest endeavours are managed by a handful of heroes.'

'I'm no hero,' Aurelius replied without even turning, 'and you know that.'

*

It snowed, that night, and it was the last snowfall of the winter. From that day on, they rode forward in the sunshine, under a sky of clouds as fluffy white as the coats of the lambs who were venturing out for the first time with their flocks to pasture. Violets and daisies sprang up overnight on the meadows facing south. Finally, one day, Ambrosinus stopped at the foot of a hill and got off his mule. He took his pilgrim's staff and walked to the top, under everyone's eyes. Then he turned around and shouted: 'Come on now! What are you waiting for? Come on, hurry!'

Romulus was the first to catch up, sweaty and panting, followed by Livia and Aurelius and Vatrenus and the others. Just a few miles ahead of them lay the Great Wall, extending like a powerful stone belt from one side of the horizon to the other, studded with castles and towers. Beneath them to their right, not too far from where they stood, glittered the waters of a little lake, as clear and transparent as air. At its very centre was a green mossy crag. Far below, to the east, rose a mountain peak still capped with snow, and on its slopes, above a cliff, they could make out a fortified camp. Ambrosinus contemplated this superb spectacle enrapt: his gaze embraced the winding fortification that joined one sea to another, then rested on the lake, the mountain peak, the fortified camp, grey as the rock itself. He said: 'We have arrived, my son, my friends. Our journey has come to an end. This is the Great Wall which crosses the entire country, and the mountain down there is *Mons Badonicus*. The lake at our feet is *Lacus Virginis*, which was said to be inhabited by a water nymph. And there, carved into the mountain itself, is the camp of the last legion of Britannia: the fort of the dragon!'

33

THEY DESCENDED INTO THE completely deserted valley and advanced towards the fort, which now seemed more distant than it had from the top of the hill. They skirted the enchantingly beautiful lake, a small rocky basin surrounded by black, white and brown pebbles which glistened under the transparent water. They then started the ascent towards the low hill where the fort stood, resting on a rocky platform.

'The interior part of the camp,' explained Ambrosinus, 'was excavated to create a flat surface on which the troops' accommodations and the stables and sheds could be built. All around, a dry wall was raised for protection, topped by a palisade and guard towers.'

'You know the place very well,' observed Aurelius.

'Certainly,' said Ambrosinus. 'I lived here a long time as a doctor and adviser to Commander Paullinus.'

'What's that over there?' asked Romulus, pointing to a megalithic monument that was beginning to emerge from behind the sides of the hill, on a raised area that had been invisible to them. It looked like an enormous stone slab encircled by four gigantic rock pillars, standing at the four cardinal points.

Ambrosinus stopped. 'That,' he said, 'is the funeral monument of a great warrior of this land, a Celtic leader known as Kalgak, who the Latin authors call Calgacus. He was the last hero of native resistance against the Roman invasion of Britannia three hundred years ago.'

'I know all about that,' said Romulus. 'I've read the pages of

Tacitus that relate his speech before the last battle, and the harsh words he uses to define the *Pax romana*.'

'"With false words they call Empire the subjugation of the world, and where they have made a desert, they call it peace,"' recited Aurelius. 'But remember,' he continued, not without a certain pride, 'these are not actually the words of Calgacus, but of Tacitus himself: a Roman criticizing Roman imperialism. This is where the greatness of our civilization lies.'

'They say that his council met gathered around that stone,' said Ambrosinus, 'and since then it has symbolized the liberty of all the inhabitants of this land, whatever their race.'

They continued their ascent towards the outer wall of the camp, but even at that distance it was evident that the place was deserted: the palisade was in ruins, the gates hanging from their hinges, the towers crumbling. Aurelius was the first to enter and witness, wherever his gaze fell, the signs of negligence and abandon.

'A legion of ghosts,' he murmured.

'This place has been abandoned for years, it's all falling to pieces,' echoed Vatrenus. Batiatus tested the stability of a stairway that led up to the sentry walk, and the entire structure crashed noisily to the ground.

Ambrosinus seemed bewildered, overwhelmed by that desolation.

'You really thought you'd still find something here?' demanded Aurelius. 'I can't believe it. Look at the Great Wall down there: there hasn't been a Roman standard flying over that wall for more than seventy years. How could you have hoped that a small bastion like this would survive? Look for yourself. There are no signs of destruction or of armed resistance. They just got up and left. Who knows how long ago.'

Ambrosinus walked towards the centre of the camp. 'It may seem impossible to you, but you must believe me: the fire has not died yet. We need only stoke it up and the flame of liberty will once again blaze brightly!'

No one was listening. They shook their heads, daunted, in

that unreal silence broken only by the whistle of the wind, by the creaking doors of the sheds eroded by time and the elements. Heedless of their dejection, Ambrosinus approached what must have been the praetorium, the commander's residence, and disappeared inside.

'Where's he going?' asked Livia.

Aurelius shrugged.

'So now what do we do?' wondered Batiatus. 'It looks like we've travelled two thousand miles for nothing.'

Romulus was crouched in a corner, closed up in his own thoughts, and Livia didn't dare go near him. She could guess how he felt and was suffering for him.

'Seeing the state of things here, we'd better look at this situation realistically,' began Vatrenus.

'Realistically? There's nothing real here! Just look around you, by all the gods!' burst out Demetrius, but the words were not out of his mouth when the door of the praetorium opened and out came Ambrosinus. Their muttering ceased and they all stared at the solemn figure emerging from the darkness with an amazing object in his hand: a silver-headed, open-jawed dragon with a purple tail, hoisted on a pole from which a banner hung. The words on the banner read: LEGIO XII DRACO.

'My God!' murmured Livia. Romulus gazed at the standard, its tail embroidered with golden scales that seemed to move as if alive, as if suddenly animated by a vital force. Ambrosinus drew closer to Aurelius, eyes blazing. His face was transformed; his tense features seemed carved into stone. He delivered the standard to Aurelius, saying: 'It's yours, commander. The legion has been reinstated.'

Aurelius hesitated, immobile before that slender, nearly emaciated figure, before that imperious gaze that flared with a mysterious, indomitable light. The wind picked up suddenly, raising a cloud of dust that enveloped them all. Aurelius held out his hand and grasped the pole.

'Go now,' commanded Ambrosinus. 'Hang it from the highest tower.'

Aurelius looked around at his silent, unmoving companions, and then slowly made his way up to the battlements and hung the standard from the western tower, the highest of all. The dragon's tail twisted free, lashed by the wind. The metallic mouth let forth an acute sound, the whistle that had so often terrified the enemy in battle. He looked below: his companions were lined up, offering a military salute. His eyes welled with tears.

Ambrosinus spoke again: 'We'll install ourselves here, and we'll try to make this place liveable. It will be our home for some time. I will try to re-establish contact with the people I knew and who perhaps still live here. When the time comes, I will report to the senate of Carvetia, if it still exists, or summon the people to the forum. I will present Romulus to the people and to the senate.'

'You promised them an army when you left this land so many years ago,' said Vatrenus, 'and you're returning with a child. What do you expect from them?'

'Heed my words: the legion has been reinstated and the soldiers who have scattered will flock around this standard and around their emperor. I will remind them of the prophecy: "A youth shall come from the southern sea with a sword . . . The eagle and the dragon will fly again over the great land of Britannia!"'

'The sword . . .' murmured Aurelius, head low. 'I've lost it.'

'Not for ever,' replied Ambrosinus. 'You shall win it back, I promise you.'

*

The next day, Ambrosinus left the camp to regain contact with the land he had so long abandoned. He set off all alone, with his pilgrim's staff, across the valley to Carvetia. With each step, his soul flooded with deep emotion. The scent of the grass carried on the wind, the song of the birds which welcomed the rising sun, the meadows dotted with white and yellow flowers, all brought him back to the distant days of his youth, and everything seemed close and familiar to him, as though he had never left. As he advanced, the sun rose in the sky, warming the air and setting the streams asparkle like silver ribbons. He watched the shepherds bring their herds and flocks to pasture, the peasants pruning the apple trees in their orchards: the beauty of nature seemed to prevail over the misfortune impending on human destiny, and this struck him as the most auspicious of signs.

He came within view of the city late in the afternoon, and recognized a familiar shape on a hillside. It was a large, ancient residence, walled all around like a fort but surrounded by green pastures and fields where farmers and workers were occupied in their tasks. Some were preparing the ground for sowing, others were removing dry branches from the trees, and still others were at the edge of the wood, loading great trunks on to oxen-drawn carts. A herd of horses ran within an enclosure, led by a long-maned white stallion who galloped unbridled, whipping the air with his tail.

Ambrosinus entered through the main gate of the vast courtyard lined with the workshops of blacksmiths, farriers and carpenters. As he entered, he was greeted by the delicious fragrance of freshly-baked bread and the festive barking of the dogs. No one asked who he was, or what he wanted. A woman presented him with a loaf of bread, their gift to all guests, and he understood that nothing had changed in that noble home since he had been away. He asked: 'Is Kustennin still the lord of this house?'

'He is, thank God,' replied the woman.

'Please tell him, then, that an old friend has returned from a long exile, and is eager to embrace him again.'

'Follow me,' said the woman. 'I'll take you to him.'

'No, I'd rather wait for him here, as befits a wayfarer who knocks at the door requesting hospitality and shelter.'

The woman disappeared through an archway and quickly went up the stairs leading to the upper floor of the villa. Shortly thereafter an imposing figure stood out against the red light of dusk. A man of about fifty with blue eyes, greying at the temples, his wide shoulders draped with a black cloak, considered him with an uncertain expression, trying to recognize the pilgrim he found before him. Ambrosinus moved closer. 'Kustennin, it's Myrdin Emreis, your old friend. I'm back.'

The man's eyes filled with joy. He ran towards him, shouting: 'Myrdin!' and he gripped him in a long hug. 'How long!' he gasped, his voice quivering with emotion. 'My old friend, how long has it been? Oh good God, how could I not have recognized you at once?'

Ambrosinus stepped back to take a look at his face, rather incredulous that he had found him again after so many years. 'I've been through every mishap you can imagine. I've suffered hunger and cold and I've had to undergo terrible trials, my friend. That's why I look so different; my hair has gone completely white and even my voice has weakened. I'm so happy to see you, so very happy . . . you haven't changed at all, except for that bit of frost at your temples! Your family is well?'

'Come,' said Kustennin. 'Come and meet them! Egeria and I have a daughter, Ygraine, who is the light of our eyes.' He led the way up the stairs and down a corridor to the women's quarters.

'Egeria,' said Ambrosinus. 'It's Myrdin, do you remember me?'

Egeria dropped the embroidery that she was working on near the window and came towards him. 'Myrdin? I can't believe it. We thought you died long ago! This is a true gift from God, we must celebrate! You'll stay here with us, I don't want you leaving ever again,' she exclaimed, turning to her husband. 'Isn't that right, Kustennin?'

'Certainly,' he replied. 'Nothing would make us happier.'

Ambrosinus was about to reply when a lovely little girl walked in. Her father's blue eyes, her mother's flaming red hair, enchanting in her long gown of light blue wool: this was Ygraine, who greeted him gracefully.

Egeria immediately ordered the servants to prepare dinner and a room for their guest. 'Just for tonight,' she assured him. 'Tomorrow we'll find you more comfortable, sunnier quarters . . .'

Ambrosinus interrupted her: 'I'm glad to accept your hospitality, but I cannot stay here with you, although I desire it with all my heart. I'm not alone. I've arrived with a group of friends, all the way from Italy. Thus far we've managed to escape the relentless pursuit of our enemies.'

'It doesn't matter who's after you,' replied Kustennin. 'You'll be safe here and no one will dare hurt you. My servants are all armed, and if necessary they can turn into a small but well-disciplined and combative fighting unit.'

'I thank you,' replied Ambrosinus. 'Mine is a long story, which I will tell you this evening, if you have the patience to listen, but why have you armed your servants? And what has happened to the Legion of the Dragon? My friends and I have taken shelter at the old fort, but it was immediately clear to us that it had been long abandoned. Have the troops been moved to different quarters?'

'My God, Myrdin,' replied Kustennin, 'the legion has not existed for years, it was dissolved long ago . . .'

Ambrosinus darkened: 'Dissolved? I can't believe that. They had sworn on the bloodied body of Saint Germanus that they would fight for the liberty of our homeland as long as they had a breath of life in them. I've never forgotten that pledge, Kustennin, and I've returned to make good my promise. But then . . . not even you have the power any longer to defend this land from those who oppress her!'

Kustennin sighed. 'For years I tried to maintain my rank as consul, and for as long as the legion existed, this was to some measure possible. I had no lack of opposition, of course, from those who tried to brand me with the defamatory title of usurper and throw me in with the tyrants of this unfortunate land, but then the legion was dissolved and Wortigern succeeded in corrupting most of the senate. He still dominates the country today with his fierce mercenaries. Carvetia is actually quite a fortunate city, because Wortigern needs our horse breeders and our port, so he cannot suffocate us. The senate still meets and the magistrates still exercise their authority, at least in part, but this is all that is left of the liberty that Germanus had succeeded in restoring to us, along with the pride and dignity of he who is master of his own destiny.'

'I understand,' whispered Ambrosinus, lowering his gaze to hide the disheartenment that had gripped him as he heard those words.

'Tell me about yourself,' insisted Kustennin. 'What have you done in all these years you've been away? Who are these friends you mentioned, and why did you take them to the old fortified camp?'

Egeria interrupted their conversation to tell them that dinner was served, and the men sat down to table. Huge oak trunks blazed in the big hearth, the servants poured frothy beer into their cups and placed platters of roasted meat before them and they all ate heartily, recalling the old days. When the table was cleared, Kustennin added more wood to the fire, poured sweet wine from Gaul and invited his guest to sit with him near the hearth.

The waves of memories and the warmth of friendship and of wine encouraged Ambrosinus to open up his heart and inspired his tongue, and so he told his whole story, beginning from when he had left Britannia to go and seek assistance from the emperor. It was very late when he finished. Kustennin looked him in the eye with a stupefied expression and murmured: 'Almighty God . . . you've brought us the emperor himself . . .'

'So I have,' nodded Ambrosinus, 'and right now he is asleep in that solitary place, wrapped in the field blanket which is the only thing he owns, watched over by the most noble and generous men that the earth has ever borne.'

34

WULFILA AND HIS MEN landed in Britannia the day after Aurelius, at nightfall. They had their horses and weapons with them, and they proceeded to disembark at once. The helmsman was persuaded to remain with them even though he was a subject of Siagrius, because he was originally from Britannia and would be precious in assisting them through that unknown land. Wulfila gave him money to encourage his desertion, and promised him more.

'What is it you want to know?' asked the helmsman.

'How to reach those men.'

'It won't be easy. I saw the man leading them: he's a Druid, or has been brought up by the Druids. That means that he'll be able to move through this territory like a fish in the sea. It means that he knows every secret, every hiding place in this land. Consider that he has a good day and a half's advantage over us; it will be very difficult to find their trail. If we knew where they were headed, it would be different, but otherwise . . . Britannia is very big. It is the biggest island in the world.'

'But there can't be that many roads; the main itineraries must be limited.'

'Of course, but who says they'll follow them? They may choose to go through the forests, following shepherds' trails or the tracks of wild beasts.'

'They won't stay hidden from me for long. I've always sniffed them out, and I will this time as well.'

He walked away down the beach and stopped to watch the undertow, brooding. He abruptly gestured for the helmsman to draw closer: 'Who's in command here in Britannia?'

'What?'

'Is there a king? Someone who holds the highest power?'

'No, the country is fiercely contested by a number of tribal chiefs, violent and quarrelsome. However, there is one man that everyone fears. He dominates most of the territory from the Great Wall all the way to Caerleon, and he's backed by ferocious mercenaries. His name is Wortigern.'

'Where does he live?'

'In the north. He lives in an inaccessible fortress that he had built over an old fortified Roman camp called Castra Vetera. He was once a valiant warrior himself, and he fought off the invaders from the High Lands who had stormed the Great Wall, protecting the cities and their institutions, but power corrupted him, and turned him into a bloody tyrant. He justifies his dominion by claiming to defend the northern border of Britannia. In truth, this is only a pretext; he pays tribute to the High Land chiefs, and makes up for it by bleeding the country white with relentless taxes, or even by allowing the Saxon mercenaries he has brought in from the continent to pillage freely.'

'You know a lot.'

'This was my home for a long time. I took shelter in Gaul out of desperation and I enrolled in Siagrius's army.'

'If you take me to Wortigern, you won't regret it. I've give you land, servants, livestock, everything you could desire.'

'I can take you as far as Castra Vetera. Then you'll have to find a way to gain an audience. They say that Wortigern is extremely suspicious and untrusting, because he knows just how much hate he has sown and how many people would like to see him dead. He's old and weak now, and realizes how vulnerable he is.'

'Let's get going then. We have no time to waste.'

They left the ship to the undertow and marched along the coast until they met up with the old Roman consular road, the fastest way to reach their destination.

'What does he look like?' Wulfila asked the guide.

'No one knows. No one has seen his face for years and

years. Some say that he's been devastated by a repugnant disease, and that his face is one purulent sore. Others claim that it's simply that he doesn't want his subjects to see the evidence of his decline: his dull, glassy eyes, his drooling, toothless mouth and his sagging cheeks. He wants them to fear him, and so he hides behind a golden mask that portrays him in the unchanging splendour of his youth. It was fashioned by a great artist from the melted gold of a chalice. Such blasphemy, they say, sealed Wortigern's alliance with Satan, and anyone who wears that mask, until the end of the centuries, will have the power of the devil.' He stole a glance at Wulfila, fearful that he had incurred his wrath by alluding to his own deformity, but Wulfila strangely showed no sign of resentment.

'You speak too well for a simple sailor,' he observed. 'Who are you, really?'

'You won't believe me, but I am an artist, and I once met the man who crafted that mask. They say that Wortigern had him killed after his work was finished, because he was the only person to have seen the tyrant's ravaged face up close. The times in which artists were considered God's best-loved creatures is long gone: is there any place for art in a world like ours? Reduced to poverty, I tried my luck on a fishing boat and was taught to govern the helm and the sails. I don't know if I'll ever have another chance in my life to model gold and silver, as I once did, or to paint images of saints in the churches, or to put together a fine mosaic, but in any case, despite my current state and condition, I shall always be an artist.'

'An artist, huh?' asked Wulfila, searching the man's eyes with a strange expression, as if an idea had suddenly come to him. 'Can artists read inscriptions?'

'I'm familiar with ancient Celtic inscriptions, Scanian runes and Latin epigraphs,' he replied proudly.

Wulfila unsheathed his sword. 'Then tell me what these letters cut into the blade mean, and when this journey is over, I'll pay you and let you go free.'

The man examined the blade and then raised his eyes to Wulfila's with a look of wonder.

'What is it?' demanded Wulfila uneasily. 'A spell of some kind? Tell me!'

'Much more,' answered the man. 'Much more than any spell. This inscription says that the sword belonged to Julius Caesar, the first conqueror of Britannia, and that it was forged by the Calibians, a people from the far east who are the only ones in the world to know the secret of making invincible steel.'

Wulfila grinned wickedly. 'My people say that a man who takes up the arm of a conqueror becomes a conqueror himself. What you've told me is the best of omens. Lead me to Castra Vetera and when we arrive I'll give you more money and you'll be free to go wherever you like.'

They drove on for nearly two weeks, crossing the dominions of a series of minor tyrants, but the number of armed warriors on horseback following Wulfila, as well as his terrifying appearance, opened the way for the group without much difficulty. Just once a very powerful lord named Gwynwird, surrounded by a thick swarm of soldiers, dared to stop them at a bridge which gave access to his territory near Eburacum. Irritated by the arrogant attitude of the scar-faced foreigner, he demanded a tribute and the surrender of their arms, which would be returned past the confines of his domain. Wulfila burst into laughter, and instructed his guide to tell him that if he wanted their weapons he would have to take them in combat, and he challenged him to a duel. Proud of his fame and prestige, the lord accepted his challenge, but as soon as he saw his adversary draw his sword – a weapon of incredible crafting and beauty – he knew he would lose. Wulfila's first blow rent his shield, the second sent his sword flying and then his head rolled between his horse's hooves, eyes still wide in incredulous shock.

In accordance with ancient Celtic customs, the warriors of the defeated lord agreed to pass under the command of the victor, and so Wulfila's band grew to the size of a small army. They continued their journey, preceded by terrifying rumours about the ferociousness of their leader and the sword that rendered him invincible, until one mid-winter's day, they finally came into view of Castra Vetera.

It was a dark, gloomy fortress set on a hill covered by a thick fir forest, surrounded by a double moat and a wall and guarded by hundreds of armed soldiers. The incessant barking of the guard dogs inside could be heard from a distance, and as Wulfila's horsemen approached, a flock of crows took flight, filling the air with their strident cries. Low clouds in an overcast sky blanketed the castle in leaden light, making it look even more dismal. Wulfila sent ahead the interpreter, on foot and unarmed.

'My lord,' he announced, 'has come from the imperial court in Ravenna, in Italy, to pay homage to Lord Wortigern and to propose a pact of alliance. He brings gifts with him, and the imperial seal that accredits his mission.'

'Wait here and don't move,' ordered the guard. He turned to whisper to a man who seemed to be his superior, who disappeared inside the fortress. Quite some time passed as Wulfila, still in his saddle, waited impatiently, not knowing what to expect. Finally the man returned to report the reply of his master: the envoy was to present his gifts and his credentials, and only then would he be received, unarmed and alone.

Wulfila was about to turn heel and ride off, but his instinct told him that the castle was the key to achieving his goal. The idea of a tyrant who was weak and ill encouraged him to take the risk; his own energies were intact, after all, and he wouldn't need his arms. Over these long years, he had too often seen men who had come from nothing and yet had managed to seize power at the very top levels. All it took was knowing how to take advantage of opportunities, in a world dominated by continuous turbulence and open to the boldest and most audacious. He accepted.

Closely watched by a picket of armed men, he strode across the courtyard, still structured like the original Roman camp, lined with stables and soldiers' quarters. He reached the main keep, built of squared-off boulders with windows as narrow as loop-holes and topped by a sentry walk covered by a wooden roof. He climbed two ramps of stairs and was stopped before a small ironclad door that soon opened, although none of the men escorting him had knocked. They gestured for him to enter and closed the door behind him.

Wortigern sat before him, alone. There was no one else in that huge, bare room and this surprised Wulfila greatly. He sat on his throne with a certain worn-out abandon. A long mane of white hair fell down to his chest and his face was covered by the golden mask. If the features were faithful to his youth, he must have been an extraordinarily striking man.

His voice sounded, distorted and unrecognizable, within that metallic shell. 'Who are you? Why did you ask to speak with me?'

He spoke a common Latin, not difficult for Wulfila to understand.

'My name is Wulfila,' he answered. 'I've been sent by the imperial court of Ravenna where a new sovereign has taken the throne, a valiant warrior named Odoacer: he desires to pay his respects and stipulate a pact of friendship and alliance. The emperor was a faint-hearted child, in the hands of scheming courtiers and he has been deposed.'

'Why does this Odoacer want to become my friend?'

'Because your power as sovereign of Britannia and your valour as a warrior are well known to him – but there is another reason, a very important one, regarding the deposed emperor.'

'Speak,' said Wortigern. Every word seemed to cost him immense effort.

'A band of deserters has kidnapped the boy with the complicity of his tutor, a mad old Celt, and they have sought refuge here on your island. They are extremely dangerous and I wanted to warn you.'

'I should fear an old man and a child accompanied by a handful of brigands?'

'Perhaps not yet, but they could soon become a threat.

Remember the old adage, my lord: 'Troubles must be faced when they're still young.'

'*Principiis obsta . . .*' repeated the golden mask mechanically. He must have been educated as a Roman in his youth.

'In any case, it will be useful for you to have an ally as powerful as Odoacer, who has immense riches and many thousands of warriors at his command. If you help him to capture these delinquents, you'll always be able to count on his support. I know that the attacks on your kingdom from the north have never fully ceased, and that this obliges you to continue a difficult and costly war.'

'You're well informed,' replied Wortigern.

'To serve you and to serve my lord Odoacer.'

Wortigern pushed up on the arm rests of his throne to straighten his back and head, and Wulfila felt the weight of his stare through that impassive mask. He could tell that he was observing his deformity and he felt hate blaze up.

'You spoke of gifts . . .' started up Wortigern again.

'That's right,' replied Wulfila.

'I want to see them.'

'You can see the first by looking out of that window: the two hundred warriors I've brought with me to put into your service. They are magnificent fighters, and can take care of themselves; they won't cost you anything. I am willing to command them myself in any mission you shall entrust me with. This is only the beginning. If you need more soldiers, my lord, Odoacer, is ready to send them at any moment.'

'He must be very afraid of that little boy,' said Wortigern. Wulfila did not answer and remained standing before the throne, imagining that the old tyrant would approach the window to see his men, but he didn't move.

'And the other gifts?'

'The others?' Wulfila had a moment of uncertainty, and then his gaze suddenly lit up. 'I have but one other gift,' he continued, 'but it is the most extraordinary object that you could possibly imagine, an object for which the most powerful men in the world would give up all their riches, if they could only possess it. It is the most precious talisman that exists and it belonged to Julius Caesar, the first conqueror of Britannia. He who holds it is destined to reign forever over this land, and never to know decline.'

Now Wortigern was immobile on his throne, head straight, intent. He would have seemed a statue, had it not been for a nearly imperceptible tremor in his hooked hands. Wulfila sensed that his words had awakened the tyrant's boundless avidity.

'Let me see it,' the old man demanded, and his voice had an imperious and impatient tone.

'The gift will be yours if you help me to capture our enemies and allow me to give them the punishment they deserve. I want the boy's head. These are the terms of our agreement.'

A long silence followed, then Wortigern slowly nodded his head. 'I accept,' he said, 'and I hope for your sake that your gift does not disappoint me. The man who conducted you into my presence is the commander of my Saxon troops. You will give him a description of those you are seeking, so that he can advise our informers, who have eyes and ears everywhere.'

Having said this, he reclined his head on his shoulder with an abandon much like death, allowing only a faint wheeze to be heard from the lips of his golden mask. Wulfila thought that their discussion must be over. He bowed and headed towards the door.

'Wait!' the voice unexpectedly called him back.

He turned towards the throne.

'Rome . . . have you ever seen Rome?'

'Yes,' said Wulfila, 'and her beauty is beyond description. I have beheld arches of marble as tall as buildings, topped by bronze chariots, drawn by steeds all covered with gold and driven by winged genii; squares circled by porticoes supported by hundreds of columns, each carved from a single block of stone, some of them as tall as this tower of yours, resplendent in all the most beautiful colours; temples and basilicas covered with paintings and mosaics; fountains in which fabulous creatures of marble and bronze pour water into basins of stone so large that they could contain one hundred men. There is a monument in Rome, made of hundreds of superimposed arches, in which the ancients put to death the Christians, allowing them to be devoured by beasts. It's called the Coliseum, and it is so large that your entire castle could fit inside it.'

He stopped because a mournful hiss was now coming from the mask, a suffered gasp that he could not interpret: perhaps the ne'er accomplished dream of far-away youth, or the avidity excited by the thought of such immense riches, or perhaps the inner torment that a vision of greatness evoked in a soul imprisoned in a body eroded by old age and disease.

Wulfila walked out, closing the door behind him, and went back to his men. He tossed a bag of money to the interpreter, saying: 'Here's the reward I promised you. You're free to go now; I know everything I need to know.' The man took the money, bowed his head in a quick gesture of gratitude and spurred his horse into a gallop, to flee as quickly and as far as possible from that gloomy place.

*

From that day on, Wulfila became the most faithful and the fiercest of Wortigern's cut-throats. Wherever rebellion arose, he appeared all at once at the head of his warriors to sow terror, death and destruction with such awesome swiftness, with such devastating power, that no one dared even to speak of liberty any longer. No one dared to confide with friends or family, not even between the walls of his own home, and the favour that Wulfila enjoyed with the tyrant grew immoderately, in proportion to the fruit of the sacks and plunder that he lay at Wortigern's feet.

Wulfila embodied all that Wortigern no longer had: inexhaustible energy, potency and lightning quick reaction. The barbarian had become the physical prolongation of the old man's craving for dominion, to the point where he no longer even needed to give him orders: Wulfila could predict them and carry them out even before he heard them in that great empty room. None the less, it was this very capability, the wicked intelligence that gleamed in his icy eyes, that made Wortigern fear him. He did not trust the apparent submissiveness of the mysterious warrior who had come from beyond the sea, although it seemed that his main desire was none other than to find that boy, in order to take his head back to Ravenna.

One day, to teach Wulfila what it would mean to betray him, or even just to think about betraying him, Wortigern had him witness the execution of a vassal whose only blame was having kept part of the booty he had taken during a raid.

There was a courtyard, alongside the tower, surrounded by a high stone wall, in which the tyrant kept his mastiffs. These tremendous beasts were often used in battle, and Wortigern's only pastime was to feed them twice a day by tossing pieces of meat from the window that opened behind his throne. The condemned man was stripped of his clothing and allowed to drop slowly, tied to a rope, over the dogs who had not been fed for two days. They started to devour him alive, feet first, as he was lowered from above. The screams of pain of the poor wretch mixed with the deafening howls of the hounds, crazed by the odour of blood and the fiercely contended meal, and echoed and dilated within the tower until they reached a pitch that would have been unbearable for anyone with a bit of humanity, but Wulfila never even blinked, enjoying that terrible spectacle until the very end. When he turned to look at Wortigern his eyes held only a disturbing arousal and an unperturbed ferocity.

35

SPRING WAS BEGINNING, and the only place the snow hadn't melted was the peak of *Mons Badonicus*, called Mount Badon in the local dialect. Many of the peasants returning from their work in the fields and the shepherds bringing their flocks in from the pasture had noticed the purple dragon fluttering in the distance. They'd seen the head of polished silver glittering on the highest tower of the fortress, a signal which awakened forgotten dreams of courage and glory.

Ambrosinus, wandering among the people at the market and among the farms in the countryside, heard and understood the restless emotions that that vision had aroused in them. Many of them were stirred by that symbol which had suddenly emerged from a remote, long unremembered past, although they dared not speak their thoughts. Once, watching a shepherd who had stopped to contemplate the legion's standard from a distance, he pretended to be a stranger to the land, and asked him: 'What is that banner? Why does it wave over that abandoned fort?'

The man looked at him with a strange expression. 'You must come from very far away,' he said, 'if you don't recognize that banner. For years it symbolized the supreme defence of the honour and liberty of this land, leading a legendary army to battle: the twelfth Legion, the Legion of the Dragon.'

'I've heard speak of that,' replied Ambrosinus, 'but I always thought it was a fanciful story, merely invented to dissuade the barbarians of the north from conducting their incursions.'

'You're wrong,' replied the shepherd. 'That division really did exist, and the man you're talking to was a part of it. When I was young.'

'Well then, what happened to the legion? Was it wiped out? Or forced to surrender?'

'No, neither of these,' said the shepherd. 'We were betrayed. We had penetrated beyond the Great Wall to pursue a band of Scots who had kidnapped the women in one of our villages, and we had left a tribal chief, one of our allies, to protect the passage through the Wall where we would enter upon our return, but as we raced back, followed by a horde of raging enemies, the passage was barricaded and our allies were pointing their weapons at us. We were completely trapped! Many of us fell in battle, but many others were spared, because a dense fog suddenly rose up and hid us. We managed to reach safety through a secluded valley which was concealed between high rock walls. We decided to disband then, and to return separately to our homes. The traitor's name was Wortigern, the tyrant who still oppresses us and bleeds us dry with his taxes and his thieving, dominating us through terror. Since then, we have lived in obscurity and shame, dedicating ourselves to our work and trying to forget what we were. But now, that standard which has reappeared miraculously out of nowhere has reminded us that one who has fought at length for his liberty cannot die a slave.'

'Tell me,' pressed on Ambrosinus, 'who was it that dissolved the legion? Who advised you to return to your families?'

'Our commander had died in battle. It was his second-in-command, Kustennin, who offered us that opportunity. He was a wise and valiant man, and he wanted the best for us. His wife had just given birth to a child, a little girl as lovely as a rosebud, and perhaps life seemed the most precious thing to him then. We all thought of our wives, of our homes, of our children. We didn't realize that had we stayed together, united under that banner, we could have truly defended what was dear to us . . .'

Ambrosinus would have liked to continue speaking with him, but the man could no longer go on, because a knot closed his throat. He gazed long and hard at the standard waving in the sun and then walked away in silence.

Struck by those revelations, the old man returned to visit Kustennin several times, to try to win him over to his cause, but it was all in vain. To challenge Wortigern's power under those conditions was equivalent to committing suicide. The semblance of freedom that his people still enjoyed must have seemed sufficient to him, compared with the enormous risks of a rebellion. The mere thought was so worrisome that Kustennin had never even gone to the old fortress to greet the rest of the new arrivals.

Carvetia was the only city remaining under Wortigern's dominion which still enjoyed a modicum of freedom, only because the tyrant needed the resources of their markets and ports on the Ocean. Some goods were still traded, and the news which arrived with the vessels from distant lands was no less indispensable for maintaining and extending his power than were the swords of his mercenaries.

*

Inside the fortress, in the meantime, the men had repaired the defences, rebuilt the turrets and the embattlements and embedded the rampart and the trench with pointed, flame-hardened stakes. Batiatus set the old forge to work again, and his hammer sounded incessantly on the anvil. Vatrenus, Demetrius and Orosius had restored the living quarters, the stables, the oven and the mill and Livia had delighted them all with freshly-baked loaves of fragrant bread and cups of steaming milk. Only Aurelius, despite his initial burst of enthusiasm, seemed to grow more sullen with each passing day. He spent long hours every night on the bastions, arms at the ready, scanning the darkness as if waiting for an enemy who never arrived – an enemy who none the less made him feel bewildered and powerless; a ghost, who resembled Aurelius himself: the ghost of a coward or worse, of a traitor. He was always up on the bastions readying his defences, preparing his strategy. When would the siege begin? When would the hordes on horseback appear at the horizon? When would the hour of truth strike out of that blue sky? Who would open the doors to the enemy this time? Who would let the wolf into the fold?

Ambrosinus sensed Aurelius's thoughts, felt a pain so intense that not even Livia's love could assuage it. He realized that the time had come to confront events head on, to force the hand of a destiny which had mocked and escaped them – and just as he was reflecting on the best course of action, Kustennin appeared on his white stallion. He brought sad news: Wortigern had ordered the dissolution of the senate by the end of the month. The people would have to forego the ancient magistratures, and within the city walls would have to accept a garrison of fierce mercenaries from the continent.

'Perhaps you were right, Myrdin,' reflected Kustennin. 'The only true liberty is what we win with our sweat and our blood, but now it's too late.'

'That's not true,' replied Ambrosinus, 'and you'll know why if you drop in on tomorrow's session of the senate.'

Kustennin shook his head as if he had never heard so much nonsense, then leapt into his saddle and rode off at a gallop through the deserted valley.

*

The next morning, when it was still dark, Ambrosinus took Romulus by the hand and they started off towards the city.

'Where are you going?' asked Aurelius.

'To Carvetia,' he replied. 'To the senate, or to the market square where I'll call the people to assembly, if necessary.'

'I'm coming with you.'

'No, your place is here, at the head of your men. Have faith,' he said, and took his pilgrim's staff, making his way with the boy along the path that meandered through the meadows, along the banks of the Virginis lake, leading to the city.

Carvetia still seemed a Roman city: its walls of rectangular stone guarded by sentries, its streets and its buildings, the customs of its people and its language. Ambrosinus found himself in front of the senate, where the people's representatives were entering for a council session. Other citizens entered as well, crowding into the atrium before the doors were closed.

One of the orators stood to take the floor: an austere, striking figure wearing simple clothing and with a look of honesty. He must have enjoyed great respect and consideration, because a hush fell over the hall when he began to speak.

'Senate and people of Carvetia!' he commenced. 'Our condition has become intolerable. The tyrant has hired new foreign mercenaries of unprecedented savagery, with the pretext of protecting the population of the cities still governed by autonomous institutions. He is about to dissolve the last symbol of the free assembly of citizens in Britannia: our senate!' A buzz of consternation spread among the senate seats and the people thronging in the atrium.

'What shall we do?' continued the orator. 'Bend our heads as we have done until now? Accept more bullying and more shame, allow them to trample our rights and our dignity, to profane our homes, to tear our own wives and daughters from our arms?'

'Unhappily, we have no choice,' spoke up one of the senators. 'Resisting Wortigern would mean the death of us all.'

'That's true!' another chimed in. 'We can't hope to face his ire. We'd be swept away. If we submit, we can at least try to preserve some of our advantages.'

Ambrosinus strode forward then, holding Romulus by the hand. 'I would like to ask for the floor, noble senators!' he shouted.

'Who are you?' asked the president. 'Who are you to disturb our assembly?'

Ambrosinus bared his head and advanced to the centre of the hall, keeping Romulus close, sensing the boy's reluctance to show himself.

'I am Myrdin Emreis,' he began, 'Druid of the sacred wood of Gleva and Roman citizen with the name of Meridius Ambrosinus, for as long as Roman law reigned over this land. Many years ago you sent me to Italy with the mission of imploring the emperor for help, and returning with an army that would re-establish order and prosperity to this suffering land, just as in the glorious time of Saint Germanus, the hero sent by Aetius, the last and most valiant of the soldiers of Rome.'

Their stupor at his unexpected appearance had plunged the room into an oppressive silence and Ambrosinus continued: 'I failed in this mission. I lost my companions during our journey as they fell to cold, to hunger, to disease and to attacks. It was a miracle that I survived. I sat for days and days, suppliant, in the court of the imperial palace of Ravenna. All in vain. I was never even admitted into the presence of the emperor, a spineless man totally under the power of his barbarian militias. Now I have returned. I'm late, this is true, but I'm not alone. My hands are not empty!

'All of you, I believe, are familiar with the oracle that announces the coming of a young, pure-hearted man who will bring the sword of justice to this land and restore her lost liberty. I have brought you this young man, noble senators!' he shouted out, and had the boy advance until he stood alone before them.

'This is Romulus Augustus Caesar, the last emperor of the Romans!'

His words met with a deep, astonished silence, then a confused murmur which grew to a widespread muttering. Some seemed awestruck by Ambrosinus's claims, others began to laugh and to make fun of the unexpected orator.

'Where is this miraculous sword?' asked a senator, raising his voice over the fracas.

'And where are the legions of the new Caesar?' asked another. 'Do you have any idea of how many warriors Wortigern has? Any idea at all?'

Ambrosinus hesitated, wounded by their words. He began again: 'The twelfth Draco legion is being reinstated. The emperor will be presented to the soldiers, who I'm sure will find the will and the strength to fight and to oppose this tyranny.'

Thunderous laughter echoed through the hall, and a third

senator took the floor to speak. 'You've been gone a long time, Myrdin,' he said, using his Celtic name. 'That legion was dissolved long ago. No one would ever even dream of taking up arms again.'

More laughter followed and Romulus felt overwhelmed by that wave of derision and scorn flooding over him, but he stood his ground. He covered his face with his hands and stood immobile in the centre of the hall. The uproar died down at the sight of him, becoming a buzz of embarrassment and sudden shame. Ambrosinus laid a hand on the boy's shoulder and began to speak again, enflamed by his indignation. 'Laugh, noble senators! Mock this poor boy. He has no way to defend himself nor to retort to your foolish insolence. He has seen his own parents cruelly butchered, he has been hunted relentlessly, like an animal, by all of the powers of this earth. Once accustomed to imperial pomp, he has had to deal with the harshest privation. He is a hero. He has concealed in his heart the pain, the desperation and the fear that are more than understandable in a boy his age, with the strength and the dignity of an ancient hero of the Republic.

'Where is your pride, senators of Carvetia? Where is your dignity? You deserve the tyranny of Wortigern. You have got your just deserts, because you harbour the souls of servants! This boy has lost everything but his honour and his life. His is the suffering majesty of a true sovereign. I have brought him to you as the last seed of a dying tree, so as to bear forth a new world, but the ground I've found here is putrid and sterile. It is only right that you refuse him, because you do not deserve him. No! You deserve the scorn of any man of honour or faith!'

Ambrosinus had finished his heartfelt speech to dead silence. A leaden weight lay upon that dismayed and confused assembly. Ambrosinus spat on the ground as a sign of his extreme disdain, then took Romulus by the arm and walked out scornfully, as a few faint voices tried to call him back. As soon as they had left, making their way through the crowd, the discussion started up again and soon rose to quite a pitch, but one of the senators hastened to a side door and slipped into a waiting carriage, ordering the driver to depart immediately. 'To Castra Vetera,' he said. 'To Wortigern's castle, hurry!'

Ambrosinus, furious over the insult, had walked out into the square. He was trying all the same to encourage Romulus to hold fast against the insults of destiny, when suddenly he was taken by the arm.

'Myrdin!'

'Kustennin!' exclaimed Ambrosinus. 'My God, what shame! Did you see what happened? Were you in the senate?'

The man lowered his head: 'I was. Do you understand now why I said it was too late? Wortigern has corrupted most of the senators. He can easily dissolve the institution today without encountering any resistance.'

Ambrosinus shook his head solemnly. 'I must speak with you,' he said. 'I must speak with you at length, but I cannot remain here now. I have to take my boy home . . . Romulus, come on, let's leave . . .' He looked around, but Romulus was nowhere to be seen. 'Oh God, where are you? Where is the boy?' he exclaimed in anguish.

Egeria had just arrived, and she approached him. 'Don't worry,' said the woman with a smile. 'There he is, down there on the beach. My daughter Ygraine is with him.'

Ambrosinus breathed a sigh of relief.

'Let them talk together for a little while. Young people need each other,' added Egeria. 'Tell me, is it true what I've just heard from the people leaving the senate? I couldn't believe my ears. Where has common dignity gone? Or at least the decency to hide one's cowardice?'

Ambrosinus answered with a nod of his head, but his eyes never moved from the boy sitting down there at the edge of the sea.

*

Romulus watched silently as the waves washed over the pebbles on the shore and he could not control the sobs which racked his chest.

'What's your name? Why are you crying?' asked the voice of a girl behind him. It was a pretty, carefree voice that irritated him, but then the touch of a hand on his cheek, as delicate as a butterfly's wing, passed on a little soothing warmth.

He replied without turning, because he didn't want her face to be different from the one that he had suddenly imagined: 'I'm crying because I've lost everything: my parents, my home, my land; because I may lose the last friends I have, and perhaps even my name and my freedom. I'm crying because there's no peace for me anywhere on this earth.'

Those words were much bigger than she was, and the girl wisely responded with silence, but her hand continued to caress Romulus's hair and his cheek, until she understood that he had calmed. Then she said: 'My name is Ygraine, and I'm twelve. May I stay here with you a bit?'

Romulus nodded, drying his tears with the end of his sleeve, and she crouched down on the sand, sitting on her heels in front of him. He lifted his face to see if her face was as sweet as her voice and the touch of her fingers. He found two moist blue eyes and a face of delicate beauty, framed by a cascade of fiery-red hair that the sea breeze tousled, covering and baring her forehead and her splendid eyes. His heart skipped a beat, and a rush of heat rose from his chest. He'd never felt anything like it before. Her gaze held all the warmth and beauty and comfort that life might perhaps still have in store for him. He wanted to say something, to let his heart speak, but just then he heard Ambrosinus's footsteps approaching, along with the others'.

'Where will you sleep tonight?' asked Kustennin.

'At the fort,' replied Ambrosinus.

Kustennin seemed worried: 'Take care Myrdin! Your words won't have gone unnoticed.'

'That's what I was hoping,' retorted Ambrosinus, but he'd understood the import of Kustennin's words and felt afraid.

'Come now, Ygraine,' said Egeria. 'We have many chores to finish before evening.' The girl stood up unhappily and followed her mother, turning back to look at the young foreigner, so different from the other boys she knew. His face was so very pale, his features and his voice quite noble. The intensity of his words was reflected in the deep melancholy of his eyes. Kustennin took his leave as well and walked away with his family.

Egeria let Ygraine skip off ahead and spoke to her husband: 'They're the ones who have raised the emblem of the dragon on the old fort, aren't they?'

'Yes,' replied Kustennin. 'Absolute folly – and today Myrdin claimed that the legion has been reinstated whereas in truth there are only six or seven of them in all. What's more, he has revealed the boy's identity to the senators. Can you believe it?'

'I can't imagine what the reaction to such a revelation might be,' responded Egeria, 'but that standard flying up there has certainly created an uproar, roused expectations. They say that some have dug up the arms that have lain buried for years. Lots of young men, I've heard, want to join up with the foreigners. There have been rumours of strange lights flashing at night up on the bastions, sounds like thunder echoing in the mountains. I'm worried. I fear that this semblance of peace, this laboured survival of ours, will be shaken by new upheavals, turbulence, blood.'

'They're only a group of fugitives, Egeria, an old visionary dreamer and a boy,' replied Kustennin. He took a last look at his friend who had reappeared as if by magic after all these years.

The old man and the boy were on their feet, side by side. Without saying a word, they were watching the waves breaking against the cliff in a seething white foam.

*

The next day, towards evening, the senator's carriage pulled up at the gates of Castra Vetera. He was allowed into Wortigern's residence, but first had to pass muster with Wulfila, who enjoyed his lord's complete trust. As they spoke, a satisfied sneer distorted the barbarian's features.

'Follow me,' he said. 'You must report directly to our sovereign. He will be most grateful.' Then he accompanied him to the castle's inner reaches, into Wortigern's presence. The old man who received him sat sunken into his throne: his golden mask was the only note of light in that twilight atmosphere.

'Speak,' Wulfila ordered and the senator spoke.

'Noble Wortigern,' he said, 'yesterday, at the senate of Carvetia, a man dared to speak out against you in public; he called you a tyrant and incited the people to rebel. He said that an old, long-dissolved legion is being reinstated, and he presented a boy, claiming that he was the emperor . . .'

'It's them,' Wulfila interrupted him. 'There can be no doubt. The old man raves about a prophecy that speaks of a young sovereign who will come from beyond the sea. He represents a true danger to you, believe me. He's not as mad as he appears. On the contrary, he's quite astute, and plays on the superstitions and the nostalgia of the old Roman-Celtic aristocracy. His goal is evident: he means to turn that little impostor into a symbol, and use him against you.'

Wortigern raised his thin hand to dismiss his informer and the senator bent over in an endless bow until he reached the door, through which he made a hurried escape.

'What do you suggest then?' the tyrant asked Wulfila.

'Give me free rein. Allow me to depart with my men, with the men I can count on. I know these bastards, trust me: I'll find them and I'll rout them out, wherever they're hiding. I'll bring you the old man's skin to stuff and I'll keep the boy's head.'

Wortigern tried to draw himself up. 'It's not the old man's skin I'm interested in. We had a different deal.'

Wulfila started. In that very moment, destiny was offering him a priceless opportunity: his entire plan was falling into place. He just had to provide the final touch, and a future of limitless power would open itself to him. He replied, trying to keep his excitement under control: 'You're right, Wortigern! In my enthusiasm for finally winding up this long hunt of mine, I had forgotten my promise for an instant. Our agreement! You let me keep the boy's head and give me the chance to wipe out these murdering deserters who are protecting him, and I will repay you with the gift I promised.'

'I see that you can always read my thoughts, Wulfila. So, have this gift that you've had me wait for so anxiously brought here. But first there's one thing you must tell me.'

'Speak.'

'Among those men you want to wipe out, is there perchance the one who cut your face?'

Wulfila lowered his eyes to hide the fierce light that flashed there and replied, despite himself: 'That's right. It's as you say.'

The tyrant had had his satisfaction. He had once more established the superiority of his perfect mask of gold over the deformed mask of flesh of his present servant and potential antagonist, because Wulfila's scar was the work of a man, while the gangrene that devoured the tyrant's face could be nothing but the work of God.

'I'm waiting,' said Wortigern, and his words sounded hollow inside the mask, like the voice of judgement.

Wulfila went to call one of his warriors and ordered him to bring the object to him immediately. The man soon reappeared carrying a long, narrow case of oak, adorned with burnished iron studs, and deposited it at Wortigern's feet.

Wulfila gestured for him to leave and drew closer to the throne himself, kneeling to open the precious case with the promised gift. He lifted his gaze to the inscrutable mask which loomed above him, and at that moment he would have given anything to glimpse the old man's expression of obscene lust.

'Here is my gift, my lord,' he said, opening the lid with a swift gesture. 'This is the Calibian sword of Julius Caesar, the first lord of the world, the conqueror of Britannia. It is yours!'

Wortigern couldn't resist the fascination of that superb weapon. He reached out his hand and hissed: 'Give it to me! Give it to me!'

'Immediately, my lord,' replied Wulfila, and in his gaze the tyrant read – too late – the lethal intentions burning within. He tried to cry out, but the sword was already sinking into his chest, stabbing through his heart, plunging all the way back into the throne. He collapsed without a whimper, and a trickle of blood dripped from his mask, the only sign of life on that immutable face appearing, in the extreme irony of fate, at the moment of his death.

Wulfila extracted the sword from the lifeless body and seized the golden mask from Wortigern's face, revealing a bloody, unrecognizable mess. He cut into the skin of the scalp all around the head and tore off the white locks with a single yank. He dragged the body, little more than a larva, over to the window behind the throne and tossed him into the courtyard below. The howling of the famished mastiffs confined in their pen invaded the room like screams out of hell. Their muffled growling continued to echo through the tower as they contended the sorry flesh of their master.

Wulfila put the golden mask on his face and pulled Wortigern's white mane of hair over his head. He grasped the blazing sword and thus he appeared to his warriors, like a demon, his temples scored with blood. They were already on horseback in the great courtyard and they gazed upon him, dumbstruck as he jumped into his stallion's saddle and spurred him on, shouting: 'To Carvetia!'

36

TWO DAYS LATER a man on horseback entered Kustennin's courtyard at a full gallop, bringing incredible news with him. He was one of the few informers Kustennin still had inside Castra Vetera, his only resource in hedging the disastrous raids of the tyrant's mercenaries.

'They've always said that Wortigern made a pact with the devil!' panted the man, his eyes wide with terror. 'It's true! Satan in person has given him back the strength and vigour of his youth, but he has increased his ferocity beyond all imagining!'

'What are you saying? Have you lost your mind?' exclaimed Kustennin, grabbing him by the shoulders and shaking him, as if that could restore his reason.

'No, my lord, it is nothing but the truth! If you had nourished hope that he was on his last legs, you were deceived! It's as if he were . . . resurrected! He's possessed by Satan, I tell you! I saw him with these very eyes. He looked like a vision out of hell, with his golden mask on his face, dripping blood instead of sweat from his temples. His voice sounded like thunder, a voice no one has ever heard before, and the sword he gripped was so marvellous that I've never seen anything like it in all my life. Its blade was as sharp as a razor, it reflected the light of our torches like transparent glass, the hilt was an eagle's head in solid gold. Only the archangel Michael could have forged such a marvel. Or the devil himself!'

'Try to calm down,' insisted Kustennin. 'You're raging.'

'No, believe me, it's exactly as I say. He's at the head of two hundred fully-armed horsemen who are sowing terror as they advance: sacking, burning, destroying with a fury no one has ever seen. I've ridden here without ever stopping. I took a short cut through the forest of Gowan, and rode on day and night, changing the horses at our properties. I heard him myself as he shouted out "To Carvetia!" It won't take him any longer than two days to get here.'

'Carvetia . . . but that's impossible! Why should he be headed here? He's never touched this city; he needs us, and besides that, nearly all the men of influence have already submitted. It makes no sense, no sense at all . . .' He meditated in silence for a few moments, then said: 'Listen, I know you must be very tired, but I have a last favour to ask you. Go down to the old Roman wharf and speak with Oribasius, the fisherman. He's one of my men. Tell him to get ready to set sail tomorrow at dawn with abundant water and supplies on board, everything he can manage to take with him. Hurry!'

The man remounted his horse and galloped off while Kustennin went upstairs to alert his wife. 'I've got bad news, I'm afraid: Wortigern and his men are headed this way, and I fear that our friend Myrdin is in serious trouble as well. I must warn him. Perhaps it was his speech to the senate that set off this whole expedition, but I can't let that old madman ruin himself and that poor boy, with all their companions – although they must be as crazy as he is, if they followed him all the way here from Italy.'

'It will be dark soon!' complained Egeria. 'Won't it be dangerous?'

'I must go, otherwise I'd never be able to sleep tonight.'

'Father, may I come with you? Please father!' begged Ygraine.

'Don't even consider it!' admonished Egeria. 'You'll have other chances to see your young Roman friend.' Ygraine blushed and walked away in a huff.

Egeria sighed and accompanied her husband to the door. She pensively remained at the threshold, listening to the sound of his footsteps going down the stairs and across the courtyard.

Kustennin chose his white stallion from the stables, the fastest he had. He leapt into the saddle as the servants opened the gate and raced across the countryside reddened by the last flame of dusk.

He could see the fort from the top of the hill that dominated the valley and the lake. His gaze was instantly attracted to the banner which hung from the highest tower: the dragon of the ancient Sarmatian auxiliary troops who had once garrisoned the Great Wall, later becoming the standard of his legion. Wisps of smoke attested to life between those old walls, and the gate opened as he arrived. He walked his horse in and was greeted by a warm embrace from Ambrosinus, who introduced him to the others.

'Romulus, you have seen my old friend once before. The rest of you, this is Kustennin, called Constantine by the Romans, our *dux bellorum* and *magister militum*, the dearest and most valiant of my friends in Britannia. I hope he has come to stay a while with us.'

A roe was roasting over a big wood fire and the men were cutting off bits of meat with their swords as it cooked. The bow and quiver of arrows Livia had shot him with were still slung at her side. They were all cheerful and it broke Kustennin's heart to think of the news he was bearing for them.

'Sit down,' Ambrosinus invited. 'Eat! We've got plenty.'

'There's no time,' replied Kustennin. 'You must leave this place. I have sure information that Wortigern is headed for Carvetia at the head of two hundred warriors in full battle gear. They may be here by tomorrow night.'

'Wortigern?' repeated Ambrosinus, stunned. 'But he's too old: he couldn't sit up in a saddle even if they tied him on.'

'I know. It's hard for me to believe the story that I've heard from one of my informers. He was ranting, saying that the tyrant has made a pact with the devil. Satan has possessed him, restoring the youth and vigour of his best years, and has apparently forged a special sword for him as well, a wondrous thing the like of which no one has ever seen.'

Aurelius drew closer: 'How could your man tell that it was Wortigern?'

'He wore the mask of gold that has covered his face for over ten years, and his long white hair fell over his shoulders – but his voice was his as a young man.'

'You spoke of a sword . . .' insisted Aurelius.

'That's right. He saw it close up. A blade as bright as crystal, and a golden hilt shaped like an eagle's head . . .'

Aurelius paled. 'Powerful gods!' he exclaimed. 'Then it's not Wortigern, it's Wulfila! And he'll be looking for us.'

They all exchanged looks in consternation.

'Whoever it is,' replied Kustennin, 'you have to get out of here. They'll be here in two days, at the very most. Listen to me, tomorrow morning at dawn, I'm sending my family to safety on a boat directed to Ireland. There's room for another two or three people: Myrdin and the boy, and the girl, I suppose . . . It's all I can do for you.'

Aurelius heaved a deep sigh and stared at Ambrosinus with shiny eyes. 'Perhaps your friend is right,' he said. 'It's the only wise thing to do. We can't keep running for all eternity. We're already at the far end of the world. We have no choice. We have to split up. Staying together will accomplish nothing but attracting all our enemies and adversaries straight to us. You must leave, you and the boy, Ambrosinus, and you go with them, Livia, please. Save yourselves. No sword can protect him any longer.'

Romulus looked at him as though he couldn't believe what he had heard, his eyes welling up with tears, but Ambrosinus rebelled. 'No!' he exclaimed. 'It can't finish this way. The prophecy tells the truth, I'm absolutely certain of it. We must remain, at all costs!'

Livia exchanged a long look with Aurelius, then turned to Ambrosinus. 'You must surrender to the facts,' she said, 'to the unhappy reality of things. If we stay here, we will all die and he'll die with us.'

She turned to the others: 'You, Vatrenus, what do you think?'

'I think you're right. There's no point in persisting; let's have the boy and his tutor taken to safety. We'll find another road for ourselves . . .'

'Orosius? Demetrius?'

Both nodded.

'Batiatus?'

The giant looked around with a bewildered expression, as if he couldn't believe that their terrible and marvellous adventure had come to an end, that this big family – the only one he'd ever had – was about to break up. He lowered his head to hide his tears and the others took his gesture as a sign of assent.

'Well then . . . I'd say it's been decided,' concluded Livia. 'Now let's try to get some rest. Each one of us will have to face a difficult road tomorrow, no matter what direction we take.'

Kustennin stood up to go. 'Remember,' he said. 'At the old Roman wharf, at dawn. May the night bring you counsel.' He took his horse by the reins.

'Wait,' said Aurelius. He went up to the battlement and took down the standard. He folded it carefully and handed it to Kustennin. 'You keep it, so that it won't be destroyed.'

Kustennin accepted it, then mounted his stallion and rode off. Ambrosinus watched that sad ceremony numbly, then put his hand on Romulus's shoulder and drew him close, as if to protect him from the chill that was gnawing at his heart.

Aurelius walked away, overcome by emotion, and Livia followed him. She found him in the dark under the sentry walk stair, and brushed his lips with a kiss. 'It's useless to fight the impossible: it's destiny that decides for us, and won't allow us to go beyond certain limits. Let's go back to Italy; we'll find a ship that's setting sail for the Mediterranean. We can return to Venetia . . .' Aurelius looked over at Romulus and he bit his lip. The boy was sitting next to Ambrosinus as the old man hugged him close, covering him with a cloak.

'Perhaps we'll see them again . . . Who knows?' said Livia, speaking her thoughts out loud. '*Sed primum vivere*; life comes first, don't you agree?' She held him tight.

Aurelius backed away. 'You've never given up on that old idea of yours, have you? Can't you understand that I love that boy like the son that I never had? Can't you understand that going back to your lagoon is like diving into a sea of flames for me? Leave me alone, I beg of you . . . Just leave me alone.'

Livia walked away, weeping, and took shelter in the barracks.

Aurelius returned up on the walkway and leaned against one of the guard towers. The night was calm and clear, a warm springtime night, but cold despair had invaded his heart. He wished he'd never existed, never been born. He remained up on the battlements, withdrawn into his own thoughts, for a long time, as the moon rose over the slopes of Mount Badon, silvering the valley. A touch from out of nowhere startled him, and Ambrosinus was suddenly standing in front of him. No noise had come from that squeaky wooden stair, nor from the disjointed planks on the walkway. He spun around as if he'd seen an apparition, or a ghost. 'Ambrosinus . . . what do you want?'

'Come now, it's time to go.'

'Where?'

'To seek out the truth.'

Aurelius shook his head. 'No, leave me alone. We have a long journey tomorrow.'

Ambrosinus clutched at his cloak. 'You'll come with me, now!'

Aurelius straightened up resignedly. 'Whatever. As long as you leave me in peace.'

Ambrosinus made his way down the stairs and went outside, heading at a quick pace towards the great circular stone surrounded by those four monoliths that stood out against the moonlight like silent giants. He reached the stone and gestured to Aurelius to sit upon it; he obeyed as if subjugated by an invincible force. Ambrosinus poured some liquid into a cup and handed it to him. 'Drink,' he said.

'What is this?' asked Aurelius in surprise.

'A passage to hell . . . if you're up to it.'

Aurelius looked into his eyes, into his dilated pupils, and felt sucked into a dark vortex. He held out his hand with a mechanical gesture, took the cup and drank it down all in one go.

Ambrosinus placed his hands on Aurelius's head. His fingers felt like sharp talons, penetrating into his skin and into his skull itself. He cried out at the piercing, intolerable pain, but it was like screaming in a dream: he opened his mouth but no sound came out, the pain remained inside like a lion in a cage clawing at him cruelly. Then the fingers dug deep into his brain, as the Druid's voice rang out shrilly: 'Let me in!' it screeched, thundered, hissed. 'Let me in!'

And his voice found a way, exploding all at once in Aurelius's mind like a scream of agony, then the legionary collapsed gasping on to the stone and lay there unmoving.

*

He reawakened in an unknown place, enveloped in the deepest darkness, and he looked around in dismay, trying to find anything that might call him back to reality. He saw the dark shadow of a city under siege . . . campfires all around the walls. Flaming meteors streaked across the sky with shrill whistles, but the sounds and the distant, muffled voices had the fluctuating, distorted vibration of a nightmare.

'Where am I?' he asked.

The voice of the Druid resounded behind him: 'In your past . . . at Aquileia!'

'That's not possible . . .' he responded. 'It's not possible.'

Now he could see in the distance the dark shape of an aqueduct in ruins; a light appeared and disappeared between the pillars and arches. The voice of Myrdin Ambrosinus rang out again: 'Look. There's someone up there.'

On hearing those words, his vision keened like that of a nocturnal bird of prey: yes, there was a figure, moving on the aqueduct. A man holding a lantern, walking on the second row of arches: he suddenly turned, and the lantern illuminated his face.

'It's you!' said the voice behind him.

Aurelius felt taken up in a sudden whirl, like a leaf on the wind. It was him, now, on that crumbling aqueduct, it was him holding the lantern as a voice came from the shadows, a voice he knew well, startling him. 'Did you bring the gold?' A face emerged from the darkness: Wulfila!

'All that I have,' he answered, and handed over a purse.

The barbarian weighed it in his hand. 'It's not what we agreed upon but . . . I'll take it anyway.'

'My parents! Where are they? Our agreement was that . . .'

Wulfila stared impassively at him, his stone face betraying no emotion. 'You'll find them at the entrance to the western necropolis. They're very weak. They never would have made it all the way up here.' He turned his back and disappeared into the night.

'Wait!' Aurelius shouted, but received no answer. He was alone, tormented by doubt. The lantern light trembled.

The voice of his guide sounded again in the dark: 'You had no choice . . .'

Now he was elsewhere, at the base of the walls, in front of a postern gate that opened on to the countryside. He opened it with great effort, overcoming the rust and the tangle of branches and vines that had concealed this gate and kept it a secret for who knows how long. He found himself outside, with his lantern in hand. Before him was the necropolis with its ancient, time-worn tombs, overgrown with brambles and weeds. He checked behind him, warily, then at his sides and finally in front of him: the ground was bare and open, apparently deserted. He called softly: 'Father . . . Mother!'

Moans of pain answered him in the darkness: the voices of his parents! He ran forward, his heart in his throat, and the lantern that swung from his hand suddenly lit up a terrifying vision: his parents were hanging from stakes, in the throes of death. The signs of cruel torture were evident on their bodies. His father raised his head, his face oozing blood. 'Turn back, son!' he began to cry out with his last breath, but before he could finish Wulfila sprang up from behind a tomb and ran him through. Aurelius gasped as other barbarians swarmed out of nowhere and surrounded him. He felt a blade tear through the flesh at the base of his neck, and then a blow to his head knocked him senseless. The last thing he saw was Wulfila's sword plunging into his mother's body, but he continued to hear sounds: the voice of the barbarian, goading his men on – 'The side gate is open! The city is ours!' – and the tread of countless warriors as they tramped through that opening. Then came excruciating screams from the city, wails of fear and of death, the clashing of weapons, and the roar of the flames devouring Aquileia.

He shouted out, with all the strength he had left, he shouted in horror, in hate, in desperation. Then he heard again the voice that had guided him through that hell and he found himself lying on that great circular stone, dripping with sweat, his head about to explode. Ambrosinus stood before him and urged him on: 'Continue . . . continue, before the opening to your past closes up again. Remember, Aurelianus Ambrosius Ventidius, remember!'

*

Aurelius drew a long breath and sat up, bringing his hands to his hammering temples. Each word cost him immense effort: 'I don't know how long it took me to come to. They must have given me up for dead . . .'

Aurelius's breathing had become calmer now. He brought his hand to the scar he had on his chest. 'The blade that was meant to slit my carotid just cut through my skin beneath the collar bone, but the pain in my head was sheer agony . . . I couldn't remember anything. I wandered aimlessly until I saw a column of refugees seeking escape on the boats in the lagoon. Instinctively I went to help. People were rushing in from every direction, besieging and even capsizing the boats. I did what I could: there were old people, women, children, sinking into the mud in a chaos of weeping and shouting, all crying out for those they had lost . . .

'Not yet satiated by the destruction of Aquileia, the barbarians were pouring out of the gates, waving lit torches and galloping wildly towards the beach, to massacre the last survivors. The last of those boats, incredibly crowded, was leaving the shore, and the boatman was holding the last place for me. He reached out his hand and yelled: 'Hurry! Get in!' But just then we heard a woman's voice: 'Wait!' she cried. 'Wait for the love of God!' She was running towards us in water nearly up to her waist, dragging along a little girl who was weeping in terror. I helped them to get on, taking the child into my arms so the woman could grasp the boatman's hand. As soon as she had found a place, I reached out with the little girl. She was terrified by all that dark water, and she held out one hand to her mother, but the other wouldn't let go of my neck. She . . . she tore off the medal I was wearing . . . the medal with the eagle . . . the symbol of my division and of my city, all lost. That little girl was Livia!'

Ambrosinus helped him to his feet and sustained his first steps as if he were an invalid. The two men walked slowly back to camp.

'I was captured,' continued Aurelius, 'and sold as a slave, until one day I was liberated during an attack of the Nova Invicta Legion. From that day forward, the legion became my home, my family, my life.'

Ambrosinus clasped Aurelius's shoulder with emotion. 'You opened the gate only because you wanted to save your parents from a horrendous death,' he said. 'You are none other than the hero of Aquileia, he who defended the city for so many months. Wulfila was the executioner of your city and your parents.'

'He'll pay,' swore Aurelius. 'To the last drop of blood.'

They had reached the gate to the camp and Ambrosinus knocked with his staff. Livia threw it open; Romulus was with her, having stayed by her side all night.

'Did you find what you were seeking?' the girl asked Aurelius.

'Yes,' he said simply. 'You told me the truth.'

'Love never lies. Didn't you know?' She embraced him and kissed his mouth, his forehead, his eyes still full of the horror they had seen.

Ambrosinus turned to Romulus. 'Come, my boy,' he said. 'Come now, try to get some rest.'

The camp was immersed in silence. Each of them was on his

own, wide awake on that tranquil springtime night, waiting for the sun to reveal their new destiny. Or their last.

'Don't leave me alone, tonight,' said Livia. 'I beg of you.'

Aurelius held her close, then led her by the hand into his quarters.

Now they stood alone, as the moon beams pierced the broken-down roof, illuminating Livia's lovely face, caressing her with their pale light, diffusing a magical aura around her head, a flowing splendour of silver. Aurelius untied the fastenings of her clothes and contemplated her there, nude before him, ecstatically caressing – with his eyes and then his hands – her majestic beauty. She undressed him, slowly, with the devotion and the trembling expectation of a bride. She brushed her fingers lightly over his body of bronze, just barely skimming the hills and valleys of his torment, his flesh furrowed by so many scars, his muscles tensed by endless bloody ordeals. Then she lay back on that poor straw pallet, on that rough soldier's blanket, and took him into her, arching her back like an untamed filly, digging her nails into his shoulders, seeking out his mouth. They loved each other hard and long, trembling with inexhaustible desire, mixing the burning flow of their breath, the torrid intimacy of their flesh. Then they fell back, and Aurelius lay close to her, wrapped in the perfume of her hair.

'I fell in love with you that night,' murmured Livia. 'When I saw you, alone and unarmed on the bank of the lagoon, awaiting your destiny. I was only nine years old . . .'

37

Aurelius awoke when it was still dark. He dressed and walked out into the vast deserted courtyard. His companions emerged from the darkness, one at a time, and drew close, awaiting the final word from him. Ambrosinus came out as well. None of them had slept.

Aurelius was the first to speak. 'I'm staying,' he said.

'What?' objected Vatrenus. 'Have you lost your mind, man?'

'If he's staying, so am I,' said Batiatus hanging his sword and double-edged axe from his belt.

'I understand,' approved Demetrius. 'We're staying behind to cover Romulus's and Ambrosinus's escape. It's only right.'

'It is right,' repeated Orosius. 'So Livia can be saved as well.'

Livia walked out in her Amazon garb, her bow hanging over her shoulder and her quiver in hand. 'Aurelius is the man I love. I shall live with him if God so wills it, but I could not survive without him. This is my last word.'

Romulus moved into the centre of the circle of his companions. 'Don't think that I'm going to run, if the rest of you stay,' he said. His firm, decided voice even seemed deeper, like a man's. 'We've got through all kinds of trouble together, and at this point my life wouldn't mean anything apart from you. You're the only ones I have left in the world, my beloved friends. I will not separate from you for any reason, and if you force me to leave I'll come back. They'll have to tie me up, or I'll jump off the boat and swim back to shore, I'll . . .'

Ambrosinus raised his hand to ask for attention. 'I love this boy like a son, more than a son, and I would give my blood for him at any moment, but he's a man now. Pain, fear, suffering and hardship have tempered him. He deserves the privilege of making his own decisions and we have to respect them – myself, first of all. Our destiny is about to come to a head in one way or another, very soon, and I want to share it with you. What has kept us together – what has prevented us from splitting up at the first signs of a threat – is so strong that it is stronger than the fear of death. It will keep us together until the end. I can't tell you how I feel, hearing these words from all of you. I have nothing to offer you but my deepest affection and the counsel that almighty God inspires in me. I'm sorry for my friend Kustennin, who will be waiting in vain at the old wharf, but there are calls that you must heed, like this one.'

Silence fell, a silence dense with emotion. A deep serenity invaded each one of them, the calm of someone prepared to face the ultimate sacrifice for love, for friendship, for faith, for devotion.

Vatrenus was the first to react with his brusque manner: 'Let's get going then, shall we?' he said. 'There's no way I'm going to let them slaughter me like a sheep. I'm going to take a few of those bastards down to hell with me.'

'You said it!' exclaimed Batiatus. 'I've always detested those freckled freaks.'

Ambrosinus could not hide his smile. 'I've heard you say that before, Batiatus,' he said. 'Maybe I have something for you, then, something I found last night when I couldn't fall asleep. Come with me.' He walked towards the praetorium. The others followed as well, and entered into the old commander's quarters. His table and field stool were still there, along with several parchment scrolls with company documents. The faded portrait of a beautiful woman was painted on a panel hung on the wall. Ambrosinus went straight to a spot in the floor and lifted a mat of woven straw. There was a trap door beneath. He raised the lid, gesturing for the others to go down.

Aurelius went first, and he could not believe his eyes: the Legion's armoury! Arranged in perfect order were at least twenty full suits of armour still shiny with grease, fashioned in the ancient manner with segmented cuirasses, helmets and shields, with bundles of triangular-tipped javelins, the kind used by Trajan and Hadrian in their heyday. There were ballistae and catapults with massive iron bolts, disassembled but in perfect working order, plus a great number of what the soldiers called lilies: deadly three-pronged devices that, buried in the ground, formed a barricade against the enemy infantry and cavalry.

'With all due respect for your philosophical propositions, I'd say this is the best contribution you've ever made to our cause,' exclaimed Vatrenus, slapping Ambrosinus on the back. 'Step up, boys, and get busy. Demetrius, you'll help me mount the catapults and ballistae.'

'Position most of them facing east,' ordered Aurelius. 'It's our most vulnerable side, and where they'll probably choose to attack.'

'Orosius and Batiatus,' continued Vatrenus, 'the two of you take your shovels and pickaxes and lay out the lilies where Aurelius tells you to: he's the strategist here. Livia, you take the artillery bolts up to the battlements, along with some arrows and javelins . . . and stones, all the stones you can find. Each of us will take a complete suit of armour: helmets, breastplates, everything, just take whatever fits. Except for Batiatus, obviously; there's nothing in his size!'

Batiatus looked around, perplexed. 'No, hold on, what about this horse's breastplate? A few hammer blows and it will fit just fine.'

They all broke out in laughter as they watched the giant lift up the heavy battle horse's cuirass and run up the stairs to get started.

'What about me?' asked Romulus. 'What must I do?'

'Nothing,' replied Vatrenus. 'You're the emperor.'

'I'll help Livia, then,' he decided and he began piling up javelins, as his friend was doing.

Aurelius came up last and started shuffling through the dust-covered scrolls still on the table. One in particular attracted his attention, with its beautiful, precise calligraphy. There were lines of verse: *'Exaudi me regina mundi, inter sidereos Roma recepta polos . . .'* 'Heed my words, Queen of the world, Rome, you who have been welcomed among the constellations of the firmament'. It was the start of Rutilius Namatianus's *De reditu suo*, the last heartfelt hymn to the greatness of Rome written seventy years earlier at the eve of the sacking of Alaric. He sighed and slipped the little parchment under his corselet, over his heart, like a talisman.

Ambrosinus was just coming up from the underground chamber and Aurelius approached him. 'When you see that everything is lost, take the boy down there and wait until it's all over. When it's dark, find Kustennin and accept whatever help he can give you. You'll manage to convince Romulus, and perhaps you'll find a place, in Ireland maybe, where you can start a new life.'

'That won't be necessary,' replied Ambrosinus calmly. Aurelius shook his head and went out into the courtyard to help the others.

They worked briskly all day, with incredible enthusiasm, as if an intolerable weight had been lifted from their hearts. At sunset, completely done in, sweaty and covered with dirt and dust, Aurelius and his men contemplated their achievements: the catapults and ballistae lined up on the bastions, piles of bolts and javelins ready and waiting next to the machines, reinforcements at the parapets, a great number of bows and arrows close at hand, right near the loopholes. Their shiny suits of armour leaned against the palisade. Batiatus's was there as well, burnished and bright, adjusted using a mallet on the anvil. Built to cover the chest of a horse, it would now protect the torso of the black Hercules in battle.

They ate together, sitting around the fire, and then prepared for the night.

'You must all get your sleep, because tomorrow you must be

ready for the fight,' said Ambrosinus. 'I'll stay awake. My eyesight's still good, and my hearing's even better.'

*

They all slept: Batiatus with his head pillowed on his armour, by the still warm forge; Livia in Aurelius' arms, in the barracks; Demetrius and Orosius in the stables, near the horses; Romulus, wrapped up in his travelling blanket, under the penthouse; Vatrenus on the bastions, inside the guard tower.

Ambrosinus was awake by the gate, deep in thought. Gently, he pushed the gate open and walked out to the great circular stone. Here he began to pile up a quantity of the wood, branches and dry bark, that lay at the feet of the century-old oaks. He approached a colossal oak and entered through a split in its trunk, extracting a wooden mallet and a large round object: a drum. He hung it from a branch and delivered a huge blow with the mallet, producing a hollow rumble that bounced off the mountains like the voice of a tempest. He then dealt another blow and then a third, and then yet another.

Aurelius, back at the camp, rose from his cot. 'What was that?' he asked. Livia took his hand and pulled him back down. 'It's just thunder, go back to sleep.'

But the sound was becoming louder, deeper and incessant, multiplied by the echo that resounded off the sides of the hills, off the cliffs and through the pastures. Aurelius strained to hear. 'No,' he said. 'That's not thunder, it sounds like an alarm signal . . . but for whom?'

Vatrenus's voice rang out from the tower. 'Come and see, quickly!' They all grabbed their weapons and rushed to the bastions. In the distance, the megalithic circle seemed ablaze. An enormous bonfire burned within the great stone pillars, shooting whirling sparks into the night sky. They could make out a shadow moving like a ghost against the glare of the flames.

'It's Ambrosinus doing his witchcraft,' observed Aurelius, 'and here we were thinking he was standing guard. I'm going back to sleep. Vatrenus, you stay out here until he comes back.'

In the houses scattered throughout the countryside, others saw that fire – shepherds and farmers, blacksmiths and craftsmen – and they lit fires of their own, under the astonished eyes of their wives and children, until the flames rose everywhere, on the mountains and on the hills, from the shores of the Ocean to the Great Wall.

The roar of the drum reached Kustennin's ear as well. He leapt from his bed and took up his sword. From the window he could see the fires and he realized why no one had shown up at the port that morning. He looked at Egeria and Ygraine's empty beds and thought of the boat that was sailing on tranquil waters by that time, towards a safe haven. He opened a chest and took out the dragon of silver and purple. He woke up one of his servants and ordered him to prepare his armour and his horse.

'But where are you going, my lord, at this hour?' he asked in surprise.

'To visit some friends.'

'Then why are you taking your sword?'

The wind carried with it the distant thunder of the drum. It was getting louder.

Kustennin sighed: 'There are times,' he said, 'in which you need to choose between the sword and the plough.' He hung his sword from his belt and went down the stairs towards the stables.

*

At dawn, Aurelius, Vatrenus and all the companions, armed to the teeth, were on the bastions and silently staring at the horizon. Romulus went from one to another with a pot of steaming soup. Aurelius was last.

'How is it?' he asked.

Aurelius tasted a spoonful. 'Good. The best that's ever been served in a military camp.'

Romulus smiled. 'Maybe we've done all this for nothing. Maybe they won't come.'

'Maybe . . .'

'Do you know what I was thinking? This is a good place to

found our little community. Maybe this camp could become a village one day, and I could even find a girl for myself. I met one down in the city, she has red hair, you know?'

Aurelius smiled. 'I'm pleased – that you're starting to think about girls, that is. It means that you're growing up, but it also means that your wounds are healing. One day the memory of your parents will cease to pain you so much and will become a soothing thought of love that will keep you company your whole life.'

Romulus sighed. 'Yes, maybe you're right, but I'm not even fourteen. A boy my age needs a father.' He poured himself a little soup and began to eat, trying to get his emotions in check. He glanced sideways at Aurelius now and then, to see if he was looking his way as well. 'You're right,' he said, 'this soup is pretty good. Livia made it.'

'I thought so,' replied Aurelius. 'Tell me something. If your father were here, what would you ask him?'

'Nothing special. I'd like to spend some time with him, like the two of us now, eating breakfast. Simple things, nothing much, just being together, knowing you're not alone, you know?'

'I do,' answered Aurelius. 'I miss my parents terribly as well, even though I'm a lot older than you.'

They stood for a while watching the horizon without saying a word. Aurelius broke the silence. 'Know what? I've never had children and I don't know that I ever will. What I mean is . . . we don't know how this will turn out, and . . .'

'I know,' sighed Romulus.

'I was wondering if . . .'

'What?'

Aurelius fingered his bronze ring with its monogram carved into a little cameo. 'Now I know that this ring is truly mine. That it's my family ring, and I was wondering . . . I was wondering if you'd accept it.'

Romulus looked at him with bright eyes. 'You mean you want . . .'

'Yes. If you accept I would like to adopt you as my son.'

'Here? Now?'

'*Hic et nunc*,' replied Aurelius. 'If you accept.'

Romulus threw his arms around his neck. 'With my whole heart,' he said. 'Although . . . I don't think I can manage to call you "father." I've always called you Aurelius.'

'That's fine with me, of course.'

Romulus held out his right hand. Aurelius slipped the ring off his third finger and placed it on the boy's thumb, after discovering that all his other fingers were too slender. 'Then I adopt you, as my son, Romulus Augustus Caesar Aurelianus Ambrosius Ventidius . . . Britannicus! And so be it as long as you shall live.'

Romulus hugged him again. 'Thank you! I shall honour you as you deserve to be honoured.'

'But I'm warning you,' shot back Aurelius. 'Now you'll have to follow my advice, not to say obey my orders . . .'

Romulus was about to answer when Demetrius's voice sounded from the tallest tower. 'They're coming!'

Aurelius shouted: 'Take your places, everyone! Romulus, you go with Ambrosinus, he already knows what must be done. Come on now, hurry!'

The prolonged wail of horns sounded at that moment; the same sound they had heard at Dertona on the day of Mledo's attack. A long row of armoured horsemen appeared on the line of hills to the east, advancing at a walk. The formation parted to reveal a gigantic warrior, his face covered with a golden mask and a shining sword in his grip.

Aurelius gestured to Vatrenus and Demetrius, who manned the catapults and ballistae.

'Look!' shouted Demetrius. 'Someone's approaching.'

'Maybe it's a deal they want!' said Vatrenus, leaning over the parapet.

A man on horseback, flanked by two armoured warriors, advanced holding a white cloth draped over a horizontal rod: the truce sign. The three of them pulled up directly beneath the palisade.

'What do you want?' asked Vatrenus.

'My lord, Wortigern, offers to spare your lives if you hand over the young usurper who claims to call himself Romulus Augustus, and the deserter who protects him, known by the name of Aurelius.'

'Wait a moment,' replied Vatrenus. 'I must consult my companions.' He drew close to Batiatus and whispered something to him.

'Well?' pressed the messenger. 'What must I answer?'

'That we accept!' shouted Vatrenus.

'Here's the boy, first of all,' yelled Batiatus. He leaned over the parapet, holding a bundle in his arms. Before the barbarian could realize what he was up to, he hurled it at him. It was a boulder wrapped in a blanket that hit its mark and crushed him to the ground. The other two spun their horses around and fled, as Batiatus was shouting: 'Wait, I've got the other one for you!'

'This will raise their hackles,' said Aurelius.

'Does it make any difference?' observed Vatrenus.

'Not at all. Be ready: they're advancing.'

The horns sounded again and the vast front of horsemen surged forwards. When they were a quarter of a mile from the camp, the line split again and a battering ram, pulled by eight men on horseback, was launched down the slope.

'They think they're back at Dertona!' shouted Aurelius. 'Ready with the catapults!'

The enemy horsemen had accumulated considerable impetus when they reached the ground planted with the lilies. The two lead horses crashed to the ground, flinging their horsemen on to the prongs of iron hidden in the grass. The machine was thrown off balance and veered to the left, picking up speed. The wheels could no longer bear up under the weight and flew into pieces, and the ram toppled over and rolled down the hill, bouncing off the rocks until it plummeted into the lake.

The catapults shot off and four more horsemen were hit as they tried to retreat. A roar of enthusiasm burst forth on the fort's bastions, but then the horns echoed once again. The horsemen had stopped and were letting through a wave of light infantry.

'Watch out!' shouted Demetrius. 'They have incendiary arrows!'

'To the bows!' ordered Aurelius. 'Stop as many as you can!'

The foot soldiers advanced at a run towards the camp. It soon became obvious that they were inadequately armed servants, sent forward to be massacred and to open the way for the heavy cavalry. Behind them, the barbarian warriors held their bows ready to transfix any of them who tried to run off. The foot soldiers became aware of the lilies as soon as they saw the first men fall, screaming in pain, their feet pierced through. They split into two groups, circling the mined area, and began to shoot off their incendiary arrows in a long arch. Some were struck by the arrows of Livia and the others and fell, but many others sought shelter behind rocks and trees and continued to send their bolts flying with unfailing aim. The wooden stakes of the palisade, old and dry as they were, took flame immediately. More foot soldiers rushed forward with ladders in hand, but they were nailed to the ground by the ballista fire and by volleys of arrows from the battlements.

The horsemen, at this point, had resumed their deliberate advance. They were evidently waiting for the burning section of the palisade to crumble so they could launch their attack.

Aurelius gathered his men. 'We have neither the water nor the men to extinguish the flames, and Wulfila will soon loose his warriors through the breach. Vatrenus, you and Demetrius continue firing; down as many of them as you can with the artillery, but when they come in, we'll have no choice but to move out ourselves. We've left a passage, free of lilies, down there by that little ash tree. Batiatus, you'll be our battering ram. Break through at the centre, and we'll be close behind. We'll attract them on to more uneven ground, where they'll be forced to split up and proceed on foot. We still have hope.'

Part of the palisade came crashing down all at once in a flurry of smoke and sparks, and the enemy cavalry charged forward at a gallop towards the breach. The catapults and ballistae were rotated on their platforms and discharged a volley of bolts, bringing down half a dozen horsemen who pulled others down in their fall. A second volley raised havoc in the crowd, slaughtering many, then the bows let fly and, as the enemy got closer, the javelins, first the light, long-range weapons and then the heavier, short-range type. The ground was sown with corpses, but the enemy continued to advance, confident of dealing the decisive blow.

'Out!' shouted Aurelius then. 'Out of the southern gate! We'll outflank them. *Ambrosine*, take the boy to safety!'

Batiatus had donned his cuirass, and the salleted helmet which covered his head and face, and was ready below, in the saddle of his gigantic Armorican stallion. The horse wore metallic plate armour as well, and his rider brandished the war axe. No mere horseman, Batiatus was a true war machine. The others were all soon behind him on their steeds, in a wedge formation. 'Now!' shouted Aurelius. 'We're out!' and the gate sprang open as the first enemy horsemen were nearing the breach. Batiatus spurred his horse into a gallop over the open terrain, followed by his friends, aiming at the gap left free of the lilies.

Romulus meanwhile had broken away from his tutor and had jumped into the saddle of his pony, waving a knife in place of a sword. He urged his pony towards his comrades, so he could do battle at their sides. Ambrosinus ran after him, yelling: 'Stop! Come back!' but he soon found himself stranded on open ground.

Batiatus was charging the lines of enemy cavalry, knocking down everyone he found in his way. His companions followed, engaging the enemy in a furious brawl, wielding sword and shield against all they met. Wulfila, who was still on the high part of the slope, spotted Aurelius and charged, sword drawn. Out of the corner of his eye, Vatrenus noticed Romulus who was racing forward to his right, and he yelled out: 'To the hill, go Romulus, fast! Get away from here!'

Ambrosinus was terrified, surrounded by horsemen riding at a full gallop in every direction. He dragged himself towards a rocky spike that emerged from the ground to his right, to see if he could spot the boy, and spot him he did, in the sway of his restive pony, racing towards the megalithic circle.

Wulfila was nearly upon Aurelius and was screaming, enraged: 'Fight, you coward! You won't get away from me this time!' He dealt the first, cleaving blow of his sword. Batiatus raised his shield, an enormous metallic disc, and saved Aurelius from the blade. The sword struck the shield with a terrible din, spraying off myriad sparks. Meanwhile the first wave of horsemen had penetrated the breach, flying through the flames and erupting into the camp. They unleashed their fury on everything they found, laying waste to the barracks and guard towers which were immediately set ablaze like giant torches.

'There's no one here!' one of them shouted suddenly. 'They've escaped. After them!'

Ambrosinus had scrambled to the top of the rock and beheld Aurelius fighting with desperate valour against Wulfila. The Roman's shield flew into pieces, his sword bent under the blows of his adversary's invincible blade, but all at once, in that chaos of wild screaming, in that din of clashing arms, a piercing, acute note rose above all else. It was a trumpet, sounding the attack. At that very instant, on the highest rim of the eastern hills, the glittering head and purple tail of the dragon came into view. A compact line of warriors advanced behind, their spears held low, their shields forming a wall, launching the ancient battle cry of the Roman infantry with every step. The Legion of the Dragon had appeared out of nowhere, and was hurtling down the slope, led by Kustennin flanked by two arrays of horsemen.

Wulfila had a moment's hesitation and Batiatus charged him with all his bulk, throwing him off balance and pushing him sideways before he could deliver the mortal blow that would finish off Aurelius, totally unarmed now. Wulfila pitched to the ground, but as he was getting up, he caught a glimpse of Romulus falling off his horse and running towards the circle of stones to seek refuge. He bounded to his feet and set off after the boy but

Vatrenus, who had guessed at his intentions, cut him off. Wulfila's sword fell upon him with frightful power, slicing through his shield and cuirass. A stream of blood spurted from his chest as Wulfila broke away, shouting to his men 'Cover me!' Four of them lunged at Vatrenus, who continued to fight like a lion. Completely drenched in blood, he backed up to lean against a tree. They pierced him through once, twice, three times, nailing him to the trunk with their spears. Vatrenus had the strength to shout: 'Go to hell, you bastards!' before his head dropped, lifeless, to his chest.

The rest of the barbarians squared off against the small group of combatants, who continued to strike with fierce energy. Aurelius took the sword of a warrior who had fallen and resumed the battle, trying to get through to where he had seen Wulfila running, towards the megalithic circle that Romulus had escaped to. Demetrius and Orosius flanked him but fell one after the other, overpowered. Batiatus finally broke through, but not in time to save them, and managed to force the enemy line so that Aurelius broke through too on to open ground, heading towards the circle of stones. Surrounded now on every side, the giant swirled his axe, chopping off heads and arms, crushing shields and cuirasses, flooding the ground with blood. A spear stuck in his shoulder and he was forced to back up against a rock. Like a bear besieged by a pack of dogs, Batiatus continued to swipe at them with frightful power, even though his blood was flowing copiously down his left side. Livia spotted him and started shooting off her arrows as she raced over on her horse, transfixing the enemies who had their backs towards her as they swarmed around the wounded giant.

The fray continued ceaselessly, ferociously. The new combatants had reached the battle field, and advanced holding high the standard of the dragon. They drove back the enemy, who were completely taken aback by their sudden appearance, and forced them downhill.

Ambrosinus, in the meantime, had seen Wulfila's move and

was racing breathlessly at the edge of the battle field, trying to reach the circle of stones and shouting: 'Seek shelter, Romulus! Run! Hide!'

Romulus had nearly reached the top of the hill and he turned around to seek out his friends in the midst of that bloody brawl.

He found before him a huge warrior with long white hair, his face covered with a mask of gold. He was very close now, rank with blood and sweat and brandishing a sword red with slaughter. He suddenly ripped the mask off his face, revealing a distorted grimace: Wulfila! Romulus drew back, terrified, towards one of the great pillars, holding his knife out in a feeble attempt at defence. In the distance he could hear the distressed cries of his tutor and the confused din of the battle, but his gaze was magnetically attracted to the tip of the blade being raised to kill him. With a swipe of the sword, the boy's knife flew to his enemy's feet. Romulus continued to back away, until he knocked against the stone pillar. His long flight was over. Anguish, fear, hope: that blade would finish them all off, in a moment, and yet the frenzy of his escape and the panicked terror which had engulfed him at the sight of his implacable enemy had given way to a mysterious serenity, as he prepared to die like a true soldier. As the sword lunged forward to pierce his heart he heard Ambrosinus's voice within him, very clearly. 'Defend yourself!' it commanded, and he dodged the blow, miraculously, with a sudden twist to the side. The sword plunged into a crack in the stone and stuck there. Without even turning, Romulus grabbed a handful of the burning embers from the great slab and flung them into the eyes of Wulfila, who backed away, howling in pain. Ambrosinus's voice inside him, again calm and clear, said: 'Take the sword.'

Romulus obeyed. He grasped the magnificent golden hilt and pulled with tranquil strength. The blade meekly followed the young hand and when Wulfila opened his eyes he saw the boy pushing it two-handed towards his belly, his mouth wide in a cry more terrible than the roar of battle. In shock and amazement, he saw the blade penetrate his flesh and sink through his gurgling bowels. He felt it come out of his back, as sharp as the wild scream of that young boy.

He fell on to his knees and Romulus planted himself squarely in front of him to contemplate his end, but Wulfila felt his hate feeding the life still within him, igniting an energy that still craved victory. He grabbed the handle of the sword and pulled it slowly out of the horrible wound, raising it with one hand as the other pressed at his belly. He lurched forward, staring at his victim to immobilize him with the terrifying force of his gaze, but as he was about to deal the blow, another blade pushed out of his chest, driven in from behind. Aurelius was at his back, so close he could whisper in his ear with a voice as harsh and cold as a death sentence.

'This is for my father, Cornelius Aurelianus Ventidius, who you murdered at Aquileia.'

A stream of blood leaked from his mouth but Wulfila was still on his feet, still trying to raise the sword which had become as heavy as lead. Aurelius's blade transfixed him once again, from back to front, protruding from his sternum.

'And this is for my mother, Caecilia Aurelia Silvia.'

Wulfila collapsed to the ground with a last rattling gasp. Under Aurelius's astonished eyes, Romulus bent over, wet his fingers in his enemy's blood and drew a vermilion line across his forehead. Then he raised the sword to the sky, launching a cry of triumph that echoed, tense and sharp, acute as a war horn, over the field of blood that lay at his feet.

The legion, victorious along the entire line, advanced in closed ranks towards the great circle of stones, following the glorious standard that had called them out of darkness and led them to victory. Kustennin grasped it in his hand, gleaming in the sun which had risen high in the sky. At the top of the hill, he dismounted and planted the standard into the ground near Romulus. He shouted: 'Hail Caesar! Hail Son of the Dragon! Hail Pendragon!'

He gestured for four warriors to approach. They crossed their four spears, placed a huge round shield on top, and hoisted Romulus so that he was standing on it. They raised him to their shoulders in the Celtic manner so all could behold him. Kustennin began to strike his sword against his shield and the whole legion with him: thousands of swords clanged against shields as thousands of voices rose even louder than the deafening clangour of the arms, infinitely repeating that shout: 'Hail Caesar! Hail Pendragon!'

Wulfila's blood was on his forehead, the glittering sword was tight in his fist, and the victorious soldiers saw Romulus as a charmed being, as the young warrior of the prophecy. Their incessant shouting, fractured into a thousand echoes over the mountains, lit up his eyes with flaming passion, but, from on high, his gaze moved beyond the men to seek out his companions, and his triumph abruptly rang hollow. His frenzied euphoria gave way to choked emotion, as he jumped to the ground and made his way through the ranks of warriors who opened respectfully to allow his passage. Silence fell over the valley as he walked mute and dazed through the field strewn with cadavers. His eyes scanned the wounded and the dying, the frightful tangle of bodies still clutching each other in their death grip. He found Batiatus with a spear stuck in his shoulder, leaning against a rock, drenched in blood, in the middle of a heap of dead enemies. He saw his friends who had fallen in the unequal struggle: Vatrenus, nailed to a tree by three enemy spears, his eyes still open, still seeking an impossible dream; Demetrius and Orosius, inseparable in life, united in death, one alongside the other. Countless enemies, lying all around, had paid dearly for their deaths.

And Livia. Alive, but with an arrow in her side, her face a mask of pain.

Romulus burst out crying, hot tears that flooded his cheeks at the sight of his wounded companions and the friends that he would never see again. He walked on almost blindly, his sight dimmed by those harrowing visions, until he reached the shores of the lake. Small waves, just barely rippled by the wind, wet his sore feet and lapped at the tip of the sword still dripping blood. An infinite desire for peace washed over him, like a gentle springtime breeze. He cried out: 'No more war! No more blood!' and he washed his sword in the water until the blade shone like crystal. He stood up and began to swing it over his head, in a wider and wider circle, finally flinging it with all of his force into the lake. The blade flew through the air, dazzling bright against the sun, and plunged like a meteor into the heart of the moss-covered stone that rose at the centre of the lake.

The last breath of wind died down at that moment and the surface of the water calmed, revealing, reflecting a magical vision: the solemn figure of his tutor who had suddenly reappeared. The little silver mistletoe twig shone on his chest. His voice was nearly unrecognizable as he said: 'It's all over, my son, my lord, my king. No one shall ever dare touch you again, for you've passed through ice, fire and blood, like that sword which has penetrated the stone. You are the son of the dragon. You are Pendragon.'

EPILOGUE

Thus the battle was fought and was won: the battle of Mons Badonicus, which we call Mount Badon in our language. At the hand of Aurelianus Ambrosius Ventidius, a humble man, the last of the Romans. And thus the prophecy was fulfilled, a prophecy that had led me to undertake a journey that no one would have thought possible: first from my native land to Italy, and then, many years later, from Italy back all the way to Britannia. My disciple, emperor of the Romans for only a few days and then sentenced to endless imprisonment, thus became king of Britannia with the name of Pendragon, 'the son of the dragon,' as he had been acclaimed by the soldiers of the last legion on the day of his victory. Aurelianus remained at his side like a father, until he realized that the name Pendragon had definitively obscured the name Romulus, and that his love for Ygraine had completely occupied the heart of his adopted son. He then set off with Livia, the only woman he had ever loved in all his life, and nothing more was known of them. I like to think that they returned to their little homeland on the lagoon – Venetia – to continue to live as Romans without having to live like barbarians, and to build a future of liberty and peace.

Cornelius Batiatus departed with them, on the same ship, but perhaps he did not follow them to their destination. Perhaps he stopped at the Columns of Hercules, the gateway to his native land: Africa. I shall never forget that it was the warmth of his heart that restored breath to my lifeless boy on the icy peaks of the Alps. May the Lord permit him to meet others as noble and generous as he, on his life's journey.

The seed which came from a dying world set down roots and produced fruit in this remote land, at the ends of the earth. The son of

Pendragon and Ygraine is five years old now, as I finish this work of mine. He was given the name Arthur at birth, from Arcturius, which means 'he who is born under the star of the Bear'. Only one who comes from the southern seas could give such a name to his son, which proves that whatever the destiny of a man may be, his most intimate memories never abandon him, until the day of his death.

Our enemies were driven back and our kingdom extended southward to include the city of Caerleon, one of the first we encountered upon our return to Britannia, but I have preferred to stay up here, to keep watch and to meditate in this tower at the Great Wall, listening to voices enfeebled by time. The wondrous sword still lies sunken into the stone, ever since that day of blood and glory. Only I now know the full inscription, I who read it that day long ago when I saw it for the first time: CAI.IUL.CAES.ENSIS CALIBURNUS, *'the Calibian sword of Julius Caesar'.*

Part of that inscription is buried deep in the stone now, and other letters have become covered by encrustations and lichens over the long years it has been exposed to the elements. The only letters still legible are E S CALIBUR, *and that is the name that the people of this land give the sword, when frozen winter mornings allow them to walk over the ice to the centre of the lake and admire that extraordinary object. They say that only the hand of the king will ever extract it from the stone, on the day when he will once again have to combat evil.*

A long, long time has passed since the distant days of my youth, and my first name, Myrdin, has changed in the mouths of this people as well. They now call me Merlin. But my soul remains the same, destined to find the immortal light, like the soul of every man created in the image of God.

The sun begins to melt the snow on the slopes of the hills, and the first flowers of spring open their corollas to the tepid wind that comes from the south. God has allowed me to finish my work and I render him thanks. Here my story ends. Here, perhaps, a legend is born.

Author's Note

The fall of the Roman World is one of the great themes of the history of western civilization, and yet remains one of the most mysterious, given the complexity of the problem and the scarcity of original accounts and sources regarding the epoch of Rome's final decline. What's more, this event – traditionally considered a catastrophe – is a mere historical convention. No one even noticed in 476 AD that the Roman world had ended; nothing that happened that year was any more traumatic than what had been going on day in and day out for years. Odoacer – the Herulian chief who had deposed young Romulus Augustulus – simply turned the imperial insignia over to Constantinople, noting that one emperor was more than enough for the whole Roman World.

Most of the story told here is the fruit of my imagination; what I've attempted to do is to render the enormous impact of this event, while bringing out the emergence of new worlds, of new cultures and new civilizations whose roots still held fast to Roman tradition. The 'Arthurian' outcome of the story can be interpreted symbolically, as a parable, but this is not its only reading. Scholars have long recognized that the events which gave birth to the legend of King Arthur, set down in the middle ages by Geoffrey of Monmouth, actually took place at the end of the fifth century in Britain. Among the protagonists was a mysterious and heroic Aurelianus Ambrosius, *solus Romanae gentis* ('the last of the Romans'), the victor of the Battle of Mount Badon against the Saxons and the predecessor of Pendragon and Arthur. We often tend to think of these characters as medieval knights, whereas in reality they were much closer to the Celtic Roman world. There is also truth in the tradition that holds that the

Roman-Britons of the fifth century invoked the assistance of the emperor in fighting off invaders from the north and south. General Aetius twice consented to their pleas and sent Germanus, an enigmatic figure, half warrior and half saint, to their aid. Other characters, like Myrdin the Celt – the Merlin of Arthurian legend – are taken from the epic tradition which revolves around the legendary sword Excalibur. This name has been interpreted by eminent Celtists as a sort of contraction of the Latin words *ensis caliburnus*, that is, the 'Calibian sword', an expression which hints at a Mediterranean origin. The mythical, symbolic hypothesis expressed in the story is thus inspired by actual historical events at the twilight of the ancient world, unfolding in that arcane moment that was to give rise to Arthurian legend.

The events narrated are seen through the eyes of a group of loyalist Roman soldiers who still embody the traditions of the past and see the barbarians as ferocious aliens bent on destruction. This attitude was probably quite widespread at the time. The short-lived Roman/barbarian realms certainly failed due to irremediable conflict between the Romanized populations and the invaders. Today, the concept of invasion tends to be re-interpreted as a phenomenon of *Völkerwanderung*, or migration, although the end result remains much the same.

In the turbulent modern day, the West – which sees itself as immortal and indestructible (much as the Roman Empire did in its heyday) – would do well to consider that all empires dissolve sooner or later and that the wealth of one part of the world cannot hope to survive long in the face of the abject poverty of the rest of the world's populations. Those who were called 'barbarians' then did not want to provoke the destruction of the Empire; they wanted merely to become part of it. Many of them even defended it with their lives, but the die was cast, and the world plunged into a long period of chaos and degradation.

Some of the novel's characters express themselves in such a way as to suggest the residual survival of pagan sentiments; although this may not be easy to sustain historically at the end of the fifth century, it is not at all improbable, in the light of certain signals appearing in late sources. Such sentiments are best expressed in the 'pagan' attachment to tradition and to the *mos maiorum*, the customs of their ancestors, perhaps not wholly extinct in this age.

Very few details are known about Romulus Augustulus; in particular, the age at which the last emperor was deposed is controversial in historical sources. In creating the character, I've preferred the account of *Excerpta Valesiana, 38*, which speaks of him as a boy: '*Odoacar . . . deposuit Augustulum de regno, cuius infantiam misertus concessit ei sanguinem*' (Odoacer deposed Augustulus from his throne and, feeling compassion for his tender age, spared his life . . .).

The specialized reader will have recognized a number of original sources woven into the fabric of the story, most from the late Latin period: Ammianus Marcellinus's *History*, *De Reditu suo* by Rutilius Namatianus, *De gubernatione Dei* by Salvianus, the *History of the Gothic War* by Procopius of Caesarea, the *Lausiac History* by Palladius, *In Rufinum* by Claudianus, *Valesianus Anonimus*, Cassiodorus's *Chronicles*, *Vita Epiphanii* and *Comitis Chronicon*, as well as occasional references to Plutarch, Orosius, Saint Ambrose, Saint Augustine and Saint Jerome. A series of sources from the early middle ages forms the base for the 'Britannic' epilogue of the story: the *Historia Ecclesiastica Gentis Anglorum* by the Venerable Bede, and the *De exitio Britanniae* by Gildas.

Acknowledgements

My deepest thanks go to a number of dear friends who have supported and encouraged me with their suggestions and scholarship, especially Lorenzo Braccesi and Giovanni Gorini of the University of Padova, Gianni Brizzi and Ivano Dionigi of the University of Bologna, Venceslas Kruta of the Sorbonne and Robin Lane Fox of New College, who listened to this whole story on a long car trip from Luton to Oxford. Precious help was also provided by Giorgio Bonamente and Angela Amici of the University of Perugia, and my former colleague and collaborator Gabriella Amiotti of the Università Cattolica of Milan. Obviously, any errors or injudicious choices are my responsibility alone. I must also express my gratitude to Franco Mimmi, who steadfastly assisted me from his residence in Madrid, Marco Guidi, one of my staunchest and oldest friends, who I often consulted regarding events of the late Roman age in Britain, and Giorgio Fornoni, who in keeping with a decade-long tradition, welcomed me to his magnificent Alpine home where I worked on the final draft of this novel in total isolation from the rest of the world. Special thanks go to my wife, Christine, my most critical and attentive – as well as my most affectionate – reader, and to my literary agents Laura Grandi and Stefano Tettamanti who accompanied me step by step on this project, encouraging me even in the most difficult moments. I also thank Paolo Buonvino, whose music was my constant companion as I wrote this novel, inspiring its most intense and dramatic pages.

Last but not least, thanks to Damiano of Albergo Ardesio, who sustained me with his delicious cuisine during my entire Alpine stay, and to Giancarla at Freccia's Bar, whose matchless espresso always starts my day off right.

Alexander: Child of a Dream

A huge international bestseller, *Alexander: Child of a Dream* is the first in Valerio Massimo Manfredi's outstanding trilogy of brutal passion and grand adventure in ancient Greece.

Who could have been born to conquer the world other than a god? A boy, born to a great king – Philip of Macedon – and his sensuous queen, Olympias. Alexander became a young man of immense, unfathomable potential. Under the tutelage of the great Aristotle and with the friendship of Ptolemy and Hephaiston, he became the mightiest and most charismatic warrior, capable of subjugating the known world to his power.

A marvellous novel of one of history's greatest characters and his quest to conquer the civilized world.

Alexander: The Sands of Ammon

Continuing the epic saga of Alexander the Great, *The Sands of Ammon* brilliantly describes Alexander's quest to conquer Asia, the limitless domain ruled by the Great King of the Persians.

In a seemingly impossible venture, Alexander and his men storm Persian fortresses and harbours, crippling King Darius's domination of land and sea. Even the legendary Halicarnassus is defeated by the Macedonian army.

But the island City of Tyre and the Towers of Gaza prove to be formidable obstacles. Undeterred, Alexander surges forth over land and sea to the mysterious land of Egypt.

And there, in the sands, lies the Oracle of Ammon, waiting to reveal an amazing truth to Alexander. One that will change his already amazing life.

Alexander: The Ends of the Earth

Alexander's epic quest continues into the heart of Asia and on towards the mystery of India.

The Macedonian army marches ever onward, crushing resistance at every turn. The beauty of Babylon is quickly ravaged and the Palace of Persepolis burnt to ashes. An empire is destroyed and a new and bloody era begins.

But there are other things on Alexander's mind. An ambitious project to unite the peoples of the empire in one homeland begins to obsess him, until the curious beauty of Queen Roxanna gives him the strength to fulfil his destiny . . .

This is a truly compelling, exciting and romantic book and a breathtaking conclusion to the bestselling 'Alexander' trilogy.

SPARTAN

An epic story of passion, courage and adventure in ancient Sparta.

Herodotus tells us that not all of the three hundred Spartan warriors died at the hands of Xerxes, King of the Persians, in the battle of the Thermopylae: two were saved bringing a life-saving message back to the city . . .

This is the saga of a Spartan family, torn apart by a cruel law that forces them to abandon one of their two sons – born lame – to the elements. The elder son, Brithos, is raised in the caste of the warriors, while the other, Talos, is spared a cruel death and is raised by a Helot shepherd, among the peasants.

They live out their story in a world dominated by the clash between the Persian empire and the city-states of Greece – a ferocious, relentless conflict – until the voice of their blood and of human solidarity unites them in a thrilling, singular enterprise.

Full of passion, courage and magic, *Spartan* is an enthralling novel of the ancient world.